SOMEONE TO

CEANE O'HA

A Sleuth Sisters Mystery
Book nine in the bewitching series

A Magick Wand Production
"Thoughts are magick wands powerful enough to make anything happen– anything we choose!"

This book is lovingly dedicated to time-travelers everywhere ~
And to my husband, Phillip R. Lincoln, who bought me my ticket.

Warm gratitude and blessings bright and beautiful to:
My husband Phillip,

And to my muses: High Priestess Beth Adams;
Janet Barvincak; William Colvin;
High Priestess Joyce Henderson; Nancy Hrabak;
High Priestess Kelly M. Kelleher;
Professor and Forensic Anthropologist Cassandra L. Kuba, PhD;
Marie Lorah; Winter Anne McKelvie; Jean and Ron Minnick;
Robin Moore; Madeleine Stephenson;
And songstress Rowena of the Glen~

For all the reasons they each know so well.

SOMEONE TO WITCH OVER ME
By
Ceane O'Hanlon-Lincoln

A Sleuth Sisters Mystery

The Sleuth Sisters Mystery Series:
~By Ceane O'Hanlon-Lincoln~

In this paranormal-mystery series, Raine and Maggie McDonough and Aisling McDonough-Gwynn, first cousins, are the celebrated "Sleuth Sisters" from the rustically beautiful Pennsylvania town of Haleigh's Hamlet. With their magickal Time-Key, these winning white witches are able to unlock the door that will whisk them through yesteryear, but who knows what skeletons and dangers dangle in the closets their Key will open?

One thing is certain– magick, adventure, and surprise await them at the creak of every opening door and page-turn.

Ceane crafts each of her spellbinding *Sleuth Sisters Mysteries* to stand alone, though it is always nice to read a series in order– for the most surprises. After all, mystery is at the heart of both creativity and surprise.

The Witches' Time-Key, book one of the bewitching *Sleuth Sisters Mystery Series*
Fire Burn and Cauldron Bubble, book two
The Witch's Silent Scream, book three
Which Witch is Which? book four
Witch-Way, book five
The Witch Tree, book six
The Witch's Secret, book seven
Careful What You Witch For, book eight
Someone To Witch Over Me, book nine of the Sleuth Sisters Mysteries: A glittering piece of the past, exotic intrigue and trickery, where titillating rumors are heard echoing down the Tunnel of Time. The Sisters' relaxing Caribbean vacation turns suddenly deadly when mystery meets history on the Eden-like island of Martinique!

Witch Upon A Star, **book ten in the series– coming soon!**

Amazon Books / www.amazon.com/amazon books

Also by Ceane O'Hanlon-Lincoln:

In the mood for something different– something perhaps from another time and place?
Autumn Song is a harmonious medley of short stories threaded by their romantic destiny themes and autumnal settings.

Voodoo, ghostly lovers, Native American spiritualism, and figures from the past– all interwoven in a collection of tales that will haunt you forever.

Read the stories in the order the author presents them in the book for the most surprises– a*nd this author hopes you like surprises!*

Each tale in this compelling anthology evokes its own special ambiance and sensory impressions. *Autumn Song is a keeper you will re-visit often, as you do an old and cherished friend.*

O'Hanlon-Lincoln never judges her characters, several of whom resurface from tale to tale. These are honest portrayals with meticulously researched historic backdrops, intrigue, *magick*, surprise endings– and thought-provoking twists.

For instance, in "A Matter of Time," on which side of the door is the main character when the story concludes?

From the first page of *Autumn Song*, the reader will take an active role in these fascinating stories, discovering all the electrifying threads that connect them.

How many will *you* find?

Available at Amazon Books / www.amazon.com/amazon

And
Ceane O'Hanlon-Lincoln's award-winning history series:

County Chronicles
County Chronicles Volume II
County Chronicles Volume III
County Chronicles Volume IV
County Chronicles: There's No Place Like Home!

"If you haven't read this author's ***County Chronicles***, then you haven't discovered how *thrilling* history can be! With meticulous research and her "state-of-the-heart" storytelling, Ceane O'Hanlon-Lincoln breathes life into historical figures and events with language that flows and captivates the senses."
~ Mechling Books / www.mechlingbooks.com

"I write history like a story, because that's what history is, a story– or rather, *layered* stories of the most significant events that ever unfolded. Each volume of my *County Chronicles* is a varied collection of *true* stories from Pennsylvania's exciting past."
~ Ceane O'Hanlon-Lincoln

~~~

"Your life is what your thoughts make it."
~ The Great Secret

SOMEONE TO WITCH OVER ME
~ Cast of Characters ~

Doctors Raine and Maggie McDonough, PhDs– Sexy, savvy Sisters of the Craft, who *are* more like sisters than cousins. With sorcery in their glittering emerald eyes, these bewitching Pennsylvania history and archaeology professors draw on their keen innate powers, making use of all their skills, experience, and magickal tools to sort out the mystery, mayhem and murder on the French Caribbean island of Martinique.

Will these mystery magnets be able to clear the cobwebs of their current mystery *and* the secrets from the past connected to it?

Aisling McDonough-Gwynn– The blonde with the wand is the senior Sister in the magickal trio known, in Haleigh's Hamlet and beyond, as the "Sleuth Sisters." Aisling and her husband **Ian**, former police detectives, are partners in their successful Black Cat Detective Agency.

The Gwynns have a preteen daughter, **Meredith (Merry) Fay**, who mirrors her magickal mother. Merry was named for the McDonough *grande dame*, who resides in the "Witch City" of Salem, Massachusetts.

Aisling Tully McDonough– The Sleuth Sisters' beloved **"Granny"** was the grand mistress of Tara, the Victorian mansion where Raine and Maggie came of age, and where they yet reside. Born in Ireland, the departed Granny McDonough left her female heirs a very special gift– and at Tara, with its magickal mirrors, Granny is but a glance away.

Great-Aunt Meredith/ "Grantie Merry" McDonough– A celebrated Salem witch and the McDonough *grande dame* whose awesome magickal gifts prove invaluable to the Sisters. In McDonough tradition, Grantie's magick is benign– though, like Raine, there have been times when Grantie was not bound by tradition, dogma or doctrine, but listened only to her heart.

The Myrrdyn/ Merlin Cats/ Panthèra, Black Jade and Black Jack O'Lantern, each a PhD/ Puss of Hubristic Divination– Descendants of Granny McDonough's magickal feline Myrrdyn (the Celtic for Merlin), these devoted "Watchers" are the Sisters' closest companions. Wholly *familiar* with the Sleuth Sisters' powers, desires and needs, the Myrrdyn/ Merlin cats faithfully offer moral support, special knowledge delivered with timely messages– and protection.

Cara– The ancient spirit in the Sleuth Sisters' poppet continually proves– as the witched little doll's name suggests– to be a great *friend* to Raine, Maggie, and Aisling.

Dr. Thaddeus Weatherby, PhD– This absent-minded professor and head of Haleigh College's history department has an Einstein mind coupled with an uncontrollable childish curiosity that has been known to cause unadulterated mischief for the Sleuth Sisters. Thaddeus and Maggie are lovers and reunited kindred spirits.

Dr. Beau Goodwin, DVM– Raine's dashing **Beau**, soul mate, and next-door neighbor is a superior veterinarian with an extraordinary sixth sense. Like Raine, this Starseed, too, is an empath and Old Soul. Each half of this remarkable couple creates magick in a singular way, together enkindling an utterly charmed *Raine-Beau*.

Dr. Hugh Goodwin, DVM– Beau's retired veterinary father– whose acute sixth sense matches his son's– has an avid appetite for mystery novels and an astonishing aptitude for solving them that the Sleuth Sisters find absolutely "wizard."

Betty Donovan– A retired librarian, Hugh's attractive new bride shares his intense love of mysteries and is fast becoming his equal in solving them.

Hannah Gilbert– The Sleuth Sisters' loyal, protective housekeeper is a wealth of homespun wisdom. Her purple sneakers and garish muumuus are indicative of her quirky personality; and like many snoopy servants before her, she's a fountain of telltale tidings– information that frequently abets and serves the Sleuth Sisters in their quests.

Jeanne Gardien– The curator at la Pagerie Museum/ le Musée de la Pagerie, Martinique, the Empress Joséphine's girlhood plantation, where the love letters on display are only a sample of the sultry passions that envelop this Eden-like site.

Drago Sournois– A creepy hotel guest, who has a suspicious habit of snooping. The begging question is– *Why?*

Odette Auteur– This author/ historian unearths a glittering treasure that triggers a torrent of trouble.

Antoine Li– A Eurasian antique dealer who knows a rare prize when he sees one.

Pierre Laperle– This Martinique jeweler has a penchant for Martinique sunsets and beautiful women. He's an expert on antique jewelry– *and appraisals.*

Dorélia Sauvage– The ardor this hotel waitress feels for her jeweler lover is indelibly etched on a heart of gold.

Jean-Jacques Sauvage– Dorélia's musician husband's ceaseless discord reaches a loud, public crescendo.

Marie Duval– This sunny *Martiniquaise* is an ardent fan of Odette Auteur's books; however, what else is Marie perusing?

Salomé Sauvage– The Sisters can't help but wonder whose head *this* Salomé might be after.

Marie-Josèphe-Rose Tascher de la Pagerie/ Empress Joséphine– one of history's most intriguing women.

Capitaine Michel Renard– The adroit principal *Inspecteur de la Police Nationale*, Fort-de-France, Martinique, is amazed at the Sleuth Sisters' crime-solving abilities.

"I rather like having someone to *witch* over me …
the right someone, anyway, at the right time."
~ Dr. Maggie McDonough, PhD

"I don't think you really want to know if I am a good witch
or a bad witch.
I'm not *just* a witch– I'm a storm with skin!"
~ Dr. Raine McDonough, PhD

"The first time I called myself a witch was
the most magickal moment of my life."
~ Margot Adler, *Drawing Down The Moon*

"You have witchcraft in your lips."
~ William Shakespeare, *Henry V*

"It is important to remember that we all have magick inside us."
~ J.K. Rowling

"For all you know,
a witch might be living next door to you right now."
~ Roald Dahl

"I do believe in magick.
My heart is a thousand years old. I am not like other people."
~ Author Ceane O'Hanlon-Lincoln

"Any time women come together with a collective intention,
it's a powerful thing …
when women come together with a collective intention–
magick happens."
~ Phylicia Rashad

,

~ Prologue ~

Known far and wide as the "Sleuth Sisters," raven-haired Raine and redheaded Maggie McDonough, cousins who share the same surname, residence, and occupation, as well as a few other things in what could only be termed their *magickal* lives, were preparing to leave for a two-week Caribbean holiday in Martinique, an overseas department of France. On summer break from their college teaching duties, the adventurous pair were eagerly anticipating a pleasant sojourn.

It was a sunny June morning, shortly after cockcrow, the baby-blue sky flecked with little white clouds, and the air as sweet as honey. Through an open window drifted a cardinal's loud string of whistles, the first bird the Sisters heard mornings, the last evenings.

As they tucked a few final things into their suitcases, their thoughts were on *mystery*, for they keenly sensed another astonishing adventure was about to unfold in their extraordinary lives.

Never was there a chance for time to hang heavy on those McDonough hands for lack of mission or duty.

Less than two months before, with Aisling McDonough-Gwynn, the senior member of the celebrated Sleuth Sisters trio, these incomparable young women sorted out the mayhem on New Moon Ranch in Montana when they were visiting their favorite cousin, Sean.

In her woodsy-themed bedroom with its green-marble fireplace, Raine slipped a cherished talisman– a gold compact, the lid a lion face– into the black, outsized shoulder bag she used for travel. The compact had belonged to Granny McDonough, and it was chock-full of protective energies.

Twisting partway round, she studied her reflection in the tall cheval glass, checking out her tight little tush and her shapely legs encased in black silk stockings. "Now that's Hex Appeal," she quipped. *Black is my **power** color. It creates an air of mystery, is elegant, dramatic, sexy, and it crafts a barrier between me and the outside world, shielding my emotions, sensitivities ... and secrets. And every witch ... every woman has secrets.*

Gothic attire was so befitting the brunette Sister, it prompted her Beau to dub the witchy chic "Raine gear."

Witches have always known that wearing black– like showering something, or someone, with water– neutralizes negative energies. Moreover, black draws in *natural* energies, enhancing the strength of the witch's personal power and connection to nature.

"Witch-trounce bad vibes that come my way," the Sister chanted to her reflection in the mirror, "so this unfolds a perfect day!"

This morning, Raine's trim body was sheathed in a black travel dress. The Goth gal loved witchy shoes and boots, and the outfit's black pumps, with saw-tooth edged vamps, possessed all the witchy-woman wow she fancied. Blowing a kiss at a silver-framed photo on the bureau, she winked at the image of her Beau. "Women who wear black lead colorful lives."

Toilette complete, Raine pinned to her lapel the glittering diamond magick-wand brooch that was her signature piece of jewelry, for imbued therein was a powerful Sleuth Sisters credo: "Thoughts are magick wands powerful enough to make anything happen– anything we choose."

Down the hall, Maggie was concluding *her* final travel preparations. Stepping back from the bureau's swivel-mirror, she checked her overall appearance. Taller than Raine and fuller-figured, Maggie, like her cousin and sister of the moon, enjoyed donning vintage clothing. But unlike Raine, this vibrant redhead delighted in color– bright colors concordant with her passionate Scorpio nature. The sleeveless, figure-hugging purple dress was just right. Seeking the matching designer bag she'd set out earlier, her eyes scanned the room.

As spacious as Raine's bedchamber, this Sister's room, too, was dignified with a substantial fireplace, though the marble here was dark red, the high-ceilinged room's palette the fiery tones of garnet and gold. Fall was Maggie's favorite time of year, and in her boudoir, it was forever autumn. "I was born in October," she liked to say, "and it is imprinted on my bones, for they ache, in the *witchy-est* sort of way, for all things multi-hued, misty– and *mysterious*."

Maggie was busy arranging at her throat a festive scarf, cheery with the colors of the Caribbean, when Raine sailed gaily into the room, carrying her suitcase, a black purse slung over her shoulder.

Flopping down on Maggie's bed, the brunette Sister announced, "I just rang off with Beau. Thaddeus is picking him up, and the two of them should be here in," she glanced at her watch, "about three hours."

Maggie gave a nod. She dropped a lipstick into her makeup kit that, in turn, she slipped into her shoulder bag. "I'm nearly ready."

Raine's feline eyes danced. "Don't take too much longer. Aisling said she was going to try and stop over this morning to witch us safe journey. Before I forget to ask, I heard you on the phone yesterday, talking with your ex. What news, Mags?"

A sad expression settled over the redheaded Sister's features. "It's strange," she said, wistful, "but looking back over the years, I don't think I ever thought of Rory McLaughlin as an ex. Not really. I mean, we began as friends, and that's how we ended. Oh, there were times when we were married that he hurt and angered me with his indiscretions; but as I've said before, it's impossible not to love that man." She placed a gauzy turquoise blouse in the valise and began rolling a strapless black dress. "When first he told me about the cancer, I honestly thought ... *hoped* he might beat it, but I know now he won't." Tears shimmered in her green eyes.

Raine reached out to pat Maggie's hand. "Granny always said, 'When it's your time ... it's your time.'"

"Rory hasn't much time, but he's managed to hold on to his courage and his great sense of humor, kidding that he can't swap jokes with the Angel of Death. He told me a hospital bed is a parked taxi with the meter running. He'll die at home, at the castle. I didn't wish to tire him, so I kept our conversation short yesterday. I do wish he'd let me visit. Thaddeus has offered to accompany me to Ireland, but Rory's still adamant that I not make the journey."

Maggie brushed away a tear with the back of her hand. "He wants me to remember him as he was."

"I'm glad he penned that heartfelt letter, baring his soul to you. It was the best thing he could have done, and a man's best is a big thing." Raine's mind darted backward, and she weighed whether to speak her next words. "I feel quite strongly that he never stopped loving you, Mags."

"I haven't been *in* love with him for years, but I never stopped loving him," Maggie pronounced softly. "So," she said of a sudden, in attempt to lift the mood, "tell me what our parents said when they telephoned this morning."

"Well," Raine gave a little sigh, "you'd jumped in the shower, so I talked for us both. They hadn't much to say– it wasn't a very good connection– only that they wished us safe journey and to touch base with them upon our return. They've wrapped their fieldwork in the South Pacific and are headed for Easter Island, then Peru, as they explore the potential connection of seafaring peoples *à la* Kon-Tiki. Though they didn't mention it, my witchy guess is that Mexico will follow, after which I feel sure, from the way they talked, they'll plan a short visit with us stateside before moving on to their next dig. However, you know how spontaneous our parents can be, so what I just related is subject to change."

"Understandable. Now that they're retired from the Smithsonian, they can go wherever they please, wherever there are research questions that intrigue them. My witchy intuition is telling me that the compilation of their archeological adventures will ultimately be an award-winning book series. I'm happy they're doing what they most love, now that they're free to do it." Maggie patted her large purple purse. "Before I forget to mention it, I've packed the small crystal ball Grantie gifted us."

The Sisters were using their affectionate title for their great-aunt, bestowed in gratitude for generosity.

"Dear old Grantie got a chuckle out of the name we gave our mini-ball. I daresay," Maggie murmured with pleased mien, "Angel Baby has proven herself to be the ideal travel companion."

"And what am I? Chopped liver?" came a reedy little voice from the bolster of Maggie's bed.

"You? You're filet mignon," Raine quipped, reaching over to give the enchanted poppet an affectionate pat.

The feisty ragdoll, Cara, was bequeathed to the Sleuth Sisters by their historic village's erstwhile enigma, an eighteenth-century hermit and fellow sister of the Craft, whose violent murder the Sisters solved when they time-trekked to the perilous Pennsylvania frontier.

Approximately eleven inches tall, the doll's head bore a mop of what used to be, over two centuries earlier, red wool yarn for hair, faded now to a pale orangey hue. The rag-stuffed head and body were fashioned of a coarse, age-darkened muslin. Two, faded but still faintly visible, black ink dots represented the eyes; and the mouth, smeared undoubtedly by countless childish kisses across the tumbled years, was crooked, giving the evident impression of a mischievous grin.

As it happened, the poppet was inhabited with the ancient spirit of a formidable Irish sister of the Craft, an entity whose powers the good Sisters were grateful to have on their side.

A green vest, the design in the cambric long claimed by Time, was pinched in at the doll's waist by a narrow, rope-like cord. The uneven skirt was pinked and somewhat tattered, the purple-ish color nearly gone the way of history; and though the poppet sported no shoes, the ink-blackened feet were shaped as though it did, the soles turning up at the toes and evoking the notion of a leprechaun.

Aiming one mitt-hand toward the Sisters, the wry poppet spouted, "Wit Beau 'n Thaddeus along, y' won't be needin' me dis trip, but rest assured, gurls, me 'n th' Merlin cats will see to da home front. Of dat y' kin be sarr-tain."

The Sisters smiled in a satisfied fashion, with Maggie reaching out to stroke the poppet's faded yarn head.

"We appreciate that," Raine replied. "Please be sure to keep an eye on the Merlin cats. Panthèra won't give you any trouble, gentle soul that she is, but Jack and Jade, Goddess bless them, can be ornery. They can't help but live up to the title of distinction I've bestowed upon each of them– PhD, *Puss of Hubristic Divination*."

"*Och*, you 'n yer highfalutin words, Raine. What's *hubristic*?"

"It's a lot of things," Raine laughed. "But simply put, it's exaggerated pride or self-confidence."

"Humph! I'll keep the little showoffs in line. Niver fret over dat. *Begorra*, I best hark back on what y'll need t' carry wit ya," Cara rattled on. "Maggie, be sarr-tain t' wear yer Nirumbee crystal. Y' niver know whin y' might have t' … how did you put it, Raine? Ah," the poppet exclaimed, tapping her head with a mitt-hand, "give someone da once-over."

The Nirumbee crystal was a powerful energy muse Maggie had acquired in Montana. In any given situation, including the person or persons therein, the crystal acted as an indicator of the surroundings, flashing a significant color across Maggie's mind's eye, at the same time inciting a sensation deep within her being.

"Both iv y' wear yer ancient talismans," Cara reminded. "Y'll need Angel Baby, sure, 'n yer tr-ravel *Book of Shadows*; but foremost, you two will need yer **wits** about ya. Bless me, I hope t' th' great Goddess y' niver travel without yer granny's healin' potion. Or her Easy Breezy f'r dat matter. Ah, an' dat reminds me, be sartain t' take some of yer friend Eva's special-brew tea. And Raine, carry an olivine stone wit ya."

"You going to tell me why?"

"*Och*, jus' do it," the poppet retorted in her officious way. "You'll *find out* why."

"Figured that's what you'd say," Raine returned. "I'll take a raw olivine from my box of gemstones."

"No worries. Magickal tools all packed for our Caribbean escapade." Maggie regarded her lapel watch. "Wait for me, Raine. I have only a few more things to pack." She started rolling an off-the-shoulder black chemise dress for the open valise. "I can't stop speculating on what mystery awaits us this adventure."

Pitching in, an ever-impatient Raine snatched up a green bikini swimsuit, rolled and handed it to Maggie. "Everywhere we go, a mystery falls into our laps. I can't fathom yet what our next puzzle will entail, but my witch's hunch has been telling me for weeks it'll focus on the ever-mysterious Empress Joséphine. I know *that* for certain."

"Indeed," Maggie agreed. She was silent for a long moment, thinking about Raine's words as she rolled a couple of lace tops and a black negligee. "*La Belle Créole*, one of history's most fascinating women."

"She is *that*," chimed Raine. "All her life, Joséphine was zealously interested in the occult, and I daresay there has always been an air of mystery about her. *Marie-Josèphe Rose Tascher de la Pagerie*, a pretty, Martinique plantation girl called 'Rose,' whom Napoléon christened 'Joséphine.'"

"Why did he do that, do you suppose?" Maggie asked. "Virtually change her name?"

"Difficult to say. However, I always believed it was because Rose had blossomed … unfurled for others before him, so," she shrugged, "by calling her the name of *his* choice, he was, in a way, making her his own."

Raine's feline familiar, Black Jack O'Lantern, entered the bedchamber and straightaway began nosing round the full-length mirror in a corner of the room.

Oblivious, the raven-haired Sister handed Maggie the flirty floral skirt she rolled for the suitcase. "Mags, as I started to say, I've been sensing for weeks there *will* be a mystery ... and likely more than one. No surprise or worry for us, but I have to tell you, I've been plagued with a *troubling* feeling. You see–"

Maggie turned with eyebrows raised, as she picked up Raine's thought. "Now, now, no point in borrowing trouble. Don't let's program anything negative for ourselves or anyone else. We've handled so many sticky situations in our lives, that–" The full red lips snapped shut, and the rest of the sentence went unspoken when Raine interposed.

"Galloping gargoyles," she spurted, pointing to the cheval glass in the corner. "Granny!"

"Merry meet, me darlin's!" The words issued with sudden force from the tall mirror, where ghostly mists were aiding manifestation of a beloved figure.

"Merry meet," they echoed in unison, though now over the initial jounce, not with surprise. "In peace and love we welcome you."

Granny– the cloud of soft white hair in its loose bun, adorned with an aurora borealis crystal snood; the unlined, pink-and-white face; the august demeanor– so angelic and profoundly loved by the two young women poised before the looking glass with their poppet.

Gazing at the radiant image, the Sisters noted that Granny was wearing Elder's attire, the long gown and cape dazzling white and sparkling with stardust of silver and gold. They remained quiet, for they knew the *grande dame* could be called away any second to the important celestial conference in the offing.

"As has been me state iv affairs th' past few times I've popped in, I'm here 'n gone in a tick; so give me yer full attention, gurls. Brief 'n to th' mark: Yer sentiments ring true. Yer Caribbean holiday will be steeped in mysteries of *all* sorts. Be ready 'n willin' t' handle tings, f'r well y' know, 'tis yer sacred destiny."

As was often their habit, Raine and Maggie responded in sync, "Mystery and mayhem again, will it be?"

"Indaid. Loomin' ahead is a brewin' cauldron o' trouble. It pains me t' say this, me darlin's, but again I must add *murder* to th' messy mix."

"Sounds like our next adventure will be a real mare's nest," Maggie said under her breath.

"Sure 'n 'tis why th' Fates aire sendin' you t' the tropics."

The Sisters knew when Granny's Irish brogue thickened that her words carried deep emotion, and her message was one of the utmost importance.

"You know b' now," Granny hurried on, "you can do whativer ya set yer minds t'." She brought her fingers together to lock them tight. *"Tré neart le chéile–* **together strong.** Now heed me counsel, f'r though y've heard dees words afore, they aire worth repeatin'." Granny crooked her snowy head to wag a bejeweled finger at the Sisters. "Make use of ivery protection I taught ya, and I taught you well. Ye're right t' pack yer talismans 'n the tools b'stowed by yer Grantie Merry. I know you gurls will handle yer new charge like true McDonoughs."

When an impetuous Raine started to speak, Granny lifted the pointing finger to beseech continued focus. "I'll take a moment longer t' pass on th' balance iv what I want t' say now, in case I'm in conference if y' try t' summon me later." Granny shook her head, and her face took suddenly a rather grim line, as her old eyes shimmered with teary emotion. "'Tis a mountain o' tings we Celestial Elders have t' sort out nowadays … a mountain o' troubles, more th'n iver in th' history iv Earth. Many more Star Children have been sent, aire bein' sent, armed with a rainbow of special gifts. One day, *our* kind will finally succeed in bringin' peace 'n love to this troubled planet. *I've* seen the visions, but it's for all to see who look. F'r now, you each have yer special assignments."

The wise woman smiled benignly, in a sad, knowing manner, and she radiated such tenderness that the Sisters could literally *feel* the warmth on their faces. "Niver f'rgit th' Star-Children's purpose: Do all the good you can, in all the ways you can, to all th' souls you can, in every place you can, with all the zeal you can, as long as iver you can.

"Always remember, too, that centuries of knowledge and wisdom reside within your cells, and ye're niver alone. As you heard me say, Star Children fr'm all areas iv th' universe have been sent, will continue to be sent, t' help Earth and its peoples. If iver y' feel alone, hark you back to me guidin' words: Th' problems that lay afore you aire niver as strong as th' ancestors who walk b'side you, and those ancestors will always, and f'river, be heralded 'n led by *me*."

With that, Granny vanished from the mirror, after blowing a kiss that reached Raine, Maggie, Cara, and Black Jack O'Lantern in the sparkling form of gold and silver glitter that spun round and round them a protective bubble of awesome white Light.

For a timeless time, Granny's parting words seemed to hang in the air like a whisper that resonated sweetly within the breast of each Sister, making them feel unconditionally and wholly loved.

Presently, Raine let out her breath. "Bless my besom, Mags, we **are** mystery magnets."

Maggie responded with a nod. "An understatement. But as Granny taught us, Old Souls, empaths, and Starseeds are different, *because we're here to make a difference.*" Again, the Sister checked her watch. "Ready with plenty o' time to spare."

"My witch's intuition is telling me we'll soon be making use of our strongest magickal tools, but we won't stress it. We'll handle whatever's coming. We always do." Raine's grin deepened the dimple in her left cheek. "And I ask you– what would our lives be without mystery? People don't call us the 'Sleuth Sisters' for nothing."

The Three Sisters were often the topic of discussion in Haleigh's Hamlet. Indeed, there was something about the phrase that conjured all sorts of witchy images, the words themselves magickal.

When tackling a new mystery, it was the Sisters' custom to throw themselves into spirit-boosting pep talks, for it quite shored up their confidence. "In keeping with the Great Secret," Raine touted, touching her signature magick-wand brooch, "the *real* magick is believing in oneself."

"At least we won't have to worry about anything here at home while we're gone. Hannah and her hubby will be staying here," Maggie commented of their loyal housekeeper. "They'll keep watch over the place and tend to whatever needs tending, including the cats and the horses."

"We're most blessed to have them," Raine answered. "Hannah and Jim have always been more like family than hired help."

Emitting a harmonious sound, Maggie moved to the dresser to apply protection balm to her wrists. All three Sisters wore magickal balms and oils of their own creation in lieu of commercial perfumes.

Raine stood to dip into Maggie's defense balm, touching it to pulse points. "Aisling and Ian are so swamped with clients, there's no way they could take off, but I wish they were going with us."

"Aisling is but an astral trek away, lass," Cara declared with her usual Celtic vehemence. "Astral wur-rk is her special gift, ye ken. Did ye iver tink 'bout the Irish meanin' iv th' braw name *Aisling*? 'Tis *vision*, *dr-ream* or *appar-rition*. Fittin' 'tis the given name iv yer granny **and** yer eldest moon-sister, is it not? Tink 'bout dat now, me darlin's."

The Goth gal's pouty lips curved upward in a catlike grin. "Whilst we're away, see you keep out of mischief, poppet." She loved Cara and ever 'n anon fretted over losing her. "But you're a wise and wizard guardian. I'll say that for you. Wiz—zard!"

Before Cara could respond, Maggie, with head cocked in wistful attitude, replied, "When you utter your pet expletive, it never fails to bustle me back to our Hamlet's elusive Wizard." Scrappy remembrances wafted across her mind. *I wonder if we'll ever discover who the mystifying advisor to our sisters, the Keystone Coven, really is?*

Raine's face presented a kittenish moue as she looked up from checking the contents of her purse. "Now *there's* a mystery!" she exclaimed, having seized her cousin and moon sister's thought. "The *Coven* has never figured out who he is; and increasingly, it looks as if that might be the one puzzle *we* never crack. Sometimes I think it's Thaddeus, other times Hugh, and then," her voice dropped, "there are *fervent* moments, I'm convinced the Wizard is my Beau."

Maggie rebounded with, "Darlin', Beau, Hugh, and Thaddeus are *each* suspect. We know from experience what finely honed sixth senses Beau and Hugh possess, the pair of them. It's why they're excellent veterinarians. After all, their patients can't tell them what's wrong. As for my Thaddeus," a Mona Lisa smile transformed her cheery air to mysterious, "well now, he's a *recurrent* wizard. Every little thing he does creates magick ... *magick with unbridled passion.* To quote Grandpa McDonough, 'Genius is talent set aflame.'" Remembering a cool, cotton dress she neglected to pack, the redheaded Sister started for the closet.

"What'd you forget?" Raine asked, not waiting for a response. "One of these days, we're going to be hashing out what we know about the Wizard, and we'll suddenly figure it out. Just like we untangle clues when we're brainstorming a mystery. As it stands, all we and the Coven are certain of is that their advisor resides in our Hamlet. The Keystone sisters don't even know if the Wizard's a man or a woman, never having met their mentor in person. Not much to go on, is it?" Raine rushed on, suppling her own answer. "Down the years, the Coven has come to refer to this enigmatic guru as the 'Wizard,' but like we've said numerous times, it could well be a *sister* of the Craft, a solitary witch who prefers anonymity."

"Indeed." Maggie rolled the salmon-colored dress she pulled from the closet and placed it in her suitcase. "And as we've reasoned, just because the Coven sisters refer to this unknown entity as their *senior* advisor, due to the steady stream of wisdom he or she imparts, it doesn't necessarily mean the so-called Wizard is a person of golden years. Why, for all we know—"

"**Whist!**" the ragdoll shrieked from the bolster of Maggie's bed, the exclamation springing the poppet several inches into the air. "Iffin' I tole y' once-st, I done tole ya a hundred times— some tings aire destined f'r mystery. Flow like water over stones," the poppet intoned, "a t'ing not seen is never known. Save yer sleuthin' f'r whaire it's needed. Now finish dat packin', an' give it th' welly! Aisling will be here afore ya know it." She tilted her yarn-covered head. "I kin *feel* her makin' ready to motor over here as we speak."

"Cara's right," Raine said, used to the poppet's bossiness. "C'mon, look sharp now, as Granny would say. I fancy a cup of tea." The raven-haired Sister rose, and slinging her shoulder bag over an arm, she picked up her single suitcase.

The Sisters always traveled as light as possible, each limiting herself to a large purse and one small valise that would easily fit in an overhead compartment. They never liked to check their baggage, for most of their things were cast with strong magick.

Seizing her purse and suitcase, Maggie followed Raine to the stair landing.

Starting down the steps, the Goth gal chanted thrice, more to the universe than to Maggie, "We've bested evil before. We can do it again, and that's for sure."

Raine was referring to their vanquishing of the ancient *Macbeth* curse from Whispering Shades, the Hamlet's "little theatre in the woods," that resulted in the most terrifying of battles. Besides ousting a bane of evil from their town and popular theatre, they managed, in the bargain, to soothe Whispering Shades' resident ghost.

Floating upward through a mist of visions and memory, she remembered what she said about their theatre phantom at the time. "A ghost is both a clue and an invitation to a world beyond our own reality, an offer to broaden our awareness to encompass anything and everything that might be possible. And, I ask you, who can resist that kind of challenge?"

"Not us for sure." Maggie gave a little titter, and her laugh sounded like crystal wind chimes on a pleasant breeze. "I'm in accord with Bess Truman when she spoke of the White House apparitions. To paraphrase– 'I'm sure they're here, and I'm not half so alarmed at meeting up with any of 'em as I am at meeting the live ghouls I encounter every day.'" The redhead thought for a moment, adding, "Ghosts are like true love, which everyone talks about but few have seen."

"Not us for sure," echoed Raine.

Maggie answered softly, "I've been blessed in that department … more than I once realized."

"Ditto that, Sister," Raine dimpled, breaking into a prompt grin.

As the pair swept down the ornately carved staircase, they passed the framed oil painting mounted on the stairwell wall, that Maggie had done of the famous Irish dolmen Poulnabrone, the prehistoric set of huge stones resembling a portal to the netherworld.

A gifted photographer and artist, Maggie executed the painting from a photograph in which she'd captured the setting sun just as it flashed, star-like and centered, beneath the horizontal slab of the great standing stones.

Several years prior, Raine and Maggie made the most significant journey of their lives– a trip to mystical Ireland, where they happened upon more than they had bargained for. There, they sought and found answers to the haunting questions connected to a very special quest of their own– and to a series of murders and legendary lost jewels at Barry Hall, a noble, old estate in County Clare. It was in Ireland where, after years of research, the pair ferreted out the magickal Time-Key, which, when properly activated, whisked them through the Tunnel of Time to yesteryear– to *any* year that they encoded.

Maggie's eyes drifted to the stair landing's tall stained-glass window that depicted the McDonough coat-of-arms with its fierce wild boar and lions *en passant*. *Granny's words hold truth*, she told herself. *We're never alone. The ancestors are always with us.*

Lingering briefly on the landing, she peered out a clear pane of the huge window to the green slope of lawn and magnificent woods beyond. "June means roses, hydrangea, wisteria, and our lovely azalea and rhododendron. The whole place will soon *sing* with color," she smiled, imaging Tara's façade splashed with red, blue, purple, pink, yellow, and white. "I sometimes think I can hear the wee voices of faerie when I walk the backyard amidst our flower beds. Those times, I gain a whole new sense of well-being. Hmmm, summer in our Hamlet is utterly enchanting."

An enchanting place *any* time, Haleigh's Hamlet was a picturesque village– a historic southwestern Pennsylvania town that conferred countless glimpses of the *used-to-be–* with a charming cluster of Victorian, castle-like homes, replete with gingerbread and old money, all built during an era when help was cheap and plentiful, and the owners– coal and railroad barons (the life's blood of the village during its heyday)– could well afford a bevy of servants.

To folks who lived elsewhere, the Hamlet's kingly mansions, each occupying a triple-sized wooded lot, were ever mysterious, bringing to mind secret rooms revealed with a touch to a certain "book" on a shelf and hidden staircases exposed by the twist of a latch disguised as a wall sconce. There was never any danger of anyone undesirable moving into one of the Hamlet's manors. The cost and upkeep prohibited that problem.

A stately, turreted Queen Anne, Tara was Raine and Maggie's nineteenth-century Victorian home, located in the quaint, storied Hamlet, on the edge of Haleigh's Wood. Anyone who visited Tara inevitably went away thinking that it was the right setting, the *perfect* setting, for the Sisters' personalities.

Perfectionists by nature, they liked the atmosphere in and about their "castle" to be flawless, and– despite creaking wooden floors, stairs, and doors– it was.

The early June sun spilled rainbows through the Queen Anne's jewel-like stained-glass windows, splashing a cornucopia of color on the already vibrant collection of curious things the old mansion sheltered within its sturdy walls, whilst the windowsills glinted with rows of vari-colored crystals– each charged with strong magick.

Among them were amber for vanquishing negativity, disease and dis-ease; amethyst for healing and inducing pleasant dreams; aquamarine for calming the nerves and lifting the spirits; citrine for cleansing; vivid green aventurine, the luckiest of stones, for inviting adventure, prosperity, and all good; moonstone, "wolf's eye," for new beginnings and intuition; peridot for release from guilt; rose quartz for unconditional love and retaining youthfulness and beauty; tiger's eye and falcon's eye for protection; sapphire for insight and truth; emerald for bliss, loyalty, and wealth; and ruby for passion, energy and vigor.

Crystals and gemstones, as candles, are essential and effective in the magickal lives of witches. The Sisters comprehended that many worlds exist and that holding special stones, crystals, or seashells, and being receptive to and welcoming of them, unlocked doors to those other realms. The Third Eye perceives far beyond ordinary sight.

On the center sill of the dining room's trilogy of castle-themed stained-glass windows, a small, smoky-glass bowl held Apache tears. To the Ancient Ones, these were frozen tears lost in the sands of time, the magickal stones proffering grounding, good luck and defense, as well as the ridding of negativity that hindered realized dreams. Like amethyst and tiger's eye, Apache tears shielded the Sisters against psychic attack– known also as the "Evil Eye."

Here too, the Sisters kept a large Herkimer Diamond, which despite the name, was not really a diamond at all but a powerful clear crystal. The Sisters understood that "Herkies," perfect conduits of the Universal Life Force, were exceptional healing crystals– the high-energy seekers of the crystal world that amplify the influence of other gemstones.

To balance moods, harmonize bio-energy, and boost resistance to illnesses, the Sisters had recently added a powerful, Reiki-infused, Third-Eye orgonite pyramid consisting of a Czech moldavite, an equal-size Herkimer diamond, seven tiny real diamonds, and nine amethysts, the smaller stones swirled in gold and set off with a golden pentacle. The green resin, metal, quartz, and gemstone pyramid was a beautiful addition to their collection, ridding the area of negativity and protecting from electromagnetic pollution.

In Tara's east windows hung hollow glass balls called "Witch Balls" to protect home and ward from detriment. Dating back to the eighteenth century, legend has it that evil spirits, attracted to these orbs, were pulled inside and trapped. It's told yet today that fishermen of old used these colorful balls in their nets to fend off evil on the high seas.

The napping black cat on the radiator cracked an eye open when the wooden floor creaked the Sisters' entrance into Tara's kitchen, where the blue opalescent glass in the cabinet doors shimmered with sunlight. It was a happy-feeling kitchen, and Maggie hummed merrily as she and Raine busied themselves with the proper brewing of a small pot of tea. Introduced to them years before by their beloved Granny McDonough, teatime was something from which these steeped-in tradition ladies took pleasure whenever and wherever they could.

The big, airy kitchen's focal point was the pretty, sky-blue, hooded stove, restored to its Victorian splendor, that had been their granny's pride and joy. The old house held most of the modern conveniences, but in the kitchen especially, Raine and Maggie preferred the Old Ways– trusted, tried and true.

Above them, bunches of dried herbs and flowers dangled from the dark, massive ceiling beams of abiding English oak. A small herb garden thrived year-round in the kitchen's bay window, and affixed to the brick chimney, a broom-riding Kitchen Witch thwarted the bad and invited the good.

A besom-riding witch topped Tara's highest gable too. Celts have always been superstitious, as well as deeply spiritual. The tradition of the witch weather vane, imbued with Irish and Scottish folktales of enchanted old women flying over castle and field, casting spells and weaving magick, dates all the way back to the 1300s– or even earlier. Legend has it that if a passing witch saw such an effigy, she knew she could rest on the chimney top and consequently would cast no mischief upon the household.

Whilst the majestic manor's waterspouts channeled rain from Tara's slate roof and rust-colored brick walls, these conduits also served as watchful gargoyles, their mouths open in the silent shrieks that staved off evil. And at Tara's front entrance, a small, decorative sign near the holly bush read: *Magickal Black Cats Guard This Home.*

Protective holly grew by every one of Tara's entrances and close to the rear gate leading into the garden, where, upon a faerie mound, spell-cast items were recharged under the full moon's energizing glow. Here, a garden plaque was engraved with a J.M. Wonderland quote: "The sun watches what I do, but the moon knows my secrets." The reference reverberated a declaration of the home's mistresses– "The moon is our loyal companion and confidante."

Like a witch's cauldron, Tara– a grand old house, one of the Hamlet's great houses– bubbled with magick, casting its spell over anyone who set eyes upon it. Invisible to non-magick people, powerful energies encircled and safeguarded the manse and its occupants. In all honesty, it was not the most beautiful residence in the district but, unquestionably, it was the most unique– *as were its mistresses.*

The large house had five grand fireplaces, plus a fire pit in the backyard– profoundly satisfying to its owners. Symbolic of heart and hearth, used in rituals and during gatherings, fire, throughout the ages, has perpetually inspired singing and dancing, plus the sharing of stories and– *magick.*

Surrounded by a black, wrought-iron fence, with *fleur-de-lys* finials crafted in France, the turreted 1890s home was crowded with antiques, the cousins' vintage clothing, and a collection of *very special* jewelry, all of it enchanted, most of it heirloom and quite old.

The "McDonough Girls," as the Hamlet sometimes called them, had a charismatic flair, each for her own brand of fashion, each possessing the gift to *feel* the sensations cached away in their collected treasures, "As if," they were inclined to say, "we are living history."

A long line of McDonough women possessed the gift for sensing, through proximity and touch, the layered stories and energies of those who previously owned the time-honored articles they acquired. Attired in their vintage clothing, these women were all gossamer and lace; but make no mistake, they bore spines of cloaked steel.

Plainly put, the McDonoughs ran to women of passionate personalities generation after generation. For the most part, they ignored convention, were headstrong and willful– with every intention of staying that way.

The family was an old one, full of tradition, mystique, and fire that dated back to the *Ard Ri* of Tara– the High Kings of Ireland.

The grand lady who named the house for Ireland's sacred Hill came, decades before, from County Meath, bequeathing her female heirs a special gift– and a great deal of magick.

McDonough women could make magick just by walking into a room. They had ages of it behind them, following in their wake like the long, fiery tail of a comet.

The witches' New Year, *Samhain*– Hallowe'en– was their favorite holiday.

And then there were the cats, known in the world of the Craft as "Watchers," though some would say "Familiars," five at the moment, three of which, Black Jade and Black Jack O'Lantern and Panthèra, were descended from Granny McDonough's unforgettable tom, Myrrdyn, the Celtic name for Merlin. After all, it was a commodious old house, and it literally *purrred* with love.

Back in the day, when Granny McDonough floated grandly into a room, the theatre, a shop, restaurant, or hall, whispers abruptly broke out like little hissing fires throughout the space. The villagers used to babble that Granny McDonough's "big ole black cat" assisted her with black magick. Black cats do that to some people, the un-magick anyway, rendering them shivery and illogical, while conjuring up all sorts of dark-night superstitions.

"Psychological poppycock! I have *no* patience with that sort of pretentious twaddle," Granny used to cite, her scoff flavored by Irish brogue, Granny whose magick was forever white. "Vile, wicked nights 'n black magick, indaid!" Her advice on the subject: "If a black cat crosses your path– **pet it.**"

In response to those harsh muggle critics of the Craft who would say, "Magick is magick, and there is no such thing as "*white magick,*" Granny would smile sweetly and reply, "There is no good or bad magick, only good and bad people. It all depends on *intent,* my dear. 'What you send forth comes back to thee, so ever mind the Law of Three. Follow this with mind and heart, merry ye meet, and merry ye part.' Magick is intended change, and *intention* creates th' change."

Her granddaughters would add: "Every intentional act is a magickal act."

Anyroad, tittle-tattle never bothered "The McDonough," as in Irish custom, Granny was rightly titled. Mostly, she laughed it off, advocating, "Sure 'n ya might as well get th' benefit of it– gossip liberates you from convention."

But that's the way of any small town. People talked, and they always would. Their tongues were never idle. Not to say that Haleigh's Hamlet didn't like the McDonoughs. They very much did, some even going so far as to flaunt pride for this longstanding Hamlet clan. Despite the whisperings of the town folk, many were the times someone of them came rapping at the back door, under veil of darkness, for a secret potion or a charm, either to satisfy a true need or stifle curiosity.

In consequence of the Hamlet grapevine, Maggie and Raine never forgot the advice they heard Granny give to one distraught woman: "*Pshaw*, fools' blather! Mark me, lass, the greatest burden– to wit *fear*– in th' world is the opinion of others. But the moment you aire unafraid of th' pack, you aire no longer a sheep. You become a *lion,*" she enthused. "A great r-r-roar rises in yer heart– and that, my dear, is the roar of *freedom.*" The Sisters found this to be pretty good advice on the whole.

Over the long years, the McDonough family home gathered within its stout brick walls its fair share of arcane, esoteric, and cloak-and-dagger mysteries. Without the least bit of puffery or purple prose, Tara could be summarized as a house that embodied a host of veiled secrets, old and new. But as the McDonough clan continually affirmed, "Devoid of mysteries, life would be dreary indeed. What would be left to strive for, if everything were known?"

The greatest secrets are hidden; the most significant, influential things in the universe unseen; and those who do not believe in *magick* will never experience it– will never uncover its mysteries. Granny always said, paraphrasing her oft-read Mr. Yeats, "The world is full of magick, patiently waitin' f'r our senses t' grow sharper."

That said, there never was a more *un*worldly person than The McDonough, who, per shades of *The Little Prince*, believed "The most beautiful things in the world cannot be seen or touched. They are felt with the heart."

No less than three generations of the Hamlet's women found themselves drawn to Granny McDonough, wanting to confess *their* secrets to her in the shadows of Tara's porch, where the sweet-smelling wisteria still grew thick in spring and summer, gracing the lattices with cascading, grape-like, pink and purple blooms.

And the Hamlet men, though they might scoff at such things, believed secretly, then and now, that on occasion a beautiful, young Aisling Tully McDonough, before she became known as "Granny," visited their dreams, igniting their carnal desires or whispering to them ways in which they might succeed in their careers.

The Hamlet learned that they could trust Granny McDonough with their secrets, and she conscientiously passed that torch on to her trinity of granddaughters– to her namesake Aisling, to Maggie, and to Raine.

A solitary, eclectic witch, Granny entrusted her accumulated knowledge and wisdom to her granddaughters by teaching them well. Of course, The McDonough didn't confuse the two– knowledge and wisdom, that is. "Never mistake knowledge for wisdom," she instructed. "One helps you make a livin'; the other helps you make a life."

Forthright and candid, Granny had always looked straight into the eyes of anyone with whom she spoke. She was never one to sit on the fence or pussyfoot around, leaving "... that to the neighborhood cats, sugar-coatin' to th' baker, and elegance to th' tailor."

It was quoted far afield that Granny McDonough was a wise woman and a healer of a great many things. "Witch and famous," mouthed the Hamlet folk. Though few held a wicked fear, and there were those who were chary, they sought her out, looking for her the way people scan the sky when there's a promise of shooting stars.

Over time, the Hamlet came to love Granny McD, even going so far as to believe that if her long, black cloak brushed against them as she passed on the street, its mere touch brought them good fortune for the remainder of their days.

Someone once asked Granny if every witch sported a cape. "Sure 'n they do," she answered with her knowing smile. "A natural-born witch requires no tools, only intent and belief, but oils, herbs, spells, and such *do* help. Wand-er nay; hence I say, 'Cloak-and-wand away!' A cape allows Nature's magnetic energy t' flow freely round th' body. And b'sides, witches spend a great deal iv time outdoors, communin' wit Earth Mother, so a cape is practical. Mine keeps me warm 'n toasty even whin I'm called out f'r a healin' on a frosty winter's night."

Suffice to say, the Celtic history of healing is a rich and powerful one, and *Celt* is synonymous with "free spirit." Never was a McDonough born who was not a free spirit.

Once when Raine was sent home from school for soundly thrashing a fellow student, a boy much bigger than she, who had relentlessly teased her for being a witch– teasing Raine was the sweep of crimson fighting cape before a bull– Granny sat her down with a glimmer in her eyes; and her words came fast, tumbling over one another. "Number One: As long as there have been human bein's, there've been witches. Two: Witches have *always* been misunderstood. We terrify folks who don't understand, don't understand what witchcraft *is* … and what it is *not*. Three: Not that I hold with brawlin', child, but sure 'n didn't ya lar-rn Grandpa McDonough's KO punch better 'n Aisling or Maggie put t'gether! You remember t' tuck yer thumbs 'n yer chin, and t' keep yer hands in front iv yer face. 'Course der's somethin' t' be said f'r th' element iv surprise too." And she could not help the smile that brightened her face.

It had been the widowed Granny who'd taken the girls in hand, when they were pre-teens, to coach them on how to defend themselves. Granny was always teaching her girls something. The lessons never stopped.

"Now lar-rn this," Granny chided, "Be yerself, *a leanbh*," she reinforced in Gaelic. "*The world will adjust.* An original is always better than a copy. Some of us create. Others can only imitate. When you dance to yer own rhythm, people might not understand you. They might not even like you–"

"I don't think they do like me, Granny," Raine had sobbed. "'N the girls are worse th'n the boys."

"*Whist, child,* let me finish! They might not understand or like you, but by the great Goddess, they'll wish they had th' courage to *be* you. Confidence, my dear, is not 'Will they like me?' Confidence is 'I'll be fine if they don't.' And remember, you not only have th' *right* to be an individual, as a *McDonough* you have an *obligation* to be one.

"Sure 'n th' gurls aire worse. They're jealous!" Granny didn't have to think too hard on that one. "Most gurls 'r innocent enough; I'll grant ya that. Like kittens. But gurls b'come women, th' way kittens b'come cats. 'Twas those Burkle gurls again, truth b' known. If they grow up to be like th'r mither ... there isn't th' like of a woman f'r devilment th' world wide. *Jealous*, I tell you, plain 'n simple. That's all 'tis."

When Raine, drying her tears, remarked that all she wanted was to be "normal," Granny drew herself up to full height to expound, with high-flying Irish temper, "Me darlin' gurl, if y' feel like y' don't fit in, in this world, it's because you are here t' help create a new one– a *better* one. I'll tell ya true, here 'n now, that bein' 'normal,' as you call it, is wholly ordinary ... *humdrum 'n utterly **unimaginative.*** And I'll tell ya flat out, lass, it rather denotes a lack iv courage."

That's all it took. In response to Granny's candor, the willful, ofttimes hoydenish Raine was cured forever of wanting a "normal" life. Ever after, she delighted in being as **not** normal as it is possible to be, quoting henceforth her adopted maxim: "Why be normal when you can be– *magickal?*"

When Raine was older, Granny advised, "Give yer heart to th' soul who loves you to madness 'n who loves yer 'madness,' who sees beauty in th' wildness of yer spirit– **not** the eejit who tries to force you to be 'normal.' And never f'rgit that whin people are intimidated by yer strength 'n happiness, they'll try t' break yer spirit 'n tear ya down. Remember, that sort iv behavior is a reflection of *their* weakness and *not* a reflection of *you*."

"I prefer cats to people, Granny," Raine had answered with the mien of a pampered feline.

"Stop inter-ruptin', child," Granny chafed. "Let me finish what I started to say. You owe *no one* an explanation f'r bein' *who you are*. Let the *amadáns* sort out yer mystery.

"Do not take this world too personally," The McDonough cautioned her granddaughters on more than one occasion. Wear it *loosely*, or it will straightjacket you. It's yer choice, me darlin's. Whativer happens in life, have th' courage, as co-creators with other Star Children and with Spirit, t' live as you aire meant to live."

Of the Sisters, Raine, especially, took that advice to heart, never letting the muggles get her down. Anyone who tried was usually thumped with the phrase, "Go smudge yourself!" As for muggle acceptance of witches, the Goth gal's response to that was, "You don't have to understand witches, just don't ever piss one off!"

After Grandpa McDonough passed on, Granny, who spoke to the end of her life with a brogue as thick as her good Irish stew, never wore anything but what the Hamlet referred to as her "widow's weeds."

With a lilt to her step and her shadowy cape billowing out behind her, Granny often walked her big, black tom, Myrrdyn, on a leash after supper in the owl light of evening. To the amazement of the villagers, the cat pranced– tail held high to form a question mark, neither twisting nor turning in any effort whatsoever to escape– at the end of a velvet lead that was fastened to a fancy, jewel-studded collar around his neck, the other end wrapped several times round Granny's bejeweled hand. As self-important as you please, proudly and demurely did that tom swagger, with attitude and countenance that clearly avowed, "I am Granny McD's cat if you please– or if you don't please."

Granny fathomed what most here in the New World of America did not– that gently stroking a black cat nine times, from head to tail, brought good fortune and luck in love (that went triple for *Samhain*/ Hallowe'en). Stroking any cat releases mental and emotional stress. Treating cats kindly, with the respect they deserve, and warmly sharing one's home with cats of any color brought a multitude of blessings from the great Goddess.

"You will always be lucky if y' know how to make friends with cats," advocated The McDonough with all the sagacity of a wise woman. "Cats possess charms a-plenty, and annyone who has iver owned a cat, if indaid one *can* own a cat, has fallen under Bastet's endurin' spell. Cats aire th' only bein's that can enter or leave a magick circle without breakin' th' energy field. Many aire totems, spirit guides, or have come into yer life as magickal familiars … *Watchers*."

The McDonough taught her granddaughters many useful things about cats, including the fact that they love to curl up and nap within a circle. Indeed, they will intentionally stay put inside a circle for long periods, sitting almost trancelike. "But," apprised Granny, "th' best ting 'bout a cat is its powerful aura, also known as an 'astral force,' which wur-rks t' repel negative energy. Cats inflate their auras t' protect th' home from negative energies iv *all* kinds, includin' evil spirits. Scares th' rubbish clean away; and since we're empaths, 'tis especially good f'r us."

As one might expect, Granny McDonough's love of cats stayed with her all her life, just as the musical lilt of Ireland remained on her tongue; and given that Raine and Maggie, for the most part, were reared by Granny, some of her expressions and patterns of speech carried over and became part of them.

Cat tales abound in the McDonough and Tully clans, and Raine especially enjoyed spinning the colorful yarns– complete with Granny's brogue.

One year, for instance, when Mrs. Jenkins' brown tabby gave birth to kittens, that everyone *knew* Myrrdyn had sired (when he darted out the door one brisk autumn night under the bewitching glow of the Hunter's Moon), it surprised the kibble out of a suddenly-younger-acting Gypsy and her owner. That tabby had thirteen years on her, if a day, and well past her kitten-bearing time was she. "The old fool!" Mrs. Jenkins had complained to anyone who would listen.

But there were kittens all right– *and what kittens!* The villagers took to calling them "faerie cats," and to be sure, there was something *magickal* about those glossy kittens, black as midnight each one, and shiny as patent leather, with bright pumpkin-colored eyes that bored clean through whomever they fixed with their mystical regard. Every child in town had fussed for one, and all these years later, Myrrdyn's charmed progeny still inhabit a few of the Hamlet's quaint old mansions. It's funny how things can stick in the mind over the mumbo jumbo of so many years– but that story has real sticking power.

Closer to the moment, Raine and Maggie were sitting at table– a heavy, round, claw-footed affair that matched its oak, pressed-back chairs– in Tara's kitchen, where the former lit a blue candle-in-a-jar labeled "Island Moonlight" that packed the tangy mélange of currant, orange and grapefruit. The candle matched the baby-blue of the kitchen walls, the braided area rug, the trim on the ecru lace curtains, and the tiny painted flowers on the faux-ivory cabinet pulls.

Raine had just lifted the new candle from its box, and she wanted to light it straightaway, for Granny imparted that it was unlucky to keep a candle in the house that had never been lit. There was *magick* in candlelight. Its soft glow not only converted a room into an entrancing space, its illumination raised psychic awareness, and most significantly– a lit candle released energies.

Granny instilled many, what some might call, "flights of fantasy" or "old wives' tales" into her granddaughters, such as a toppled chair upon standing was a bad omen. Spilled salt was too, unless you promptly tossed a pinch of it over your left shoulder to stave off the bad luck. Needless to add, if you were benighted enough to build a house over a faerie fort, you'd have infinite ill fortune. It was also unlucky to drop a glove and pick it up yourself. If someone else picked it up for you, good fortune would follow.

The summer she was nine, Raine dropped a glove on a New York City street. A handsome young man picked it up and handed it to her with a warm smile. Standing there watching him hurry down the avenue, she noted to Granny and Maggie, "That was an angel. He's here on a special mission. I should've thanked him." At that point, the young man was about a block distant, and there was no way, with traffic noise, he could have caught Raine's words; but at that express moment, he stopped, turned, and waved her a sort of salute– that she never forgot.

Remembering Granny, as she always did when she made tea, Maggie poured herself and Raine each a fragrant cup of the special brew they ordered from Ireland. Nary a tea bag ever found its sorry way into Tara's traditional door. As was their habit, the pair used the eggshell-thin cups their granny had carefully carried, years before, from the "Old Country." At Tara, tea was never taken from a mug, or as Granny used to call it, a "beaker."

Raine sighed wistfully, looking across the room to the old Boston rocker, where The McDonough had often sat by the kitchen window to read her arcane books. It was the chair in which the proud granny held her granddaughters for the first time, cradling them gently in loving arms, where she'd rocked them to sleep, crooning Irish lullabies during restless nights of infancy.

We love you, Granny.

Following Raine's gaze, Maggie gave a knowing nod. Her eyes shone brilliant green as she brought the cup to her lips, her rings catching a beam from the early-morning sun that sparked a rainbow off a stained-glass window.

Through the window, the redheaded Sister could see Tara's small, cupola-crowned stable, home to their horses, Raine's ebony gelding, Tara's Pride, and Maggie's cherry chestnut mare, Isis. The stable's weathervane, a broom-riding witch, identical to the one atop Tara itself, told her there was a stiff wind out of the west.

Maggie looked absorbed, reaching up to flick back the wave of fiery hair that frequently dipped over one eye. "I'm proud of Aisling and Ian for the success of their Black Cat Detective Agency, but I so wish they were going with us to Martinique."

Raine nodded. "It would be nice if Merry Fay were going too, but she's leaving for cheerleading camp in a few days."

Maggie dabbed at the corners of her mouth with a paper napkin. "By the bye, Sister, I did some further research on the Empress Joséphine, and you won't believe what I uncovered ..."

Some moments later, the conversation over tea got round again to Granny.

"Even from her lofty position in the Summerland, Granny continually reinforces," Maggie was saying, "that it's our destiny to solve crimes, come to the aid of innocents, and put things as right as we can." She pursed her brow. "Though she's always been keen that we should not stop living to do it. As always, she knows more than she was at liberty to say."

Raine caught at Maggie's presentiment and made a kittenish face, wordless.

Wordless, however, was a rare condition for the verbose, brunette Sister. Often effusive, at all times bold and ever more-than-ready for a new adventure, Raine was a sexy, somewhat naughty pixie who was destined to keep her looks and her youthful appearance. Pixies, after all, are enduring as well as endearing.

Whimsical Fate had ordained that Maggie, too, find that ladder to the stars to climb every rung and stay forever young. In addition, this Sister was most enchantingly *sensual*, and it wasn't just her fiery hair, peachy skin, feline eyes, and voluptuous figure.

Her voice was soft. It fell on the ear like a love song, and she had an especially attractive, lilting expression of amusement. Perchance it was her wittiness and vibrant sense of fun that helped retain her beauty and allure. "She who laughs, lasts" was one of her choice dictums.

Maggie loved to laugh. She did so often, and it was the sound of easy laughter.

"Granny instilled confidence in us that we can do *both*, enjoy life's special moments *and* fulfill our destiny," she reminded.

Raine chortled. *I'm more concerned with what Granny didn't say.*

The short laugh Maggie pitched in response carried a trace of trepidation. "Goddess forbid we encounter anything as dodgy 'n dangerous as our last shock of mysteries. Fire burn and cauldron bubble," she quickly amended, "boil away all our trouble! We won't let our imaginations take flight. We'll *witch* our way through, like we always do," she rhymed.

A hint of alarm sparked an old misgiving in Raine's core, but she blew it off, not allowing it to flame. *My imagination **was** beginning a wild dance*, she admitted to herself. "Fear not, I'm back on track, Sister."

Their ability to read each other's minds bonded Maggie and Raine; and though they sniped at one another on occasion, they were close– much more like sisters than first cousins.

For one thing, the magickal trio– Raine, Maggie, and Aisling– had identical eyes, arresting to anyone who looked upon them. The "McDonough eyes" the villagers called them– tip-tilted and vivid green, the color of Ireland itself, fringed with long, inky lashes and blazing with insatiable life.

"God's fingers waire sooty whin He put in th' eyes of me lovely Irish granddaughters," Granny used to say.

Like their blonde-with-the-wand cousin, Aisling, raven-haired Raine and redheaded Maggie accentuated their eyes with intense makeup, too theatrical for most– dramatically stunning and signature sexy for the Sleuth Sisters. And like their granny before them, the McDonough lasses had beautiful complexions– rich cream, glowing and flawless.

Granny recognized, from birth, how extraordinary each of her granddaughters was– even for a Tully or a McDonough–

predicting that they would be able to see what others, including their own kind, could not.

And from the instant the McDonough girls entered puberty, it was like bees to honey. Boys suddenly couldn't keep away from them. Just looking at them left most males so giddy, they acted like they'd had too much of old Buck Taylor's 'lectricfyin' applejack. Would-be suitors followed the McDonough gals home from high school and college, tied up their phones evenings, and fought over who would escort them to dances and such.

"You don't find yer worth in a man," Granny schooled her granddaughters when they reached adolescence. "You find yer worth within yerself, and then find a man who's worthy of you. Or better yet, let *him* find you. There's no greater power than that of the sun, the moon– and a woman who knows her worth. *Remember that.*"

Perhaps it was Granny's special olive-oil soap the threesome used that made their skin so luminous and turned their auras so bright that people– well, those who believed in magick, anyway– virtually saw them in dazzling, sparkly radiance, like the beautiful leaders of splendor and light they actually were. Or maybe it was simply the self-confidence Granny instilled in her granddaughters that made them shine so. Poise has an enchanting way of doing that. Granny unerringly quipped that "Sex appeal is fifty percent of what you've got, and fifty percent of what people *think* you've got."

Whatever the reason, the McDonough lasses radiated something that was impossible to ignore.

Their theatre friends summed them up by saying, "Raine, Maggie, and Aisling have that intangible *je ne sais quoi* that makes them unforgettable."

No one ever forgot a McDonough woman.

In all fairness, they did not collect hearts as one collects seashells or butterflies, and yet …

A few seconds ago, Raine, who was usually fearless about plunging into tomorrow, felt that fantastic McDonough confidence and optimism slip a notch. *Mystery, mayhem and **murder– again!*** The harrowing thought, delivered on Granny's caveat, had quaked along her spine with the icy fingers of Fear, the disquiet making itself evident on her face. *Granny took time from another important celestial conference to pop in on us, so that makes me think our upcoming challenge will be beset with …*

Instinctively her hand flew to the antique talisman suspended on a thick silver chain around her neck. She brushed her ringed fingers across the large emerald embedded in the center of the amulet's broad silver-and-black-enameled surface. A glittery sprinkling of tiny, pinhead-size gems of moonstone, garnet, emerald, ruby, sapphire, amethyst, citrine, and various hues of quartz and topaz glittered in the treasured heirloom.

For a spun-out suspension in time, Raine regarded the inspiring piece, as Granny's words rocketed back to rouse her: *The enemy is Fear. We think it is Hate, but it is Fear. Everything you want is on the other side of Fear.*

Looking to Maggie, Raine uttered another of Granny's dictums, "'Fear is a reaction. Courage is a decision.' Beau always teases me that the mere mention of a mystery quickens my pulse, and he's absolutely right." She shrugged. "From experience, I recognize my uneasy feeling is due to the unknown. I just like to know what we're up against is all."

Maggie declined to respond, except to comment that the Merlin cats– the bold Black Jade and Black Jack O'Lantern with the elusive Panthèra, perfectly aligned, were, in the twinkling of an eye, sitting before them in the kitchen, their combined steady *purrrrrr* growing louder.

Raine scrutinized their Watchers for a charmed moment. "They're warning us that this forthcoming mystery will be even more fraught with danger than the last one, because the killer this time is a professional, case-hardened criminal." The Sister cocked her head, hoping to pick up more information telepathically. It was one of her special powers, the ability to communicate with animals. She made it a point to pay close attention when she saw her familiars stare– for magick was most definitely near.

"Black Jack especially is warning us to be careful. '*Beware*,' he's saying. 'This killer is especially dangerous … elusive, cunning and exceedingly crafty.'"

A very unpleasant prospect. Maggie contemplated with a pensive nod, picking up Raine's train of thought, as the latter's mind sped on. From under her clothing, the redheaded Sister extracted the talisman she habitually wore on a strong silver chain around her neck.

Understandably, Maggie's heirloom piece matched Raine's, save that the big center stone was a blood-red ruby. Tracing a finger over the amulet's gem-encrusted Triquetra– or more precisely, over her talisman's *third* of the Triquetra design– she said, imaging their accomplished Leo cousin Aisling, whose talisman hosted the focal stone of sapphire, "There's indeed something to be said for the Power of Three.

"We'll prove ourselves yet again," Maggie managed to insert with quiet Scorpio force. "As Granny is prone to remind, Old Souls, Star Children, and empaths are charged with duty. She left us more than just this house and a great trust fund. We've been blessed with many gifts, but with those gifts have come obligation. We worked long and hard to earn the Key to a mystical portal, a gateway that unveils a world of ancient mysteries and hidden knowledge. Among our utmost responsibilities is to guard the Time-Key's secret– and to use it for good."

A surge of witchy-woman power fired Raine's Aries *chutzpah*, and she flashed her cousin and sister of the moon an appreciative grin. *Woman In Total Control of Herself ... that's what it means to be a witch. And what a **delicious** word it is!* "At times like this, I'm reminded of what Granny liked to quote from Abraham Lincoln, whom she believed was a mystic: 'The best way to predict the future is to create it.'" Reaching into her pocket, she extracted a little tin of calming balm she and Maggie concocted that they'd christened Serenity Now! Serenity Now!! After applying it to the inside of her wrists, she handed the tin to Maggie. "That trifle more of vetiver we added did the trick."

"Thanks." Maggie rubbed the sweet-smelling balm into her skin, then stood to carry the tea things to the sink. "Let's not dally. Aisling will be pulling in at any moment now."

As the Sisters rallied, they chanted softly, "Still around the corner a new road awaits. Just around the corner– ***another secret gate!***"

In the entrance hall, Raine scooped up a muscular black cat that on silent paws had shadowed her to Tara's front door, where dangled a set of antique Witch Bells. Like their familiars, the bells, on each of Tara's exit doors, helped to keep negativity and evil at bay. Extending a hand, she gave them a brisk flick, the jingle causing the cat's ears to twitch, as she spellcast thrice, "Guard my home, Bells on the Door. Let only blessings walk this floor. Block all evil and the Dark Arts. May only *good* approach our hearts."

For a long moment, Raine stared, through one of the glass panels that bordered the front door, at Tara's new porch mat that brandished the bewitching words *Enchanted Castle. A fanciful first impression to visitors,* the Sister thought, *a sweet reminder to us.*

Her eyes returned to the cat she cradled in her arms. Gazing into the depths of Black Jack O'Lantern's mesmerizing pumpkin-colored eyes, the Sister recited her pet tale, "Once upon a time, there were two pioneering college professors and one former police detective turned private eye– young but possessed of very old souls– from an unheard-of little hamlet in the backwoods of Pennsylvania. Nevertheless, the good works of this magickal trinity were widely noted, winning them the well-earned soubriquet the 'Sleuth Sisters.'"

"All we need do," Maggie was asserting some minutes later, as she joined Raine in the downstairs hall, where they set their bags, "is keep to our path. That's how we ferreted out the Time-Key. It's how we crafted our dissertation on time-travel so that it was accepted by our fellow colleagues of letters, and how we defended it successfully to gain our doctorates. In addition, we've solved a run of wicked crimes the past few years. And we did it *all* by keeping to the path of the Great Secret."

Tilting her dark head, Raine's fair cheeks took on a rosy tint. She ran her ringed fingers through her short, sassy asymmetric hair– as black and lustrous as their cats– the point-cut bangs dipping seductively over one eye. "Likewise, we've safeguarded the secret of the Time-Key through, I might add, *eight* nerve-jangling time-travel missions."

At that, Raine's cell sounded with the enchanting music of Rowena of the Glen's *Book of Shadows.*

"Dr. McDonough," her deep voice rumbled. After listening for a few moments, she uttered into the phone, "We're ready and waiting for you. So shake your wand, Sister!" Disconnecting, Raine related to Maggie, "Aisling's on her way. She'll be here in ten."

"Cara sensed she left over a half-hour ago," Maggie replied.

"Cara wasn't wrong, but just as Aisling was about to step out the door, Merry Fay asked to go to the movies this afternoon *with a boy*," the Goth gal prattled on, wandering a tad off point. "Aisling wanted to have a heart-to-heart, along with a compromise, before granting permission, for which Merry was keenly pressing, you see."

Raine paused a beat in reverie. "Bless my besom, *Merry Fay's first crush!* I can't believe it. Seems like only yesterday when we sang her to sleep in Granny's rocker, and now she's–"

"Going on a date," Maggie finished the sentence, evoking with relish her own first heartthrob. The memory still wielded the power to make her heart carol pleasurably.

"Merry told Aisling it's *not* a date, that she and this boy are only friends," Raine countered.

"*It's a date,*" Maggie said wistfully.

While they waited for the sound of Aisling's black Cadillac Escalade in Tara's driveway, the brunette Sister strode past the life-size knight-in-armor in the foyer to the pillared entry that led into Tara's parlor with its massive Victorian furniture, green velvet drapes, and wall of books, the shelves crammed with leather-bound tomes teeming with arcane esoteric knowledge. Instantly her eyes locked with the pair, so like her own, of her grandmother whose fascinating portrait hung above the ornate fireplace.

The oil painting by Charles Dana Gibson captured Aisling Tully McDonough at the height of her beauty, the soft cloud of red hair, upswept in the famed Gibson-Girl coiffure of the era, graced the flawless oval of the face, the low-cut, off-the-shoulder, shimmering green gown accentuating the hour-glass figure. Streaming down over one white shoulder, a long tendril of fiery red hair formed a perfect question mark. Gibson had entitled the captivating image *The Eternal Question*, and thus read the neat, brass plate at the base of the portrait.

There, Raine hovered for a solemn moment, deftly voicing her thought aloud, "Granny, it's *empowering* to know, from our past endeavors, that we can travel down the Tunnel of Time, at will, to unlock the door that'll whisk us through the thrills and chills of yesteryear. It's easy to get carried away. *Dreadfully* easy ... especially for me. Hence we entreat and welcome your continued guidance in making prudent choices."

The eyes in the portrait seemed to kindle, causing the corners of Raine's pouty, candy-apple-red mouth to lift in a grin. "I can't help but apprehend that, with each new adventure, Aisling, Maggie and I advance to a whole new degree of skill and achievement for which, I must say, we are grateful."

In playful manner, she dressed her normally husky voice with a thick coat of drama, topping off her words with an eerie laugh,

"But as I always say, who knows what skeletons and dangers dangle in the closets our Time-Key will open? Along with those secreted perils– magick, adventure and surprise await us at the creak of every opening door."

Coming up behind her, Maggie interjected, "If and when we run into a snag– you *know* there'll be twists and tangles– we'll make good and proper use of *all* our magickal tools, including our Time-Key. With it **and** the powerful gifts bestowed on us by Granny and Grantie Merry, we should be able to solve virtually *any* mystery that History has cloaked in shadow. With each new challenge, there's the unknown, sure; but one thing's certain– our lives are never dull. Again, we've some exciting days ahead."

"Peril and risk?" Raine posed rhetorically. "Comes with the territory, but remember what both *grandes dames* imparted: 'To be forewarned is to be forearmed.'"

"Right," Maggie put in, raising a brow for emphasis; "and a word to the *wise … woman* should suffice."

Raine's gaze left the redhead in the portrait to travel to the one beside her, as she tilted her head to hear a car engine. "Aisling just pulled in."

Maggie concurred with a nod, her eyes shifting to the riveting canvas. "Guide and guard us, Granny Angel."

"So mote it be," Raine swiftly ordained.

As the Sisters hurried to answer the door, Maggie, with a fiery witch's passion, repeated the time-honored phrase, "So mote it be."

From her cozy nest in the side pocket of Maggie's shawl, the poppet Cara, watching the trio of Sisters embrace in Tara's entrance way, fortified the magickal mantra with her own fervent invocation–

"With the Power of Three– so mote it be!"

La Pagerie, Martinique, birthplace of the Empress Joséphine.
Above, the foundation ruins of the plantation house and
(right) the former kitchen, now the museum.
Below, the standing ruins of the plantation's *sucrerie*, sugar refinery.

"It's never too late– in fiction or in life– to revise."
~ Author Ceane O'Hanlon-Lincoln

Chapter One

"Time check," Raine prompted, lifting the lighted lantern high to lead Maggie and Aisling up the dark, narrow stairwell to Tara's attic.

"Thad and Beau should be here in about an hour and a half," Maggie answered. "We've sufficient time."

"Good, then we needn't rush. It's never good to hurry magick," Aisling stated.

As always when magick was afoot, the three black Merlin cats shadowed the Sisters.

Tara's other two cats– Tiger, the distinctly striped brown tabby, and Madame Woo, the seal-point applehead Siamese– preferred the cushioned comfort of one of the manse's sunny window seats to spellcasting.

At the top of the stairs, Raine and Maggie set about snapping on table lamps, as well as a Himalayan salt lamp in a black metal design of sun, moon and stars. The lamp's healing salt chunks, bathed in a soothing amber glow, cleansed the atmosphere and heightened mood.

Supporting their granny's grimoire and occupying a place of honor before three grand stained-glass windows was the antique wooden bookstand that bore the Sisters' ultra-thick *Book of Shadows,* the McDonough witches' diary of magick and rituals. The bookstand that supported this all-important tome had been prized by Granny McDonough because it was the lectern used by the celebrated orator William Jennings Bryan when, decades before, he delivered an eloquent speech on women's suffrage at the Hamlet's Addison McKenzie Library. By accident of Fate, the reading stand was crafted of the same dark English oak and finished with the same gleam as the woodwork throughout Tara.

The huge grimoire's black leather cover was embossed in gold gilt with full-blown Triquetra, the ancient Celtic knot symbolizing all trinities– *and infinite power.* Above it, from a thick oak beam jutted a sturdy hook; and that's where Raine hung the lantern, the small lamps splashing the colorful, hodgepodge room with the soft glow of light and the mystery of shadow.

A former maid's quarters, Tara's sloped attic was eclipsed by its trilogy of stained-glass windows, the ceiling-to-floor, center one exhibiting the national symbol and soul of Ireland– a golden harp. The two smaller, flanking, stained-glass windows each depicted a bright-green shamrock, another symbol of Ireland, and one of the supreme Trinity.

There were two stairways, the "front" and the "back" (the back being the "servants' stairs"), leading to the attic, the Sisters' sacred ritual room that they referred to as the "Heavens." This seemed a fitting name since it was the place where they conducted the spiritual procedure of spellcasting, weaving powerful magick; and it was here they conjured their dear granny. This morning, however, the Sisters would be conducting a protection spell.

"Which," Aisling remarked to her sisters of the moon, "we will craft, using Granny's travel blessing."

The tall, cool blonde, with the warm and generous heart, released a sigh, as her green eyes scanned the surroundings. "I love this old attic," she turned partway round, "with all its memories."

Aisling was the senior member of the witchy McDonough Girls and the married Sister of the magickal trinity. Queenly, with a slim, long-legged way about her, she was a regal lioness, from her royal bearing to her personal style. Fiercely loyal to her sisters of the moon, Aisling could always be counted on. A wife and mother above all else, this Leo woman, despite her sweet nature, did not tolerate anyone meddling with her family. Adversaries sensed straightaway that unless they wanted to see claws, Aisling was no one to provoke. "Every time we come up here, I'm haunted by things that tug at my core," she told Maggie and Raine.

"Blessed be, Sister," Raine and Maggie replied with witches' heart.

The spacious attic's furniture was a collection of odds and ends, touched by Time and not fitting enough for the rest of the manse, but too steeped in memories to cast away. Granny and Grandpa McDonough had purchased a few of what became the attic's keepsakes during the "Grand Tour" of their overseas honeymoon, such as a Louis XV room-divider screen with hand-painted floral panels that they found in a quaint antique shop in

Montmartre, a green velvet couch and two– somewhat lumpy but still handsome– easy chairs in a claret shade of a fabric from *Belle Époque* Paris. When Raine or Maggie wanted to escape from life's pressures, they always found the attic's old furniture a welcome, comfy haven in which to settle with a good book and something good to drink.

On the attic wall, between the easy chairs, hung a framed, nostalgic picture of a cozy old house nestled in a charming woodland setting. Granny always loved the poem printed under the image, which was entitled "Reflections of Home" and read in part: *An open fire, an easy chair/ My sewing basket waiting there. A reading lamp that's always near/ To send forth rays of warmth and cheer. The flowers that I picked myself/ My glasses on a corner shelf/ A book I love within hands' reach/ Seashells from a far-off beach ...*

A peculiar spinning wheel, tucked away in a dark corner, had a female ghost attached to it. The apparition was a crone named Nancy Hart, who was born when Thomas Jefferson was President of the United States. A much later owner gifted The McDonough with the wheel when Granny healed the woman of a most virulent winter fever. Every once in a while, one of the Sisters got a flash of the original owner, old Nancy, at the spinning wheel before her hearth, and sitting near to her, her black cat staring drowsily into the dancing flames.

A treadle sewing machine with a lovely filigree cast-iron base stood against a wall of the old attic's dusty gems, the top closed to serve as a table upon which rested Granny's hand-painted sewing box with labeled drawers for buttons, snaps, needles and such. The long bottom drawer was for scissors, the thought of which prompted Maggie to remember how, years before, Gypsies used to come round, asking to sharpen household tools. Granny ofttimes bade these fascinating rovers come into the house for a snack and something to drink, after which a reading usually followed.

Most of those Gypsy readings were right on target, Maggie recalled. *I remember the one Gypsy woman especially, the seventh daughter of a seventh daughter. Her eyes were the most **piercing** eyes that ever held mine. I felt she could see inside me, into my soul. She told me so many things that have come to pass. About my* *studies in Ireland, my marriage there, about my professorship, travels, property hugely significant in my life ... so many things.*

The whole of Tara's attic was a treasure chest of remembrances. Next to the sewing machine, a mannequin displayed a chic Victorian *ensemble en vogue* that Raine had worn once upon a time in a play; and across the space, a fainting couch never failed to remind the Sisters that those tiny waists came at a price.

On that same wall, Aisling's seeking eyes lighted on an aged oil painting of Grandpa McDonough's favorite dog, a huge Irish wolfhound he'd called Séamus, pronunciation *Shamus*. (It was actually Granny's nickname for her husband, since his given name was James, of which Séamus is the Irish equivalent. Granny joked that her husband and his dog were alike, both stubborn as mules, and so it was fitting they bore the same name.) The dog and Grandpa had passed over well before the Sisters were born, but Granny entertained them with scores of poignant stories.

For instance, Séamus saved Grandad McDonough's life on one occasion. The pair were at the McDonough hunting lodge at the time. (Years later, the lodge was converted into Aisling's home and detective agency when that Sister married.) Grandad used the lodge to get away when he felt the need to take a break from the pressures of his work; and those times, he always took Séamus with him. The incident occurred in April, but the nights were still cold. Rising just after dawn, a shivering Grandad pulled on his jacket and started for the door, intent on snatching more wood for the stove from the stacked pile on the porch. However, Séamus positioned himself before the (at the time) one-and-only exit, refusing to let Grandpa out. When the impatient man tugged on the huge dog's collar to move him, Séamus remained put, doing something he had never before done. He growled at his insistent master, who, giving up, went back to bed to try and get warm. Séamus lay down too, stationing himself in front of the door. Later, when James McDonough woke, he again started for the exit, *determined* to gather wood for the fire. This time, Séamus let him pass, following his master outside, where Grandad saw fresh tracks in the dusting of snow– of a large mother bear and her two cubs.

Grandpa McDonough's fancy wooden pipe stand, with pipes and humidor, ornamented a shelf in Tara's treasure trove of an attic. Raine smiled when she remembered how Granny never let her granddaughters play with the pipes. "You wouldn't want t' spoil th' nice memory these tings give yer granny, would you, me darlin's?" she asked in her gentle way that made anyone want to conform to her wishes and confide in her.

In another corner of the beguiling garret was a stack of curious old hat boxes, a couple from Edwardian London that held cunning little hats with black nylon netting that dropped down over the upper half of the face. The sexy Maggie, especially, enjoyed donning these witchy chapeaux for the added mystery their veils afforded.

Atop two cabriole end tables rested the pair of porcelain lamps the redheaded Sister had snapped to life. Chipped from years of use, the glowing lamp bases depicted romantic scenes of eighteenth-century lovers *en dansant*. Once, after a particularly strong conjuring session, Raine reported to Maggie and Aisling that she'd actually seen *and heard* the dancing couples swirling in a spin-two-three Viennese waltz.

On each end of the roof space, two domed trunks occupied places under the eaves; whilst the center of the scarred-wood floor was enhanced by a worn, though still valuable, French carpet, its floral design faded by Time, sun, and the treading of countless feet. There was a soft sheen about that once-luxurious rug that glinted in the mellow attic light and whispered *silk*– along with a myriad of reminiscences.

Grandad McDonough's brass maritime spyglass lay atop a small stand, and next to it, a charming child's rocker, its white paint scarred and peeling. Regarding it, Maggie instantly saw her child-self, rocking her teddy to sleep as she *tura-lura-lural-ed* her way through Granny's favorite Irish lullaby.

Teddy occupied the chair now, his plush beige fur stained from long-ago tea parties, his missing eye still covered by the swashbuckling black patch crafted by Granny to still the deep-feeling Maggie's tears.

"Sure 'n doesn't he look like a pirate now, lass? I tink it shows how brave Teddy is, don't you?" She drew the child Maggie close. "There, there now. Nothin' wrong wit sentiment, if it's what you truly feel. And you feel so much, me darlin'. You always have, and you always will."

Granny's preference for vintage toys for her "gurls" was evident in a faded pink wicker pram and a rocking horse carved from a single piece of plantation-grown English oak. The saddle on the wooden steed was leather, the mane and tail real horse hair. Raine, especially, had ridden "Ogma" for all the pair of them were worth; and to be sure, the steed, named for an ancient Irish warrior-god, bore the evidence of the toddler Goth gal's zeal.

One piece of furniture in Tara's Heavens was not chipped, faded, worn or shabby, though it was most certainly old. This was the tall cheval glass that accompanied Aisling Tully McDonough, "Granny" as the Sisters called her, on her fateful journey from Ireland to America. The mirror was likely worth a fortune, so ornate was it in carved giltwood with Irish symbols and heroes from the Emerald Isle's turbulent past. Bestowed on her by a doting uncle, when she was just a slip of a girl, it had been Granny's most cherished keepsake from the Old Country.

Ronan McDonough struck it rich, mining for gold in Australia. Centered on a page of Granny's old photo album was a dashing sepia of him, in buckskins, gun and holster, his long mustache curving upward at the waxed tips. "Never forget your heritage," he commanded upon gifting the mirror. "This will help you remember who you are!"

The Sisters wanted to preserve as much of Granny's essence in the Irish cheval glass as possible; and so they kept it draped, when not in use, in their sacred attic space under a protective ghostly sheet. Hence, no one else ever handled and confused the energies of this precious family heirloom.

On one side of the mirror dangled an unusual necklace, a long, thick rope of pure silver from which hung two round, silver Gypsy bells. Granny had purchased the charmed necklace as a lass in Ireland, "… from an especially talented tinker," who had traded a donkey for the magickal bauble. The bells' pleasant jingling soothed away her troubles and brought to mind the tinkling shell chimes she remembered hanging in the windows of the Old Sod's seaside cottages. From the mirror's opposite side hung Granny's Irish knit shawl. In a spiderweb pattern, the black-as-jet shawl sparkled with dozens of tiny aurora borealis crystals. Granny's widow's weeds had enfolded style, as well as a great deal of magick.

Raine abidingly made it a point to choose something of Granny's to hold in her hand from a small coffer of bits and bobs that rested on one of the cabriole tables. Today, 'twas a wide silver and brass band ringed by gold elephants with linked trunks, a lucky charm that Raine sometimes wore as a thumb ring. The old Nepal treasure had been a gift to Granny from Raine and Maggie's archeologist parents. Holding the ring between her hands, she made a wish before slipping it over her thumb. Its magick was strong and never did it fail to bring her a blessed day.

As was her custom, Raine tarried a few quiet moments at the tranquil trilogy of stained-glass windows, peering out, through the clear portions, at the faerie-tale Hamlet below. In a mysterious way did an ethereal mist oft hover over the beautiful but contrary Youghiogheny River.

To center herself in preparation for spellcasting, the Sister drew a deep breath, letting it out with measured release. The sight of the curving river never disappointed. On every occasion, it relaxed her, freeing her mind of unwanted thoughts and anxieties, a must for successful spellcraft.

From that spot, she could see a few small boats on the water. Of a murky early morn or evening, she sometimes heard the nostalgic sound of a horn from one of the boats as it navigated the fog pockets that crept along the winding ribbon of river like a stealthy cat on silent paws. In fog, sounds carry a long distance, seeming ofttimes to echo. It was a beguiling thing, that. On occasion, Raine imagined she heard voices in that misty vapor.

Today she did.

As she stood stock-still, hardly daring to breathe, a female voice in soft husky whisper gave her notice in French– *I'm waiting for you ... wait–ing ... waiting for you.*

Magick was so much a part of the Sisters' lives that the happening did not fluster her. Cool and composed, she was almost certain she knew who the voice belonged to and what the message meant. The Goth gal remained before the window, staring through the clear segments of stained-glass at the early-morning Hamlet. A light, cleansing rain that had fallen overnight burnished the trees below, making them glisten. Presently, a sudden notion caused her to move to one of the eaves' domed trunks and lift the lid.

"What're you looking for?" Maggie asked, curious.

"A lace shawl," Raine answered, as she carefully rummaged through the lavender-scented chest's contents, at the bottom of which were Granny's wedding dress and dried bouquet in preservation boxes. In a few moments, the Sister found the shawls atop a couple of evening dresses. She quickly chose a black lace one, started to rise, but decided to look through the storage space at the bottom of that which Granny had called her "Sweetheart Trunk."

It had been a long time since she poked through those old attic chests. Everything in them held a story. The drawer was stuck, and it took a bit of finagling to open it. There, a midnight-blue bead and sequin evening bag that, opened, revealed Granddad McDonough's gold pocket watch engraved on the back with Granny's poignant words, *From the first look, you captured my heart*; a thin decorative box of initialed handkerchiefs around which Granny had meticulously crocheted scalloped edging with black tatting. A small bundle of old letters tied with a pink, satin ribbon; yellowed newspaper clippings with faded print; and handwritten in Granny's slanted, curly script, a wee poem. *Memory is the golden bridge/ That keeps our hearts in touch/ With all the long-past yesterdays/ And those we love so much.*

Raine closed her eyes and pressed the things to her bosom, remembering snippets of stories from Granny and Grandad's global honeymoon. She opened the antique, maroon-velvet photo album.

In Alexandria and Cairo, the newlyweds had marveled at the great pyramids. They'd sailed lazily down the Nile; toured the maze-like old quarter of Nepal's Kathmandu, then the valley with its Buddhist temples and resident monkeys; and somewhere in India, the couple had their photograph made with four British dandies. Frozen in time, against a backdrop of flora, the James McDonoughs look blissfully happy in the center of the Englishmen, who, sporting tropical white suits and spiffy safari helmets, are smoking long, thin cigarettes.

Raine rummaged further through the drawer's contents. *Wonder why Granny kept these recipes here?* she asked herself, perusing the handwritten instructions for Buttermilk Crispy Fried Chicken, Picnic Potato Salad, and Old-fashioned Raisin Pie. *Food for the road. June is a fine month to go on a picnic, and when we return from our Caribbean break, that's what I intend to do,* she decided, casting an eye toward the picnic baskets suspended from the rafters, before delving deeper into the hope chest's jumble.

"Mags, look! I'd forgotten about Granny's antique fans. Let's take a couple with us to Martinique. Pretty, feminine fans are all the rage there."

"Yes, let's," Maggie replied with enthusiasm etched on her soft voice. "That would be lovely." Flirting by use of fans was an artform, and she was remembering the signals Raine had taught her, such as pressing the closed fan to the lips to mean "Kiss me."

Raine chose two of the romantic heirlooms, a black lace and a green silk fan hand-painted with a spray of colorful flowers. Gathering them up, she set them on one of the small side tables till they were ready to go back downstairs, where she planned to tuck them into their bags.

On the river, a boat signaled its lonely cry, stirring her to the task at hand. When she stooped to pick up Black Jack, the cat began purring loudly– his Number-Three Purr she called it– as she stroked his velvet ebony fur.

Maggie, meanwhile, was using her wand to draw a circle of protection around the attic room, calling upon the God-Goddess; the spirits of the four elements, the guardians of the watchtowers; as well as their angel and spirit guides, to secure their sacred space.

Aisling was busying herself with the lighting of four white candles, whilst Raine, having placed Jack inside the circle with Black Jade and Panthèra, moved to touch her lighter to a dragon's blood incense cone that she set in a brass burner. With the aid of a large, purple feather, she fanned the smoke, allowing the aromatic fragrances to permeate the entire area before placing the activated cone on a stand.

In turn, Maggie lit three small bundles of white sage, each in a big, fan-shaped seashell; after which, she handed them to her sisters of the moon, retaining one for herself. Taking the pungent, smoking sage in a clockwise motion round the attic space, the Sisters cleansed the room of negativity, all the while chanting a smudging mantra, as they carried out the ancient art of purifying.

"Negativity that invades our sacred place, we banish you with the light of our grace. You have no hold or power here. We stand and face you with no fear. Be you gone forever, for now we say– this is *our* sacred space, and you will obey!"

"Together, we cleanse this area," Aisling continued, initiating another chant, "completely free of any and all negativity."

Walking deosil, the Sisters spellcast in accord, as Tara's attic room took on the pleasing mingled aromas of burning white sage, candle wax, and the soft, amber-like scent of dragon's blood.

Satisfied that their space was properly and thoroughly cleansed, the gifted McDonough witches positioned themselves within their circle before their altar and the Merlin cats, sitting patiently on their haunches with a somewhat drowsy look to their pumpkin-hued eyes. There was no need to check their *Book of Shadows*, for they knew the travel spells by heart.

"Grantie always told us we should feel wholly protected when we use these charms to safeguard our travel, but that we should never allow ourselves to be careless," Aisling reminded, casting a pointed look at the too-daring Raine. "I'll remind you that this spell has been in our family for years. It's tried and true and part of who we are." She raised her eyes. "We ask the ancestors to guide us."

"As well we know, *intent* is the *key* element to this or any spell work, not to mention– and this is a given– that we *believe*," Raine, ever the lecturer, remarked. "To make *any* magick work, we know a witch must believe, and *strongly*, in his or her own abilities. Intent and belief, the two primary keys to witchcraft." The Sister smiled. "We know all this, but it's always good to review. Repetition increases retention and rule."

"Right," Maggie replied. "Now, before we begin, are we unplugged?"

"We are," answered her sisters of the moon.

"Though we're not skyclad, you're set to travel, so you're each wearing comfortable clothing, as am I. Granny and Grantie always advised comfort when doing magick." The senior Sister then ordained, "We don't just *do* magick, Sisters, we *are* magick."

"Blessed be," chimed Maggie and Raine in response, which Aisling promptly echoed.

"Mojo bags at hand," Aisling bade. "I take it you both set the opened bags in direct sunlight yesterday."

"We did, Sister," Maggie and Raine answered simultaneously.

Raine, then Maggie, extracted from a pocket a yellow felt bag tied with red ribbon, yellow the color of sunshine, air, and travel, red the color of defense. Inside each of the two pouches were stones and crystals to aid in safe travel– black tourmaline, tiger's eye, turquoise, yellow jasper, malachite, aqua marine, moonstone, and in each, a pearl, since the Sisters would be traveling over water. And since they were flying, there were wild birds' feathers too– cardinal, seagull, owl, and blue jay. The remaining charms were a rowan twig and a dried fig, that Granny always asserted brought good luck when traveling.

The Sisters smudged their travel mojoes, guiding the good-smelling white-sage smoke inside the pouches to cleanse the charms therein, after which they cupped their hands to bring the smoke over themselves as well.

"Talismans at the ready!" Aisling commanded. The Sister pulled her amulet free from its resting place beneath her blouse to lift the silver chain over her long, blonde hair. Her talisman's center-stone sapphire and scatter of tiny jewels glittered and flared energy in the candlelight.

Thus encouraged, Raine and Maggie removed their amulets from around their necks. Then the Sisters extended their hands to fit together the trilogy of necklaces bequeathed to them years before by Granny McDonough, whose influential presence her granddaughters sensed more keenly with every passing moment. In each pair of Sisterly hands, the powerful talismans actually warmed the skin as they verily hummed with energy.

At Aisling's signal, Maggie and Raine chanted, "Patrons of travel, watch over me when I journey in air, on land, or the sea. For talismans in pocket these charms will I tuck, for they encourage safe passage and bring me good luck."

"Keep those talismans with you at all times," Aisling charged. "Raine, I see you're wearing Granny's elephant ring from Nepal. That's a great choice for travel."

"And, of course, we're both wearing our ancient moonstone rings," Maggie pointed out.

"Good on you," Aisling reinforced with a nod.

"I gave Thaddeus' car– his everyday VW, not the Model T– a cleansing and protection spell yesterday, with instructions for him to refresh it this morning at the carwash during the rinse cycle. With him casting the spell on the inside of the car, and the water cleansing it on the outside … you know what I'm saying. That will protect us on the road to the airport. We'll refresh the spell anew when we return to Pittsburgh International en route home," Maggie finished.

"A negativity cleanse at the carwash during the rinse," Aisling restated almost to herself, "that's a witchin' idea!"

"Oh, I can't take credit for it. 'Twas Raine's brainchild," Maggie laughed, indicating the Goth Gal, who was looking like a contented kitten with a nice bowl of cream.

"Now," Aisling began, "let us take a few moments to image you both, with Thaddeus and Beau, arriving safely in Martinique. We all know how powerful imaging is, and what it can do."

The Sisters three closed their eyes to conjure this vision, fueling it with profound feelings of happiness, gratefulness– and love.

Aisling raised her arms skyward. "God and Goddess, hear my prayer. Guard my Sisters' through the air. From the time they leave this, their house, luck increase and dangers douse. From the time they leave the ground, increase protection all around. Smooth landing at the end, shield them till they're home again." The senior Sister chanted the spell two more times, concluding, "For the good of all, with harm to none. By moon and stars, this spell is done."

"The spell is cast. The spell doth last," the trinity of Sisters ordained. "By the Power of Three, so mote it be."

"Blessed be!" Aisling avowed. Turning to Maggie, the second eldest, the senior Sister handed the redhead her talisman. "I'm loaning you this for your trip. You wear mine *with* yours. That way, you're closer to harnessing the Power of Three."

"Thank you, Sister," Maggie and Raine replied, stepping in for a three-way hug.

"Wear it in good faith and good health to do all the good you can," Aisling finished. "If you need me, I'll astral travel to your sides, but my witchy intuition is telling me you will be fine without me," she smiled. And it was Granny's smile. "Now, let us properly conclude our rite, thank, and release the conjured energies."

No sooner had the Sisters completed their ritual when the sound of Tara's antique doorbell, loud enough to reach the attic, announced the anticipated arrival of Thaddeus and Beau.

"Magick is not for everyone.
Only those willing to take full responsibility
for themselves need apply."
~ The Sleuth Sisters

Chapter Two

"Thank the God-Goddess we finally got through customs," Raine exclaimed with a sigh, as she tucked her passport safely into a zippered compartment of her purse.

"There were more tourists than we fancied for what I'd call the *off* season," Maggie commented, slipping on her sunglasses. "From what I've read, June starts the rainy season."

"We'll get some wet days, but there'll still be lots of good weather." Raine glanced about. The airport was very modern and clean with a variety of amenities, including a pharmacy, bank, money changing station, tax-free shopping, florist, hairdresser, car rentals, restaurant, cafés and bars. *Wiz-zard*, she told herself, *lots of agreeable changes since last I visited.*

"Wait here," Thaddeus verbalized to the others, "I want to change some money to euros."

The idea struck Beau as a good one. "I'll go with you," he said.

Raine and Maggie gave the men some of their money to convert whilst they waited nearby, people-watching, as was their habit.

"C'mon," the Goth gal urged some minutes later, taking a step toward the airport's front doors. "Let's hail a taxi for l'Hôtel Bakoua. Be advised that dusk falls early and quickly in the Caribbean. We want to get sorted out in time to relax and enjoy the sunset, which I promise will be awesome."

"How far is the hotel from here?" Beau asked, hoisting his and Raine's suitcase to follow the zealous Sister outside to the curb.

She breathed in. The sweet smell of molasses hung heavy on the air. "Ah, I remember it well," she said *à la* Maurice Chevalier. "To answer your question, the hotel is about a half-hour's drive," the raven-haired Sister informed, picking up her pace. "It's not so far in miles, but traffic on the N5 and Lamentin, the airport region where we are now, is always high-density during the morning rush hours and in the pm, from around 3:00 to 7:00."

Looking at his watch, Thaddeus determined, "It's about four now, so we'll hit that traffic."

Raine put two fingers in her mouth to whistle, whilst her free arm shot in the air, "Taxi!"

En route to the hotel, the Sisters and their other halves took pleasure in the scenic ride, their route lined with stately, graceful palm trees, the shimmering azure sea, and the lush green mountains ever visible in the distance.

"Lot of changes since I was here last," Raine stated, her emerald eyes scanning the view from the cab.

"Like what?" Beau's question broke through her reminiscence.

"The name of the airport for one thing," she replied. "It was called *l'Aéroport Lamentin* until a few years ago when the name was changed to *l'Aéroport Aimé Césaire*. It's the international airport."

"Named for a local author, isn't it? I caught a bit of info from a plaque inside the terminal," Beau said.

"That's right," Raine answered. "Aimé Césaire was a celebrated author, poet, and politician. He passed away in 2008, if memory serves, only a few months after the airport was named for him." She studied her Beau's strong profile for a long moment, as he drank in the passing landscape. "I can't believe you're actually here with me and not slaving away back at Goodwin Veterinary Clinic." Leaning toward him, she kissed his cheek, rough with afternoon shadow.

Tall and powerfully built with wide shoulders, trim waist, and the muscular legs that do proper justice to a kilt, Beau Goodwin was blessed with the jet-black hair and scorching blue eyes of a long line of Scottish and Scotch-Irish ancestors. In his thirties, his body was all lean muscle— muscle that moved with the kind of intensity and power that comes to men who get plenty of exercise a good deal of the time outdoors. Relentless farm calls afforded "Doc Goodwin" continuous bodybuilding workouts.

By and large, both Raine and Beau preferred the company of animals to people. "To restate Freud," Beau once remarked to Raine, after she related the details of a particularly macabre murder that she and her sisters of the moon had just solved, "some folks think wild animals are cruel, but to be cold-blooded and merciless is the privilege of civilized humans."

Like-minded in many ways, the couple shared several preferences and opinions. For instance, they both enjoyed spending their free time, the turning wheel of the seasons, in Nature's rejuvenating company. Like his Celtic father, Hugh, Beau hyped the Natural World: "Witchcraft is the most *natural* thing in the world," he revealed to a surprised Raine years before when she told him she was a witch. And he meant that quite literally. "Witches," he concurred with her recently, "possess a keen and unique sensitivity to the natural world. You and I have always connected on this.

"A witch is one with Nature," he avowed. "If you're thrown into turmoil, thrust your hands in the soil or walk barefoot on sand or earth to feel grounded. Wade in stream, river or ocean to feel emotionally cleansed and healed. Fill your lungs with fresh air to feel mentally clear. Raise your face to the sun to feel your *own* power. It's like wishing upon a star. Witch or no, doesn't matter who you are– it's free and accessible to all."

Raine's favorite acumen gained from the Goodwin doctors was this: "The best medicine for humans or animals is love. If a patient asks, 'What if it doesn't work?' The answer's simple– Increase the dose."

There was something, simply stated, *extraordinary* about Dr. Beau Goodwin that people– and above all, animals– noticed straightaway. Perhaps it was that *special something* that peered from his eyes, a soulful softness that revealed a good and pure heart.

Animals reap a "knowing" when a human possesses empathy and kindness through the vibrations the human emits, and this provides the "fur, fin, and feather people" with an instinct of safety in the company of that human. On the wall in the Goodwin Veterinary Clinic hung a plaque that displayed a Buddha dictum: *Be kind to all creatures.* ***This*** *is the true religion.*

If his patients could talk, they would undoubtedly say that Beau was a born healer with perfect bedside manner. Like the Sisters, he was an Old Soul and an empath. (Empaths always connect with animals and Nature, and animals and Nature always heal empaths. It should be noted, too, that most empaths *are* Old Souls.) Raine knew, from Granny's teachings, to treasure what the McDonough clan termed Soul Clickers, "… people who walk into your life and straight off click with you– for these are souls known before."

Raine believed profoundly that Celts have the power of prophecy and intuition and that the voice of the Goddess called to Beau and her from another time and place.

Often did she experience a keen Irish knowing, just as he frequently did of her, that Beau had come from somewhere else– somewhere not of this earth. At times, each felt a "soul-clicking" homesickness for a place they weren't even sure existed. "For that elusive, faraway star," Raine alleged, "the Pleiades perhaps, where my heart is full, my body loved, and my soul understood."

Beau understood. More and more, it seemed to Raine, Beau apprehended her needs, her desires, and her dreams. To be sure, each half of this remarkable couple created magick in a singular way, and together these two Star Children enkindled an utterly magickal *Raine-Beau.*

Like all Starseeds, who are intrinsically programmed to find others like themselves, both opted to work in fields that allowed them to use their innate but heightened talents– healing, imparting knowledge and truth, and searching for their own truths. "Truths beyond the ken of men," Beau was apt to philosophize on the infrequent occasion when he could relax with a tall glass of the Scottish ale he favored.

Raine had a saying of her own regarding their relationship. "It's said some lives are linked across time, connected by an ancient calling that echoes down the ages. We're like magnets, Beau and I, with each incarnation, reaching out and soaring through space to reunite. We cross oceans of time to find one another."

Magick calls to magick.

Spiritually evolved souls, the couple shared a basic philosophy of life with several common denominators as well as untold memories of the heart, *these the love letters of past lives*; and though there had been others in each of their current lives, this was *why*, after so many years, Raine and Beau still were mutually enchanted.

"Life should be magick," Raine was inclined to impart.

"Life *is* magick," Beau answered, to which Raine added, "We've lived enough to know that there's a mystery behind it all, and we are all a part of it."

Only a few things triggered Dr. Beau Goodwin's temper– a product of the wild, warrior heritage of Scottish Highland clansmen, as his father was wont to say– causing him to lose his Leo chivalry. First and foremost was animal cruelty. He did *not* tolerate animal cruelty in the least. Those times, the glitter in his hot blue eyes narrowed to twin slits of ice-cold fire. And, at more restrained times, his temperament was tested by Raine's too-daring, impetuous Aries disposition, along with her unwavering outlook on the woes of marriage, conventional muggle marriage, at any rate.

"I shan't even try to put into words how glad I am that you decided to escape the grind at the clinic for this well-earned vacation," she told him now. "But tonight," she breathed into his ear, "I'll *show* you just how much I appreciate it."

"I believe nearly every vehicle on this island is either white or pale blue," Maggie was saying to Thaddeus, as she peered out the taxi window, where trucks, cars, and buses moved in constant succession. Everywhere, there was a sense of drive and effort.

"White and pale blue are the best colors for the tropical climate," the professor responded, picking up her hand to kiss it. "It's hot and humid here all year round. January to mid-April is relatively cooler and drier, with constant trade winds. The rest of the time, the trade winds blow irregularly with some breaks, increasing the feeling of sultriness."

"I can't believe our cab is a Mercedes," Maggie observed, stretching then resetting herself comfortably into the seat.

"A pleasant aspect of taxi service here. I read that about eighty percent of the taxis on Martinique are Mercedes-Benz," Thaddeus stated in his usual edifying manner before his voice dropped. "Fares are somewhat pricey, but travelers usually find themselves in the lap of luxury. Not surprising since this island's economy depends heavily on tourism … in addition to sugarcane and rum, bananas, avocadoes, and light industry."

As the esteemed head of Haleigh College's history department, Dr. Thaddeus Weatherby had been the perfect advisor to

Raine and Maggie when they were working toward their doctorates in history. His mentorship bonded him with the McDonoughs and aroused his fervent love for Maggie, who, before Thaddeus, lived by the free-spirit credo, "Fall in love whenever you can."

Over time, the Sisters came to discover, the inimitable Dr. Weatherby was well-versed in a wide range of subjects, and he possessed an intriguing spectrum of talents. Not to intimate that he was a jack of all trades, but he most assuredly was a master of many. Friends and colleagues were apt to say that Dr. Weatherby knew something about everything.

Furthermore, and to the point, Dr. Thaddeus Weatherby, PhD, was the textbook absent-minded professor with a brain like a steel trap. To put it another way, the highly respected Dr. Weatherby was a bona fide genius, and like most intellects, he was distinguished by his quirks. For one thing, he believed IQ tests were "... a piss-poor way to evaluate intellectual ability, failing as they do," he said, "to account for *magick*, which has its own significance, both by itself and as a compliment to logic."

For another thing, Weatherby occasionally displayed a childlike nature, or more precisely what, owing to his passionate curiosity, associates *mistook* for a childlike trait that, at times, drove his fellows in the history department, to use *his* word, "bats." But then, as those of the Craft know well, the secret of genius is to carry the riddle of the child into old age.

"I am happy to report that my inner child is still ageless," he liked to inform his colleagues at departmental meetings. Dr. Weatherby was fond of self-made maxims. "You're never too old to enjoy a happy childhood. Take time *every* day to do something amusing. Play is the highest form of research." Thaddeus Weatherby was not one to flout his own advice. From his teen years, he bounded out of bed each morning with the affirmation, "And so the adventure begins!"

All truth is simple, and through the looking glass, the professor's take on this was such: "We all of us have a little of the mad hatter. You have enough of it, and you're called a *genius*."

His fellows at the college liked to say that Dr. Weatherby looked as though he were listening to distant voices. In the professor's own words, he fancied he could hear and see things no one else could. "... unless you're open to them. There are wizards out there, cosmic seekers. Make no mistake– they're out there!"

Over the years, there developed a long, colorful list of people who thought of the professor as a magician of sorts.

One of the most special characteristics about the electrifying Thaddeus Weatherby was that he possessed extraordinarily accurate and vivid recall, both visual and audial, an "eidetic memory" some might call it. The amazing man's sharp Scorpio wit and courage, or as Hemingway penned it, "grace under pressure," served the Sleuth Sisters well on more than one close-call circumstance in the past.

Dr. Weatherby held that "The brave may not live forever, but the cautious don't live at all," a stance in spot-on sync with the Sisters. "In the end," Thaddeus told his confrères, "you won't treasure the time you spent working those extra hours, cleaning or repairing the house, or mowing the lawn. Did you ever hear someone on his deathbed say, 'I wish I'd spent more time at the office'? The big question is whether you are going to say *yes* to your adventure. Climb that damn mountain!"

As one might suspect, the professor was an exceptional teacher because while schooling others, he continually remained the student. This was another soupçon of wisdom he didn't have to impart to the Drs. McDonough. Raine and Maggie already lived it.

A wiry and surprisingly muscular middle-aged man, Thaddeus' hair was not streaked or speckled with grey. More accurately, it was the solid iron-grey of a Maltese cat; and thanks to Maggie's influence, no longer was it wildly reminiscent of Einstein's. Rather, it was professionally and becomingly styled.

"It doesn't look as if you comb your hair with firecrackers anymore," Raine ribbed when first she'd seen Thaddeus' new look.

His once careless manner of dress was now "country gentry," Irish tweeds replacing the rumpled, mismatched "Weatherby wear" about which, once upon a time, his students did genially jest. However, he retained, regardless of what he was wearing, his cherry-red bowtie, this signature mark as much a part of his personality as his quick wit and old-world charm. He was wearing his crimson bowtie now, clipped to a pale-blue cotton shirt, slightly damp from perspiration, with khaki trousers and navy-and-tan leather boat shoes.

Due to his significant other's sway, nowadays the professor sported a neat van dyke mustache and beard; and though he wore his contacts more often than he used to, this afternoon his brilliant blue eyes peered from behind his workaday Harry Potter spectacles that adjusted to light. He blinked owlishly. From the taxi window, the sky looked pleasingly azure against the smudgy green of a grove of tamarind trees.

"Shades of paradise," he pronounced with feeling.

"Is this your first time on Martinique?" their driver asked in pronounced French accent.

"Not for me," Raine blurted. *"Moi, j'adore la Martinique,"* she finished in French.

"Ah, vous parlez français, mademoiselle," he smiled at her reflection in the rearview mirror.

"Oui," she returned. *"Mais alors désolée pour mes fautes."*

"Pas de fautes, mademoiselle," he gestured with a flick of hand, telling her he heard no mistakes in her French. "You know, *bien sûr,* that our island is known as *l'Ile aux Fleurs,* but we have, in addition, another name. *Le Pays des Revenants,* the Land To Which One Returns."

"Bien nommé," Raine swiftly pronounced. "Aptly named. Something always remains of a love affair," she said after a pensive pause, "and my love affair with Martinique is ongoing."

"Voici l'Hôtel Bakoua!" the driver announced a few minutes later, as he pulled up to the attractive vanilla-hued stucco building with its orange tile roof.

On the Caribbean side of the island, overlooking the bay, the Bakoua's arched windows were prettily framed with open hurricane shutters. Throughout the grounds, tropical flowers and plants grew in structured perfusion, bringing to mind Martinique's bloomy soubriquet. The shrubs lining the driveway on which they strode from the taxi to the canopied front entrance were studded in pink, red, purple, orange, and yellow hibiscus. On either side of the main door, royal palms stood straight and tall like proud sentries to the noble resort establishment.

The lobby, from which flowed the main bar and formal dining room, was virtually empty when the Sisters and their escorts entered. Across from the reception desk, an enticing shop displayed quaint art works and crafts of local artisans.

Within a few minutes, the English-speaking concierge welcomed the new arrivals and checked them in, after which an attendant showed them to their adjacent cabana rooms on the glistening white-sand beach.

Whilst the Sisters' party stood for a moment to gaze at their accommodations' charming exterior, Raine informed, "You know, don't you, that this hotel began life as a Colonial residence."

"I can readily see that," Maggie replied. "It has a nostalgic appeal."

"Martinique is tropical forests and beaches, but it never lets you forget that it is a slice of France," the chatty Sister reminded.

Before they entered their rooms, Maggie asked if they should change out of their travel togs.

"No need to change. Let's just freshen up and rendezvous at the *Coco*. There," Raine pointed, "the bar hovering out over the water on stilts. We can unpack later."

Maggie caught Thaddeus' eye. "Sounds good to us."

Beau set their suitcases down on the luggage rack at the foot of the king-size, canopied mahogany bed and glanced about. *"Very nice."*

The bedchamber's walls were painted a deep ocean blue, whilst the wood-paneled, shuttered sitting area boasted a gleaming mahogany-and-cane table and chairs that conjured the ambience of an eighteen-century sugarcane plantation.

"Oh Beau, look," Raine called from the bathroom. "A double-sink vanity has saved many a relationship."

"I'll have to remember that," he said on a low chuckle, pulling her into his arms.

Less than twenty minutes later, Maggie and Thaddeus rapped on the door, a perfunctory rap to draw attention. "Ready?"

"We are," Raine replied.

Maggie took a moment to peer into Raine and Beau's room. "Looks just like ours, except that our bedroom walls are a delicate peach color.

The foursome accessed the Coco Bar via the long, wooden pier from the hotel's beach.

"I just happened to think that the straw– or whatever that thatch is– roof resembles the pointed *bakoua* hat for which this hotel is named," Maggie noticed.

"It does, doesn't it?" Raine answered. "You have a good eye, Mags. An artist's eye. The *bakoua* hat is *symbolic* of Martinique. Its conical crown encourages airflow to keep the wearer's head cool; but the fishermen who wear the hats found another use for the cone, safely secreting the day's cash receipts beneath the hat's towering peak. Crafty … in a witchy sort of way, *n'est-ce pas?*" She thought for a moment. "Just so you know, *coco* is the word for coconut in French."

Raine's emerald eyes scanned the area. "People come to the Coco Bar for the sunsets, for the spectacular views across the bay to the capital of Fort-de-France, and," she added with a twinkle, "to ogle the topless beauties on the beach."

"Ah, I've noted that," Thaddeus mumbled. Catching Maggie's expression, he amended his words. "Noticed the ogling, I mean."

"Oh, it's only Americans who ogle," Raine snickered. "With Europe's open, body-loving culture, topless is *no* big deal. Because of our puritanical history, we US Americans are, generally speaking, more prudish about nudity than most European countries. What's ironic is that we frown on nudity while we lead the world in pornography."

Beau sat up and raised a brow. "Maybe that's *why* we lead in pornography."

Rubbing his hands together, Thaddeus asked as they chose a table and sat down. "What shall we order? Raine, what do you suggest?"

"If you want a traditional Martinique rum drink, you should order either *le planteur* or *ti punch*. Both are made from white *rhum agricole*."

"What do you mean by *rhum agricole*?" Beau asked, and his face took on a receptive expression.

"If I recall," Raine began, "it's the French term for cane-juice rum, a style of rum distilled in the French Caribbean from freshly squeezed sugarcane rather than molasses."

"OK, so what's in *le planteur* besides the rum?" Maggie questioned.

The brunette Sister pursed her mouth. "Let me think … orange juice, guava juice, mango pulp, and sugar-cane syrup."

"And the *ti punch*?" Thaddeus asked, picking up a drink menu to peruse it.

"Sugar-cane syrup, white *rhum agricole*, and lime. Both drinks pack a punch, so sip slowly. They can fool you, wallop you sudden-like, if you know what I mean," Raine laughed, remembering her first encounter with *les planteurs*. "It was hot. I was thirsty. They tasted like fruit juice, and I downed three in a row on an empty stomach. The shadows of twilight were hardly falling when I teetered to my room and slept through dinner to the next day, noon."

"Can I get a cold beer?" Beau queried, as a waiter, attired in spick-and-span white, approached their table.

"Sure can," Raine replied. "The local beer is good, Bière Lorraine, what they call here 'blonde,' a pale lager that's copped more than a few awards over the years. Give it a go."

Whilst Beau sampled the island brew, Raine and Thaddeus sipped *ti punch*, and Maggie nursed a *planteur*. All about, picture-postcard sailboats bobbed on the tranquil blue-green water, and a catamaran glided softly out of the bay. Nearby, a small group of children were at play on the beach, their happy squeals rising to excitement as each wave swept across the sand, sending their small, brown legs scurrying in retreat.

"I almost expect to see the Sea Witch riding in with the tide, on the waves like foam, singing a Siren song, her seaweed hair, adorned with starfish and shells, floating out behind her, the strands aglitter from algae bloom and sea glass." Maggie leaned back in her chair to gaze wistfully across the bay. "It would be real hard not to be happy here," she sighed.

"It takes only five minutes for first timers to fall in love with Martinique," Raine acknowledged. "You'll love the people," she said of a sudden. "I find the local population here adorable. They're mainly of African descent, generally mixed with French and Carib Indians. Here, too, are descendants of immigrants from India, as well as intermarriages with Chinese and with Europeans other than French. A melting pot, as we Americans say."

"From what I've seen thus far, the *Martiniquais* seem quite friendly," Maggie remarked.

"Indeed," Raine replied, taking a sip of *ti punch*. "An enthusiastic people, always ready to help tourists. They laugh a lot, throwing their heads back to let loose contagious chortles, *and* they throw *themselves* into their dances and music with abandon. I have to say that, despite its small size, the music of Martinique has gained in international renown. Now, I've heard some say that the people here are aloof, but I've always found the natives to be wonderfully friendly and personable. But then again, I do try to speak their language. A thing every 'Ugly American' should attempt to do," she added, using the term applied to her countrymen who behave offensively abroad, remaining ignorant of local culture and judging everyone and everything by American standards.

Raine took a nip of punch, feeling its warmth all the way down to her toes. "You'll note also that these people are beautiful. The women, especially, are famous for their looks."

"I read once that French sailors adoringly nicknamed the ladies of this island *les femmes du paradis*," Thaddeus commented.

Raine gave a brisk nod. "They're strikingly handsome, with a proud, poised bearing, carriage and walk. A sparkling melody of people, *les Martiniquais*."

"On the ride from the airport, I enjoyed catching sight of the fishing villages. So picturesque with their multi-colored nets strung out to dry on poles, the wooden boats painted in such bright, happy shades." Maggie's eyes shifted to Raine. "What did you say the little fishing boats are called?"

"*Gommiers* or gum-tree boats. Without a doubt, the oldest type boat here."

"More colorful things than just the fishing nets and boats," Thaddeus commented. "*Quimbois*, for example, Martinique's answer to Voodoo." He set his glass down to expound. "When we were still in the area of Lamentin, I spotted, at a four-way intersection of the highway, what looked to be hexing wares, a small coffin, feathers, and such items of sorcery. Practitioners of black magick often place the like at a crossroads to enhance the strength of a spell."

"True that is," Raine conceded, "but I warn you, the people here don't speak openly of *Quimbois*. And though I've heard drums in the hills, they … well, they just don't talk about it. Widespread belief in concepts of sorcery and the evil eye, what I've heard some locals call 'devil's work,' has been supplanted by psychiatric and other scientific explanations for extraordinary behavior and phenomena."

The professor looked thoughtful, as he absently stroked his van dyke beard. "Let's make a plan for tomorrow," he suggested quite abruptly. "We want our first full day here to be memorable."

"That's a no-brainer," Raine put in swiftly. "I've arranged with the museum curator for a private tour of la Pagerie, Empress Joséphine's girlhood plantation here at Trois-Îlets." She snapped her fingers with a sudden thought. "That reminds me. We *must* rent a car at the reception desk, and we'd better do it soon, because it takes longer for things to get done around here. Island life is slower paced than we're accustomed to in the States, and you'd better get used to it in cafés and restaurants too. WE don't want to be labeled 'Ugly Americans.'"

Beau turned toward Thaddeus, "How about you and I taking care of the car rental in a few. It shouldn't take us long, then we can return for a second round."

"Good plan," the professor agreed.

Maggie checked her watch. "Raine mentioned that sunset this evening is 6:34, so you've time."

"I did some research of my own on the Caribbean," Beau replied. "Because of the location of the islands, twilight is shorter than it is in Europe or America. The afterglow of sunset stretches to dusk and full night in an hour at most."

"Right," Thaddeus said, "and that short time-frame produces the intense and varied colors as the sun dissolves into the sea."

"Raine," the professor asked, "how's the Internet situation here?"

The Goth gal set her glass down on the table. "Like small-town America."

Rising, Dr. Weatherby posed the foreseeable question, "Do you want to clarify that?"

"In small towns, the Internet is slow, but the gossip fast," she giggled. "Just kidding. We should get good cell phone and Internet reception here at the Bakoua and most spots on the island."

"C'mon, Beau," the professor urged, "let's rent the ladies their carriage for the fortnight of our stay."

"Don't dawdle," Raine cautioned. "You don't want to miss the fab sunset our first night here."

A sinister man with penetrating, blue-grey eyes, who was sitting off to himself and studying everyone in the bar, rose and walked past their table to leave, his eyes glacial.

Maggie leaned toward Raine. "What a strange man! Did you notice how he looked to be sizing everyone up?"

"I did," the raven-haired Sister answered. "The eyes were hypnotic, seemingly able to pierce through even carefully constructed layers." *My keen witchy hunch is we'll be seeing more of him.*

The men came back to the table some minutes later to announce that they had rented a compact car for their two-week island holiday.

"We were going to opt for a luxury vehicle," Beau said, reclaiming his seat next to Raine, "but the concierge recommended we choose a nice little city car, good for tight squeezes."

"Hence," the professor concluded, "we rented a Renault Twingo, a four-passenger hatchback."

"I bet it's a stick," Raine commented, sliding Beau's second beer toward him.

"It is. No way round that, but three of us can drive a stick." Catching Maggie's eye, Thaddeus sent her a wink.

- 63 -

"A moot point," she said. "The only stick I drive is my broom, and I never drive anything in a foreign country."

"You hardly drive at home," Raine returned, the lightness of her tone robbing the words of tartness.

"Blessed be, I don't," Maggie laughed. "Well, at least they motor on the right side of the road here."

"Roads are well-maintained," Raine informed, "but there are speed bumps everywhere; and be forewarned that this island's steep hills and curving jungle traces– which, by the way, can present themselves simultaneously– aggressive drivers, and congested traffic make driving a stick tricky business."

"We'll survive," Thaddeus replied, lifting his replenished *ti punch* in a toasting gesture.

"Incidentally," Beau raised a question along with his glass, "how large is this island?"

"Martinique's about fifty miles long and twenty-two miles across, at its widest," Raine answered without pause.

"What time did you say we're scheduled to be out at la Pagerie in the morning," Maggie asked, glancing over at Raine.

"Ten sharp. I hope they have our rental here in time." Noting Beau's wordless, thumbs-up response, the Goth gal checked her watch to sunset. "I thought, when we finish our tour at la Pagerie, we might drive the short distance to the Village Créole. You'll love it, I promise. The place is designed to look like a classic Martinique village. It's a delightful complex of shops, restaurants and such, the structures an array of beachy colors."

"We could take lunch there in one of the charming cafés Raine told me about," Maggie said, looking to the men who both received it as a fine idea.

"We won't want to rush our visit at la Pagerie," Raine advised. "I've visited the museum several times in the past, but they always seem to get new acquisitions. One of the most popular items is Joséphine's childhood bed. Amazing it's still around, considering the plantation house was destroyed in a devasting hurricane when the future empress was a child.

"Another big draw," Raine swept on, "are Napoléon's sensual love letters to Joséphine. Handwritten, of course, and signed. Even if you don't read French, you'll get the idea they are," she raised an ebony brow, "fairly risqué. And when you consider that just *one* of the emperor's letters to her sold recently at auction for more than half a million, American, it makes seeing a collection of them at la Pagerie a bargain at five euros."

"What other things does the museum have on display?" Beau asked.

"Oh," Raine reached back in time, "there's a spectrum of period art and artifacts. Paintings, sculpture, furniture, lamps, vases, flatware … tea sets. The museum is a picturesque stone building that was once the family cookhouse. As you know, a plantation's kitchen was housed in a separate structure to minimize the risk of fire. All in all, la Pagerie is a lovely site, beautifully landscaped, with a profusion of tropical flowers and lush vegetation."

Beau took a long pull of his beer. "This *is* good. I wonder if the Pagerie suffered much from the hurricane that battered the Caribbean a few months back?" he mused aloud.

"I think that storm pounded this whole island," Thaddeus answered. "I'd wager islanders are still recovering from it."

"Though it wasn't nearly as devasting as the one that destroyed the toddler Joséphine's home in 1766," Raine could not help but say.

Two women passed by their table, and from their carriage and chic beach attire, Raine guessed correctly they were Parisians even before she heard the distinctive, elite French sliding, in sexy *liaison*, from their throats. *French is so pleasing to the ear*, she thought.

Her eyes scanned the setting– the crystal clear, blue-green sea; the bobbing boats scattered on the bay; the lush, green hills of tropical forest; the beguine swaying palms; the vivid bougainvillea with Carib hummingbirds in merry attendance; and everywhere, *everywhere*, the bright splashes of color redolent of the Impressionist palette of Paul Gauguin. She sat back and sighed, and it was almost as if Martinique were hers alone.

"I can understand how visitors come to his island for a fortnight's vacation and end up staying for the rest of their lives," Thaddeus admitted.

It is the most bewitching of times, the hour before the sun lapses languidly into a shimmering turquoise sea, and the mountains' peaceful green changes to the mystery of deep purple.

As they sipped their drinks, no one spoke. Rather, they listened.

On all sides, in the hush of descending West Indian twilight, hummed a soothing murmur, a continuous low blend of sounds– the rhythmic cadence of the pervasive tree frogs, the gentle rustle of branch on branch, the sensual soughing of the sea as it surged to embrace the strand, and in the surrounding hills the distant beat of drums.

Then, in what seemed but moments, *magickal* moments, the Divine traded the azure-blue sky for a sky *ablaze* with purples, pinks, reds, orange and gold, as the huge fiery ball of sun sank slowly into the sea– and sunset settled over Martinique like a Benediction.

Raine sat paused in splendor. As an insect trapped in Antilles amber, she could not move.

"I know now what you meant, Raine, when you said that a Caribbean sunset was a faultless conclusion," Thaddeus revealed. "Here, night does not fall. It sails in softly, in poetic beauty."

"It's," Maggie drew in the exotic, heady scent of jasmine, recounting in witch's rhyme, "the smooth collusion of sky-burst fire and light into the calm and lull of tropic night."

"It's the waves, the wind, the trees all moving in concert, humming to one another in whispered awe of Earth Mother's creative genius." Beau enfolded Raine's hand in his, holding her gaze and reflecting on the first time he set eyes on her. "I experienced a similar bewitchment once before," he pronounced tenderly, "so I've a hunch this place is about to cast a spell over me."

This was the tropics such as one dreams of finding, moonrise silvering the palm fronds and drawing a broad ray of light, in breathtaking glimmer, across the bay, veiling with a poetic dusk the outline of the distant mountains, known in that part of the world as *mornes*.

The air is cooler after the long day's heat, and the surrounding *mélange* of tropical colors grows more subtle after the day's glare. Shadows lie level along road and beach. The mountains, a tangle of bamboo, fern and vine, of palm, mango and mahogany, of the breadfruit trees brought long ago from Tahiti– are violet now in eventide, save for the splash of scarlet, yellow or white, where a tree is in blossom with its promise of eternal summer.

However, as the distant drums grew in shamanic intensity, the Sisters, with their keen witches' intuition, sensed this paradise would soon be plagued by a lurking evil.

"We don't meet people by accident.
They are meant to cross our paths for a reason."
~ The Ancients

Chapter Three

Several wide steps led from the beach to l'Hôtel Bakoua's terraced open-air restaurant. Under its tent-like roof, the seafront *la Sirène* was illuminated with dozens of flickering candles, creating a romantic setting. Across the moonlit bay twinkled the faerie-tale lights of Fort-de-France, the capital's reflection on the glassy water rendering the scene dream-like.

"The info sheet in our room says a steel band will be performing here tonight," Maggie stated, settling into the chair Thaddeus held for her. Over her shoulders, she adjusted the aqua wedding-band shawl she was wearing– called thus because the weave is so fine, it can be pulled through a wedding band. The evening trade wind felt a bit cool, and the delicate wrap was just right.

Granny's black shawl was draped over Raine's shoulders, and she could feel the *grande dame*'s warm vibes enveloping her.

No sooner were they seated when a waitress approached their table with a glow of welcome. "*Bonsoir*, my name is Dorélia, and it is my pleasure to serve you," she greeted in French. Graciously, she handed the restaurant's fancy corded menus to all four at table.

Raine took the liberty of responding. "*Bonsoir et merci. Dites-moi, s'il vous plaît, parlez-vous anglais?*"

Dorélia smiled again, showing lovely teeth. "*Oui*, I speak English, *mademoiselle*. Not perfect English, but most of us at the hotel speak a leetle English." She seemed to study them for a protracted moment. "I knew the minute I saw you that you were *des Américains*."

"Is it that obvious?" Maggie asked with good-natured tone.

"I *saw* how you looked at all the candles when you came in … *en admiration*. Europeans are not so filled with wonder as Americans, *je crois*."

Maggie extended a hand in response with a quick chuckle. "We are demonstrative. I'll say that about us."

Dorélia appeared to be in her thirties, a pretty woman with café-au-lait skin, soulful dark eyes, and a fine, warm figure. Like all *Martiniquaises*, her carriage was ramrod straight and proud, and as the other waitresses, she sported a long, flouncy skirt of orange madras, the emblematic fabric of Martinique. Her off-the-shoulder blouse was white cotton eyelet. Large gold hoops adorned her ears and wrists, and her hair was covered with orange madras tied atop the head in two knots.

"Let me see if I remember what Raine told me the knots signify in a woman's traditional head-wrap," Maggie contemplated. "One knot means the lady is single. Two that she's married. Three that she's either widowed or divorced, and four, *ou la la*, that she's available to anyone who tries."

"*Voilà*," Dorélia laughed. "*C'est vrai, mademoiselle.* You are correct."

Thaddeus, who had been engrossed in the menu, looked up then to ask, "What do you recommend … for starters?"

"Everything here is good, *monsieur*; but if you're asking what *I* like, or what is typically Martinique, then I must recommend, *pour commencer, la salade Créole.*"

"Why don't we all try that?" Raine suggested. "It's got stuffed crab and the local sausage that I remember as scrumptious," she translated from the menu.

When everyone agreed, Dorélia jotted it down on her pad.

"Oooooh," Raine enthused, "the *langouste* … lobster here is to die for. *Pour l'entrée, pour moi, la langouste, Dorélia, s'il vous plaît.*"

Thaddeus ordered the same, whilst Maggie opted for the snapper with Créole sauce. For a few moments, Beau was undecided between the lobster and the entrecôte, but finally went with the latter, which was prepared with a green pepper sauce.

"A rib-eye steak is usually one of the tastiest steaks any restaurant can offer, so I can't go wrong," he said, returning his menu to the waitress.

"I promise you will be pleased, *monsieur*," she answered in easy-going island manner. "Our chef is *un artiste*. Martinique food is a *mélange* of African, French, and Caribbean, with a nod to Asian traditions. The *best* of each," she conveyed in her native tongue, and her laugh was, as the Americans had heard, contagious.

Having collected all four menus, Dorélia set them aside. "You will want to choose a dessert later," she beamed. With that, the waitress headed for the kitchen, as an attendant poured ice water and took the drink order to the bar. For Beau, a Cabernet Sauvignon, Chardonnay for the others.

While the Sisters' party awaited the food, they sipped their wine, chatting pleasantly. After several minutes, an elevated male voice carried to their table from across the way where the steel band was setting up, the French words that reached their ears explosive with anger.

Maggie heaved a sigh, looking to Raine. "Wow, what's that about? Did you catch any of it?"

"Not much," she admitted. "They were speaking *Patois*, the French-based Créole, which I don't understand. The people here speak it when conversing with one another, but they don't usually use it with anyone else. I caught a snatch of it though. I think a band member is late."

Their salads arrived, and the talk shifted to food and local delicacies.

"The crab in this salad is very tasty," Maggie commented. "The sausage is good too, but the crab is excellent."

"Lime juice gives it a nice kick," Thaddeus replied, squeezing more over his salad, "as do the hot peppers, enough just to warm the palate, but they don't overpower the other flavors."

In a moment, their attention was again drawn to the area where the band was preparing for the night's entertainment. This time, when the leader raised his voice in anger, his ire went a step further. Like a can of soda that had been hard shaken, he erupted, springing forth to yank the errant musician by the front of his madras shirt.

Maggie leaned in closer to Raine. "Galloping gargoyles, what's going down now?"

"All I could decipher is that the tardy musician is *habitually* late, and … oooh, here comes the hotel manager to speak to them," the Goth gal concluded.

As they watched, the manager spoke quietly to the men, after which things settled down.

When Dorélia returned to their table to check on them and relate that their entrées would be soon served, she cut a forlorn figure, standing there looking as if she had been crying. Her eyes were somewhat red, and she sniffed continuously. Unable to restrain herself, Raine posed the question on all their minds. "What's happening between the band members?" The Sisters both sensed that the incident was somehow connected to their waitress' distress.

With a groan, the affable *Martiniquaise* replied in barely audible words, "The band leader is my husband. He loves his music, and he enjoys it very much, *mais*," she plucked a handkerchief from the deep pocket of her madras skirt to dab at her eyes, whilst she lapsed softly into French, and it looked as though she were about to burst into fresh tears. "*Jean-Jacques se met très facilement en colère.*"

"Yes," Raine said almost to herself, "he certainly appears to have a hair-trigger temper."

They all turned toward the band, as the enchanting steel drums rang out with the ever-popular *Yellow Bird*.

Dorélia coughed apologetically. "I … er," she attempted English, but gave in to the emotional pull of her own language. "I don't know why I told you that. I never confide in *les étrangers*, but *you*," she regarded Raine and Maggie for a studying moment, "don't seem like strangers."

Raine translated the woman's words, sending them telepathically to Maggie, who answered in her easygoing manner, "We've been told that before. Many times, in fact."

"We're empaths," the redheaded Sister clarified. Then, not certain Dorélia would understand, she turned to Raine, who instinctively adjoined–

"*Intuitive … nous sommes tous les deux psychiques.*"

"People tend to tell us their woes. They sense that we can help them," Maggie explained further, after which Raine put the words into French for the waitress' benefit.

"*Merci*," the sad-eyed woman whispered, glancing quickly round to see if anyone else had noticed her anguish. "You are very kind. *Je suis désolée.* I am so sorry about the trouble," she voiced quietly. "Now that the music has begun," she forged a weak smile, "*tout ira bien.* Everything will be fine."

The disturbing thought rose to Raine's mind, whereupon she sped the omen to Maggie. *Music to soothe the savage beast.*

When they finished what turned out to be a most delicious dinner, the foursome drifted over to a table near the band. Several tables skimmed the dance floor, on which a few couples were swaying to a delightful beguine.

"That coconut flan was scrumptious, wasn't it?" Maggie said to no one in particular. "I think," she cackled, "it's what *witches* eat."

"Nooo," Raine giggled, "witches eat marzipan. I have it on good authority. It's easy to gain weight here," she warned with serious tone. "My first visit put ten pounds on me. I'm small-boned. I returned home looking like *le bonhomme Michelin*."

"Well, what's say we work it off on the dance floor," Thaddeus proposed, extending his hand in courtly gesture to Maggie, who asked the professor to clarify Raine's comment.

"The Michelin Tire Man. His whole body is made up of inner tubes," he explained.

"C'mon, Beau," Raine urged, pulling him to his feet. "This is a beguine, and it's essentially a slow rhumba. Just sway like a palm tree in rhythm with the music."

The string of golden-age beguines that followed was wonderfully happy music, showering good spirits over the audience like Martinique rays of sunshine.

Even the tetchy Jean-Jacques looked joyful as, switching from the steel drum, he led with an artful clarinet. Dorélia was right. Her husband was an extraordinary musician. It was impressive how he smoothly traded clarinet for trombone, changing back to steel drums, now and again taking up the *chachas*, the rudimentary maracas, as his band, the Trade Winds, entertained with beguines, mazurkas, waltzes, and salsas. The waitress, however, had confided that music was an avocation. Her husband's day job was loan officer at a bank across the bay at Fort-de-France.

Jean-Jacques Sauvage was a tall, well-built man, strikingly handsome in a Harry Belafonte sort of way. Even his singing was reminiscent of the King of Calypso, the clear, silky voice soothing, belying the seething anger just below the surface. There was no mistaking he was a forceful personality. But it was also clear that Sauvage loved being on stage. He was a natural. It was where he belonged, conveying the sense that he was at his best, making his music. It made the Sisters wonder if perhaps the man suffered from the disenchantment of an unfulfilled dream.

When the band took a break, Raine and Maggie happened to catch sight of him in a far corner, a hand gripping Dorélia's arm, his face close to hers, his expression, again, mirroring anger.

***

"I'm relieved the hotel had our rental waiting for us," Raine said, as they motored out to la Pagerie the next morning in the white Renault Twingo. Around them spread a beautiful Martinique day. Thaddeus was behind the wheel, Maggie in the front passenger seat, with Raine and Beau ensconced in the back. "I remember pushing the concierge years ago to hurry a rental to me at the hotel. 'Oh,' he answered like a cat lazing in the sun, 'whether that car's here or not, the sun will come up in the morning. You Americans rush about far too much. You're here to relax, so do what you came here to do. *Relax.*'"

Raine tilted her head, remembering. "I did learn to relax … in Martinique at least. This is the only place in the world I can just *be*. Time stands still here, and I don't seem to worry about a thing. I can just … *be*," she giggled, flicking her fingers in the air, her expressive hands framing her face. In the blink of an eye, she caught Beau's disbelieving expression. "Well, it takes a day or so to kick in, if I recall," she amended sheepishly. "Anyway, summer's humidity renders the tempo of life *and me* languorously lazy. What's that you used to say? 'For fast-acting relief, try slowing down.'"

"There's more to life than increasing its speed," Beau agreed. "I'm just sorry we settled for a continental breakfast in our rooms in place of that tempting buffet breakfast in the hotel's main dining room. Did you get a look at what we're missing? That was a breakfast *banquet*."

"We'll do the buffet tomorrow," Raine replied. "No time for it today. We don't want to keep the curator waiting, after she agreed to give us a private tour. That would be rude."

"Raine's right," Maggie concurred.

"I quite see your point," Thaddeus imparted to the Sisters, "but Beau's made a valid point too. Tomorrow, the breakfast buffet. I can resist anything but temptation," he laughed.

"We might see Dorélia at the plantation," Maggie commented. "She told me she sometimes works there during the day. Her schedule at the hotel is the dinner shift, so she's free days to volunteer her time at la Pagerie. Apparently, the museum depends somewhat on volunteer help."

"Raine, do you know when this museum opened?" Thaddeus asked.

"The museum's origins date to 1929," the Goth gal replied without falter. "But in 1940, a Martinique scholar dedicated to the humanities, Dr. Robert Rose-Rosette, saved la Pagerie from destruction and oblivion. He's considered the founder of the present museum on the site."

"How beautiful!" the redheaded Sister exclaimed, some minutes later, when a neat green sign welcomed them to the birthplace of the Empress Joséphine.

La Pagerie was nestled in a setting lush with palm trees, flowers, and carefully planned vegetation of all sorts, conjuring the impression of a tropical paradise. When the Sisters, Thaddeus and Beau walked from their parked rental to the picturesque stone museum, they noticed several people at work, tending the numerous flower beds on the property, raking the newly cut lawn, and trimming shrubbery.

Maggie drew in a long breath. *Such an enchanting place, with the sense of the Summerland*, she told herself.

On the manicured park grounds stood a charming pavilion, where tourists could rest out of the sun's glare to ponder the foundation ruins of the plantation house, as well as the standing ruins of *la sucrerie*, the sugar refinery.

When the Sisters' party entered the stone museum, they were relieved to be out of the tropical heat. Though it was only ten in the morning, it was an especially hot, humid day. Inside, an air conditioner hummed quietly on a wall.

"Feels good in here," Raine whispered. "I think that brunette lady over there," she jerked her own dark head to the side, "is the curator. She looks like the photo on the museum website. I'll go and see."

No sooner did Raine approach the woman when she stepped forward to offer her hand. "Are you here for a private tour this morning?" she asked in beautifully French-accented English.

"Yes," the Goth gal replied, introducing herself.

"*Mais oui*, we spoke on the phone. I'm Jeanne Gardien, curator here." She gently squeezed Raine's hand. "I'm delighted to welcome you to la Pagerie."

"Thank you. We're happy to be here. The rest of my party is just over there."

"Doctors McDonough, you have been here before?" Jeanne queried in a voice that told them she had an inkling of an idea of the response. The curator was a pleasant, slender woman, medium height, who reminded the Americans of the whimsical yet classy French actress, Leslie Caron.

"*I* have been here several times in the past, but this is the first visit for the others in my party," Raine responded.

"You are all history professors, *non?*" the curator asked. They were standing in the entrance area, not having yet begun the tour.

"Three of us are history professors," Maggie said, indicating with sweep of hand herself, Raine, and Thaddeus. "Dr. Goodwin," she gestured toward Beau, "is a veterinarian."

"Maggie and I are also professors of archeology," Raine added.

"*Bien*. Due to your history backgrounds, I'll keep my presentations devoid of heavy detail, more to create mood than to instruct. However, I will interject items of human interest about Joséphine as we progress through the exhibits. This, I believe, will be good for all." Jeanne smiled, indicating that they should begin walking through the museum. Only a handful of visitors were there that early, which made it easy to view the items on display.

"As you know," Jeanne began, "the woman distinguished in history as Empress Joséphine came into the world on 23 June 1763, here on this sugarcane plantation. Her birth name was Marie-Josèphe-Rose Tascher de la Pagerie. The family into which she was born belonged to the ancient country gentry of France. *Les grands blancs*, or *békés*, these white Créole aristocrats were called here in the sugar islands; and they brought to Martinique, Guadeloupe and elsewhere echoes of their French homeland. Créole, *au fait,* is a person of either French or Spanish extraction born here in the islands.

"For these landed gentry, life held a certain air of ease and gallantry, comparable perhaps to plantation owners' *bon vivant* in the southern region of your country prior to your Civil War. Gracious hospitality, a richness of dress that on grand occasions reflected the fashion modes of Paris, a passion for gambling– certainly Joséphine's father was afflicted with this fever– and a ready resort to dueling were all marks of *béké* island society.

"Reminiscent of a manor in medieval Europe, la Pagerie was a world unto itself. Here were the enfolding fields of sugarcane, the huts and kitchen gardens of the slave families, the barns full of stalks used as fuel, and most important of all, *la sucrerie*, the sugar refinery, where the cane stalks were crushed by rollers, the liquid collected, and raw sugar produced. Tamarinds, palms, mango, orange, and breadfruit trees provided shade; and tropical flowers and birds bestowed splashes of bright, happy colors everywhere.

"An ill-matched pair, Joséphine's parents struggled financially after a hurricane– the worst in the history of our island– destroyed the plantation house in 1766, when the future empress was three, and her nurse carried her to safety, moaning and muttering with terror. The stone foundation is all that remains of the plantation house– a big, picturesque, white wooden mansion with large, open windows, a verandah decked with blossoms, and a tree-shaded courtyard.

"Joséphine's mother, Rose-Claire des Vergers de Sannois, was descended from one of Martinique's oldest and wealthiest families when the phrase 'rich as a Créole' was in daily use. The empress' father, Joseph-Gaspard de Tascher de la Pagerie, a naval officer and minor French aristocrat, who married up, had neither ambition nor money to rebuild the house, though I daresay, he promised his wife numerous times that he would. Rather, he preferred languishing about, telling stories of his glory days at the French count of Versailles, Paris, where in his youth he had been a page. I suppose we could say, he was an incompetent, a poor, pretty-boy charmer with an eye for the ladies. Characteristically, after the hurricane destroyed their home, *Monsieur* de Tascher moved his family to the top floor of the *sucrerie*, upon which he did some minor additions, such as an outside gallery. With that verandah added, he called it a day.

"Nonetheless, in the future empress' own words, her island childhood was a most happy time: 'I was a spoilt child, allowed to do as I pleased. I ran, I frolicked and danced, from morning to night, and no one restrained the wild movements of my childhood in a paradise of pleasure, where I splashed in the sea like a dolphin and sucked on sugarcane plucked from the fields.'

"To be sure, the child shared in the stories, the songs and the dances of the plantation slaves; and conceivably, the witchcraft and prophecies, so prevalent in the tropics, was the basis for her lifelong interest in the occult. Joséphine would always find having her cards read irresistible.

"As a young girl here on the island, she was called by the soubriquet *Yeyette*. Her petname until, at age fifteen, she married her first husband, who would declare the name totally unsuitable, 'juvenile and silly.'"

The curator recommenced after a brief pause in which she seemed to be musing over something. "This fascinating woman would have several names in her life, but History addresses her with *one*, that which Napoléon christened her, but let me not get ahead of myself.

"In 1779, the benighted, starry-eyed teenager went off to Paris to marry Alexandre Vicomte de Beauharnais, becoming the Vicomtesse de Beauharnais. Alexandre looked to be a dream husband, rich, titled, and handsome in his military uniform. It was an arranged marriage and, as it turned out, a very **un**happy one for both husband and wife."

"We know that the advantageous marriage was arranged by Joséphine's paternal aunt, who was the mistress of Alexandre's father," Raine interjected. "Aunt Edmée was the marquis' mistress for over two decades, and with her paramour getting on in years, her position was becoming a bit precarious. Thus, the auntie hatched a scheme to keep the old Beauharnais money in the hands of the

Tascher family. Marry one of her brother's daughters to the marquis' son, Alexandre, who went along with the plan, mostly because he wouldn't come into his inheritance *until* he married."

"*Exactement*," Jeanne replied. "Although Rose– the name the future Joséphine was now using– bore Alexandre two children, Eugène and Hortense, the vain, heartless man was ashamed of his wife, of her provincial manners and lack of sophistication. Throughout the time they were together, so embarrassed was he, Alexandre declined to present Rose to the court of Marie-Antoinette at Versailles. He never took the lonely *demoiselle* with him anywhere, leaving her at home with lesson plans 'to at least cultivate her mind.' Rose was less than enthused.

"Actually, Alexandre was in love with *his* mistress. He neglected Rose so badly, she finally obtained a legal separation. *The dream had turned into a nightmare– a runaway.*

"Alexandre's pregnant paramour was the last straw. The cunning Laure de Longpré brewed in her cauldron of deceit all sorts of foul lies about Alexandre's naïve little wife, the most damaging being that since their second child, Hortense, was born a couple of weeks early, the baby was not his. Alexandre and his mistress, working her snakelike charms on her lover, embarked for Martinique to gather evidence against Rose from her early years, hoping, in that way, to rupture the marriage. Alexandre could not divorce Rose, *impossible* in France then, but he could exile her.

"Here on Martinique, they bribed and threatened slaves for lies, doing everything in their power, to the chagrin of the family Tascher de la Pagerie, to destroy Rose's reputation at her birthplace. When the schemers returned to Paris, Laure swept into the Beauharnais home armed with a most horrid letter, which she brandished before a tearful Rose's face.

"Sophisticated and stylish, the older woman took evil pleasure in presenting the communication from Alexandre, calling his innocent young wife the 'vilest of all creatures ... beneath all the sluts in the world.'" Jeanne clicked her tongue. "The missive ordered Rose to take herself to a convent.

"Chubby, awkward, and artless enough to have allowed her vain, pompous husband to see that she'd fallen in deep enchantment with him from the moment she stepped off the boat, poor little Rose didn't stand a chance, responding with shock and hurt, rather than a Créole curse."

By this point, the Sisters' party was standing before a large portrait of Joséphine hanging against a stone wall, the woman therein gazing indolently, across the years, at curious visitors.

None of the likenesses of this captivating woman ever did her justice, Raine said to herself, casting the thought to Maggie. *Napoléon once said that her portraits fell short of the reality.*

As if she could read minds, the curator said, "I have always felt that no artist ever captured Joséphine's real beauty. I suppose that was because she was possessed of more charm and sex appeal than classic beauty. She was about five feet, a respectable height for a woman of her era. Her best features were her beautiful porcelain skin, beautifully formed neck, shoulders and arms, and her dreamy, bedroom eyes, eyes of a peculiar hazel shade with bright amber flecks. From all the studies done of her, both paintings and sculptures, we can safely say she had strong cheekbones and a delicate, straight nose. From all accounts, too, her hair was a lustrous, dark chestnut color, and she came to wear it upswept at the back, with little wisps and curls around the face, over the forehead and ears. We see a small, slightly pinched mouth in nearly every image. *Pourquoi?* Sources tell us that Joséphine had rotting teeth, the result of all the sugary goodies she consumed as a child here on Martinique. She was passionately fond of sucking on sugarcane. Before a mirror, she practiced talking and smiling without showing the teeth."

A sudden surge of voices behind them prompted the curator to turn round. "Let's let this tour group pass us while I continue my talk with you. That way, when I've finished, we'll have a clear way.

"To revisit our story," Jeanne Gardien went on, "though her mother begged her, via letter, to return to the bosom of her family in Martinique, Rose remained in Paris, learning the ways of the fashionable world. Here is how that came about, and to be sure, the convent was, for the future empress of France, a huge blessing in disguise. During her separation from Alexandre, she and her children lived, at *his* expense, at Pentémont Abbey, which was run by a group of nuns. The boon for the unsophisticated Rose was that this was *the* place wealthy Parisian ladies went to live if they could not live with their husbands for whatever reason. The highborn ladies seeking independence were provided tasteful apartments, and they could come and go as they pleased. The gauche country girl from a backwater plantation found herself in a sort of finishing school, where the aristocratic ladies were eager to share their secrets.

"At the Pentémont, Marie-Josèphe-Rose learned everything she could about how to behave in high society. She learned how to do her hair, makeup, how to talk and walk. She developed a very elegant, indolent walk that was really enchanting. Understanding that she had nothing but her charms to rely on in what she was discovering was a cruel world, a man's world, she watched the titled women around her and soon mastered the art of graceful movement and conversational allure. A born coquette, she perfected the art of whispered suggestion, softening her voice to a husky Créole drawl that would become one of her chief attractions– a ravishing sound according to several of her lovers.

"She became accomplished at covering her small, neat mouth (that in and of itself projected refinement rather than sensuality) with a mysterious smile and, when she laughed, a fancy handkerchief to hide the teeth. She lost weight and discovered how to enhance her new-found curves with clinging, low-cut dresses, shawls, and regal carriage. Gone the way of history were the stiff, heavy gowns that thrust out so far from the hips that ladies had to turn sideways to get through doors. The new draped gowns and softly curling natural hairstyles perfectly suited Rose's face and figure.

"The soft, flowing gowns more easily revealed the feet. Since Rose had small, attractive feet and dainty ankles, she made certain to expose hers at every opportunity. In that time and place, the glimpse of a pretty ankle was more likely to drive men wild than a generous bosom.

"Napoléon would later say of his Joséphine: 'She was a woman in the fullest sense of the word, vivid, vivacious, and with the best of hearts.'

"And lest I forget to mention Rose's mastering of the art of rouge– craftily applied to recall sexual flush. At twenty-one, the 'Rose of la Pagerie,' with her silvery voice, sensual grace, and the heady, sweet fire of her Créole soul, blossomed into a *very* intriguing lady. By far, her most appealing feature were her big, luminous eyes, eyes that glittered green or amber, depending on the light or what she was wearing– and they stopped men in their tracks.

"She learned to shade her eyelids with kohl and elderberries and even applied the kohl with soot to her brows and long, thick lashes. In days to come, women might question why men were so infatuated with the vicomtesse, drawn to her by an irresistible force. Men didn't have to figure it out. She made them think of the boudoir. Was it the sexy, beautifully modulated low voice, the way she moved, or the bedroom eyes?" The curator raised her shoulders. "*Eh bien*, it was the whole package. Simply put, there was something about Rose's aura that *enchanted*.

"*Bien sûr*, the future empress had learned much more at the Pentémont than which fork to use for salad and which for dessert. She emerged from her 'finishing school,' a sexy, savvy woman of the world– as sensual as Martinique itself. Perhaps not a great beauty, but *striking*."

"Was makeup accepted back then?" Beau asked. "Seems kind of racy for aristocratic women to wear makeup in the eighteenth century, don't you think?"

Jeanne shook her head, her tone slightly censorious. "In England, it would have been considered racy, but not in France, *monsieur*. Highborn French women used makeup freely, and would not have dreamt to leave their homes without it. The 'Rose of Martinique' came to make her own cosmetics, one in particular in a very secret ritual."

Her youth-cream concoction, Raine whooshed to Maggie, who responded with a subtle nod.

The group proceeded on, through a gallery of additional portraits of Joséphine from her later life, as wife of Napoléon and crowned empress.

"Hoping to get some needed funds from her father, in 1788, Rose made a snap decision to return to Martinique for a visit that extended into a two-year stay. Besides, she was homesick for her island home and her aging mother and wanted to spend time with her parents before they left this earth. In addition, she wanted to show her birthplace to her little daughter, Hortense.

"Alexandre had taken their son, Eugène, into his care, for now he was old enough, at the age of seven, to begin boarding school in preparation, in his father's footfalls, for a military career, though the courts had granted Rose the right to spend summers with her son. The same courts declared her innocent of the nastiness spewed by Alexandre and his mistress, who were forced, as you Americans say, to eat crow. Alexandre's own father, the Marquis de Beauharnais, testified *against* his son in Rose's favor. Rose could now live anywhere she chose, and her conniving, mean-spirited husband was ordered to pay her support."

"Was that the only return visit Joséphine made to Martinique?" Beau asked.

"As destiny would have it, it was," Jeanne answered. "She set sail in the summer of 1788 on the *Sultan*." The curator indicated that they should move on, to view the other items on display.

"After her torment at the hands of her heartless husband, Rose left the Pentémont to reside with her aunt at Fontainebleau. The Belle Créole was free to enjoy herself in Paris for the first time since her arrival in the City of Lights several years before, but such enjoyments came with a large price tag. She needed extra money, beyond what Alexandre was paying her, for gowns, jewels, and entertaining new-found friends. Thus, she decided to try and get some of the money her father had promised her when she married."

"Do you give credence to the rumblings in history that, at this stage of her life, Joséphine had begun to depend on the generosity of older men, wealthy married men, for those extras?" Raine asked.

The curator's smile was almost as mysterious as the one the empress was wearing in the portrait before them. "She was a pretty woman, desperate to have the luxuries of the era, and she discovered that her attractiveness gave her certain advantages. She didn't care about polite society, and more and more, she was able to shirk off public opinion. *Oui*, Rose began, as you said, to depend on the favor of older gentleman friends. Men of her own age, she found difficult and demanding. Older man praised and petted her, appreciated her charms, and best of all, they gifted her with expensive presents, including jewelry, for which she had a penchant." Jeanne reached a hand to the string of pearls she was wearing. "I should say an *insatiable* desire.

"The country, however, was near bankrupt. Not only were the royal coffers depleted, but over two decades of poor harvests, drought, cattle disease, and skyrocketing bread prices kindled unrest among the peasants and the urban poor. The Have-Nots were living in terrible conditions, while the Haves, the French aristocracy, continued to spend lavishly down what could only be termed a debauched road. Rose had set her pretty feet squarely on this path, and with the spirit of Revolution sparking all around her, it was a *dangerous* game she was playing."

"I'm inclined to concur with several historians who believe the real reason Joséphine… er Rose was taking flight to Martinique is that there was already gossip," Thaddeus interjected. "She'd been spending rich men's money like water. I suspect she was fearful Alexandre would learn of her indiscretions and perhaps try and take her children away from her. Hence, she thought it best to absent herself from the Paris scene, at least until the talk died down. Think about it. There she was, always a poor traveler with the migraine headaches travel gave her, embarking on a dangerous sea journey during hurricane season to the Caribbean, when the high seas were thick and hostile with enemy British ships."

"Agree!" both Raine and Maggie resounded as one.

"Sometimes, running away means you're headed in the exact right direction," Raine added.

"And *I* think you'd be correct in your reasoning," Jeanne granted. "To return once again to our story: The *Sultan,* carrying Rose, her five-year-old daughter Hortense, and Rose's maid, Euphémie, arrived in Martinique in August of 1788. Rose was delighted to see her family. At the capital across the bay, she reveled in the balls and various soirées and receptions, basking in the attention sophistication and her new look conferred on her. It thrilled her that she could coquettishly wave a fan before her face and reel a man in with her eyes from across a crowded ballroom. The vicomtesse became quite skilled at this game, and she had great fun playing at it.

"But there was trouble brewing among the slaves of the island. Social unrest and the spirit of Revolution were intensifying with every passing day. Anti-slavery literature was circulating like wildfire across the Caribbean, and freed slaves were forming groups and making demands.

"On 31 August 1790, a slave uprising erupted in Saint-Pierre that quickly flamed into a full-fledged revolt when underprivileged Whites joined the slave ranks. Rose, with Hortense, and the faithful Euphémie, who had been with Marie-Josèphe-Rose from the time she was born– accompanying her to Paris when she married Alexandre, never leaving her side through all the stressful times, returning to Martinique to visit family– now took flight with her back to France.

"With her *café-au-lait* complexion, chocolate-brown hair, and greenish eyes, the comely Euphémie might well have been

Joséphine's half-sister, for it is known that plantation owners often had offspring with their slaves, and there was such a close bond between the two women.

"La Pagerie's slaves– as many as 300– by all indication, were treated kindly, that is for the norms of the times. Neither the plantation nor the owners were harmed during the slave uprisings. What has never been proven is that Joséphine convinced Napoléon to reinstate slavery in Martinique. I'm sure you know," the curator said, looking to the Drs. McDonough and Dr. Weatherby, "that France abolished slavery in 1789, but soon after Napoléon and Joséphine assumed their thrones, in 1804, it was *re*-established. Many believe it was Joséphine who pushed for the change to benefit her family's failing plantation interests here on Martinique."

In pensive posture, Jeanne cocked her head. "Personally, I think this is to attribute to Joséphine a power she may not have had, though she did have influence over Napoléon. However, imagine being a former slave living as a free man or woman for more than ten years, then being forced back into bondage at the alleged behest of your home's most famous citizen.

"To be sure, many *Martiniquais* harbor a strong sense of pride over the lofty station the Rose of Martinique attained. *Eh bien*, the complexities still swirling round the love-hate feelings for the empress are on full display with her marble statue at *la Savane*, the park across the bay at Fort-de-France– a mystery unsolved now for years.

"You see, in 1991, the statue was furtively beheaded in the dark of night and splashed with red paint. *Bien sûr*, the decapitation echoes the Reign of Terror during the French Revolution when aristocrats like Joséphine were beheaded, the red paint blood. The vandals, who were never caught, wrote on the statue's pedestal: '*Respe ba Matinik. Respe ba 22 Me.*' Translated, the Créole French means: 'Respect Martinique. Respect 22 May.' The reference is to 22 May 1848, the date of the slave rebellion that eventually led to the abolition of slavery in the French Colonies." *Madame* the Curator held the Sisters' party with a solemn regard. "Be sure to visit *la Savane* during your time here on Martinique. The park gardens are beautiful, and you can ponder our rich history on one of the benches overlooking the sea."

Jeanne blew out her breath. "Now, where was I in my presentation?" She thought for a moment, then went on after the

Sisters reminded her that she had been talking about the slave unrest during Joséphine's one and only return visit to Martinique.

"*Ah oui*, Martinique was the first of the islands to explode into conflict, causing widespread fear among the plantation owners. When Rose's uncle, port commander at Fort-Royal– the fortification's former name– was taken captive, the slaves took over. Paranoia among the white population hit a fever pitch, causing Rose to make another snap travel decision.

"In a literal run for their lives, loudly interrupted with cannon shot landing near their feet, she, a whimpering Hortense, and the ever-faithful Euphémie raced through the streets, swarming with prowling and rioting slaves, for the port, where they were given passage aboard the *Sensible* bound for France, without luggage or the opportunity to bid farewell to the family. Before the ship could set sail, it was nearly capsized in the harbor by cannon fire. Both the run for the *Sensible* and the crossing itself were nightmare journeys. A postscript to this chapter of Rose's life is that her father died about three months hence, leaving enormous debts for his wife to pay off.

"For the future empress, it was back to Paris, where the danger for aristocrats was ever broiling as the Have-Nots grew more and more hungry for blood, where in the not-too-distant future her vicomte husband, Alexandre de Beauharnais, would be guillotined, and where Rose herself would be imprisoned for four harrowing months, narrowly escaping death when the Revolutionary leader Robespierre himself was beheaded and the Reign of Terror ended.

"The terrifying sound of the guillotine crashed down to sever the last head, and the streets of Paris ceased running with blood. Needless to say, Rose's encounter with the instrument of death was a close shave, excuse the pun, for that same morning, her bed had been taken from her prison cell, a sure sign she was next on the docket to be beheaded. Rose was released from Carmes Prison on orders of the anti-Robespierre political group led by Jean-Lambert Tallien.

"While imprisoned, Rose had become a close friend with Tallien's mistress, the spicy Spanish Créole, Thérésia Cabarrus. It was the glamorous Thérésia who orchestrated Rose's release.

"Falling into her old habit of seduction and making use of all her coquettish tricks, Rose began embarking on love affairs with France's new leading political figures, including Paul Barras, who, of course you know, became the leader of the new Directory government." *Madame* the Curator lifted her shoulders in another of her Gallic gestures. "I think Rose reveled in debauched affairs with powerful men."

She pursed her lips. "She thoroughly enjoyed sex, the full physical expression, as much as she enjoyed spending the money of the men she seduced. I think she felt in *control* of men during–" the curator stopped herself. "Less than a year after she was released from prison, this thirty-two-year-old widow, with hardly a *sou* to her name, was presiding over the most powerful table in Paris. With her two closest friends, Créoles like herself, Rose blossomed afresh, trading on her reputation as– seductress.

"In the new French society of the *Directoire*, these ladies were known as 'les *Merveilleuses*,' the 'Marvelous Women.' They scandalized Paris with the new style of dresses they devised– transparent gauze termed 'woven air.' Displaying more than just cleavage, the dresses hugged curves in such a way, they left little to the imagination and did not allow pockets. Ladies had to carry small purses known as *reticules*. Expensive rings adorned fingers *and* toes on feet in sparse sandals, with several circlets of gold on ankles and wrists alike."

"Makes me think of the Roaring Twenties, a consequence of the shell shock of World War I," Thaddeus remarked. "In both eras, religion and social mores were all but obliterated, and the only thing left was hot Armageddon sex."

"At risk of sounding salacious," the curator went on, "with wine flowing and *les Merveilleuses* wearing barely any clothes, *Directoire soirées* were known to degenerate into orgies. On one occasion, Rose, Thérésia Tallien, and another Créole friend, Fortunée Hamelin, disrobed completely during the soup course, after which Thérésia dipped her breast into Barras' glass of champagne. During the salad course, Fortunée, using a napkin as a prop, performed a most erotic dance. By dessert, Thérésia was on the floor, imitating the undulations and stealth of a panther. The cheese course saw Rose on Barras' knee, fondling him unabashedly.

"Consumed later with bitterness against Napoléon, a disesteemed Barras would condemn Joséphine as a 'lewd Créole,' blustering that she was motivated solely by money and would have '… drunk gold from a lover's skull.' This from the man who made a parade of their affair! Truth is, Rose was hungry for money *and* love. She wanted a protector– someone to watch over her.

"You know, of course, that she even had a steamy affair in prison with the young General Lazare Hoche, a couple of years her junior, dashingly handsome with a mop of curly black hair and a most manly physique. Though Hoche had just taken a wife before he was imprisoned, he could not resist this charming Créole's alluring way of talking, her flirtatious eyes, and soft hands, a lover's hands that performed magick.

"Though that fetid cesspool of a prison known as the Carmes was infested with rats and lice, the walls spattered with blood from the September Massacres, Hoche, a privileged prisoner, had his own cell, where he dined on excellent food complimented with fine wines. It didn't take Rose long to seduce him, stealing night after night to his cell. Inmates were free to … *fraternize* with one another. If there is one true aphrodisiac in this life, it's the feeling that the apocalypse is nigh. Their intense," she pursed her lips, "*liaison* resumed after they were both free. I think he grew tired of her constant entreaties for money." Jeanne pursed her lips. "Throughout her entire life, Joséphine would never learn to curb her spending.

"However, not so very long after being released from the Carmes, Rose met Napoléon, who, like a string of others before him, was swiftly smitten– *starstruck*– and her destiny was sealed."

"How *did* Joséphine come to meet Napoléon?" asked Beau.

Jeanne smiled, pleased that the member of her private tour with *no* history background whatsoever appeared fascinated. "*Eh bien*, this indeed is a romantic tale. The year was 1795. Following an order for unauthorized weapons to be handed over to the government, Joséphine's son, Eugène, visited military headquarters in Paris to entreat permission to keep his deceased father's sword. Napoléon granted the impressive teenager this favor, and later, Joséphine called upon the young artillery commander to express her thanks. Napoléon fell instantly under her spell. He would say later that while he won battles, Joséphine won hearts.

"The afternoon they met," *madame* narrated, "Napoléon was busy at his desk, at the headquarters of the Army of the Interior. This was a man notorious for temper when interrupted at his work. When his orderly announced, 'A lady to see you, sir. All dressed in white, and the most beautiful sight I have ever seen,' Bonaparte roared, 'Her name, you fool!'

"When she stood before the earth shaker– and Time stood still as Destiny raised a glass– the general stared unabashedly at her to say, 'I remember *you*. I saw you at a ball several days ago. The room was full of attractive, scantily dressed women, but I recall little save *you*.' He thrust out an arm, indicating a chair. 'Sit!' he commanded, as if speaking to one of his aides.

"Oblivious that she looked slightly affronted, he boldly continued to gape at the woman before him with his hands clasped stiffly behind his back, feet apart, balancing himself lightly on his toes. 'You are, of course, well used to being stared at,' he stated flatly, shifting his weight from toes to heels. 'You were all in white then too. I like you in white. And you danced frequently with Paul Barras.' That last he added with noticeable contempt in his expression. Eyeing his visitor fixedly, he continued to slowly rock back and forth, from toes to heels. 'What are you? Spanish?' When she told him she was French from Martinique, he exclaimed, 'Ah, a Créole! That accounts for many things, including your gracefulness. You are the most graceful woman I have ever beheld, though I think I like your voice even more. It makes you *fascinating*.'

"'Really, General,' Joséphine, known yet as Rose, replied, somewhat taken aback by his forwardness but ever the coquette.

"'Yes, *really*,' he retorted, unashamed for his boldness. 'There are many beautiful women in Paris, my dear, but only one I deem *charming*. Beauty fades, you know, but charm … ah, charm lives on.' He tilted his dark head, adding, 'You, *madame*, have both. The exotic about you appeals to me. *Very much*.'

"With his eyes fastened on hers, he began asking a series of probing, even personal questions, which she told friends made her feel as if she were under some sort of interrogation.

"Now," said the curator, "it was *her* turn to stare at what she saw as an uncouth, shabby little man in a badly tailored uniform. The young General Bonaparte was painfully thin, with shaggy, lank brown hair, a very pale pallor, and a sensuous mouth. It was the piercing dark eyes, though, that held her, for they were of an almost frightening intensity, and she found herself having to quash the unsettling sensation of intimacy caused by his words.

"'General,' the widow in white began, resolute to master the bit of jumpiness he roused, 'I shall disclose why I came. I apologize for my son's impetuous behavior. Much as he values his father's sword, he ought not to have intruded on you as he did. However, we are grateful.'

"'I admire your son's courage, and I assure you, I was happy to restore the sword. I understood perfectly.' Bonaparte spoke with short, bullet-like sentences, as if he were issuing military orders.

"'You are too kind, sir.' Rose stood determinedly. She said later she needed to escape his probing eyes. *'No, no!'* the general bellowed, vaulting across the room to place his strong hands on her shoulders and force her back into the chair, his dark eyes piercing her soul. 'Remain a little longer and talk to me. If my manner seems rude, ignore it.' He could not help himself. The woman spoke and moved and breathed sex. He was putty in her skilled hands. He had never met anyone like her. At that juncture in his life, he had known few women, perhaps only one, and was, in fact, naïve and unworldly when it came to amorous experience.

"Before the glittering woman in white left, he apologized for making her uncomfortable, effecting a clumsy little bow that brought a half-smile to her rouged mouth, before he kissed her hand with lingering lips. I know, as a historian, I can safely say that if she never saw him again, it might well have been too soon. But they *would* meet again. *It was destined.*

"Speaking of Destiny, you probably know that Napoléon's wedding gift to Joséphine would be a gold ring inscribed with the words, *Au Destin*, 'To Destiny.'" She noted with sparkle, "He was that certain of his star."

A bit of discussion ensued between the curator and the three history professors, after which Jeanne resumed her tale.

"Not long behind the sword incident, at a dinner party orchestrated by government-head, Paul Barras, Joséphine's teenage daughter, Hortense, found herself at table between her *maman* and General Bonaparte. 'In order to talk to my mother,' she said in her memoirs, 'he kept leaning forward so often and with so much vivacity that he tired me, and I was forced to push back my chair. The general spoke with great animation, devoting his entire attention to my mother.'

"Joséphine could be a good listener, and truth be known, the man was riveting. She was especially struck by his words: 'I have a star, a glorious star that I will follow to the end, whatever that end might be.' At one point, she looked closely at the artillery officer, saying, 'You, sir, are very ambitious. I shall watch your career with the greatest of interest. I feel you will go far.' She said later that if she'd stroked Bonaparte any further with her flattery, he would have purred."

"He might well have done that," Raine laughed. "Napoléon was a Leo."

Jeanne gave a nod. "Yes, he was."

"The Leo man tends to tighten his paws round the object of his affection with possession and jealousy," Raine stated with a darting sidelong glance at Beau, who, she saw, was looking askance at her. *Yeah, big boy, I meant that for you. The Royal Lion can be a royal pain in the tush.*

Cocking his head, Beau raised a brow in such an astute manner, fixing her with his hot blue gaze, that she nearly drew in her breath.

Dragons and trolls, it's as though he can read my mind! she started. *And this is not the first time I have felt this way. Always makes me wonder if–* Her thought was cut off by the curator's next words.

"Before the dinner party broke up, Napoléon maneuvered Joséphine off to himself, on the moonlit terrace, to impress her with all he knew about her, including the fact that her mother's family was a very old one, sated in tradition and breeding, with all the mystique of the French landed gentry. 'It seems, General, you've been talking with Barras. I wouldn't doubt you know the location of each of my beauty spots.' 'Oh no, *madame*,' he answered glibly. 'I prefer to do my own reconnaissance.'

"Every time Hortense came home from boarding school for a visit," the curator informed, "she found General Bonaparte more assiduous in his attentions to her mother. Once they married, both of Joséphine's children came to respect, love and trust their stepfather, and he them. From the beginning, I believe he felt a compelling need to watch over Joséphine and her children, to protect them."

Jeanne's face grew a tad somber. "No sooner did Napoléon forgive Joséphine for a blatant love affair shortly after they wed, during his absence at the front, when, throwing herself wholeheartedly into the gaiety of a Paris wild with joy over her husband's military victories, she began to indulge openly in further affairs, casting all caution and discretion to the wind. He wrote her, saying, 'You, *madame*, do not write your husband. What, then, do you do with your time?' He was mad for her, and his jealousy was driving him wild.

"Though Paris was already treating Joséphine as a queen, Napoléon's family *loathed* her. Consequently, they were happy to indulge him of chapter and verse of her infidelities, hoping it would convince him to rid himself of her. Indeed, it was Joséphine's children, whom Napoléon always treated as if they were his own, who interceded with persuasive tears for their mother." Jeanne's face went pensive. "The children's tears combined with hers … pretty potent stuff. Joséphine knew the power her tears had over her husband, though on that occasion, his discovery of her affairs, combined with the humiliation those indiscretions brought him, it took the whole of the night for their power to work their magick on the man she had come to call the 'Earthshaker.'"

The curator's voice took on a decided melancholy tone. "Bonaparte did not divorce his wife for infidelity; but henceforth, Napoléon did not scruple to take any woman he desired, and Joséphine's tragedy was that, all too late, her indifference to him, in wistful regret, turned to genuine love.

"But prior to that happening, the general wrote his beloved passionate *lettres d'amour* before they were wed and later from the front, some of which we have here in our collection. Take the time to read them." The pretty French woman summoned a coy expression. "They sizzle.

"The morning after their first night of intimacies, he wrote her: 'I awake full of you. Your image and the memory of last night's intoxicating pleasures have left no rest to my senses.'

"The exotic Joséphine was the talk of Paris. A glamorous survivor of *la Terreur*, creator of the new fashions– her name was on everyone's lips. *Ah oui*, her days as a gauche country bride were far, far behind her. Now, she was a glittering seductress, her mysterious smile suggesting all sorts of sensual delights. What *was* the secret of this Créole temptress' ravishing charm?"

"*Unquestionably*, Joséphine was an enigma. One really has to consider the many facets of her life before passing judgment. What men," Raine ventured, "*before* Napoléon, did she have to look up to in her life? Certainly not her father or her first husband. And not the blasé lovers who were cheating on their wives to romp about with her. It's no small wonder that once she discovered her prowess as a woman, she would use that power to turn things round and finally get what she wanted in life, financial security at the top of the list. Romance and sex became a path to status, just as a decree of fate made her Empress of the French."

"And *as* empress, misunderstood wife or cunning tactician in her own right? *Both.* Definitely both. She excelled where the, yes, rather *uncouth* Napoléon did not, as master of diplomacy and etiquette. Come," Jeanne beckoned, "let us proceed through the museum. I hope I have set the mood for an exciting journey."

At *Madame* the Curator's words, a flicker of excitement rushed through the Sisters' witchy essences.

I know something astounding is about to happen, Raine whizzed the thought to Maggie.

Yes, the redheaded Sister shot back. *Oh yes, in due course. However–*

By the pricking of my thumbs, Raine returned, *I pray nothing wicked this way comes!*

Rose's small, canopied childhood bed was a most riveting exhibit.

Maggie, who could often conjure visions, closed her eyes for an image. "I can see the young plantation girl, who was destined to be Empress of the French, in long, flowing white nightdress, climbing into this bed and folding her arms over her chest to make a wish."

"A wish, no doubt, to marry a wealthy man and live a life of luxury in Paris," Thaddeus commented. He, too, envisioned a coddled Créole *demoiselle*, making a wish upon a star.

"I feel obliged to say that in fairness to the unprincipled phases of Joséphine's life, it must be admitted that her motives were not entirely those of personal greed. I think," said Jeanne, "most historians would agree that her strong maternal feelings prompted at least some of her lascivious behavior. For instance, thanks to the money Barras provided, her children were sent to good schools and looked after adequately, even luxuriously."

Madame the Curator's expression was bright with the thought that popped into her head. "Say what you will about the Empress Joséphine," she said with a glimmer in her eyes, "but she is still one of the most famous people from Martinique, if not the entire Caribbean; and two hundred years later, through her son Eugène and her daughter Hortense, both of whom Napoléon adopted, and because Napoléon placed his family on the various thrones of Europe, Joséphine is the ancestor of five dynasties that still reign in Europe. The ruling families of Sweden, Norway, Denmark, Belgium, and Luxembourg descend directly from her, and she is also related to the Prince of Monaco, as well as the royal houses of Italy, Romania, Yugoslavia, and the last queen of Greece. Did I mention Holland?"

Jeanne Gardien halted briefly, suddenly pensive. "I'm certain you know the story about the empress' prophecy. It is a *true* story and one that Joséphine told long before she met Napoléon and was crowned empress. In fact, when her cot was taken from her prison cell at the Carmes, an omen that forecast rendezvous with the guillotine, she leapt to her feet to declare, 'I will *not* be beheaded. It has been foretold. I will be more than a queen!' After Napoléon placed the crown of France on her head, she liked to tell the tale for the magick it conveyed to listeners.

Joséphine was intensely fascinated by the occult, much to Napoléon's frustration. She had interest in tarot, necromancy, and other occult arts. You know of the prophecy, *n'est-ce pas?*"

"We do," Raine replied, jolted free of her daydream, "but, please, *je vous en prie*, tell us the story in *your* words, *madame*."

"*Bien sûr.*" The curator glanced at her watch, thought a moment, and said, "After which, I *must* make a telephone call, but I'll catch up with you. In my absence, take your time. Be sure to see everything. You are welcome to stay as long as you wish." Then she launched into her tale of mystery and magick.

"Rose was fifteen when she and two friends decided to visit *Madame* David, a local witch. The old woman lived in the hills a short distance from la Pagerie and was known far and wide for her potions, cures, and her predictions. In a world of dis-ease and disease, she had a good trade. Then and now, few can resist the seductive pull of the occult.

"When the trio of teens sat on a straw mat before her, the crone, attended by a small, naked child who fanned her indolently, clutched the ready hand of each girl in turn, taking Rose's hand last.

"'Aaaah, *M'm'selle* Rose is born for greater things than to remain on Martinique and make an unimportant local marriage,' she drawled in *Patois*-laced French. Summoning her skill, she studied the palm a lingering moment before continuing. Then, tracing a gnarled brown finger over a branch of the life line, she revealed, 'First a long voyage across the water–'

"'I am to go to France?!' Rose blurted, leaning forward despite the strong odor of an unwashed body in the small hut's oppressive heat.

"'*Eh bien, ti-fi*, where else does one go across the water from Martinique but to France!' the witch rejoined waspishly, vexed at being interrupted. 'You will marry a rich man and live in Paris.' A ruminative rumbling sound issued from her throat. 'It will be an *unhappy* union, *most* unhappy, though your …' she waited till she was certain, '*two* children will always be a joy to you.'

"The old sorceress bent her madras-wrapped head lower, to study closer the hand she was holding. Then ensued a silence that lasted several minutes, after which the crone mumbled something unintelligible, the *Patois* words garbled and jumbled. She sucked in her breath, becoming visibly excited, which caused the impatient Rose to ask, 'What do you see? Tell me!' Again, there was silence in which the witch raised her free hand to shush the girl, keeping her head lowered over the presented palm. She was still mumbling gibberingly, her *Patois* lost to the trio of *béké* plantation girls, her foul breath rattling out the strong incantations and ancient crooning sounds for what seemed like an eternity to the anticipating Rose.

"'You will marry again,' the *Quimbois* woman witched over the *demoiselle*, who awaited, in near unbearable suspense, for the remainder of the reading, 'a dark man of little fortune,' her voice progressively rose in volume and vigor, '*who will cover the world with glory ... and make you more than a queen!*'

"Rose was at once thrilled and baffled over the reading. Her thoughts were spinning. Due to the hut's foul smell and stifling heat, combined with the excitement, nausea threatened to overwhelm her. *Et remarquez* ... mind you, this was *before* the young lady knew from her parents that *she* would be the daughter boarding a ship to Paris to marry the Vicomte de Beauharnais. In fact, at that moment in time, her younger sister was the one chosen to wed Alexandre.

"*Mademoiselle* Rose's eyes had grown suddenly large and round, and for a spun-out moment, she was speechless. Swallowing bile, she struggled not to retch. 'More than a queen?! What is more than a queen? How could I be more than a queen? Is there more? Do you see anything else?' she entreated, spilling forth a tirade of anxious questions. She was so dizzy, it was difficult to grasp all that the hag was telling her.

"In response, the crone scowled and muttered, then, looking the eager young woman in the eyes and holding her gaze for a timeless time, she pronounced in lowered, level tone, '*Oui, ti-fi*, more than a queen. It is the decree of Fate. But even so,' she pointed the gnarled brown finger at the stunned girl, 'you will die unhappy; and often in your life, you will *yearn* for the ease of life here on Martinique.'"

The curator concluded her tale. "Joséphine believed that island-born people possess the power and sensitivity of the sea, gifting them thus with a sixth sense. To be sure, she was to lie in the bed of Marie Antoinette and wear the heavy crown of Empress of France." The French woman reflected for a long moment, saying, "Joséphine loved Paris but she always held Martinique in a special place in her heart. *Always*."

Thaddeus nodded. "Makes me think of the signature song of another famous Josephine," he said. "Josephine Baker's 'I Have Two Loves, my birthplace and Paris.'"

"*Ah oui*," Jeanne concurred with a knowing smile on her lips. "*Moi aussi, J'ai deux amours, mon pays et Paris.*"

Beau's expression was noticeably pensive. "You said Napoléon fell madly in love with Joséphine. I'm a bit confused on that one point. Do you think she ever really loved him?"

Jeanne shook her dark head. "Not at first. The widow Beauharnais was not in love with this man who was six years her junior, but Paul Barras was growing tired of her; and she felt, at that moment in time, that the up-and-coming young general was her best bet for the future. So, for her, it began as a marriage of convenience. There are some historians who believe that Barras offered Napoléon a promotion along with his mistress."

"Unrequited love is boring," Raine cut in, "for the one whose heart is not involved. At first, Joséphine was, I think, a trifle bored."

"*Oui*," the curator answered, "but the bottom line is that Napoléon, in his own words, revealed that he was instantly enamored, dazzled by the widow's ... *sophistication*. And, as Napoléon began to gain power and social clout, Joséphine *came* to love him. Oh yes, she kept him waiting for her devotion until she had captured his heart. And then, *then* she offered him a passion he had never known before ... or after.

"*Et qui sait?* Perhaps she was thinking of the crone's prediction so many years before. *Napoléon et Joséphine*. Linked for eternity. They were both unfaithful, she in the beginning, he later on, but I believe truly theirs was one of History's greatest love stories. Even after he divorced Joséphine– and it was a perfectly amicable divorce– Napoléon continually exhibited his love for her, allowing her to retain the title of Empress of the French. In his words: 'It is my will that she retain the rank and title of Empress, and especially that she never doubt my sentiments, and that she ever hold me as her best and dearest friend.'"

"Exactly why did he divorce her?" Beau queried. "You said it was not for her indiscretions."

"He needed an heir for the empire he created, and she could not bear any more children," the curator replied dryly. "Only when she could not give him an heir did he end their tempestuous marriage and lock their secret passage to love. Joséphine had a son and daughter by her first husband, *bien sûr*, but most historians believe that though she was past forty, likely the real reason for her barrenness during her marriage to Napoléon was that she had," Jeanne broke off, groping for a genteel way to phrase her next words, "done things during her sexual exploits that rendered her sterile." Jeanne gave a sad little smile. "Theirs was one of the most impassioned romances in history. And in the end, Napoléon would say to his Joséphine, 'To you alone I owe the little happiness I have experienced in this world. No woman was ever loved with more devotion, ardor, and tenderness.'"

Beau posed yet another question. "How old was Joséphine when she died?"

"Fifty-one," the curator answered. "She passed away of pneumonia, in May of 1814, at her beloved Malmaison, the beautiful estate on the outskirts of Paris that the emperor purchased for her.

"As she lay dying, she often called the exiled Napoléon's name in her delirium, and her family and personal maid related afterward that she 'died of grief.'

"As soon as she had lent grace and elegance to Napoléon's court, Joséphine poured herself into *la Malmaison*, spending huge amounts of money making it a show place. Whenever she had ample means to purchase whatever she wanted, her habit was to spend lavishly. Napoléon once said that the only thing that could ever *really* come between them were her ever-mounting debts.

"Following the divorce, he often dropped in unexpectedly to visit her at *la Malmaison*. After his ill-fated Russian campaign, it was there, to Joséphine, he went, in quotes, 'to warm himself,' telling her that after the cold and snows of Russia, he would '... likely never feel warm again.'"

Jeanne considered what she'd just said, adding, "As I am certain you professors are well aware, historically speaking, weather can be the Great Determinator. No flesh-and-bone general defeated Napoléon. *Mais non*, it was General Winter in Russia and later, General Mud at Waterloo.

"But to continue with what I was saying about Malmaison, it became famous for the empress' vast art collection, her *ménagerie* of exotic animals, and especially for the splendid rose gardens. Joséphine had a passion for roses. She not only hosted the first rose exhibition, in 1810, she produced the first written history of the cultivation of roses that same year. She and her horticulturalists were the first to begin modern hybridization of roses." Jeanne tilted her head in musing attitude. "Rose was the empress' name, you recall, in her youth, and so it seems fitting, *n'est-ce pas,* her affinity for roses?

"Back on point with Joséphine's passing: When Napoléon was in exile on the small Mediterranean island of Elba, he was *shattered* by the news of her death, which he received via a newspaper. He locked himself alone in his darkened room, refusing all food, refusing, too, to see anyone for days on end. The woman he called his 'little Créole,' his true wife, his tormentor, his happiness, the hope and soul of his life was gone. He was devastated–*inconsolable.*

"She would haunt him forevermore on restless nights. And forevermore, his life would be replete with restless nights.

"Ten months after her death, when Napoléon returned to France to try to recapture his lost empire, it was no surprise that it was again to Joséphine's Malmaison where he first hurried, pressing those who were with her in the final hours to tell him every detail of her passing, every word she uttered. He wandered the gardens there, as though in a daze, tears streaming down his face, speaking in the lyrical way he always did about her: 'I still seem to see her walking along the paths and collecting the flowers she so loved. Poor Joséphine! Truly, she was resplendent with more charm than any other person I have ever known. *Ma pauvre Joséphine,* how I loved you! From the moment I met you, I never stopped loving you, not one day, not one hour.' The empress' daughter, Hortense, said later how '... his dark eyes burned with the oil of truth.'

"From Joséphine's garden that day, he collected violets, one of her favorite flowers, pressed and wore them in a locket until his death. A few years after her passing, the emperor too died in the month of May, in 1821, at the same age Joséphine left this world, fifty-one.

"All during his second and final exile, on the bleak and lonely isle of Saint Helena in the Atlantic Ocean, far, far from the shores of *la Belle France,* Napoléon never stopped thinking of his grand love. He surrounded himself with images of his Joséphine, taking them out of an old chest to study them time and time over, touching them, as if to feel the touch of her skin back through the years, running his fingers over the shape of her body, as though, through tactile memory, from mind to fingers or the other way round, he could *actually* run a hand, soft and easy, over her across the miles and years. Oh, how he wanted it all again!

"His preferred image was one, in profile, just before he placed the crown upon her head. I don't know if I've mentioned it, but it was widely quoted that Joséphine's loveliness at that moment was truly the beauty of an angel. He ofttimes stared at the likeness, utterly carried away by her radiance, quite as he was on the day of the coronation.

"*Mon Dieu*, Napoléon even took his meals off plates bearing her face."

"As with every man who ever loved," Thaddeus interposed, "he was being aware of the howl of Time, of the fading and passing of this curious thing we call 'Life.'"

"And understanding," Beau felt the need to add, "that it was all so transitory."

"*Oui*," the curator said with heartfelt agreement, "*mais oui*."

The empathetic Sisters looked to one another, keenly touched by it all.

"On his death bed, in his delirium," Jeanne continued, "Napoléon cried out that he saw his '... good Joséphine. She disappeared at the moment when I was about to take her in my arms ... she is not changed ... she told me we are about to see each other again, never more to part.'

"And when Napoléon drew his last breath, it was, indeed, *her* name he whispered–

"'*Joséphine.*'"

Chapter Four

"Napoléon's handwriting is difficult to read," Raine murmured. "Doubtless 'cause he dashed off so many missives from the front." The Sisters' party was standing before the air-tight glass display of the museum's collection of Bonaparte's love letters penned to Joséphine. "But I'll do my best to translate."

As that Sister stood perusing the legendary epistles, yellowed with age and seemingly brittle to the touch, on each the signature bold, something stirred in Maggie's brain, and she remarked to Thaddeus, "I read once that a handwriting expert said Napoléon had what's called a Type-A personality. If memory serves, A-Type people are natural leaders and thrive in positions of authority. They tend to be ambitious and competitive, hard-working ... *driven*, and because of that, they're often successful. Let me think. They're decision makers. They can be controlling, impatient and aggressive, tending to over-react. I remember reading that they're in constant need of stimulation, and relaxation is something with which they aren't at all familiar."

"Fits what I've ever read about Napoléon," Beau took the liberty to put in.

Raine began translating from one of the letters on display, "'Sweet, incomparable– thrilling– Joséphine, what strange power you have over my heart! Your image and the intoxicating pleasures of last night allow my senses no rest. I draw from your lips, from your heart, a love which consumes me with fire. I shall see you in three hours. Until then, my sweet love, a thousand kisses. But send me none in return, for they set my blood ablaze!'"

"Napoléon, the romantic. Much different from Napoléon, the conqueror, dictator and tyrant," Thaddeus noted.

"What do the French think?" Beau asked. "Do they see him as a tyrant and dictator?"

"That's still a subject for debate," Thaddeus answered flatly.

"You know," said Raine, "Napoléon wrote a romantic novella entitled *Clisson et Eugénie*."

"Are you serious?" Beau guffawed, and his look was dubious. "*Napoléon* wrote a romance novel?"

"He did," Maggie and Thaddeus responded nearly at the same time.

"A novella. A long short story really," Raine interposed. "About twenty pages that were pieced together not *so* very long ago, circa 2007, from half a dozen fragments of the manuscript that survived from private collections to museums, from California to Moscow. He wrote it when he was twenty-six, prior to his meeting Joséphine. I suppose, like writers throughout the ages, he found that he liked expressing himself on paper."

Beau pursed his lips. "Who would've thought? What's it about?"

"The story, first of all, is somewhat self-revealing," Raine informed. "Clisson is a heroic soldier who is weary of war. He meets Eugénie; they fall in love, marry, and live in bucolic bliss until another war prompts Clisson to again serve his country. When he's injured in battle, he makes the grievous error of sending a charming comrade to notify and console his wife. The so-called friend seduces Eugénie, who stops writing Clisson. Heartbroken that his marriage has been destroyed, Clisson pens a final letter to his unfaithful wife before engineering his death at the front. In a heroic charge toward the enemy, he goes out in a blaze of glory."

"Doesn't the story parallel Napoléon's love affair with Eugénie Désirée Clary?" Maggie queried. "The woman he was courting before he met Joséphine?"

"Oh, I think it likely inspired him to write a love story," Raine answered. "In fact, Napoléon was *engaged* to Désirée, but broke the engagement when he fell head over heels for Joséphine."

The Goth gal's emerald eyes scanned the display. "Let me read you a paragraph Napoléon wrote in his *memoires* about his one true love. 'Everyone knows the extreme grace of the Empress Joséphine … and her sweet and attractive manners. My acquaintance with her soon became intimate and tender, and it was not long before we married.'"

Raine's gaze swept the letters and documents inside the glass case. "Ah, this is interesting," she said after several moments. "A brief description of Napoléon, shortly after he met Joséphine, written by his personal aide. I'll read it. Hmmm, says he bore an air of grandeur that was quite new, with an ever-increasing sense of his own importance. But I'll get back on point. 'As to Joséphine,' the aide chronicled, 'Bonaparte was in love in the full sense of the phrase. Though she no longer had the freshness of youth, she knew how to please him, and we know that to lovers the question "Why?"

is superfluous. One loves because one loves, and nothing is less susceptible to explanation and analysis than this emotion.'"

Raine chewed her lower lip. "I must contend Bonaparte's aide. If anything, Joséphine grew more attractive with time. With middle age, her soul bloomed."

"Read us another of the *billets-doux*," Maggie urged, placing a hand on Raine's shoulder.

The raven-haired Sister concentrated on the romantic letters behind the glass. After several moments, she said, "Here's a juicy one. I'll translate what I can make of Napoléon's scribble. 'I keep remembering your kisses, your tears. How happy I would be if I could assist you at your undressing, the little white breasts ... springy and firm; the adorable face; the hair tied up in a scarf à la Créole ... *Joséphine*, mmmmm, good enough to eat.

"'I cannot wait to give you proofs of my ardent love. You know well that I have not forgotten the elysian visits to the little black forest. I give it a thousand kisses and impatiently await the moment I will be there again. To live in Joséphine is to live in paradise. Ah, to kiss your mouth, eyes, shoulders, breasts ... everywhere ... everywhere– *everywhere*.'

"And this," Raine saw fit to add, 'I idolize you and send you a thousand kisses!'

"Here's a scrap from yet another message penned between the roar of battles," Raine began tentatively, studying the communications longer. "After bemoaning the fact that Joséphine did not write as often as *he* did, Bonaparte lamented, 'Your letters are the joy of my days, and I assure you, my days of happiness are not many.' The Sister paused. "I can't decipher the rest of it from his scrawled handwriting, but he ends with, 'I hope to hold you in my arms before long, when I shall lavish upon you a million kisses, burning as the equatorial sun.'

"Oh, you'll like this one, Mags," Raine exclaimed, reading on, "'By what art have you learned to enchant all my faculties? It is **witchcraft**! To live for Joséphine– that is the story of my life.'"

"Those last letters you read were written from Italy," the curator said, coming up behind the Sisters' party to rejoin them. "I don't believe Joséphine had ever met with anything, or anyone, so romantic or so heavy with longing.

"Three days after they were married, Napoléon left to head the army in what History calls the 'Italian Campaign.' He very much missed his wife, who we know was a master in the art of love. The short time they had been together, she changed her appearance constantly, giving her lover the illusion of infinite variety. She'd paid meticulous attention to the romantic design of her bedroom. Her fondness for mirrors, for example, multiplied the image of their love. Sexy bacchanalia but ba–ad feng shui," Jeanne laughed.

"Joséphine was at her best when she was *amoureuse*, then she could forget everything but the thrill, the excitement, the fire to which her body responded. To her, this was as insidious as a drug, as stimulating as a glass of fine wine. She longed for it, craved it, felt that life was empty and pointless without it. However, I don't think that the men who produced those feelings mattered in themselves. Until she actually fell in love with Napoléon, she was attracted until satiated, then, like a man with a harlot, she forgot each lover as soon as he was out of sight.

"During Napoléon's absence, he wrote Joséphine frequently, sometimes twice a day." *Madame* the Curator regarded the historic letters for a considering moment. "One dashed-off note says, 'Since I left you, I have been constantly depressed. My happiness is to be near you. Incessantly, I live over and over in memory your caresses, your tears, your affectionate solicitude.'"

Jeanne nodded her head in a musing gesture. "Joséphine once told a friend, 'Bonaparte is all day in adoration before me as though I were a goddess.' There's no question he adored her and was entirely in thrall to her sexuality. As for her tears, he was swept away by the erotic image of her in tears. To him, tears were proof of her deep emotion and her femininity, and Joséphine's ability to turn on the waterworks was one of her powers over him. It worked. Not always," the curator smiled, "but in many, many instances did it work."

"I've been meaning to ask you," Maggie happened to think, "does the museum have any of Joséphine's fabulous jewelry? Given her passion for jewels, there must exist a great deal of her treasures."

"I wish we did have some of her jewelry," Jeanne answered with zeal. "I suppose you know that in 2013, the empress' engagement ring from Napoléon garnered what would be to you Americans a million dollars at auction."

"Tell us about that, if you would," Beau asked, the request casting an amazed air over Raine.

"The betrothal ring must have emptied Napoléon's *portefeuille* ... wallet," the curator stated. "At the time, he was a young and promising officer, *oui*, but certainly not rich. It's a quality piece of jewelry, then and now. There," she pointed to the display case that held the love letters, "is a picture of the precious token.

"The auction, which was held at the Osenat Auction House at Fontainebleau, just outside of Paris, was timed to coincide with the 250-year anniversary of Joséphine's birthday. The solid pink-gold ring is in a popular eighteenth-century setting called *Toi et Moi,* 'You and Me,' with closely nestled, tear-shaped jewels– a sapphire and a diamond, about a carat each. Even after their divorce, Joséphine continued to wear and treasure the ring, leaving it to her daughter, Hortense, whom Napoléon made Queen of Holland.

"Hortense, who was married to Napoléon's brother, Louis, passed it on to their son, Napoléon III, the last French monarch, and his wife, Empress Eugénie. Napoléon III's son died without descendants, so the ring passed to Victor, grandson of Napoléon's youngest brother, Jérôme. *Eh bien*, for over two centuries, the ring remained with the extended Bonaparte family before it was auctioned."

"Who purchased the ring at auction?" Beau queried.

The curator cocked her head. "That person has remained anonymous."

Maggie uttered a sigh as she grasped for a vision but came up short. "There's nothing like the sparkle of a ring to capture the romantic imagination," she breathed. "And small wonder that rings worn by famous people from the past hold special magick."

"Small wonder the engagement ring of one of History's most famous couples would reap a mighty sum at auction," Raine added. "Yes, when the hammer fell, Joséphine's engagement ring went for nearly a million dollars." She shook her dark head. "However, that ring is priceless."

"The family was only expecting to get about $20,000 for it," Jeanne informed. "*C'était le gossip*. For a fact, that's the amount the auction house estimated in the catalogue." She grimaced in thought. "Curious that they decided to determine the auction estimate based solely on the ring's materials and design. *C'était ridicule!*"

"Utter nonsense," Raine promptly agreed. "The ring remained in the family till the auction. I can't *believe* they sold it. It's not only a family heirloom, it's a piece of history, for goodness sake! Nothing could have induced *me* to sell." The ardent Joséphine aficionada looked wistful. "I would've kissed that ring every night and guarded it with my life."

Her words seemed to register deeply with Beau, who again pursed his mouth as if mulling over something of weighty significance.

"If we had, in truth, *any* piece of jewelry we could connect with provenance to Joséphine, we would stage a grand exhibition to attract wealthy donors." *Madame* the Curator cocked her head. "A fundraising dinner perhaps. Oh, such a treasure would bring us worldwide recognition, not to mention the visitors it would draw. It would be a great boon to la Pagerie.

"In her lifetime, Joséphine would come to possess an empress' ransom of jewels," Jeanne commented. "Millions of francs' worth of valuable pearls, diamonds, rubies, and just about every other precious and semi-precious stone you could name. Since Joséphine is the ancestor of five dynasties that still reign in Europe, many items of her jewelry are among the crown jewels of those countries, in addition, of course, to France.

"Joséphine's jewelry boxes spilled over with more diamonds, for instance, than Marie Antoinette once owned. As empress, Joséphine would acquire hundreds of rings, bracelets, earbobs, necklaces, and she was forever having the settings changed to suit a passing whim. As many of these pieces were gifts from Napoléon, they must have reminded her of treasured and beloved events, of the constant ascent of her star– *of so many things.*

"Soon after Napoléon was appointed Head of the Army and the young general began achieving victory after victory, if Joséphine showed herself at a window, the huge crowd outside her house shouted the name with which Paris christened her– 'Our Lady of Victories!' As wife of the Head of the Army, a *victorious* army, her prestige was infinitely greater than it had been as mistress of Barras."

Madame the Curator paused for a beat, as though to be sure of the accuracy of what she was about to say. "Joséphine adored the trappings of power. During her life, she would play several roles– mistress, courtesan, revolutionary heroine, art collector and patron of the arts, horticulturalist, diplomat and empress, to name but a few. In the succinct words of one of her close friends, 'Joséphine was a consummate actor who could play all roles– and play each well.'"

Nearly an hour later, the Sisters' party walked with the curator out of the museum into the bright Martinique sunshine.

When Beau's phone sounded, he took a few moments to chat with his father and Betty, to let them know all was well. "Dad, Martinique is paradise on earth. You and Betty should think seriously about taking your next vacation here."

"Hugh and Betty *would* love it here," Raine said, when Beau rang off. "We'll send them some nice picture postcards to prove our point. Did Hugh have any news?"

Beau shook his head, returning the phone to his pocket. "No news from the home front."

"Mags," Raine said unexpectantly, "I just happened to think of one of Joséphine's secret youth-cream concoctions for tightening and lifting the skin. Bananas, olive oil, and honey puréed to create a face mask. Worked like a charm."

"I believe I read that she used egg whites too," Maggie replied, "for tightening the skin."

"Yes," Raine answered. "And rice powder to make the skin look whiter."

Slipping on her sunglasses and glancing round, Raine caught sight of Dorélia, leaning against a stone pillar of the pavilion, taking a cigarette break. Like a cat watching a mouse hole, the waitress' attention seemed to be fixed on a female volunteer digging in one of the flower beds yonder. Her brow was furrowed, and an almost disagreeable expression darkened her pretty face. In a moment, however, she looked their way to see Raine and Maggie lift their hands to signal a greeting. Waving back, the *Martiniquaise* sent them a cheery smile.

"Permit me, *je vous prie*," *Madame* the Curator intervened, "to escort you about la Pagerie's exterior property. Afterward, take the time to enjoy. We don't close until 4:30 this afternoon. You can see, we have several workers here today, all volunteers. The cleanup and repairs from the hurricane that struck last fall have been done. At present, we're only tending to aesthetics. Under my direction, our helpers are adding a couple more flower beds to the grounds." She gave a little laugh. "Can never have too many flowers, not on Martinique.

"La Pagerie's volunteers come to us from all walks of life, from all socio-economic levels. Over there," Jeanne indicated the woman digging with a trowel in a flower bed, the woman at whom Dorélia had been staring. "That's Odette Auteur, a local author and historian. She's known all over France, and especially here on Martinique, as an expert on the Empress Joséphine."

"Yes," Raine realized reflectively, "I've come across several examples of her work." She peered with renewed interest at the historian, sending Maggie the thought, *From my research, I would pithily define Odette Auteur as a glossy woman with a mind of her own. Opinionated, perhaps even biased, but every author has a point of view.* Aloud she said, "Auteur does her homework, and I tend to agree with her most of the time on the subject of Joséphine."

Jeanne gave a crisp nod. "As do I. Let's walk, shall we? *There*," the curator indicated the large rectangular stone foundation, "as I mentioned earlier, is all that remains of the plantation house, which was constructed of wood. The *sucrerie* ... the sugar refinery survived the hurricane because it was stone, and it was built under the lee of a hill."

Glancing in the direction of the *sucrerie's* ivy-covered ruins, Maggie said softly in a musing voice, "I don't imagine it was very comfortable for the family, after the mansion was destroyed by that hurricane, to live upstairs in the sugar refinery."

"*Non,* it was not," *Madame* the Curator answered. "It was noisy and smelly amidst the suffocating steam from boilers. Not very classy for the *béké* ... er Créole society of the time here in the French Antilles, to be sure.

"I don't believe I mentioned it, but la Pagerie was founded in the seventeenth century by Joséphine's maternal grandparents as one of the *largest* plantations on Martinique, over 500 hectares. The current golf course here in Trois-Îlets was part of that vast property."

"So the original plantation was over 1,235 acres," Thaddeus swiftly calculated.

"*Mais oui,*" Jeanne responded with an admiring nod. "Cotton, coffee, indigo, cassava, cocoa, and, most of all, sugarcane were produced here. Come, let us walk."

The Sisters' party treated themselves to another hour at la Pagerie, during which their hostess shared with them several more stories about the Rose of Martinique. All in all, it was a fascinating, informative tour, and one that would prove painfully prophetic to the mystery that was about to unfold.

When the Sisters' party left la Pagerie, they motored onward to the Village Créole, a sort of outdoor mall with a collection of twenty-eight shops, cafés, and restaurants housed in charming Créole-style buildings painted in pretty island colors with lacy, white trim.

"Wiz-zard," Raine gushed, by means of her favorite exclamation. "This place rocks."

"Going to be difficult to make a choice of café," Maggie said, glancing about. "There're so many."

"Let's just pick one," Thaddeus replied. "I'm starved." He checked his watch for the time. "We only had a croissant and coffee for breakfast, and it's nearly two now."

"I'm with Thad," Beau concurred. "In this tourist area, any one of these cafés will be good."

They wandered into the nearest eatery, La Belle Créole, where they took seats at a corner table.

In a moment, a waiter brought them menus and then moved off with their drink order.

"I'm still trying to get my head around the fact that artillery tactician Napoléon was a *romantic* son of a gun," Beau quipped without preamble.

Raine gave a little chuckle. "At least he was handsome … in an Armand Assante sort of way. When Assante played the emperor in a TV film back in the Nineties, he looked more like Napoléon than Napoléon. Like I said, *handsome*. Over two centuries after Ben Franklin's death, people are still trying to figure out how a paunchy, balding, bifocaled septuagenarian managed to put French ladies, including the Queen of France, into sexual flutter. Ben was a babe magnet."

"*Touché*," Thaddeus returned.

"I've said it before, and I'll say again," Maggie laughed, "Benjamin Franklin is the founding father who winks at us."

"Joséphine was a cunning *tactician* in her own right," Raine giggled, pouncing on Beau's word. "I wish I knew what her *zigzags* were. Napoléon mentioned them with yen in his love letters to her. She did something in bed called 'zigzags,' but I don't think any historian has ever uncovered exactly what it entailed."

"Oh, I think with a little imagination, we can guess," Maggie responded with her mysterious smile. The sensual Sister planned on reaching for a vision later.

"Joséphine was a very tactile person," Raine remarked. "Real touchy-feely. She liked to sit on Napoléon's lap and run her fingers through his hair, with feather-light touches skimming his face, ears … his lips."

"When we were discussing Napoléon's handwriting earlier," the professor happened to remember, "I wanted to mention that his autograph changed over the years. As his career declined, his bold signature suffered greatly, shrinking with his star. And," Thaddeus thought to add, "he was not really that short. A tad over five foot, six, average height for a man of his era."

"Listen, let's not eat anything too heavy," Raine suggested abruptly. "We want to enjoy another great dinner tonight at our hotel."

"Good idea," Maggie answered, as her eyes skimmed through the bill of fare. "I'm for the avocado salad with the wine I ordered."

"A salad sounds good." Raine turned to Beau. "How about ordering me the crab salad, baby?" She stood. "Maggie, shall we visit the ladies'?"

The Sisters were just exiting the restroom, when Raine chanced to notice a man, seated in a shadowy corner, his back against the wall, using his phone to take pictures through a hole in the newspaper held before his face. Poking Maggie, she whispered, "It's the Creeper."

"The who?"

Declining to answer, Raine grabbed her sister of the moon's arm to usher her along, past the strange man's table and through the dim café to rejoin Beau and Thaddeus.

"We've ordered," Thaddeus announced. "Beau and I are having the *poulet boucané,* Martinique sugarcane-smoked chicken. Not to worry, we're getting the lunch portion."

After taking her seat, the Goth gal leaned toward Beau. "Over there," she whispered, jerking her head in the direction of the man still hidden behind the newspaper, "it's the Creeper. He's taking pictures with his phone through a hole he made in his paper, and he was aiming the camera directly at you and Thaddeus."

Beau looked incredulous. "Why would he want pictures of *us*? That's your over-active imagination at work, Raine-Storm." He leaned in to pat her bejeweled hand before glancing around. "Perhaps he was capturing a picture of that businessman there," he inclined his ebony head toward a Eurasian gentleman, with a Fu Manchu mustache, in an immaculate white suit seated at the table next to theirs, "or that group of mirth-making tourists over there. *Or*," his brilliant blue eyes scanned the quaint surroundings, "perhaps he was just snapping images of the interior of this café. Could be he's an architect or somethin'."

"Un-huh, and that's why he's taking pictures in such a sneaky manner," Raine retorted.

Beau's features enlivened with a sudden thought. "Maybe he's a café owner himself, and he's scouting the competition." He patted her hand again before bringing his beer to his lips.

Raine's ebony brows rushed together in an instant scowl. "Don't patronize me, big boy. Maggie, you saw him yesterday, staring at us in the Coco Bar. Well," she amended, "that's not quite right. He was staring at *everyone* with those ghoulish, though strangely compelling eyes and that wooden, expressionless face of his. And, Beau, was it my imagination last night, when we *both* saw him creeping round the hotel at two in the morning? Yeah, it's true. We were just getting back from our moonlit stroll on the beach," she clarified for Maggie and Thaddeus' sake, "when we saw him."

Thaddeus watched the subject of their discussion as the man lowered the newspaper. "He's dressed like a tourist," he stroked his van dyke beard in meditation, "but I don't think he is one. Appears to be a solid, ex-army type … special forces maybe … recently retired."

"Military? I think not. Raine's right," Maggie rejoined. "He's not only mysterious. He's got an agenda."

"Maybe he's a hired killer," Beau said in an attempt at jest. "Or a soldier of fortune."

"Don't trifle with Mags and me." Raine's deep voice bore a thinly veiled caveat. Her eyes darted back to the Creeper. "Though … he could well be a hired killer."

Unbeknownst to the Sisters, the pristine businessman at the next table overheard their discussion. Making a show of looking at his watch, he brusquely stood, flung some euros on the table, and hastily exited the café.

Oblivious, Maggie was staring fixedly at the Creeper, who also rose to hasten past them to the exit. "Whoever the Creeper is, he's the type who never laughs or even smiles much. He quite looks like a gangster. A *hired* gun? Hmmm," she considered, "perhaps."

Her eyes followed the man till he disappeared out-of-sight. "Not American. Noooo, I don't believe American. And the way he's always skulking about ... oooh, he's got an agenda all right. I wonder who and what he is?" she said to no one in particular.

"I haven't a clue, Mags," the raven-haired sister answered, "but I've a keen witchy feeling we'll find out before we leave Martinique."

"Don't fret and worry– be witchy!"
~ Granny McDonough

Chapter Five

Whilst the Sisters, Thaddeus and Beau spent the morning relaxing in sun and sea at their hotel, Odette Auteur, the author/ historian whom the group had seen the previous day at la Pagerie, took the ferry across the bay to Fort-de-France. There, she located a shop she had researched online that specialized in antiquities of all sorts, especially antique jewelry.

Catching sight of the sign in the window, *Spécialisation Bijoux Anciens*, Odette entered the charming store. The shop's illustrative name, *l'Objet Qui Parle,* attracted her, for she always wished antiques *could* talk, to share their histories and secrets. Walking to the counter, she rang the bell. In a moment, the owner, Pierre Laperle, appeared from behind the curtain that separated the showroom from his work area.

"*Bonjour.* May I help you?" he addressed his customer in Parisian French, his manner as elegant as his appearance.

"I hope so." She removed her sunglasses and set them on the counter.

Odette was a slender, medium-height woman, chic in both appearance and manner, with classic features and very black, glossy hair parted in the middle and caught in a low bun at the nape of the neck. The regal style suited her face and comportment. Her complexion was almost olive, the eyes as dark as night. When she opened her mouth to speak, the voice was silky and refined, her French precise.

Reaching into her bag, she extracted a maroon velvet case. "I was cleaning out a closet yesterday and came upon this bracelet that I forgot I had. I'm originally from Paris, and I used to frequent the flea markets there years ago." She tilted her head in a reflective posture. "I loved leisurely browsing *le marché aux puces* Saturday and Sunday afternoons. I'm thinking you know the most popular one to which I'm referring, the *old* one between the eighth *arrondissement* and St. Ouen."

The jeweler gave a nod. "*Certainement, madame*, I know it well."

"I was confident you would, *monsieur*. This piece was in a small carton of things I purchased from an old woman, who was selling off all her merchandise. By the time I discovered her stall–

you know there're about 2,500 stalls at Ouen– she had only a few items left. I bought a mélange of things in one of the small boxes that remained, this bracelet among them. The bracelet wasn't in this case originally. I put it in there this morning.

"It was only a few days after I purchased the trinkets that I relocated from Paris to Martinique." She allowed herself a little smile. "I've always gone where my heart takes me, you see. When I was finally settled in my cottage here, the box got shoved to the back of a closet. As I said, I forgot I even had it. It took me a long time to transfer my life to Martinique, and nearly five years have lapsed since my move. *Le temps passe, n'est-ce pas?*" She handed the jeweler the bracelet.

Monsieur Laperle was a distinguished gentleman in his early forties, well-soigné, read, and traveled. His styled dark hair, threaded with silver at the temples, neatly trimmed mustache, and meticulous suit and tie bespoke a mature man proud of his looks, all of which prompted the woman before him to think of the urbane French actor, Louis Jourdan. With a writer's scrutiny, she could tell that Laperle was a serious-minded fellow.

Turning the bracelet slowly in manicured hands, he said nothing as his expert gaze assessed the piece. After several quiet moments slipped by, the jeweler pronounced in smooth, mellow speech, "Needs a good cleaning, but I'm certain these stones are rubies. There're no hallmarks, not unusual for certain antique pieces. However, I should be able to put this bracelet in the proper time-frame without the presence of such marks." He stopped talking to study the object attentively. "Looks to be gold, but I'll test it, of course."

Furrows of apparent surprise formed on Odette's high forehead. "I must say, I didn't think the bracelet was anything but paste. I only paid a few euros for the lot. This is an attractive piece, *oui*, but since the other baubles in that jumble were so *obviously* costume, I just assumed … ." Words failed her, and she let the rest of her thought drift away. "I tried cleaning the bracelet up a bit with a mild dishwashing soap and an old toothbrush, but it's *so* dirty, my efforts didn't make much difference. I was afraid to do more. I didn't want the stones to end up down the drain. The thing looks old."

The bracelet was a semi-bangle of sorts, the top of which was fashioned in a floral design, rather like a rose, and encrusted with unfaceted red stones. Each side of the band created a fancy *fleur-de-lys*.

Monsieur the Jeweler was examining the stones closely now, using a loup he pulled from below counter. "*Oui, madame*, this bracelet is *quite* old. Of that I am most sure. Rococo. One of the ways I can tell that it is not a replica is by the clasp, this S-link ... which is bent."

"Yes, I know. I couldn't get it to fasten properly. If, when you clean it, you find the bracelet to be of quality, then please repair the clasp and, if you can, without harming the integrity of the piece, perhaps add a safety chain, so that I might wear it without fear of loss." Odette noted how intensely Laperle was studying the bracelet. "If you think it's really worth something, perhaps you should do an appraisal for me as well," she added.

Pierre Laperle locked eyes with Odette. Of a sudden, with a slow gauging interest, he seemed to be appraising his *customer*, who lowered her gaze on pretense of looking for something in her purse.

For a long moment, the jeweler did not speak, then he took a pad of repair tickets from beneath the counter, along with a pen. "It's rare to find a bracelet this old in near-mint condition." He began making notes on the ticket. "You want the bracelet cleaned, the clasp repaired– I don't think any of the stones are loose, but *bien sûr*, I shall check them all– and an appraisal."

She opened her wallet. "And a safety chain, if you think–"

"I do not think you should alter the bracelet in any way, *madame*." His tone was resolute.

"*Très bien*," she replied. "I am sure you know best. Do you require payment in advance?"

"*Non, madame*. I have your bracelet, *après tout*," *Monsieur* the Jeweler responded with dry humor. "What I need is your name and telephone number. There are a couple of small jobs ahead of you, but I should have this item ready in about three days. If not, I'll ring you."

Later that day, the Sisters' party decided to take a drive to Diamond Rock and the Anse Cafard Slave Memorial on the shore of le Diamant, about a five-mile drive from their hotel. Since they'd partaken that morning of the hotel's sumptuous breakfast buffet, they opted for a light lunch of fruit, before taking Dorélia's suggestion to motor out to le Diamant. The waitress had made the recommendation at dinner the previous evening, even going to the trouble of ferreting out a guidebook for them.

"One of the hotel guests left this at *la réception* about a month ago," she told them. "He never returned for it. *Alors*, you take it and put it to good use. It's in English, and it contains Martinique's places of interest, with history and cultural information."

Theirs was becoming a comfortable relationship, with the Sisters feeling as though they knew Dorélia all their lives.

The drive to Diamond Rock, off Martinique's southern coast, was quite a pleasant one.

"Rising vertically from the sea, Diamond Rock gets its name from its gem-like shape and the fact that, in certain light, the Rock appears to glitter," Raine read from the tour book.

"While Diamond Rock is geologically interesting, it is best known for its unusual history," Thaddeus declared with his strong, sure hands on the steering wheel. "I like this quirky little Renault. Handles well, and the interior's bright colors are growing on me."

The professor cleared his throat, a habit of his when he had something of significance to say. "During the Napoleonic Wars, a small British naval squadron took up station in the waters around Martinique, harassing French warships, privateers, and merchant ships. In 1803, the squadron's commodore had cannons placed on Diamond Rock, two 24-pounders on the summit, a 24-pounder in a cave mid-way up the side, and two at the base. The Rock is situated in the straits between the islands of St. Lucia and Martinique; and because of its height, those cannons, not only commanded the straits, they could fire upon ships entering and leaving the capital of Fort-de-France.

"Accordingly, the British took guns from their ships and hoisted them up the Rock's sheer sides– a herculean task to be sure– whereupon the sailors and officers, around a hundred total, made their quarters in the caves. Hundreds of bats were driven out by burning bales of hay. The sailors used pulleys and ropes to raise supplies to the summit." Thaddeus nodded his head at a thought that struck him. "Dangerous duty all round. The men ran the risk of falling from the heights– it's 600 feet above sea level– or being bitten by the *fer-de-lance*, a venomous snake inhabiting the place, one of the deadliest vipers in the Americas, in fact."

"When you ponder the matter, the whole affair is incredible," Raine interposed.

"One night," the professor swept on, disregarding the interruption, "a party of slaves from a nearby plantation made a clandestine visit to Diamond Rock to trade bananas and other fruit. They carried news that a French lieutenant colonel of engineers had arrived at their plantation to survey the heights, opposite, for a mortar battery that would shell the Rock.

"The slave doing the talking had been sold by his English owner to the French when the former left the island. The informant didn't like his new master and claimed the protection of the British flag. The commodore granted that protection, promising the slave he could serve in the Royal Navy as a free man, *if* he guided the British to the plantation where the French engineer was staying. As you might suspect, under cover of darkness, a party set out straightaway, taking the French engineer and several other soldiers prisoner. Hence, no mortar battery materialized.

"Because," Thaddeus went on, "this was entirely a Royal Navy operation, the commodore classified the Rock as a stone frigate, christening it the 'HMS Fort Diamond.'

"Napoléon eventually sent a fleet to do battle with the Rock. However, the attackers simply could not scale its vertical sides. The garrison there was desperately short of water. Due to an earth tremor, their stone cistern had cracked. After seventeen months, the British finally surrendered, but not until they'd completely run out of ammunition, water, and food."

"With you along, professor," Beau laughed, "we don't *need* a guidebook."

"Bats and snakes," Maggie gave a shiver, "sounds dreadful."

Professor Weatherby chortled. "Wasn't a picnic at the beach, that's for sure. To augment their uncertain food supply, the garrison had a small herd of goats and a flock of chickens that survived on the meager foliage. They turned one of the caves into a hospital for those men with fevers and injuries.

"It's over two centuries, but Britain still views the Rock as part of the Royal Navy," Thaddeus stated. "All Royal Navy ships passing it are required to accord the appropriate honors. Personnel on the upper deck stand at attention and face the old HMS, whilst the bridge salutes."

"Is the Rock inhabited in any way today?" Beau inquired.

"No," Raine answered. "It's uninhabited, though I've read it's a sanctuary for birds. Because it's sunnier and drier than mainland Martinique, it's covered with undergrowth and cacti."

"Here's something interesting," Maggie said, reading from the guidebook Raine had handed her upon request. "According to folklore, the French floated barrels of rum toward the Rock, then waited till the Brits were sloshed before overpowering them."

"I don't give much credence to that tale," the professor returned.

"Yipes," the redheaded Sister exclaimed after perusing the rest of the page, "the book says there're still snakes out there."

Maggie turned the page. "Oh," she read on, "not the poisonous kind, but a grass snake that's extinct except for the Rock. I'd wager people on Martinique's mainland confused that harmless snake with the poisonous *fer-de-lance* viper.

"History aside," Maggie resumed reading, "it's the scuba experience that draws visitors today. Kind of rare really." She scanned the subsequent paragraphs. "Says there's a triangular cave beneath the Rock that enables divers to swim under it from one end to the other. The cavern is filled with several varieties of colorful fish, coral, and sea fans. Hmmm, interesting … divers have reported seeing one of the cannons that toppled from the summit. Says too this is no place for novice divers due to the strong currents."

A few minutes later, Thaddeus parked the Renault at the beach. "There's the pier that reaches far out into the sea," he gestured. "Let's walk it to get as close to Diamond Rock as we can."

"Then we should drive up the hill to the viewing platform," Raine pointed. "There're a few parking spots up there, along with interesting information panels."

The Sisters' party savored the majestic views of the famous HMS from the pier, as well as the viewing terrace on higher ground, after which they motored onward to the nearby slave memorial.

Within sight of Diamond Rock, they experienced the unique stone commemorative on a grassy field that sloped gracefully to meet a roaring sea.

"Wow, the waves here are high!" Raine exclaimed. "Gives the phrase, 'The surf pounded the shore,' appreciable significance."

"The Anse Cafard Slave Memorial, created by celebrated Martinique artist Laurent Valère, was completed in 1998, in commemoration of the 150th anniversary of the emancipation of slaves in the French West Indies," Maggie quoted from the handbook. "The statues are *chilling*," she said in a near whisper, as they exited the Renault and began walking toward the memorial.

The fifteen concrete figures were *huge*, each eight feet tall and weighing four tons. "They stand in a triangle to represent the slave trade between Africa, the Caribbean and America," Maggie read on, "their faces bearing stoic, brooding expressions, their heads and shoulders bent under the evil of slavery. They face Africa and the sea that claimed their lives when the ship they were on went aground, crashing against the rocks to sink. Over forty would-be slaves, shackled together in the hull, drowned. A local plantation owner, with his slaves, managed to save eighty-six of the African captives."

"There's an unmistakable sense of loss and bereavement here," Beau stated evenly. "*Heavy*. As the yoke of bondage." His blue eyes scanned the area. "There're no guards, no ropes, no fences between us and the statues. I suppose we can go right up and walk among them."

"It is permitted," Raine answered. "Let's do that."

As the group made their way between the figures, it was impossible not to feel the raw emotion of the place. Listening to the pounding surf, the Sisters meditated for several solemn minutes, the stark contrast between the memorial and the beautiful natural setting creating a most powerful experience.

"I'm glad we made it back to the hotel in time to freshen up and get out here to the Coco Bar for another Martinique sunset," Raine said, as she lowered herself into the chair Beau held for her. "Do you know what the French for *sunset* is?" she asked, not really expecting an answer in return. "*Le coucher du soleil.* The sun's bedtime. Isn't that precious? I love the French language. So expressive. Melodious … easy on the ears and quite logical too."

"It's ever so relaxing to sit and sip a drink here before dinner," Maggie breathed with a satisfied sigh.

"What's on the agenda for tomorrow," Beau raised. "You know what? I'm becoming so acclimated to Martinique, I might just try a *ti punch* tonight in lieu of my beer."

"I promise you'll like it," Raine said, leaning over to kiss him. "*Deux,*" she told the waiter, holding up two fingers to order the same.

After Maggie and Thaddeus decided to follow suit, the coterie began discussing what they would do the next day. When the drinks arrived at table, Raine lifted her *ti punch*, "Rose-lipped maidens, light-foot lads!" after which the others echoed the old, visceral, paradise-longing toast.

"We went south today," Thaddeus suggested; "so tomorrow, why don't we head north to Mount Pelée? Maggie, let me see that guidebook, please." The professor perused the section on Martinique's infamous volcano, saying after a few moments, "It's about forty-two miles from here. If we take the N5, we should be there in a little over an hour and a half, all things considered. The N5 is a seaside route, so the scenery should be most refreshing."

"Thad, I can drive tomorrow, so you can relax and enjoy the ride," Beau volunteered.

"Sure, we can alternate drivers," the professor replied.

"We should take lunch in the Pelée area," Raine put in. "It's like dining in the clouds."

Thaddeus snapped his fingers, as an impulse thumped him. "That reminds me. We better get up early and set out immediately after breakfast for Pelée," he cautioned. "Early morning is best for climbing. Clouds often shroud the mountain's windward side, so the

Aileron Trail yields the clearest views in the morning. I think that trail's the right fit for us," he pronounced.

"It's steep but incredibly scenic." Raine brought her hands together in growing excitement, then lowered her gaze to the guidebook, which Thaddeus tilted toward her. "Stairs and switchbacks lead to Pelée's crater rim, and there, we'll get to experience top-of-the-world panoramic views. The mountain reaches an elevation of 4,583 feet. That's 1,397 *mètres*, one of the highest peaks in the Antilles."

Maggie reached for the guide and began skimming the section on Mount Pelée. "The book says the Aileron Trail is generally in good condition, but can be muddy and slippery in places, so there might be a few scrambles. We need to wear sensible walking shoes." Her eyes strayed further down the page. "Dense mist and strong winds most days. Hmmm, says you can either descend into or walk round what they call the 'Cauldron,' which is almost always surrounded by a thick, foggy mist, creating a mysterious, eerie atmosphere."

"Oh, it's wizard," Raine interposed. "*Wiz–zard*. Climbers can hear the ominous bubbling sounds in Pelée's nefarious cauldron."

"When did you say the disaster occurred?" Beau asked, taking a sip of his drink. "This *ti punch* is very good, by the way."

"The volcano blew its top in 1902," Raine answered, "and within only a minute or so, the mountain's fury killed about 30,000 people, destroying the entire town of Saint-Pierre, known then as the 'Paris of the Caribbean.' It was literally *hell on earth*.

"The cataclysm started with a deafening roar, an atomic-like *blast* of gas, ash, and rock, heated to 1,000 degrees Celsius, that completely eclipsed the sky. Pelée's volcanic mudflow rushed down the slopes toward Saint-Pierre at incredible, terrifying speed, killing and burying everything in its path to the sea, where it generated a tsunami and flooded the lowlands. About twenty boats and ships in the bay were instantly destroyed. Their remains still lie at the bottom of the ocean. Homes swallowed, people incinerated within a blink of an eye– the worst volcanic disaster of the twentieth century."

"Did Saint-Pierre have any warning?" Beau wondered aloud.

"Pelée moaned, groaned, and rumbled days before, and there was some ash and a strong smell of sulfur, as well as various other signs, but the authorities proclaimed there was nothing to be afraid of," Thaddeus answered.

"That's right," Maggie confirmed, "they didn't want anyone to leave the area, since an important election was upcoming. Remember Saint-Pierre, that lay in the shadow of Pelée, was the capital of Martinique then. Its citizenry were mostly descended from African slaves, but the wealth and political power were in the hands of the Créoles and French officials. However, change was in the air, and that election was going to tell the tale of who would be in power. Thus, people were told not to panic, not to leave– and no one did. There was plenty of time to evacuate, if the people would've heeded the warnings Pelée itself emitted, but they were too caught up in the political goings on."

The Goth gal tapped a finger to her mouth in pensive gesture. "There's a particular *auberge*, inn, near to Pelée that has the most *exquisite* view. We should take lunch there. I remember it well. The food used to be good, likely still is, and close by are the old ruins of Saint-Pierre."

"Ruins?" Beau questioned. "Didn't figure they'd be any ruins."

"Only a couple. Old theatre ruins and the cell of the only man to survive the disaster, a prisoner, who was locked up for a bar brawl. The walls of his jail were so thick, he was spared a horrible death. The man toured with the Barnum and Bailey Circus for years after."

"No kidding," Beau murmured.

"That playhouse had been an extravagant, 800-seat theatre," Raine informed, catching the eye of their waiter to refill their drinks.

"We'll be hungry after our climb, which will take till, or past, lunchtime," Thaddeus said, "so we should eat when we get down from the summit, then take in the ruins and the museum. The *Musée Volcanologique* houses items plucked from the rubble, as well as photographs of Saint-Pierre before and after the disaster."

"Has Pelée erupted since?" Beau probed, nodding his thanks to their waiter for the refills.

"It did, thirty years later, in 1932," Raine replied. "It blew out lava, but it was a minor eruption, nothing so devasting as 1902. There were no casualties, and it's been dormant ever since."

A thought rushed to meet her. "The same artist who created the Slave Memorial also designed the underwater, twenty-ton interpretation of *Manman Dlo*, which is *Patois* for Mermaid. The huge sculpture was installed under the sea in 2004, at a depth of about twenty-five feet, just off the beach at Saint-Pierre. The water's so crystal-clear, you need only a mask and a snorkel to view it from the surface.

"The mermaid's face is trained up, toward the surface, the better to watch all the boats sailing by overhead. You know, sailors were always wary of the *Manman*, as these creatures were said to overturn ships. *Manman*'s the second of a collection of Valère's underwater sculptures for divers to enjoy in the depths of Martinique waters. His renderings," Raine concluded, "are intended to engender respect for the sea."

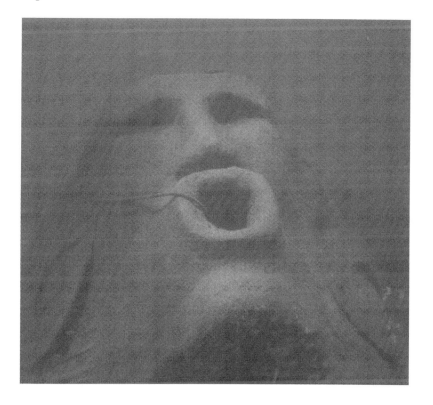

"OK, so we've got tomorrow planned out. Then the following day, let's go shopping," Maggie bubbled with zeal.

"I'm for that," Raine readily agreed. "We'll catch the ferry over to Fort-de-France after the buffet breakfast, and we'll visit the beheaded statue of Joséphine at *la Savane*, stroll the park, then scurry over to *le Grand Marché*, where we can shop till our hearts' content. *Le Marché* is the local market where the locals shop, and it has everything from spices, to Créole delicacies, to clothing, to perfumes, to artisans' crafts, to antiques, including jewelry. Won't be any need to break for lunch, 'cause the Marché offers all sorts of food choices."

"Perhaps while you girls are shopping, Thad and I can do some exploring of our own," Beau suggested, "there in the capital. Whatdya say, Thad ole boy?"

A look passed between them, an expression not missed by Raine.

Now what's he up to? She sent the *pensée* to Maggie, who gave a little shrug. The redheaded Sister felt in her witch's bones she knew the answer to Raine's query, which is expressly *why* she kept it to herself.

Once the magick of the Martinique sunset enveloped the Sisters and their escorts with another of the Goddess' blissful Benedictions, they drifted down the steps from the hotel beach to *la Sirène,* the candlelit restaurant, where Dorélia welcomed them. By that point in time, Trade Winds, her husband's steel band, was setting the mood with *Beyond The Sea/ La Mer.*

"I've always loved that song," Maggie commented. "Evocative. Conjures seascapes and dreamscapes from the past in such a nostalgic way, it almost hurts."

"Jean-Jacques," Thaddeus began, "has made his naturally mellow voice sound like Charles Trénet, the fella who originally recorded the briny tune he wrote back in the Forties while gazing out a train window at a sunlit bay in the south of France. Jotted it down on a piece of scrap paper, and," the professor smiled, "as they say, '*Voilà!*' It's become a classic and one of the songs most associated with France, sort of like Édith Piaf's *La Vie En Rose.*"

After ordering Créole salads and skewered grilled chicken with sweet and sour sauce, the party sat back to sip their wine and enjoy the music.

"Look," Raine whispered, leaning forward and keeping her words low, "it's the Creeper."

Dressed in casual clothing, the man came forward to take a seat, alone, at a table of the restaurant that provided him an inclusive view of the area. He glanced stealthily about, ordered what looked like a gin and tonic, then sat back to do his usual thing– observe everyone and everything around him.

It was at that juncture the Sisters noticed the Eurasian businessman with the Fu Manchu mustache whom they encountered on previous occasions. He was sitting alone as well, eating a salad. From time to time, he picked up his phone to text someone.

Those two must be guests here, Raine zapped the notion to Maggie. *We're in the vicinity of our hotel each time we see them. Somehow ... they have a connection.*

It's quite possible, Sister. Warning signals hummed along Maggie's nerve endings. *And we haven't seen the last of 'em.*

***

Just after sunrise, the Sisters, Thaddeus and Beau, sporting safari shorts, tees, jackets, and comfortable walking shoes, set out for the village of Morne-Rouge, the jumping-on site for the Aileron Trail to Mount Pelée, where they would begin the challenging climb to the summit.

The hike was a virtual forest experience of lush emerald-green. Though the trees were small and flowers few, the trail was luxuriant with thick, low shrubs, as well as a variety of ferns and grasses. The air was cooler than down below, misty, with the mountain enveloped in fluffy, white clouds.

"This drizzle is making me feel like a drowned rat," Raine huffed, pulling herself up the current set of steps. She straightened and pushed her jagged, ebony bangs back from her face. "Martinique seems to sparkle after a rain, doesn't it? Anyway, I'm glad we wore these light, rain-repellent jackets. Do you notice? Snails seem to be everywhere up here. Everywhere I look." A flamboyant, jewel-like hummingbird darted near to check her out, its wings sounding like a tiny helicopter. "And so are these hummers.

Curious little rascals, aren't they?" With help from Beau, she pulled herself over a protruding boulder. The climb was a series of stairs and boulders, straight lines and switchbacks.

"I didn't know if we'd smell sulfur," Beau remarked. "After what you guys said about the mountain yesterday, I half-expected to."

"No sulfur fumes," Thaddeus replied. "No gasses coming out of the earth." He looked at Pelée looming before them. "The giant is slumbering again."

Raine put her pert nose in the air to sniff. "The smell of salt from the ocean is wonderful." She paused to catch her breath. Though she and her companions were all in good physical condition, sections of the varied climb were torturous. Whilst scaling a particularly tricky set of boulders, her foot slipped, and she fell forward to skin her knee. "Damn, that smarts!"

"Lucky the concierge loaned us this backpack," Beau said, lifting it off to ferret out the small first-aid kit inside. Within a few moments, he cleaned and bandaged the Goth gal's scraped leg.

"That's a perk of having a doctor for a boyfriend … even if he is a horse doctor," she laughed blithely, kissing him on the cheek. "'Course, I trust a good horse doctor more than I do a people one any day." She sent Beau a wink. "Always have."

The party took a short break at the third *Refuge,* where they followed the eerie path round the bubbling Cauldron with its mysterious mist, whence the old lava field conjured a sleeping dragon. Afterward, they set off on Pelée's steepest segment to conquer the highest elevation on the island, trudging on in determination.

At one point, Maggie reached out to steady herself on the slippery slope, when something furry brushed against her hand. Turning her head, her eyes flew wide open. It was the largest spider she had ever seen. Letting out a scream that split the atmosphere, she swiftly withdrew her hand, taking a stumbling step backward and pointing, "**Tarantula!**"

Thaddeus put his arms around the panicked Sister to draw her close and comfort her. "Shhhhh, my Maggie, calm down."

"Simultaneously, Raine was scrambling over wet rocks to her sister of the moon's side, her fingers feeling inside her jacket for a special vial. The Sisters never traveled without Granny's healing potion. She had purposely refrained from using it on her skinned leg in the event they would have a serious need for it. "Great Goddess, Mags, did it bite you?" She swiped sweat from her forehead.

"I don't think so," the redhead rasped with a sob, checking her hand for a telling mark.

"It's OK. That tarantula is not poisonous. It's a tree spider, very docile, and in fact, sought after as a pet. That one's an adult. I know from its dramatic, bright colors." The professor placed a finger to her lips. "Hush now, it didn't harm you, though its hairs can be itchy to the skin." He kissed her forehead, then pulled her close again, and she sensed him smiling against her hair as she inhaled the earthy masculine scent of him. It was preeminently the smell of a human body after it had been pushed to the limit, such a scent that has poignance to any athlete, or lover. "I think you frightened him more than he frightened you, luv." Thaddeus handed her a tissue, then a bottle of water Beau passed to him from the backpack.

"Well," Maggie breathed out to admit, "it's a pretty spider." The creature, about six inches across, was a rainbow of colors– red, pink, blue, metallic-green, grey and brown. "Creepy but pretty in its way." She kissed Thaddeus's cheek as he mopped his forehead. "I love how protective you always are of me, darlin'. Thank you."

Watching the Antilles Pinktoe Tarantula scurry away, she said, "I hope no one captures you. You belong in the wild, not in captivity."

Later, at the hard-earned summit, Thaddeus blew out his breath, to say over the strong wind. "It was a bit of a sport, but well worth it, my good fellows. Look at that view!"

Raine adjusted the hood of her jacket, glad for its warmth. "This has been an exquisite adventure I, for one, shall never forget." She grasped Beau's hand, and the pair stood amorously close, gazing out at the far-reaching vista.

Pelée could be capricious, but it was as if the ubiquitous clouds waited to veil the panorama just so the Sisters' party could savor it.

"The toughest four-plus miles I ever hiked," Maggie voiced into the wind. "Sure, we weren't staring into a pit of molten lava, but I feel as though I've flirted with Death in the safest way possible."

"Beautiful, wild, and challenging," Beau pronounced, his eyes sliding from the seascape to Raine.

"We did it," she whooped aloud. "We climbed Pelée, the highest point in Martinique and the third deadliest volcano on earth. Blessed be!"

"Blessed be," her companions echoed.

After several moments, a quiet spell spent in meditation, Thaddeus said, "Let's get moving. We want to lunch and take in the ruins of old Saint-Pierre before we call it a day." His intense blue eyes swept the outlook. "This mountain's a cloud magnet. Fog's starting to roll in, and the lack of visibility could make our descent dangerous."

As it turned out, the entire Pelée experience was not half as dangerous as the mystery about to ensnare them.

Chapter Six

"She's holding a rose," Raine pointed, as the Sisters, Thaddeus and Beau stood before the beheaded statue of Empress Joséphine in *la Savane,* the noble old park at Martinique's capital of Fort-de-France. "Symbolic of the name she preferred in her youth, as well as her lifelong passion for roses."

"And the fact that she is known as the 'Rose of Martinique.' An exquisite statue … such beautiful Carrara marble. I can't help but feel sad," the tenderhearted Maggie murmured.

"The statue was erected in 1859, just forty-five years after Joséphine's death," Raine informed. "In France and across Europe, the empress was … is a *beloved* figure. 'Our Lady of Victories' in France. The French were convinced that Napoléon's luck went south after he divorced her to marry a womb and secure an heir. There is absolutely *no* historical proof that Joséphine convinced Napoléon to reinstate slavery. There *is* proof *he* wanted to revive the lucrative Caribbean sugar trade to aid in solidifying his political authority."

Raine halted her recitation to look at a vintage, black-and-white photograph in the guidebook of the statue before it was beheaded, the eyes gazing out to sea, in the direction of France.

"On the other hand," Raine went on, "there's *much* historical evidence chronicling Joséphine's generosity, extreme kindness of heart, and ready willingness to forgive any wrong done her. To quote from several contemporaries, 'She was everywhere adored.' History acknowledges that Joséphine visited the slave cabins to minister unto the sick, to bring comfort and nourishment to the old and the weak, and to pray with the dying. We know she even acted as mediator when a slave was accused of some offense or other. The Empress Joséphine provided for her former Martinique nanny, the slave Marion, with freedom, in addition to a comfortable pension. We know she provided for her personal maid and companion, Euphémie, as well. The good-hearted Joséphine even provided for her first husband's mistress, Laure de Longpré, who, remember, once cruelly conspired against her."

"Here on Martinique, the old adage, 'Time heals all wounds,' seems not to apply," Beau mused. "But then again … then again …"

After strolling *la Savane*, the group walked on, to the center of town. The Sisters were eager to begin their shopping spree at *le Grand Marché*.

"OK, ladies," Beau said at the entrance to the large open-air market, "you've got plenty of euros, so happy spending. Thaddeus and I are off on our own. We'll meet you right here, on this spot, at 5:00. Don't be late, so we can catch the ferry across to our hotel in time for our sunset siesta at the *Coco*."

When the two men walked far enough to be out of ear-shot, Thaddeus turned to Beau to ask, "What's the plan? I know you've got one."

Beau chortled, slapping his cohort on the back. "I do, and I need your help to carry it off."

Excitingly exotic and bursting with wares, vendors and shoppers*, Le Grand Marché* was a covered open-air market that bustled from sunup to sundown.

"This market reminds me of the French Market in New Orleans, but on a grander scale," Maggie remarked. "And so colorful! I'm glad it's covered. We'll be protected from the broiling sun, and if we get a sudden rain, we won't get soaked."

Raine sniffed the air. "Mmmm, hmmm. A wonderful mélange of smells– all the spices and curries. This place has great vibes, doesn't it? Not waiting for a response, she grasped her sister of the moon's arm. "C'mon, Mags, we don't want to waste one precious moment."

The Sisters stopped first at a spice table to choose packets of Martinique seasonings for fish and chicken, of which they planned to make good use at home. "Mmmm, this colombo spice smells divine," Raine lauded. "So does this Créole packet. Stop me from going mad and bringing home loads, though I have intention of sharing with Aisling and Ian."

A few minutes of continued browsing led them to a stall with island clothing. Pulling a large, loose-fitting madras dress free of the rack, Maggie asked, "Who does this muumuu remind you of?"

"Hannah would absolutely *love* that," Raine answered, imaging their loyal housekeeper *à la Martiniquaise*. "Let's both choose a really nice one for her, each in a different color."

"Now, let's scout something special for Aisling, Ian, and our Merry Fay," Maggie suggested. "Oh, look!" She indicated the table stacked with the symbolic Martinique sunhats. "A *bakoua* would make Aisling a great gift. I heard her comment just the other day that a beak doesn't shade her sensitive skin enough when she works in their garden." The Sisters moved to the targeted table and, within moments, selected a hat for their fair blonde cousin.

Raine scrunched her mouth in thought. "You know what? We should get a *bakoua* for Hannah's hubby too. Jim does a lot of work for us outdoors, and I think it would be a welcome, practical gift for him. Have you any idea what we should get for Ian?"

Maggie thought for a reflective moment. "Hey, how about a chef's apron with Martinique on it? He's the gifted cook in our family. What do you think?"

"That's wizard, Mags. We could also get Ian and Aisling a joint gift of a good bottle of Martinique rum. There's a rum table yonder. Let's check it out."

It took the Sisters quite a while to select the rum, for there was such a vast selection in an array of bottles. In time, however, they were happy with the choice they made.

After careful browsing, they also found the sought-after I ♥ Martinique chef's apron for Aisling's gourmet hubby. The Sisters were having a wonderful time watching the shoppers interact with the friendly, helpful vendors, some of whom spoke a little English. From a nearby stall, the sound of steel-band music, from a CD, drifted to their ears. To accommodate their parcels, they each purchased a strong Martinique carryall, "… which," said Raine, "are themselves nice souvenirs."

"How I would love to buy several of those hand-woven baskets," Maggie commented, gesturing toward a large, impressive display close to where they were paused. Sitting on a bench at one of the market's cafés, they were refreshing themselves with freshly squeezed fruit drinks. "*But* we don't want to have to check anything at the airport, so let's confine our purchases to things we can put into our luggage. We left room for souvenirs, and we can always impose on the guys for space in their suitcases. We'll have to wear the *bakoua* hats."

"Agreed. I like 'em. They kind-a look like straw witch hats. Now, what about Merry Fay?" Raine stood, glancing about. She handed Maggie another of the pistachio nougat candies so popular on the island. "Mmmm, are these *bonbons* yummy! Which do you prefer, the pistachio nougats or the *filibos*, the ones made from sugar cane?"

"Both. In response to your question," Maggie began, "Merry's turning into quite a little lady. Let's keep our eyes peeled for perfume. Oh, on second thought, we should get perfume at the duty-free shop at the airport before we board our flight. It won't take up much space in our purses." The pair began strolling again through the market. "I know what we can buy for Merry Fay here," she exclaimed after a quiet lull. "Something in the way of local crafts. Wooden, hand-painted jewelry or a small, wooden treasure box perhaps. I opt for jewelry. We can wear it home."

"Or one of those handcrafted straw purses at that table over there," Raine pointed.

"Oh, Raine, for my doll collection, look!" Maggie indicated a table crammed with Créole dolls in assorted, bright madras

Martinique costumes. "C'mon, help me select just the right one. It'll have to be a tiny one though."

The Sisters' next move was a stroll through the antique segment of the Marché, where Raine was elated to find a vintage sterling silver spoon, the top of which was crafted like a *Martiniquaise* wearing the traditional, knotted head-wrap, the reverse of which was engraved with the word *Martinique*. Maggie bought an antique, carved mahogany figurine for Thaddeus, whilst Raine chose a vintage seashell picture frame for Beau.

"For his office at the clinic," she declared, "so he'll think of all the fun we had every time he looks at it. I plan to slip a nice photo from our trip inside before I give it to him."

"Ooooh look, that lady over there is selling handcrafted jewelry. I want to get a pair of huge Martinique earrings for myself," Maggie cooed with delight. "I've always been a Gypsy at heart."

As it turned out, the savvy Sisters purchased a flat, straw clutch purse for Merry Fay, as well as handcrafted jewelry for her, Aisling, Hannah, and themselves. The *Martiniquaise* who sold them the items captured their immediate attention– and held it.

Dressed in a long, white cotton frock with green madras foulard and matching head-wrap, tied with three knots, the crone seemed to sense that the Sisters were witches, just as their keen witchy intuition told them *she* was a sister of the Craft.

"Have you any items infused with magick?" Raine asked in clear French, though she made certain to hold her voice to a near-whisper.

The crone's eyes, black as jet, bore clean through them. *"Oui. Les colliers que vous venez d'acheter tiennent magie."*

Raine translated for Maggie. "She said the necklaces we just bought are infused with magick." The Goth gal turned to the *Quimbois* woman, whom the Sisters were convinced was the real deal. *"Dites-nous les sortilèges, madame, s'il vous plaît."*

I asked her with what spells she cast the necklaces, Raine rocketed to Maggie.

"*Je jette la même magie sur tous mes colliers, mademoiselle*," she replied with stoic expression. "*La bonne chance, la bonne santé, la joie et le bonheur.*"

Raine turned back to Maggie. "She said she cast all her necklaces with the same spells– good fortune, good health, joy and happiness."

Maggie held the necklaces close to her bosom and closed her eyes, welcoming the energies. "Oooh yes … they radiate with *good* blessings." She faced the crone. "*Merci, ma soeur.*"

"*Voici.* Perfect for you," the woman said, handing Maggie a pair of large seed earrings dyed with vibrant Caribbean colors. "They are cast with the same magick," she pronounced in French.

"*Bon*," Maggie replied, already hooking the dangling ornaments in her ears to regard her reflection in the mirror the good witch held for her. "They suit me," she nodded. "I'll take them too. *Merci, madame.*"

The wise woman scrutinized the Sisters for an inspective moment before she spoke again, and when she did, she continued to speak in French, devoid of *Patois*. "You two have the brightest auras I have ever seen. You each have many spirits surrounding you, watching over you, guiding you, and inspiring you. One especially strong spirit." She eyed the Sisters steadily, unblinking, her dark eyes narrowing in concentration. "But you already know that. Would you like for me to read your palms?"

Raine shot the translation to Maggie, who nodded her approval, after which the former answered in the affirmative. "*Oui, madame, si vous voulez.*"

With anticipation and an elbow nudge from Raine, Maggie extended her hand to go first.

The old woman bent her head to look carefully at the rosy palm. After several quiet moments, she made a soft, low sound deep in her throat that came off almost like a groan, as she continued to meditate in silence– and it was the silence of the grave. "I see a final farewell," she revealed at last, her voice somber, "of a never-ending gift of love."

Tears flooded the impassioned Sister's emerald eyes. For a private moment, she stared into space and said nothing. There was no need to ask a question to which she knew the answer. With eyes that came back from a long distance, she gave a quiet nod, then stepped to the side to let Raine proffer her hand to the soothsayer.

The crone studied the raven-haired Sister's hand a bit longer than she'd done with Maggie's, saying after several nonverbal minutes, punctuated only with a trilogy of grunts, "A surprise, *mademoiselle*, is coming to you."

Raine loved surprises, and her green eyes opened wide with eagerness. "A surprise?" she blinked. "Will it be good or bad?"

The witch cackled, tilting her head and looking for the Sister like a wise old owl. "Oh, it will be good, *ma petite*. There is nothing more precious than a gift from the heart."

The *Quimbois* woman's coal-black eyes seemed to kindle with an inner fire. "There's something else," she pronounced in French. "With each of your gifts," the eyes moved from Raine to Maggie, "will come the need for a weighty decision."

The Sisters stared back at the crone in wordless curiosity, then looked to one another.

"Choose carefully, *mes petites*," the witch finished with solemn air. "Choose carefully."

She sent forth a warm smile. "Heart reckoning and mind reckoning are two different things," she continued in French. "Decision-making can be a battle between mind and heart. Sometimes the heart needs more time to accept what the mind already knows." Again her black eyes sparked. "Sometimes the opposite is true. I have lived many years, long enough to know that the heart is usually the wiser of the two."

Sensing the Sisters' uncertainty, the *Quimbois* concluded, "You'll know you've made the right decision when there is peace in your heart."

Chapter Seven

Whilst the Sisters were souvenir shopping in Fort-de-France, Historian Odette Auteur, a few blocks distant, was retrieving the bracelet she had left in the care of Jeweler Pierre Laperle.

"Ah, *Madame* Auteur," the antique dealer remarked in his polished French, "your bracelet is in the back. Excuse me. I'll get it for you." He ducked behind the curtain, reappearing a moment later with the maroon velvet box Odette had used to cradle the piece.

"I waited to this afternoon to collect the bracelet," she said in Parisian French, "to make sure it would be ready."

Pierre opened the lid of the case, took out the restored bracelet and placed it lovingly on a black velvet display tray that was resting on the counter. The historian literally gasped when she saw the dazzling piece of jewelry under the overhead light, the fiery inner world of the rubies sparking her imagination.

"*Mon Dieu!* It is not the same bracelet surely."

"I assure you it is, *madame,*" Laperle smiled proudly. He waited while his customer admired the bangle, basking in the metamorphic change he brought about.

"Never in my wildest dreams did I think that filthy," she reflected on what the piece had looked like, "old, worn-out bracelet, the stones so dull and cloudy, the metal scratched and damaged, could be restored to such splendor! You are a genius, *monsieur!*"

Pierre Laperle was used to such praise, but that did not mean he grew tired of it. With a subtle bow of his head, he replied in as humble a voice as he could muster, "*Merci, madame.* Note the bright luster and weightiness of this exceptional example of Rococo jewelry. Gold is heavy but soft, hence the bent clasp, which, *vous voyez*, I repaired. The bracelet is nearly pure gold, even better than 22 karat. In addition to the twisted clasp, it bore many scratches, which I buffed out to the best of my ability, restoring it virtually to mint. The fourteen cabochon stones, creating the impression of a rose atop the bracelet, are high-quality pigeon-blood rubies, the deepest and most sought-after shade of red. Small stones, quarter to half-carats, but of the finest quality."

His astute eyes fastened on those of the author. "Would you be kind enough to tell me again how you came to ... *acquire* such a treasure?"

Odette swallowed. It wasn't what he said so much as *how* he said it. "I-I told you, I'm Parisian. I used to love to browse the flea markets the weekends, and the Saturday before I relocated to Martinique, I stumbled across an old woman who was selling off everything she had. The bracelet was in a mixed box of trinkets I bought from her. When I moved into my cottage at Trois-Îlets, the carton got shoved to the back of a closet, and I forgot about it. Actually, it's a miracle the box didn't get tossed away, because I haven't much storage space, and–" his penetrating gaze stopped her.

In spite of the façade of a formal, self-contained demeanor, it was clear he suspected her of something deceitful.

She lowered her eyes to the bracelet. "And," she concluded, "I suppose it was a good thing I did forget about it. As I told you before, I was cleaning out that closet, when I came across the box of baubles and decided to bring the bracelet to a jeweler. Did you appraise the bracelet for me, *monsieur*?"

Laperle chose not to answer. Rather, he handed her a jeweler's loup, then asked that she look at the inner band. Squinting through the magnifying glass, Odette was expecting to see a hallmark or jeweler's mark of some kind. Instead, she saw faint engraving in an almost scrawling, hand-crafted script: *Pour ma belle Rose.* With: *M.J.R. Lapagerie de Beauharnais.* The historian drew in her breath.

"*Est-ce possible?!* Can it be?!" she exclaimed, her dark eyes round with astonishment. A thousand questions began swirling in her mind, but the significance of the situation held her captive, rendering her speechless.

"*For my beautiful Rose,*" he read the French message. "A token of affection for Joséphine from a lover perhaps? Engraving can be forged, but I do not think this a forgery. The hand-engraving looks, to me, to be authentic. I have been in this business all my life, following as I have in my grandfather and my father's footsteps. I would date the bracelet to the second half of the 1700s. In addition, I had another antique dealer look at it, someone who buys and sells internationally. He is also quite knowledgeable, the best in the business. He completely agrees with my assessment." The jeweler fixed her again with penetrating inquiry. "By dint of your story, I assume you have no documentation to prove a connection to Joséphine," he pronounced in a half-question.

"*Non, bien sûr,* I- I do not," Odette murmured. "I'm sorry," she said, bringing a slightly shaking hand to her bosom, "this is … quite overwhelming."

"To answer *your* question," Pierre began, "I have appraised the piece only for its intrinsic value, the component parts of the bracelet, its materials and workmanship. As for its historical value," he tilted his head and lifted a brow, "a rare item such as this … it's almost impossible for me to attach a value to it." The jeweler slid a brown envelope across the counter to her. "You know, *madame*, I named my shop *l'Objet Qui Parle,* because *each* of the antique items in this showroom holds a story." His eyes scanned the *objets d'art* around them. "If only they *could* talk, tell their stories." His gaze fell on the bracelet. "I especially wish this piece could talk, tell us its tale. I know it would captivate."

Odette opened the envelope and perused the appraisal. When her eyes met Laperle's, she read again *Suspicion*.

"It is a qualified, competent appraisal, though, in this case, a conservative one. If you had history of ownership for this piece, the power of provenance would skyrocket the value." Pierre misread the confused expression on his customer's face. "To make clear, *madame*, the documented history of a piece of jewelry is called its *provenance*. Of course, one never knows what background search will yield. As a celebrated historian– I realized who you were after your first visit here– you know the value and rewards of research. I would suggest you take this bracelet to the curator of la Pagerie, and–"

The historian's dark eyes widened, and she became instantly aware that her manner suggested a secret. Quickly, she glanced at her watch in pretense of something other than fear. "I must go, *Monsieur* Laperle, I need to be somewhere else before they close for the day. Perhaps we can discuss this further at a later time. Indeed, I will be in touch with you." She hurriedly secured the bracelet into its velvet nest and popped the case into her purse, zipping the compartment. Then she paid the jeweler and swiftly exited the establishment.

Stepping outside into the dazzle of the Martinique sunshine, Odette reached into her bag for her sunglasses. When she failed to find them, she realized she'd left them on the counter. Since they were prescription lens, she knew she had to go back for them.

Quietly, she opened the shop door and ducked inside. No one was about, but she could hear voices coming from behind the curtain that separated the showroom from the jeweler's workshop.

"There's something suspicious about this," Laperle was saying. "What are the odds of a historian, who has always had an affinity for the Empress Joséphine, coming upon such a bracelet at a Paris flea market, then rediscovering it in Martinique? I'm wondering if I should report this to the proper authorities."

A woman's voice answered. "Did someone just come in? I thought I heard the door out front." Odette could only see the back of the woman through a chink in the curtain, but the words froze her reaching for the sunglasses atop the glass showcase. Snatching them up, she ducked down behind the counter.

If the jeweler comes out and finds me, I'll say I came back for my sunglasses and found them on the floor, she told herself.

When the voices resumed, the historian eased to the door, opened it, and sidled out unnoticed. Crossing the street to a popular outdoor café, she dropped into a seat, her wide-brimmed straw hat and outsized sunglasses blending her into the touristy crowd. From her position, Odette could watch the entrance of the antique store.

It's nearly closing time, she told herself. *I'll wait here to see the mystery woman Laperle was talking with. I know that voice from somewhere. I just can't place it now. I **must** find out who she is.*

Nursing a cold drink while she waited, Odette's anxiety was enhanced with her swirling thoughts. *Oh, why did I take the bracelet from la Pagerie?! I must have been out of my mind to do something like that. I never stole anything in my life. I honestly did not think it was worth anything. I thought it was paste, a pretty bauble lost by a tourist. Never did I dream when I picked it out of that flower bed— oh God! What am I going to do? I can't take it back to La Pagerie. Not now. I have a sterling reputation as a historian and author, and I'd be labeled THIEF! I might even be sent to prison!*

How wasn't the bracelet found years ago? As a volunteer, I know they're always doing renovations, additions, all sorts of improvements at la Pagerie, especially in the past few years. A thought fell upon her. *The hurricane! It somehow pushed the bracelet to the surface. I've heard about such things. Let me think. Laperle said the bracelet dates back to the second half of the 1700s. That's when Joséphine made her return visit to Martinique, in 1788. It fits. She must have lost the bracelet at la Pagerie during the two-year span of time she was on the island.*

Odette trolled her realm of knowledge about the empress. *I'll wager she lost it the night she and her little daughter Hortense had to run for their lives, the night of the slave rebellion. If Joséphine would've lost the valuable bracelet before that night, she would likely have found it. Somehow, it got trampled down into the earth ... in a deluge of rain! Yes, yes, I recall reading in her daughter's memoirs that a storm was raging the night of their escape from Martinique. I'm too stressed now to recall if a lost bracelet was mentioned in Hortense's memoirs ... which would be provenance for the bracelet ... but I couldn't possibly use it, because my story is that I purchased the bracelet at a Paris flea market.*

Suddenly she remembered something. *Oh God, Laperle said he told another antique dealer about the jewel.* Her lips tightened, and the muscles tensed along her jawline. *That means **three** people know about this in addition to me.*

Odette sipped her drink, her eyes glued to the front of the antique shop across the way. *If I had known the bracelet was of any value whatsoever, I would have immediately turned it over to the curator at la Pagerie. Now, it's too late for honesty. I must stick to my story. The jeweler knows who I am. I had to use my real name. And good thing I did too. He recognized me. I never dreamed ...*

The more I'm thinking, the more I am starting to believe that this bracelet was destined to come to me. I own a piece of history! I can't believe it. It's surreal, the chance of a lifetime!

I've always believed I lived before, that if I wasn't Joséphine, I was someone quite close to her. I truly believe that. I have always defended her in my writings. I have always known her mind, her heart.

The overwrought historian's brain continued to churn with tumbling thoughts, until finally she knew she could not part with the treasure that she decided Destiny had bequeathed her.

If only I could place that woman's voice! I'm stressed now, but it'll come to me. Get hold of yourself, Odette. You're a renowned historian. No one will doubt your word.

I was genuinely surprised by nearly everything the jeweler told me. Surely the pompous ass noted that.

So here's the plan: I wait here to see who the woman was behind the curtain. Then I convince the jeweler of my story. Ooooh, he's coming out.

Odette watched as Laperle exited the shop and locked the door. *He's alone! La merde, there's a back door to his shop! Now, I **must** rely on my memory to put the voice with a face. And if I can't? Then I use my historian's detective skills to find out who that* *woman is. If she left by the back door, she obviously doesn't want to be seen in public with Laperle. Maybe she's married, and they are involved in– He's getting into his car. I'll tail him!*

Odette threw some euros on the café table, hastened to her car, started the engine, and peeled out onto Rue Victor Hugo, Martinique's parallel to New York City's Fifth Avenue, nearly running down two men who were attempting to cross the street.

Beau and Thaddeus jumped back onto the sidewalk, watching the yellow Citroën Deux Chevaux roar away.

"Hey, wasn't that the historian we saw out at the Pagerie?" Beau asked with a start.

"Looked like her," Thaddeus replied. "She sure was in an all-fired hurry," he added, as they watched the small auto disappear in traffic down the boulevard.

Odette followed Laperle out of town as closely as she dared. At one point, her heart sank when she was sure she'd lost him, until she spied his white Mercedes up ahead rounding a sharp curve in the road. Gunning the Deux Chevaux, she urged the little car along N2 in the direction of Schoelcher. Twenty minutes later, she tailed him up a steep hillside to a secluded chalet overlooking the sea. Easing her vehicle off the road, she ducked down, as he pulled into the private driveway.

Odette glanced across the way to see a side road half-hidden in jungle. Quickly backing up, she drove into the trees, out-of-sight. Then she turned off the ignition and waited, needing to collect her thoughts and plan what she intended to say to Laperle.

*I've got to convince him that the story I fed him is true, that I bought that bracelet in a box of worthless trinkets years ago at a Paris flea market. Things like this do happen. After all, truth is stranger than fiction. As a historian, I know **that** to be true. I'll ask his advice on insurance. He struck me as an arrogant sort. After three husbands, if it's one thing I know about, it's the male ego. I know, too, I cannot part with this bracelet. I can**not**. I intend to keep it no matter what I have to do!*

Odette glimpsed her watch. Then she exited her car, locked it, and started the short climb to Pierre Laperle's chalet. Walking briskly over the paver stones to the door, she took a deep breath and wrapped thrice. Within moments, the opened door revealed the jeweler. He had swapped his suit jacket for a smoking blazer, over one arm of which was a tea towel. In the other hand he held a lime. His eyes peered questioningly into hers, though his greeting was cordial.

"*Bonsoir.*"

The two continued to speak in their native French, Odette delivering her excuse as she plotted it.

"*Bonsoir, Monsieur* Laperle. I'm sorry to interrupt you at home, but in the shop this afternoon, I was too overwhelmed to think logically. In fact, I was in a surreal daze, *monsieur*. I still can't believe this. Could you grant me a scrap of time to answer a few of my questions … now that I've gotten over the initial shock? I promise I won't stay long."

"*Entrez, madame.*" With a sweep of his free hand, Pierre ushered her inside. "Forgive my manners, but I was surprised to see you at my door. I'm in the process of preparing myself a *ti punch*. Won't you join me? It's my habit to sip a drink on my balcony evenings, while I enjoy the sunset over the sea. The spectacular view is the reason I bought this chalet."

She followed him into his kitchen, where a large window previewed the delight of which he spoke. There was a glorious view of the sparkling turquoise water dotted with white boats of various sorts, the lush-green mornes, and nestled into the hillsides, a rainbow of colorful island residences.

"Please make yourself at home," he said, indicating a chair. "You can talk while I tend to the drinks." He proceeded then to squeeze fresh lime juice into a pitcher, in which he had already poured white rum and sugar-cane syrup.

"I appreciate this. I trust you, *Monsieur* Laperle. I can tell you're very good at what you do. I daresay *expert*. I was thinking that I should get the bracelet insured as soon as possible. Perhaps you could suggest an agency and if you think I should exceed the appraisal value. I also want to ask the name of the other dealer with whom you conferred about the bracelet. After all, you told me he's the best in the business, so I'd very much like to speak with him myself. As a historian, it's my habit to garner as much information as I can, you understand."

When Laperle did not respond, she rattled on, "I wish I knew the name of the vendor from whom I purchased the bracelet years ago, but I had no reason to get her name. For all I know, she's deceased. In truth, I felt sorry for the woman. She was quite old and looked as if she were suffering from ill health. That's why I bought the box of trinkets. I really didn't want them, especially since I was in the process of relocating. I suppose that's another reason I was so unnerved when we spoke at your shop. It's a miracle I didn't toss the carton out. I nearly did twice. However, a few days ago when I came across the box, I finally had time to go through the *bric-à-brac* inside."

Stop. You're rambling, Odette told herself. Pierre Laperle's silence was making her nervous. His back was to her, and on the table where she was sitting lay a knife, a serrated, wicked-looking knife she could not help noticing. In fact, she could not drag her eyes from it. *It would be so easy, so easy.* It was only when Laperle turned around that her gaze shifted to him.

He handed her a *ti punch*. "Come, let us adjourn to the balcony. We don't want to miss the sunset. I can answer your questions there, *madame*. This way," he indicated with elegant sweep of hand. "After you."

The jeweler shadowed Odette through the connecting dining area with its beachy rattan furniture– the island-print cushions reflecting the *calme et zen* placard adorning the pale azure walls– and through an open sliding-glass door to the balcony overlooking the sea and rocks below.

"Please, make yourself comfortable, *madame*," Pierre said, indicating a chair. "Perhaps as time goes by, you'll uncover, in your research, provenance that will beyond doubt connect the bracelet to Empress Joséphine."

Odette settled into the proffered chair. "In your expert opinion, what do *you* say? I was so flustered in the shop, I can't recall exactly what you said. Do *you* think it was hers?"

"I've my own opinion about this entire affair," Pierre answered cryptically. His brow furrowed, and he cocked his dark head a little to the side. He was looking at Odette the way he might look at an *objet d'art* brought to him for appraisal. Raising his drink to his mouth, he took a swallow of *ti punch*, intensely watching the woman before him over the rim of his glass. "Let me put the same question mark before you, *madame*. Surely, as a historian and an expert on 'la Belle Créole' in your own right, *you* must have formed an opinion." It was only the faintest suspicion of a question mark, but Odette responded– though inwardly.

What is he thinking? she asked herself, struggling to regain her composure. She sensed strongly he was toying with her, and it was not only making her nervous, it was vexing. Nonetheless, she knew she could not insult this man. Now it was her turn to take her time answering.

The author assumed a musing posture, but her thought was not on what he asked. Aloud, she said, "*Monsieur*, I trust your knowledge of antiques. My research told me you are one of the best jewelers in Martinique, if not *the* best. *That* combined with the bracelet's inscription … the way Joséphine's name is inscribed is precisely how she signed herself during the era in which you've placed the bracelet. The words *Pour ma belle Rose*," she pulled a pensive face, "*eh bien*, I know she had many lovers in Paris during that time-frame."

"Yes," Pierre remarked, his eyes locking on hers, "from what I've read she was a sensual woman." He still hadn't answered her queries, as he sipped his drink, continuing to study the increasingly nervous historian before him.

At what game is this man playing? she asked herself. *He has beautiful manners when he chooses to display them, but he's deliberately trying to unnerve me.*

After several charged moments lapsed, the astute jeweler pursed his mouth in thought. "Let me ask you this: Many people tend to visit the same vendors at flea markets. Did you have that kind of relationship with the elderly woman from whom you purchased the bracelet?" He gave a slight shrug. "Oh, but you said you didn't know her name, yet you felt sorry enough for her to purchase a box of things you didn't want *and* at the time you were moving an entire household to a different part of the world. You told me you bought the bracelet right before your move to Martinique. Did you mention Martinique to the vendor that day? Did the old woman mention to you that she had ever been to Martinique?" He held her captive with his penetrating stare.

Odette was stunned, and it was several moments before she replied. "Why would you ask me these things?" she blurted, becoming *visibly* nervous now. *All those questions! The man's insufferable.*

Pierre's mouth curled in a victorious smile, and his voice was disdainful in its arrogance as he zeroed in for the kill. "When you retrieved the bracelet at my shop, and I asked you again how you came to acquire such a treasure, you repeated your story the same way you told it to me the first time, with virtually no deviation. Since you hadn't changed the basic details, it should have rung with truth. However, it struck me as a good story created by a good author, suspiciously appropriate, and it sounded rehearsed. You, *madame*, are a much better writer than thespian, *je crois*."

His dark eyes snapped. "What are the odds of you, shall we say, *chancing upon* a piece of jewelry that harmonizes with the period Joséphine returned to Martinique?" He raised one ebony brow to give her a look of scorn. "I did my research too. I had to when I did the appraisal."

He leaned back against the railing, as if resting his case, the triumphant expression on his face suddenly vanishing as his eyes widened in fear when the railing gave way, and he plunged, screaming, to his death on the rocks below.

For several moments, Odette could not move, so shocked was she by what transpired. She didn't know if she, too, had screamed. It had all happened so fast and furiously.

Lowering a hand from her mouth, she gripped the arm of the chair for support to stand on wobbly legs, her heart pounding in her ears louder than the roar of surf beneath her. Presently, she became conscious of the fact that she was still holding the *ti punch*, which she downed in one gulp, before easing herself over to the edge of the balcony to gaze at Laperle's broken body sprawled on the rocks below, the arms akimbo.

"What are the odds?" she echoed his words in a pant as though she'd run a long distance, her breath coming in ragged spurts.

Drawing back to the wall of the house, she prayed no one had seen or heard. Scanning the scene, she realized she was trembling and struggled to hold on to her sanity. *Tout va bien. This place is so isolated. There's no one about, not a living soul.*

How long she stood there, staggered, her back against the wall, she did not know; but all at once, her brain began to race, and leaving the sliding-glass door open, she hastened back inside to the kitchen.

There, she carefully washed her glass and put it away in the cupboard, neatly, to blend with the others on the shelf. Next, she used the dish towel to wipe anything and anywhere she might have touched. Finally, she ripped off a paper towel, snatched up her bag, and with the towelette in hand, opened and set the lock on the door, from the inside. Peering furtively out, to make certain the coast was clear, she pulled the door closed with a reassuring click behind her, stuffed the paper towel into the pocket of her dress, walked briskly down the road to her car hidden in the trees, and drove off.

What're the odds, huh? she repeated to herself on the drive home, mimicking Laperle's pointed question. *What're the odds indeed ... of me being the one to unearth the bracelet at la Pagerie after what? Two hundred and thirty years. Think of the thousands of people, over more than two centuries, who could have discovered that bracelet! And what are the odds of going to that pompous jeweler's home to protect myself and watching him fall to his death in a well-timed accident of Fate?*

It all happened for a reason, she justified to herself. *Everything happens for a reason. Laperle's death is further proof the bracelet is meant for me.* She took three deep breaths. *I've got to get hold of myself. I could easily get paranoid, and my colitis will fire up. Besides, I've work to do. I must find out who the woman was in that backroom with Laperle, as well as the identity of the other dealer with whom he discussed the bracelet.*

I haven't done anything wrong. I never thought that bracelet was going to prove to be a national treasure, and I never laid a *finger on Laperle. What're the odds? The odds are Joséphine's bracelet was destined for **me**!*

The thought calmed her, and that night, in her jasmine-scented townhouse, she drifted into the balm of restful sleep.

"Happiness is when you feel good about yourself without feeling the need for anyone else's approval."
~ The Sleuth Sisters

Chapter Eight

Early the subsequent day, when the beaches of Martinique were brightening with the golden radiance of morning, the Sisters, Thaddeus and Beau rented a catamaran sailboat, with a skipper, to sail round the southern tip of the island. *Endless Summer* was the ideal choice of "cat," manned by an American skipper who left the corporate world to sail the Caribbean in perpetual pursuit of a serene, idyllic lifestyle.

"Three years before I set sail on this quest," Skipper Kai Nelson related, "I'd never sailed a boat or even knew I wanted to. In my heart, though, I knew I yearned for a change. It all began when I took a much-needed break to Martinique. I went sailing, like you're doing today, with a skipper on a cat very like this one, and I fell in love with her. The next day, I took my first sailing lesson. The die was cast.

"In the months that followed, I rented a boat and lived on it for a year, forgive the pun, to test the waters. Fortunately, I had a respectable savings, so I didn't have to stress over money. I sold my pricey penthouse apartment in Manhattan. Sold most everything I had to downsize my life. Then I bought my own boat, all the while learning as much as I could about sailing, the sea," he smiled, "and myself. *Endless Summer* is my second cat, upgraded from the first. I like to tell folks, I came to Martinique for a week's break some thirty years ago and never looked back."

Tall, middle-aged Kai Nelson possessed the swoon-worthy good looks of cinema or romantic fiction. He was exotically handsome in a swarthy, almost Continental way, cordial and naturally courteous, reminding the Sisters of something Granny used to say that echoed Abraham Lincoln's famous quote: "The mark of a truly educated person is one who treats others with respect."

"You can never cross the ocean till you have the courage to lose sight of the shore," Kai declared, his capable, sun-browned hands on the wheel, as he effortlessly maneuvered the cat out of the Pointe du Bout Marina near l'Hôtel Bakoua. He drew in a deep breath. "So I say to you this day: Smell the sea and feel the sky, let your soul and spirits fly. *Nothing like it.* Never have missed my former years of hustle, bustle. I turned everything negative in my life into a positive, but getting off that ladder to the top was the best. Never regretted my decision, not once."

Nelson's weathered face took on a look of reminiscing. "I have an ongoing love affair with the sea. Guess with a name like 'Nelson,' I should, right? But I'll tell you somethin'. I grew up in the landlocked Mid-West. Then I attended Harvard, where I earned degrees in business and finance to prepare me for Wall Street." The skipper gave another shrug, and it was the gesture of a man who clearly understood human behavior. "For me, education was the key to unlock the door of freedom. *This* is freedom.

"Funny how things turn out, but life is full of surprises. You never know who or what you're going to encounter that will change your life forever." Kai breathed in again. "Salty air, blue skies and sunshine, trade winds, white sand and swaying palms, starry nights … relaxed island life. This is what I'm talkin' about. Every time I see a beautiful beach, the waves seem to whisper to me, 'If you choose the simple things and find joy in Nature's treasures, life and living need not be so hard.' Take it from me," he grinned, confirming his poetic spirit, "happiness comes in waves."

"I envy you," Thaddeus commented, now that they had set sail in the open arms of the sea. He looked to Maggie. "We plan a similar lifestyle one day, and before long, I hope."

In good time, she told herself, casting him her Mona Lisa smile as a strange and sudden expectancy suffused her.

The Sisters could readily see how neat, clean, and cared-for *Endless Summer* was. It was obvious this skipper took a deep pride in his vessel. A good sign for a good sailing experience, to be sure.

"Martinique offers idyllic sailing conditions," Kai was saying, reading the sky through his sunglasses. He readjusted the white captain's hat he was sporting. "Good day for it. We're going first to a place I know where you can swim with the dolphins if you like. Let me append that by saying that ninety-five percent of the time, we spot them. They like to showoff for boats, ships, all sorts of crafts. With a bit of luck, they'll make a good showing today, and if we're real lucky, we might even spot sea turtles.

"You can do some snorkeling if you choose. All the equipment you'll need is on board. Or you can simply relax and enjoy the wind and sea mist in your face, read a good book, or do a little fishing. It's totally up to you. A Créole lunch will be served at noon. My chef will supply you, throughout the day, with snacks, appetizers, and drinks. We've an open bar. Two heads ... bathrooms, and we have two staterooms for anyone who cares to take a nap.

"We'll be sailing all day, dropping anchor when we spot dolphins, again to snorkel at Grand Anse d'Arlet and Anse Dufour, where I'm optimistic we'll find the sea turtles.

"I'll drop the hook toward the end of our cruise at Joséphine's Bathtub, a shallow patch of sea nestled between two pristine islets– Îlet Oscar and Îlet Thierry. *La Belle Créole*, it is said, bathed there often. I strongly urge you to take a dip in the Empress' Bathtub. Its waters are cool and soothing, and they provide the unique sensation of standing safely atop a nice, soft sandy floor right in the middle of the briny deep.

"We'll put in, back at the marina, in time for sunset, a final drink, and parting *adieux*."

"Sounds great," Raine enthused.

Their talk was briefly interrupted when the First Mate, Bertrand, a somewhat laconic man with hair like a wire brush, appeared on deck with refreshments.

Later, Raine told Maggie, "I don't know if a dolphin feels more like slick, wet rubber or smooth like a peeled, hard-boiled egg. I just know how good I feel when I interact with them, but it's hard to do the experience justice with words. 'Jubilant' comes to mind and 'awed.' You know, of course, that numerous times, dolphins have sensed humans in peril and have come to their rescue, even saving swimmers from sharks. Ooooh, they can beat living hell outta sharks. Anyway, I loved talking with the dear, sweet creatures. They are ultra-intelligent, and this experience has made me even more *grateful* for my gift of animal communication."

"You must have asked for a lot of kisses," Maggie laughed, and her expression was reminiscent of the merry tinkling of wind chimes.

"Wasn't it a perfect day, Mags!"

The Goth gal was right. It was a perfect day in every way–until, that is, they returned to their hotel that evening.

***

Early that same morning, whilst the Sisters, Thaddeus and Beau were relishing the joys of sailing, Jeweler Pierre Laperle's body was discovered on the rocks below his chalet by some local fishermen, who in turn reported it to the authorities.

That evening, after showering and dressing for dinner, the Sisters' party entered their hotel's *la Sirène* dining room to encounter a visibly stressed Dorélia. Stepping quickly between the Sisters, she slipped an arm round each of their waists to whisper anxiously, "I must speak to you as soon as my shift ends tonight. Please, it's important. I finish at ten."

Raine shot Maggie a startled look with the thought, *She's really rattled, and she's been crying.* The Goth gal turned her head to see Jean-Jacques preparing to croon a song into the microphone. *I wonder if ...*

But her thought was halted, full stop, when the waitress pleaded with troubled eyes, "*Je vous en prie, mes amies.* Please. ***Please.***"

Maggie placed a comforting hand on their new-found friend's shoulder. "Are you all right?" When Dorélia gave a quick nod, the redheaded Sister said, "We'll meet you on the beach–"

"*Non!*" the *Martiniquaise* stopped her short. "I don't want anyone to see me talking with you."

"Come to Cabana Nine," Raine cut in to settle matters. "We'll parley there a few minutes past ten."

The rest of the evening unfolded without incident, the food, wine, and music ever pleasing, as the minutes ticked slowly away, and the Sisters waited for the hour when they would rendezvous with Dorélia.

About two hours later, excusing themselves from Thaddeus and Beau, whom they left on the terrace, sipping drinks and listening to Jean-Jacques' band, they met the distraught waitress.

Cached in the shadows near the entrance to their rooms, Dorélia was nervously smoking a cigarette. Flicking the butt into the sand, she snuffed it out with the toe of her shoe. "*Merci d'être venues.*"

Unlocking the door to Cabana Nine, Raine ushered her inside and switched on the light. "*Of course* we came," she answered in French. After glancing up and down the near-deserted beach, she closed and relocked the door. "Please sit down. I'll pour you a glass of wine." To Maggie, Raine tossed the thought: *Galloping gargoyles, the poor gal looks covered with sweat and confusion.*

Dorélia sank down in a chair and swabbed her forehead with a handkerchief she drew from the pocket of her waitress, orange madras skirt.

Raine poured the wine and handed the *Martiniquaise* the goblet. "Drink. It'll help you relax."

The woman appeared even shakier than she'd been earlier. Once she took a couple of sips of the red wine, Maggie urged, "Now take a deep breath and tell us what has happened to make you so distressed."

"*Mon Dieu*, I don't know where to begin." The waitress downed a long swallow of the Beaujolais.

"From the beginning," Raine said flatly. "Start from the very beginning. Speak slowly," the raven-haired Sister saw fit to add, knowing the woman's English, in her emotional state, would be heavily punctuated with French words and phrases, "and don't leave anything out."

Dorélia drew in her breath, expelling it with force. "First, I have a confession to make. This afternoon, before I left for work, I visited my sister-in-law. I used her computer to research you. I remembered you both said you were psychics, and how you help people all the time. I wanted to find information on the computer."

Her eyes shifted from one Sister to the other. "I know you unravel mysteries. I know you've solved crimes where you live in America. I need for you to do that here, for me."

The Sisters looked at her with an interested, surprised expression.

"There's been a crime?" Maggie questioned, neatly switching gears, "Sorry, you tell your story from the beginning, as we said, your way."

"I had another reason," Dorélia went on, "for going to my sister-in-law's house, but I don't want to get ahead of myself." She stole another swallow of wine. "A dear friend's body was found this morning on the rocks below his home. He's … *dead*," she sobbed, bringing Maggie to her feet from the edge of the bed, to draw a chair up alongside the waitress and comfort her.

"*Je suis désolée* … I'm sorry," Dorélia rasped. "This is *très difficile pour moi. Pauvre Pierre. Mon Dieu. Mon Dieu. Mon ami est mort! Dead … he's dead!*"

"We're so sorry about your friend. Try to relax, and take your time," Raine said. "We told the fellows to leave us alone with you. Take your time," she repeated. "We won't be disturbed."

"*Merci.* You are very kind." The island woman finished the wine, sucked in a fresh breath, blew it out, and picked up again.

"The fishermen who found my friend's body reported it to the police, who believe his death to be an accident. The railing on Pierre's balcony gave way, and he fell a great distance to the rocks below. His home is located atop a high cliff, outside Fort-de-France, in the direction of Schoelcher, off N2." She swiped at her eyes with the hankie she'd pulled from her skirt pocket. "*Mes amies*, Pierre's chalet was not an old house. He bought the land and had the chalet built only about four or five years ago. It is a well-built home. This was *not* an accident as the police are saying. I know of what I speak. Pierre was murdered!" Again, she began to sob.

"Dorélia, if you have information about a crime, then you must take that information to the police," Maggie cautioned. She picked up her chair, drew it forward, then sat to face the woman.

The *Martiniquaise*'s expression mirrored fear, and throughout her whole countenance there reigned a stony rigidity.

"Non, non! Je *ne peux pas faire çela!* I-I can**not** do that. I don't want my husband to know–" She stopped abruptly, covering her face with the handkerchief to vent her tears.

Maggie looked to Raine, then posed their unified thought. "Would you think it frightfully impertinent if we asked you some personal questions?"

Dorélia fidgeted a little, then appearing to take her courage in hand, she replied, "I'll do my best to answer." Moistening her lips, she reluctantly uttered the words, "What would you like to know?"

"What exactly was your relationship to the victim?" Maggie questioned kindly, enfolding the woman's hand between her own. "I think you know what I'm asking."

Dorélia bridled and, at first, made no response. *"Un ami.* A friend," she replied at long last in what sounded like an honest, heart-felt response. "He was my friend, *mon bon ami* ... a **good** friend. When Jean-Jacques and I were separated, Pierre and I became lovers, but after my husband agreed to– oh, *comment dit-on en anglais? Therapy* for his anger, Pierre and I ceased all *intimités* ... intimacies, but he remained ever my friend. I admit, I hid that from Jean-Jacques. I continued to see Pierre, *mais seulement ... only* as a friend. I could," she dabbed at her eyes, "talk to him with ease. *Pour moi,* he was a much-needed confidant."

Maggie, getting what she always referred to as a 'flash,' flicked the glimpse in Raine's direction. *Much of her life has been a cadence so measured, it's made her want to scream. The man she calls Pierre helped her silence the scream, so she could* **cope**.

"Pas un amoureux? So this Pierre was not your paramour?" Raine probed bluntly.

Dorélia shifted uneasily, and the muscles round her mouth twitched in tiny spasms. "He was no longer a lover. He was my friend," she answered with dignity, circumspect and refusing to say more.

"What was your friend's full name?" Raine asked, grabbing a pad and pencil from the desktop.

"Pierre Laperle. He is ... was an antique dealer and jeweler. His shop is on Rue Victor Hugo in Fort-de-France."

"Please," Raine prodded, "go on with your story."

"You told me to start at the beginning, *alors* that is what I am going to do. The other day when you were taking the tour at la Pagerie, and you saw me there," her voice bore inflection as though she were asking a question.

"Yes, we remember," the Sisters replied.

"The historian, Odette Auteur, was there too. *Vous vous souvenez?* Do you remember?"

"Yes," the Sisters answered tonelessly. "We do."

"Like me, she is a volunteer at la Pagerie. I've seen her there often. That day, she was digging, planting a flower bed," Dorélia stated.

"We remember," the Sisters reiterated.

Though that historian didn't seem to me the type to like to potter round with a trowel, Maggie pondered.

"*Bon. Alors et là,* I saw her do something that, at the time, I didn't think anything of, but later, I did think something of it. Something **significant**," Dorélia waffled, pausing to blow her nose into the well-used hankie, after which Raine handed her a fresh tissue from a box on the dresser.

"What did you see the historian do?" Raine spurred with a bit of impatience wavering on her voice.

"*Eh bien*, I was taking *une pause cigarette–*"

"A cigarette break," Raine interjected for Maggie's behalf.

Dorélia gave a brisk nod, then her words surged forth, stumbling and tripping over one another in her haste to get them out. "*C'est ça*, and I saw her pull a handkerchief from her pocket, drop it on the earth in front of her, then pick it up to stuff it back into her clothing. She did *not use* the handkerchief, only dropped it and picked it back up to *cache-le*, hide it away, in her pocket. You might say, '*Quel problème?* A handkerchief in the pocket?' *Mais*, it was the *way* she did it. She looked quickly … *cautiously* around to see if anyone was watching her."

I saw the historian do that too! Raine realized, but the Goth gal didn't want to think about that now. She would think on it later. Now, she wanted to remain focused on what Dorélia was sharing with them.

"*Comme j'ai dit*," the waitress was saying, "I never thought a thing about it until something else happened, *later*. Something in my friend's antique store.

"The following day," the waitress rattled on, "Odette Auteur came into Pierre's shop with a very old and valuable bracelet. I know, because I was in the backroom of the shop. A curtain separates *l'espace de travail* ... the work area from the showroom. *Vous comprenez?*"

"We understand," the Sisters replied.

"*Continuez*," Raine urged.

Dorélia related all that transpired when Odette made her initial visit to Laperle's place of business. Subsequently, she said, "Three days later, the historian returned for the bracelet. Pierre had it ready, and he informed her of its age and value. Again, I was in the backroom when she came in. There was another antique dealer back there too, a man who stops at the shop to buy and sell to Pierre when he's on Martinique. While he was there, Pierre asked his *évaluation* ... assessment of the bracelet. But more to the point, I heard *every* word that was spoken between my friend and Odette Auteur *both* times she visited the store.

"*En tout cas*, the day she came back for the bracelet, *Madame* Auteur sounded nervous, *notamment*, especially, after Pierre revealed its value to her."

Dorélia then recounted all that occurred during Odette Auteur's second visit to Laperle. "After Odette exited the shop with the bracelet, Pierre slipped back behind the curtain to say that he suspected something was wrong with her story. He thought there was something *méfiant* ... *suspicious* about the whole thing, and he wondered if he should contact the proper authorities.

"I remember that Odette looked especially worried– I was watching her from an opening in the curtain– when Pierre suggested she take the bracelet to la Pagerie, you know, since it was engraved with Joséphine's name," Dorélia pressed on; "and since Pierre and the other dealer both believed the bracelet to be *authentique*. *Oui*, Odette looked *inquiète* ... *tense*, and *that's* when she stopped the conversation and hurried with the bracelet out of the shop like le Diable himself was after her."

Dorélia's eyes widened at her next words. "I think she dug that bracelet out of the earth at la Pagerie the day she was digging in that flower bed. That's what I think." Her dark eyes moved from one Sister to the other in search of empathy and understanding.

"A minute after Odette exited Pierre's shop," the waitress again took up the story, "I *know* I heard the door open and someone come in. That was when Pierre was speaking the words about contacting the authorities. When we looked, no one was out there, but she could have cached herself behind a counter *peut-être*, because I *know* I heard someone come in. Pierre didn't hear the door because he was focused on his suspicion, but I did. *I heard it.*

"*Et alors qu'est-ce qui se passe?* And what happens next? The very eve of his suspicion, Pierre falls to his death from his balcony. *Coincidence?*" Dorélia gave the word its French pronunciation. "*Je crois que non.* I think *not.* As I started to tell you earlier. There were *two* reasons why I went to my sister-in-law's house this afternoon. The first was to research *you* on her computer. The second was to get a reading from her. She's a *Quimbois* woman, a very gifted one. *Comprenez Quimbois?*"

"Yes," the Sisters responded that they did understand what was meant by *Quimbois*.

"It comes from an African word that means *knowledge.*" Dorélia lowered her voice, "There are more *Quimbois* here on Martinique than most people would believe … and this I know.

"But I must tell you the rest of my story." The waitress seemed to draw breath to center herself. "The news about Pierre's death was on *la télévision*, and I just *had* to get out of the house. I had to tell someone, someone I could trust. My sister-in-law heard the news too. She looked into her crystal ball, and she told me, *sans équivoque*, that my friend's death was *not* an accident. '*Il a été assassiné.* He was murdered,' she said, her eyes wet and blazing. '*Murdered!*'"

Dorélia sucked in a huge sob, and this time, she did not attempt to stifle her tears. "There's more, *mes amies*. My sister-in-law said she saw a *woman* on the balcony with Pierre. A white woman with glossy, black hair."

The Sisters let their friend pour out her feelings.

"Odette Auteur took that bracelet from la Pagerie, and then she murdered my … Pierre to prevent him from reporting her to the police. I know it!"

The Sisters slanted one another a glance, then looked at Dorélia sharply and suspiciously. And it was the more loquacious Raine who spoke.

"You don't know that for certain. But you must go to the police with what you *do* know. There's a law against withholding evidence in a murder case. At least in the US there is, and I'd wager there is in French law too."

"You don't want to get yourself in a sticky spot of trouble," Maggie interjected with concern.

The waitress immediately became flustered. *"Non, non!* I cannot do that!" she shrieked obstinately. "I cannot speak of this to anyone else. *I won't!* That's why I confided in *you*. You must help me. *Please*," she implored in a quieter tone. "I want my friend to rest in peace." She brought the tissue to her face and wiped away a tear streaming down her cheek. "You are my only hope. I cannot talk to the police. *It's too risky!*"

"It's risky if you *don't* talk. Dorélia, *you* will *have* to take your suspicions to the authorities," Raine heaved a groan of exasperation, "but that doesn't mean we won't help you. Tell the police you are frightened for your own life. They will not reveal your identity."

The *Martiniquaise* uttered what sounded like a wail, her head dropping into her hands. "Oooh, what you must think of me," she whimpered, red-eyed and weeping.

"We think you'd better do as we suggested," Raine let slip with blunt expression.

Maggie coughed as a signal to the Goth gal to cool it, though she said, "Raine's right," after which the redheaded Sister's voice dipped even softer. "We'll help you, but you are going to have to trust us. I assure you that we shall endeavor to justify that trust."

She was picking up a lack of self-confidence in Dorélia that needed assurance and even comfort.

An extraordinary want of confidence, Raine thought, having snatched Maggie's *pensée*.

"Is your friend's home within the jurisdiction of the capital? Under the protection of the police stationed at Fort-de-France?" Maggie queried.

"*Oui*, his home is in an *environ* of Fort-de-France."

Raine said, "You are our friend, and we will very much try our best to help **and** protect you, but to do that, we need more information. Was your friend married or single? Was he seeing anyone at the time of his death? Did he have a lover at the time of his death?"

"Pierre was a ladies' man, as you Americans say. He loved women, but he respected them too. He *was* married … once. He divorced years ago and never remarried."

"Was there animosity, do you know? Between him and his ex-wife? Any children?" Raine demanded in French.

"*Non. Pas de mauvais sentiments.* No bad feelings. No children. Pierre's *ex-femme* remarried several years ago. He told me he was happy that she found someone more … *suitable* for her." Forgetting herself, the waitress carried on in French, "*Il est sorti avec plusieurs femmes, mais rien de sérieux. Pierre a apprécié sa liberté.*"

Raine translated for Maggie: "Pierre went out with lots of women, but he wasn't serious about anyone. He enjoyed his freedom."

The Sisters sent each other a look– and a weighty thought.

"Dorélia," Raine began, "you said Pierre had an eye for the ladies and relished their company." She fixed the waitress with her witchy stare. "How did it make *you* feel when he went out with other women?"

The pretty *Martiniquaise* looked uncomfortable, quite like a guilty child, and the empathic Sisters picked up that she had been possessive of her jeweler friend. *Most possessive.* She flushed a little, then seemed to rally her dignity and strength before murmuring rather incoherently, the blush fading in her café-au-lait skin to a pallor that rendered her almost pasty.

"We're stepping off the subject, *mes amies. Ecoutez*," she admonished, sitting up very straight and holding up a finger for regaining attention, "you are pursuing a misguided line of thought.

My sister-in-law told me Pierre was murdered, and she is *never* wrong about what she sees in the crystal ball," Dorélia concluded with conviction. She gave the Sisters a flickering glare from her dark eyes, then looked quickly away.

She was in love with the fella all right, Maggie directed to Raine.

*But was she **still** in love with him at the time of his death?* the raven-haired Sister pondered in her wily mind. *It's **romance** she craved ... craves.*

A look of dark malevolence rose to Dorélia's eyes, and she struck an attitude. "Who else could it have been but that woman, that *creature* Odette Auteur?!" she burst out aggressively, continuing her tirade in French. "She is a cold, selfish woman, and she has a way of annoying people, you know. I've heard her do it many times at la Pagerie, to anyone who makes a ... rash statement. She'll look at them and say, in that *precise* way of hers," and the waitress' voice took on a clipped, high-class tone, "'I'm afraid that is *not* borne out by facts. Most historians would agree–'" Dorélia broke off, finishing in English, "Or something like that. She is always scolding somebody about something or other to do with Joséphine."

"Did you ever have words with Odette Auteur? Angry words, a quarrel?" Raine heaved at the waitress.

"Not exactly a quarrel, but she, er ... *elle s'est mis en colère contre moi* ... became angry with me once for making what she fancied was a derogatory remark about Joséphine," Dorélia admitted. "She is not a *Martiniquaise* and therefore does not share ... understand *our* feelings. What Odette Auteur is, is *vexing*, what you Americans call a 'know-it-all,'" she declared with finality.

"If you are not a fan of the Empress Joséphine," Raine thought suddenly to ask, "why on earth do you volunteer your time at la Pagerie?"

Dorélia seemed for an instant to be taken aback. "There are those of us who harbor negative feelings against Joséphine, *oui*, but I ... I have *mixed* feelings about her. *Encore*, we are stepping away from the subject," her voice hardened and rose in volume as her emotions took hold, flaming her anger, "and the subject is Odette Auteur and what I told you about her. *She* is the one who murdered my friend. I need you to prove it, *mes chères sorcières*. Who else could have done it?!"

Raine nudged Maggie with her bare foot, and again the Sisters traded glances. "Who else?!" they echoed as one.

"Darlin', from all you've shared with us, in our estimation, there are other suspects." Maggie lowered her voice. "In addition to the historian, your *husband* is a prime person of interest. Then there's the other antique dealer who was present in Pierre's shop and who knows the value of the bracelet." The Sister refrained from mentioning that Dorélia, too, was a suspect.

"Jean-Jacques would not kill anyone," Dorélia avowed loyally. "He has a temper, *oui*, but he would not commit murder," she added unconvincingly with obvious doubt on her mien, as she twisted her hands nervously. They were lovely hands, with long, slender fingers and well-manicured nails lacquered with a pearly-pink polish.

"What about that other antique dealer?" Maggie posed. "Tell us everything you know about him, please."

"It wasn't him either." The waitress paused to reflect. "I remember him using his phone to do something. Then right after Odette left the shop with the bracelet, he said he had to dash for a flight to Rio." Dorélia wiped her nose. "He's Chinese. *Non, non,* I misspoke. Eurasian, I think. *Antoine Li*, that's his name. He and I exited the shop at the same time, by the backdoor.

"*Monsieur* Li was a guest here at the hotel. I'm certain he has checked out ... I *think* he has. He travels the world, buying and selling antiques. Pierre mentioned once that he respected the man's expertise. He said he never met anyone who knew more about antiques than Antoine Li." She thought for a moment, tussling with Time to bring something back from the recesses of memory. "Pierre said Li's work was *quelque peu* ... a little dangerous."

"Any particular reason he said that?" Maggie asked.

Dorélia gave a typical Gallic shrug with turned-up palms and extended lower lip. "I suppose because he deals in such valuable *objets d'art*." The *Martiniquaise* waited a protracted moment in thought. "I remember *Monsieur* Li talking about buying emeralds in Columbia." She completed the tale in French. "Because of their value internationally, Columbian emeralds spawn illicit trade. Dangerous smugglers poach the mines and waylay buyers leaving with stones. Often, bandits compete with one another for the same loot, most of which generate large profits on the black market. I heard *Monsieur* Li tell Pierre he came close to losing his life once to bandits, and I recall something else too. I heard him tell Pierre that he feared hired thugs following him with the intent of killing him for emeralds and other treasures he carried."

Raine translated the story for Maggie, after which she said, "Give us all the info you can about that antique dealer and the historian, Odette Auteur. We also need to know your husband's schedule for the whole of yesterday. He and his band didn't play at the hotel last night."

"I don't really *have* anything more to tell you," Dorélia replied.

The Sisters swapped looks, noting the signs of rising anxiety.

"Suppose you try," Raine pushed in snappy response.

The *Martiniquaise* closed her eyes to concentrate on the information the Sisters wanted. "I don't think I know anything more of *Monsieur* Li, except that he only visits Martinique about once a year. Odette Auteur is a known French historian and author. She has written several books. I believe she is *parisienne*." Her eyes narrowed for an instant, and again, her voice took on an edge. "Just because she is well-known doesn't mean she can't be guilty of theft and murder!"

The Sisters pressed on with further questions, but with no gainful result.

Maggie sent Raine a thought before the latter said, "Your jeweler friend was a successful businessman with an elite shop. Businessmen make enemies sometimes. Ofttimes without even realizing it, people whose ambitions they might frustrate, others who regard them as a threat or a menace."

"Is there anyone you suspect?" Maggie asked.

"I told you who did it!" the woman shrieked with passion, her anger venting itself on the Sisters, though she quickly got hold of her ire, their calm eyes juddering her to a halt, ashamed.

The waitress' embarrassed expression endured for several seconds, and her eyelids blinked in a discomfited manner. "*Pardonnez-moi*. I've told it all so clumsily. I'm afraid I've made a fool of myself," she stated quietly in French. "And it wouldn't be the first time I have acted the fool."

"Now, now," Maggie replied with tactful sound, "don't get yourself all muddled up. We're not trying to make things difficult for you. We're trying to help you."

"*Je comprends* ... I know." Dorélia nodded her thanks to Raine after the latter refilled the wineglass, which shook slightly when she raised it to her lips to take a drink. "As for Jean-Jacques, my husband worked late yesterday. He telephoned me to say he would not be home for dinner, that he was staying at the bank, after hours, to catch up on paperwork. He always has so much paperwork that it piles up at times."

Alarm suddenly peered from her dark eyes. She gave a small frightened gasp, and her hand shook even more as she set the goblet down on the mahogany-and-cane table next to her, adjusting herself in the chair, the routine act as though to regain control. In the tick of a clock, she became a picture of dogged resolution– if not for the eyes, which registered something between hesitation and fear.

Both Sisters read desperation in the depths of those eyes, masked almost completely by fierce determination.

Turning to Maggie, Raine tossed her sister of the moon the pithy thought, *I hope Monsieur Jean-Jacques Sauvage has someone to corroborate that alibi.*

Chapter Nine

An hour later, after Dorélia took her leave, the Sisters and their escorts were in Raine and Beau's room, brainstorming to connect the dots and piece together the full picture of the mystery that had fallen into their laps.

"Dorélia promised," Raine reminded, "to share her suspicions with the police in the morning."

"She promised, yes, but do you think she *will*?" Beau questioned.

"We do," the Sisters replied.

"After we convinced her what could happen, she became more afraid of withholding what could be valuable information, if indeed there has been a murder, than what Jean-Jacques might do," Maggie stated.

"And," Raine mused, "if there has been a murder, then there's a murderer at large ... or among us."

"I've been thinking of that historian," Beau said in reflection. "Thad and I encountered her in Fort-de-France when you girls were shopping. She pulled out like a bat outta hell onto that fancy boulevard. What's it called, Thad?"

"Rue Victor Hugo," he answered.

"Hey, that's the street where Pierre Laperle's antique shop is located," Raine blurted. "What happened?"

"Burned rubber from the curb like a mad woman. Looked to me like she was tailing someone. Thad and I were attempting to cross the street, and she nearly ran us down," Beau finished.

"Hmmm," Maggie pondered. "What time was that? Do you recall?"

"Remember, we were running a bit late. Ooooh, I guess a couple minutes after 5:00," Thaddeus answered. "When that incident happened, we were headed back to the *Marché* to rendezvous with you."

"Likely Laperle closed shop at 5:00," Raine commented. "Perhaps Odette Auteur was tailing him to his home. Based on what Dorélia's sister-in-law saw in her crystal ball, a woman who matches the historian's description was with the jeweler on his balcony."

Maggie lifted a hand to her forehead. "Wait! I just got a vision, though it was only a flash. A woman … there's a woman who harbors jealousy for Dorélia. It," she groped for more, "could be a friend or a relative. I think it might be, not sure. Jealousy? Y-y-yes," Maggie considered, "and this woman might feel *threatened* in some way by Dorélia."

"What does the woman look like?" Falling into one of her habits, Raine began pacing up and down the room in a fairly good imitation of a caged panther near feeding time. "Did you see her face?"

Maggie shook her red head. "No, sorry. It was, as I said, a mere flash."

"Could the woman be Odette?" Thaddeus questioned.

Maggie drew her full lips in a straight line. "I don't know. It could be, but then again, it could be someone else, someone we haven't met." She slowly nodded her head in pensive gesture. "One thing's clear. Dorélia is jealous of Odette."

"I wonder just how much that woman really knows about all this," Raine murmured to herself. This Sister, too, was lost in reflection. "I've an idea the woman knows something more of this business than appears."

"You lost me. Which woman?" Maggie questioned.

The pacing Raine responded with puckered brow, stopping dead in her tracks to snap her fingers. "*Witch* woman. W-I-T-C-H. Dorélia's relative, the *Quimbois* woman. I wonder if there might be something dark there. Could *she* possibly have a motive? Could someone have put her up to a trick or two perhaps?"

"Hmmmm," Maggie contemplated. "Motives can be fantastic, or they can be absurdly slight. I wonder if Dorélia might herself be a *Quimbois*? Even with my–" she stopped herself, for the Nirumbee crystal was something she shared only with her sisters of the moon. "*That* might be difficult to detect, depending on how good *she* might be at–"

"I don't follow," Thaddeus interjected. "What're you driving at? Do you think something else is at work here? Black magick?" But his query was left unexplored, when Beau put forth his thought.

"As far as I'm concerned," he began, "Dorélia's husband is a top suspect *if* a murder has been committed. Jean-Jacques could have found out his wife was still seeing Laperle. Even if they were no longer lovers, she admits she lied to her husband about staying in contact with the jeweler."

Something stirred in Raine's memory. "Yeah," she murmured, "it's only a murder of crows if there's probable caws."

"What are you talkin' about?" Beau asked, bemused.

"Something I thought of from a past case. What you said about Jean-Jacques ... I have a witchy feeling that would've been a real *blow* to his ego," Raine brooded as she flopped down into a chair.

"Right, and we've all seen instances of *Monsieur* J-J Sauvage's temper," Maggie put in.

"We asked Dorélia for a detailed description of the antique dealer, Antoine Li– who was in the backroom of Laperle's shop when Odette picked up what turned out to be a most valuable bracelet. And guess what? Her depiction matches the Chinese ... could be *Eurasian* man we've spotted several times in the vicinity of our hotel." Raine paused to catch her breath. "Fu Manchu mustache, pristine white suit and all."

"From what our waitress friend told us," Maggie declared, "Jeweler Laperle had a lot of respect for Antoine Li." The inquiring redhead noticed the ruminative expression on Raine's face. "I can almost hear the wheels in your wily head turning, Sister. What are you thinking? Give!"

"I was thinking of motive. If Laperle's death was not an accident, what motive would each of our suspects have for killing him?"

"I'd say Jean-Jacques would have the strongest motives," Beau stated with conviction. "Jealousy and revenge are the top two motives for murder, and he certainly had opportunity."

"Yes, but is he a murderer? Historian Odette Auteur and the Chinese antique dealer's motives would each be greed, another strong motivation for murder," Thaddeus proffered.

"But the historian's motive may be *more* than greed," Maggie ventured. "She, after all, is a noted expert on the Empress

Joséphine. If the bracelet, as Pierre believed, was once owned by Joséphine, what wouldn't Odette Auteur do to possess something of such historic significance? Something, in her estimation, to die ... er, *kill* for?"

Raine was of the same mind. "I told you, I too saw Auteur drop that hankie on the ground, pick it up, and stuff it into her pocket, after glancing round to see if anyone was watching." The Goth gal's legs were crossed, one over the other, and the slender foot that dangled shook with excess energy, an indication that her Crafty brain was racing. "Motives appear to be multiplying all around."

"You know," Maggie ventured, "some folks don't really need a cause to feel or do what they do. They're just made that way. A bad seed. No conscience whatsoever."

"Or maybe they're just unbalanced," Beau put forward.

"Could be. All I know is, you can't reason with evil." Raine bit her lower lip in thought. "I've been thinking of Dorélia's sister-in-law's crystal ball. We've work to do before we can consult ours, which, of course, we'll do when the time is right. Our ancient oracle isn't apt to share anything with us before we do *our* part. We must get an early start on the required legwork in the morning, right after breakfast."

"Hmmm," Maggie considered. "Just a few more clues ..."

"Our holiday here in Martinique will be over before we know it," Thaddeus said.

"Right," Maggie began, "we'll have to clear this all up quickly before we leave."

"I propose," the professor set forth, "to save time, we divide our research. How about you and Raine investigating Odette Auteur? Concurrently, Beau and I will dig up whatever we can on Jean-Jacques. You know what I'm saying, any past incidents of violence, criminal record, whatever. I doubt the bank where he's employed would want anyone working for them who has a criminal record. We can't very well go *there* to ask personal questions about one of their employees, which I'm certain they would not answer; but I have an idea how we can rummage around for info about Jean-Jacques. Beau and I can also have a go at ferreting out whatever we can on the elusive antique dealer, Antoine Li, as well."

"Raine and I should go back out to la Pagerie and talk to the curator there about Odette," Maggie decided. "We could speak with the librarian at the Schoelcher Library in Fort-de-France too. As an author and historian, Odette probably visits that library often."

"Since the police think Laperle's death was an accident, the place probably isn't roped off as a crime scene," Thaddeus mused aloud. He stroked his van dyke beard, a habit of his whilst mulling over something. "It's risky, going onto private property to scout about for clues in what just might be a murder case, especially in a foreign country, but it's a risk we've taken before. If we're agreed to do it, we'd better go there *first* thing after breakfast, before the police change their minds and decide to cordon it off. We'll be careful not to touch or disturb anything."

"Sounds good," Raine and Maggie concurred in concert.

Beau didn't look too sure. He started to say something, but stopped himself when Thaddeus seemed to give him a subtle nod of assurance.

"When we leave Laperle's place, we can go about our separate research, then meet up later to exchange information and brainstorm," Thaddeus finished.

"Our investigations should take us most of the day tomorrow, so why don't we just agree *now* to start out as a group at Laperle's chalet, then split up to use the rest of the day for our separate sleuthing. We'll keep in touch via our cell phones, and we'll meet back here at the hotel, at the *Coco*, to compare notes whilst we enjoy our sunset drinks," Raine evoked.

When everyone subscribed to the plan, she happened to think, "There's one more person of interest we don't want to skip in our investigation."

"Who?" Beau asked.

"Isn't it rather obvious?" Raine replied a mite sharper than she intended.

With one mind and voice then, the coterie echoed, "The Creeper!"

***

Immediately following an early breakfast, the Sisters, Thaddeus and Beau drove to Pierre Laperle's secluded home outside Fort-de-France. Dorélia told them where he lived the evening before, so they expected to have no trouble finding it.

Motoring along N2 in the rented Renault, in the direction of Schoelcher, Thaddeus, acting once again as their driver, commenced to review their plan for garnering clues. "Raine, it's you who should act as our all-important lookout."

"I'm usually the lookout, but I can't drive a stick," Maggie said needlessly, "so it has to be Raine. Plus, she's the one of us who speaks fluent French."

"Quite right. I think this is the best idea we can devise." Dr. Weatherby looked to the Goth gal. "You'll pretend that the car is stalled. I'll position it, and you can stand beside it with the hood up, where it will block anyone from driving up the hill to Laperle's chalet. Dorélia said it's a private road with only one way in and out. If someone comes, the police, *anyone*, wanting to go up that lane, you say, 'My car is stalled, and I've flooded the engine. Please be patient, I'll try and start it again in a couple minutes.' Then get back in the car, windows up, and with your cell, you warn us with the economy of two words, '*Get out!*' Stall, pun intended, for as long as you can, then start the car and drive down the road. After five or ten minutes, drive back to the same spot, and if the coast is clear, pull off the road into the jungle. Dorélia mentioned, in her description of the place, that there are several side roads bordered by thick foliage."

"Before I neglect to bring it up," Beau said with verve, "we tell no one we scouted Laperle's property. *No one*, including Dorélia and, if we talk to them later, the police. Especially the police."

"*Agreed*," the coterie replied.

"What exactly will we be looking for in that chalet?" Beau asked.

"Anything and everything that might suggest that Laperle was murdered," the professor answered. "Raine, are you sure you have your lock picks with you?"

"Always," she replied, patting her bag. "I keep a set in my purse and another in my car at home."

"Good," Thaddeus responded. "Let me have them, please. I know a thing or two about lock picks. Unless there's a deadbolt on Laperle's door, I should be able to open it."

Raine handed the professor the tool, after which he said, "Beau, if I can get us in, you check out the balcony; but mind you watch your footing. Maggie and I can split up inside the chalet."

When they arrived at the private lane to Laperle's clifftop home, Thaddeus pulled the car across the entrance, got out, and lifted the hood. "Raine, station yourself here, outside the car. I'll ring your cell when we get to the chalet. You know what to do if anyone wants to drive up this lane. I have every confidence in you," he jested. "I've seen your performances in our community theatre. Always thought you missed your calling."

"Oh, I'm a woman of many talents," she answered, taking up her position next to the Renault.

When Maggie, Thaddeus and Beau arrived at Laperle's chalet, the professor rang Raine, then using her lock picks, he easily opened the front door to allow them access. Not wasting a moment of time, Beau hastened to the balcony, Thaddeus to a land phone, where he used his handkerchief to reveal Laperle's messages.

Simultaneously, Maggie prowled all about the living-dining room area, whence she edged soundlessly through the door to the kitchen, poking through drawers and cabinets, taking note of the items on the counter– the cut lime, a knife and spoon, cane syrup, an opened bottle of rum, and a bowl of water that she assumed had held ice. *The makings for ti punch*, she told herself.

Finding not a single clue within Laperle's phone messages, Thaddeus moved to a desk, where he again used his handkerchief to search nook and cranny, shuffling through various papers and files.

Meanwhile, Beau was having better luck. Taking out his cell, he proceeded to capture a few pictures, careful not to touch or disturb anything.

Back inside, he relocked the glass door with his handkerchief. "Thad, you ready?" he called, bringing the professor out of the master bedroom, where he and Maggie had been gingerly going through dressers and closets.

"Nothing we can connect to a murder," Thaddeus reported with disappointment on his voice.

"Let's get out of here," Beau advised. "I believe I found what we're after, and I don't fancy ending our tropical vacation on Devil's Island. I'll fill you in when we get to the car."

"The railing's screw holes are virtually clean," Beau revealed once they were back inside the Renault. "If the railing gave way from weathering or *broke away* from the weight of Laperle's body, there would be telltale signs of that. There's no damage … no breakage, splintering or abrasion to speak of. The threads are clean in the holes. I'd wager someone *unscrewed* the bolts that held that railing. There's no other explanation."

"Why didn't the police discover that, I wonder?" Maggie challenged.

"Well, the logical answer is they found the railing below, on the rocks near the body, and when they reconnoitered Laperle's house, they saw there was no break-in, no signs of a struggle, no blood, nothing to indicate foul play," Thaddeus reasoned. "In fact, contrary to Dorélia's sister-in-law's crystal ball, I found no evidence that anyone was with Laperle when he died. To me, it looked as though he was alone in the house. Likely, the police thought the same thing. That's why they ruled the death a tragic accident."

"I didn't see a used glass from the *ti punch* that Laperle either fixed or *was* fixing for himself. If he was holding a glass of punch, it went off the balcony with him. I didn't see a glass on display anywhere, not in the kitchen or out on the balcony, so your opinion that he was alone, could be correct, notwithstanding Dorélia's sister-in-law's vision in the crystal ball. However, I've another question," Maggie wondered. "If the bolts were unscrewed, wouldn't the railing have fallen off– right *then*, when the murderer tampered with them?"

"There were two huge bolts on each side of the railing, holding it on. I'm thinking the killer might've unscrewed one on each side completely, and left the other two *nearly* unscrewed, perhaps all but an eighth of an inch or something. Then all Laperle would've had to do was lean against the rail … hell, rest an arm on it to be a goner," Beau reasoned.

Raine grew pink and nodded vehemently. "Wiz–zard, Beau! Wizard!"

Discussion followed, with everyone congratulating Beau on a job well-done.

"*Mes amis*, we're no longer at a point where we've seen no evil, heard no evil, and aren't speakin' any evil," Raine stated with certitude. "We know now that a murder has been committed."

"We know too," Maggie said at one point in the energetic discussion that followed, "that to plot and carry out a murder, the killer– and we've seen this time and again– must possess a large dose of conceit, in addition to motive. I can't help thinking back on all the crimes we've solved over the years. Murderers are a conceited lot."

"Yep," Raine felt compelled to agree. "We've had a good deal of experience on the seamy side of human nature, and I daresay, you are spot-on with that observation, Sister."

"I agree," Thaddeus cut in, "**when** the murder is plotted and schemed. However, lest we neglect to reason that the jeweler's death could well be a crime of passion." The professor went on to explain, in careful and somewhat elaborate detail, what he meant.

"Not to worry," Maggie replied in turn. "We aren't likely to rule passion out of the mix."

"Guess we'll be visiting the Fort-de-France police station after all, but I say we should collect more evidence before we do that," Raine said.

"Raine's right," Thaddeus concurred. "If we're going to the police with evidence, let's make it as thorough as we can. We don't want a 'It's-all-theory-and-conjecture' reaction; that's for sure. We must be sensible about this."

"True," Raine acknowledged. "France is the most bureaucratic nation in the world. The French drown themselves in a sea of paperwork. Trust me; it's a national characteristic."

"We can intimate to the police that they check the railing's bolt holes when we present them with whatever additional clues we uncover," Beau advised.

"That's precisely what we'll do," Raine responded, kissing him on the cheek.

"What was that for?" he asked.

"Do I need a reason?" came the crisp reply. She blew in his ear, whispering something only he could hear.

"We're coming into Fort-de-France," Thaddeus announced. "How about we park at the Savane? There's street parking there, you remember. That way, the car will be half-way between the library, where Raine and Maggie can dig up what they can about Historian Odette Auteur, and Rue Victor Hugo, where Beau and I can uncover all we can about the victim, Pierre Laperle, as well as the Chinese antique dealer, Antoine Li. Not a long tramp for anyone then."

When everyone agreed, the four sleuths started off on their various quests, but not before Maggie charged, "Let us each keep an open mind."

With which Raine enhanced, "Good hunting, and let's cover as much ground as we can."

"Doesn't look like your average Caribbean edifice, does it?" Maggie remarked, when they reached Schoelcher Library. The pair stood on Rue de la Liberté, staring at the magnificent structure, an elegant, multicolored basilica crowned with an eye-catching, byzantine glass dome.

"That's because it isn't," Raine replied. "The entire library was built in France for the *l'Exposition Universelle*, the World's Fair held in Paris in 1889, then shipped, piece by piece, to Martinique as a monument to Victor Schoelcher, the French abolitionist writer from the early nineteenth century. It was he who drafted the decree that abolished slavery in the French colonies. By the bye, the Eiffel Tower was built for the same World's Fair to commemorate the centennial of the French Revolution and show off France's industrial prowess. C'mon," she caught Maggie's arm, pulling her toward the extraordinary library. "Let's go inside. I can't wait to show you how grand it all is."

They took in the striking portrait of Victor Schoelcher in the atrium and gazed in awe at the glorious glass dome.

After making a sweeping tour of the interior, marveling at the enormous collection of books, the Sisters started forth, to approach the desk.

"Wait," Maggie whispered, grasping Raine's arm. "I've just gotten one of my flash visions. I saw Odette here in this library, in what looked like a reading or reference room. Problem is I don't know if it was past, present, or future." She closed her eyes for a meditative moment. "I think, that is I *sense*, it just happened or is happening as we speak."

Raine considered what Maggie said. "Remember, Dorélia said Laperle mentioned to Odette that he felt research would produce provenance for the bracelet. I betcha when he said that he was telling her, in a subtle way, that *he* intended to do further research, but as a historian, research is *her* middle name. Uh huh, I'd wager—" the Goth gal cut off, saying instead, "Follow my lead." She quickly steered Maggie toward the reception desk.

"*Bonjour*," she greeted, her French pronunciation suddenly and surprisingly bad. "Do you speak English?"

"I do," the librarian answered. "May I help you with something?"

"We were supposed to meet Author-Historian Odette Auteur here today. Has she arrived; do you know?"

"You just missed her," the older woman answered. "She left about twenty minutes ago."

"Oh dear," Raine sighed audibly. "I don't speak fluent French, and it seems my high-school French has failed us," she commented, looking to Maggie. "We'll have to make our apologies." She turned back to the desk. "You see," she spoke to the librarian, "we are working with the historian on a joint project. I read French so much better than I speak it," she fabricated. "Tell me, if you can, was she doing research while she was here?"

"She was, yes." With a wordless smile, the woman handed a bookmarked volume to a gentleman at the desk.

"We will be rendezvousing with Odette this evening for dinner," Raine murmured as if to herself. "Would you be able to bring us the same book or books she was using, so that, when we catch up with her later, we're on the same page, so to speak? That would expedite matters for all concerned."

The librarian smiled again, this time at the Sisters. "I would be happy to do that. Why don't you go into the reference room, just there," she indicated, "and I'll pull the book for you. You can't take it out, but you're welcome to stay as long as we're open today to study it."

"Thank you," Raine and Maggie echoed.

As soon as the librarian set the thick tome down on the Sisters' table and exited the room, Raine noted the title on the faded blue cover, whispering to Maggie. "The first volume of the published memoirs of Joséphine's daughter, Queen Hortense," she indicated.

Maggie stretched a hand toward the book, when Raine stopped her.

"Books tend to open to the place where they were last opened." She stood the volume upright, allowing it to fall open into her waiting hands. "*Voilà!*"

"Look," Maggie breathed, pointing to the dates, 1788-1790, "it opened right to the period when Joséphine made her one trip back home to Martinique."

The Sisters moved their chairs close together so Raine could read the targeted pages, then translate their content to Maggie. After several minutes of quiet reading, Raine sat back with a cat-who-ate-the-canary expression on her kitten face. "We were right, you and I, when we figured Joséphine might have lost the bracelet when she ran for her life, the hectic night of the slave uprising."

"Hmmm, though I see no actual mention of the word *bracelet*, and my memory's dust on that score. It's several years since I read this book." Her eyes scanned the page. "Hortense relates that, due to the unexpected and sudden manner that she and her mother fled Martinique, they hadn't time to bid proper farewell to their dear ones that frantic, stormy night. Nor did they have time to pack their bags, grabbing only a couple of things which Joséphine hastily wrapped in a shawl."

"Oh my Goddess!" the raven-haired Sister exclaimed a few moments later, nearly forgetting to hold her voice to a whisper. She reread the passage that seized her attention. Then, with her smart phone, she quickly captured photos of two of the pages from the gripping volume. Some minutes after, Maggie returned the book to the reception desk.

When the pair exited the library, Raine poked her sister of the moon. "Mags, I can't believe Historian Auteur doesn't own *The Memoirs of Queen Hortense*. It's available in print."

"While you were looking around, I mentioned that very thing to the librarian. Seems Odette has a collectible, first-edition set that she stores in a protective box. When she wants to read those memoirs, she goes to the library. I suppose the historian's townhouse doesn't afford much storage."

***

Meanwhile, Thaddeus and Beau were making the rounds of the posh antique shops along Rue Victor Hugo.

When the pair entered *Du Temps Perdu,* they asked to speak to someone who spoke English, preferably the owner. In a moment, the proprietor appeared, a well-dressed, middle-aged man with greying dark hair and a close-clipped mustache.

"*Bonjour.* I am the owner, Monsieur Genoud, and I speak English. Is there something I can help you with, *Messieurs*?"

"We are here with our wives on holiday," Thaddeus began, "and we'd like to purchase something quite nice, for each, to remember our very pleasing sojourn here on Martinique. Our hotel manager was kind enough to suggest your shop, along with a few others. Accordingly, at this point, we're browsing." He stroked his beard. "Another guest at the hotel mentioned an antique dealer by name of Antoine Li. Do you, perchance, know of him? We were told he has impeccable taste for exquisite collectibles, and we were wondering if you ever purchased anything from him, something perhaps you might show us."

Monsieur Genoud thought for only a moment before responding. "I know *Monsieur* Li. He is an international antique dealer who stops here once in a while, but I'm afraid he has not been in for over a year. I have nothing from him at the moment. Of course, I have many fine items I'd be happy to show you."

Gazing about, Beau answered, "We'll most certainly look around. We want to visit each of the places recommended to us before we make our purchases. You understand."

The proprietor bowed his head slightly, answering, "Very good, *monsieur.*"

"In case we ever do connect with Antoine Li in person, or in the event we'd come across any of his *objets d'art*," Thaddeus beseeched, "would you say he's a dealer of good reputation? We wouldn't want to deal with anyone who wasn't."

Monsieur Genoud pressed his lips together in thought. "I really don't know much about Li except, as I already told you, he buys and sells worldwide. From what he has said, he travels constantly. If you're asking if I ever heard anything negative about him, the answer is *no*, I have not. By all indication, he's a respectable business man."

"Thank you," Thaddeus replied. "It's difficult to choose a reputable firm when one is a foreigner. We can only go by word of mouth. I trust I haven't offended in some way."

"*Non, certainement non.* I quite understand," Genoud answered, again with a genteel bow of his greying head.

"We aim to visit all the shops recommended to us," Thaddeus began anew, "but the first one we tried was closed. *L'Objet Qui Parle*, just across the way," he gestured toward the large display window, to the shop across the street. "Do you think it will be open tomorrow?"

Monsieur Genoud shook his head sadly. "I think not. The owner has died."

"Really?" Beau feigned revelation. "Well, I guess the hotel manager didn't know that. The death must be recent."

"*Oui*, a terrible shock," Genoud returned with a bob of his head. "We were all taken by surprise."

Thaddeus posed the begging question. "What happened?"

"*Monsieur* Laperle, the owner of *L'Objet Qui Parle*, met with a fatal accident," the shop owner answered with gloom on his voice.

"Sounds sinister," Beau commented, playing his role to perfection and astonishing himself. "I trust there wasn't foul play."

"*Mon Dieu*, nothing like that," Genoud replied. "Everyone liked and respected Pierre Laperle. I doubt he had an enemy in the world. He'll be sorely missed."

Unbeknownst to the Sisters' party, who, like today, were out and about afternoons, and even to Bakoua waitress Dorélia, whose shift was confined to evening, Historian Odette Auteur had a habit of taking lunch at l'Hôtel Bakoua's informal terrace café. What *Odette* didn't know was that she was being stalked by an unseen predator who was keeping close tabs on her.

Shielded as it was from view by potted palms, Odette's preferred corner table was cozy and private. Since she often brought notes with her on her current book, she habitually asked for this table, so she could have the privacy she craved. Today, however, she was not alone.

A shadow figure was skulking through the reception area to the adjacent terrace café, only to peer at the historian through the huge potted ferns and palms. The stalker did not long dawdle, for he did not wish to be observed by hotel staff and patrons. After only a few moments, the sinister character slunk off, melting into a group of garish tourists, who had drifted in from the garden path to the hotel's terrace.

Beau and the professor visited two more shops, both with nearly the same results. Finally, they made their way back to the Renault, parked on the Savane, where the Sisters were waiting for them under the tall palms.

Once everyone piled into the rental, Thaddeus put forth a plan. "How about we have a piece of that fruit you brought for us, Raine, for our lunch break, then I propose we drive back to Trois-Îlets. You ladies can drop Beau and me at the Village Créole. I believe I've thought of a way to harvest some info about Jean-Jacques. Then you can motor out to la Pagerie and talk to the curator about Odette Auteur. The Village is right next to our hotel. Once we wrap our investigation, Beau and I can easily hoof it back to our rooms to clean up in time for our sunset rendezvous with you ladies at the *Coco*."

"Sounds good," Maggie agreed.

"Have you a plan for pulling info about the historian from la Pagerie's curator?" Beau queried Maggie and Raine. He bit off a piece of the banana the latter had handed him.

"We always have a plan," Raine answered.

At la Pagerie, the Sleuth Sisters felt lucky to chance-meet the curator, Jeanne Gardien, on the lawn in front of the museum.

"Ah, my American friends, how fine to see you again!" she greeted in French. "La Pagerie has drawn you back with its enduring magick I see."

"*Oui, c'est ça!*" Raine responded in the affirmative. "We hoped we might have a few moments of your time, if you're not swamped. I apologize that we don't have an appointment."

"*Mais oui.* Of course," Jeanne answered with sincerity. "What can I do for you today?"

"We were wondering if you could tell us a bit about the author and historian, Odette Auteur," Maggie stated. "We didn't have a chance to speak with her the other day, and we thought it might be nice to arrange a meeting before we leave Martinique. However, we don't know if she would be open to that. What do you think?"

"Oh, I think if your proposal would be to talk about Empress Joséphine, she would absolutely love to chat with you. I thought she was coming out here today, but she phoned to say her colitis is acting up, so she isn't coming."

"Colitis. I hope it's not serious," Maggie said.

"Odette told me once that it could be, but she keeps it under control." *Madame* the Curator's face took on a wistful expression. "I never met anyone who is more engrossed in the subject of Joséphine than Historian Auteur, and she defends the empress every chance she gets. *Vehemently.* I'll share with you a secret. Many times, I've watched Odette speculatively when she's here. *Ça alors*, she's in a world of her own *à la Pagerie. C'est vrai.* You know something? If I believed in reincarnation, I would be quite certain Odette was Joséphine in another life."

Could be, Raine told herself and Maggie, *but more likely, she's a wannabe.*

"So what's your plan for finding info on Jean-Jacques?" Beau put to Thaddeus as they headed for one of the Village Créole's café-bars.

"Musicians have favorite haunts. They tend to hang out together in cool places for gigs, such as that café," he pointed, "where we were the other day. I remember seeing a few guys with horn cases, sitting together and having a drink. I figure we can talk to a few of them and see what we can glean about Dorélia's musician husband. Whatd'ya think? There's something to be said for gossip."

"You mean where there's smoke, there's fire?" Beau queried.

"In a way," Thaddeus rambled musingly, "though ours is not a political agenda. Ours is a *hidden* agenda."

"I don't follow," Beau said, confused.

"Supposedly," the professor began, "once upon a time, when politicians wanted to know what their constituents were thinking, they'd send surrogates into taverns to eavesdrop, along with the directive, '***Go sip*** some ale.'"

Beau's teeth flashed in a roguish grin. Slapping Thaddeus on the back, he chuckled quietly as the pair entered the pub's cool, semi-dark interior.

Straightaway, Thaddeus approached the bar. The barkeep was a brawny fellow of mixed race with a huge, rather strange ring on his right hand, whom the professor heard speaking English to another customer. "Excuse me, do you per chance know a musician by name of Jean-Jacques Sauvage?"

"Jean-Jacques?" He continued polishing the glass he was holding. "Sure. He comes in here once in a while, in what I call one of his flying visits. Why are you asking?" His tone wasn't unfriendly, but the message therein was somewhat daunting, or it would have been for someone with less pluck than the professor. Beau could almost feel the active wheels turning in Thaddeus' resourceful mind.

"We're interested in getting a few good musicians together to cut an album of authentic Caribbean music." The professor paused as if in thought. "Feel-good sounds from a spectrum of island genres. Something as diverse as the Caribbean itself– reggae, salsa, calypso, pop-calypso, beguine, zouk, perhaps even a bit of kumina. You know what I'm talkin'– soul sounds, *groove*, a resonant mix that we expect will sell in the States. We heard Sauvage is good, but he might be hard to work with," he concluded in a low tone. "We've heard things, and we can't afford to take a gamble on someone who will waste our time and money."

The beefy bartender ran a hand over his close-cropped dark head, the gesture indicative of his unwillingness to proffer his opinion. "I never worked with J-J, but," he pointed, "those two over there have. They used to be in Jean-Jacques' band. They're brothers. They could answer your question better than I could."

"Thanks," Thaddeus said, jerking his head, for Beau's sake, toward the two men sitting in a corner. He ordered drinks for Beau and himself, as well as refills for the brothers, asking that the barkeep bring them over.

At the siblings' table, Thaddeus opened with the same lure he used with the bartender.

The brothers, both tall and slender with chiseled features, stared at the two Americans, exchanged looks, and for a weighty moment, Thaddeus thought they might not wish to say anything about one of their own.

"John Charles," the older of the two spoke flatly in the English of the neighboring island of St. Lucia, extending a hand, which Thaddeus firmly grasped. "This is my brother, Archie."

The latter offered his hand. Thaddeus obliged, then introduced Beau as his associate, who, in turn, shook hands with the Charles brothers.

"We played in Jean-Jacques' Trade Winds for about a year, then we left him to form our own group, Island Vibes," John stated. A waiter brought the drinks to the table, after which the brothers raised their glasses, "Cheers."

"I promise that whatever you tell us will *stay* between us," Thaddeus said. "I just don't want to waste time or money on a hothead."

"When we played with Trade Winds, it was Jean-Jacques' way or no way. There was no room for creative freedom for us, but the real problem was his temper. It's *legendary*," Archie said with a curt nod of his head. He glanced over at his brother, who, for the moment anyway, was keeping his own counsel.

Another musician approached the table, where he took a seat to join his friends, setting his horn case on an empty chair. "*Waa gwaan?*" he greeted with the Jamaican *Patois* for "What's going on?"

Archie leaned close to the newcomer. "Talkin' 'bout Jean-Jacques Sauvage." He let that suffice as an answer.

"One bad dude," the Jamaican laughed, showing very white, perfect teeth. His eyes were hidden behind a pair of sunglasses.

The brothers introduced Thaddeus and Beau, then enlightened their friend, whose name was Leroy Clarke, on what the Americans were seeking. Clarke was a strapping fellow, muscular, with mocha-brown skin, a shaved head, gold hoop earring, and a ready smile.

"Did you ever work with Sauvage?" Beau asked straight up.

Leroy laughed again. "I don't know, mon, if I'd put it quite that way." He removed his shades and set them on the table. He had nice eyes. Honest. "J-J hired me just after Christmas, a couple of years ago, and by Carnival ... *Mardi Gras*, I was history."

"Would you mind telling us what happened?" Beau queried, taking a sip of his beer. He motioned for the waiter, who took Leroy's order for a Jamaican breeze.

"I don't mind. It was a hostile environment, mon. But, to be fair, he was goin' through some t'ings at the time with his marriage. His wife left him, and when J-J found out she was steppin' out with a new mon," he shook his head, using his blown-out breath and large hands to mimic an explosion, "he went *ballistic*. His head's nuh good when it comes to his wife," Leroy chortled. "Used t' think maybe she put Guzumba ... Obeah on 'im, but nuh, nuh spell. Badmind, mon– *jealous*."

The teeth flashed a wolfish grin, "Did you ever see his wife?" Before Thaddeus or Beau could answer, he made a low sound of admiration, continuing, "*Ouch*. She sends a fiery tingle to my blood. Once when we was jammin', I asked her t' dance, and J-J went off like a rocket. I backed away, wid m' hands in the air, tellin' him t' breathe easy, to level, but ..." Leroy's thought trailed off with another shake of his head. "Real love kan be dangerous, mon," he said with a sort of half chuckle. "A girl kan be your best fren 'r your worst enemy. All depend how y' treat 'er. Yeah," he muttered under his breath, "yeah," as though remembering something else, for his eyes went split-second sad.

"The breakin' point for me," Leroy went on after a moment, "was when I was late for a gig. J-J always insisted we show up early, so technically, I wasn't late. I had to take my wife to hospital.

She cut her hand. There was a lot of blood, and she was afraid. I didn't ring him. I just showed up, 'bout fifteen or twenty minutes past da time he told us t' be there. J-J didn't give me a chance to explain. He just went off on me like a time-bomb. I picked up my horn, walked out, and so di ting set– *that was that*."

"Old sins cast long shadows," Archie declared with a half-smirk.

Thaddeus spoke in a questioning tone. "Long shadows?"

A hard block of silence followed with the musicians trading what looked to be conspiratorial glances.

"What exactly do you mean by that?" the professor queried in a more precise tenor.

"Nothin' much," came Archie's terse response, his eyes dropping to the toes of his shoes.

"Uh-huh," Thaddeus huffed, sensing a door had closed and locked. He set his *ti punch* down on the table. "Essentially, you guys are telling me the rumors about Sauvage are true."

Ignoring the question, Archie opted to say, "J-J's got a big talent, though he's never taken it far. Maybe doesn't t'ink big. Me," he poked his brother in jest, "I like livin' soft and talkin' big," he concluded with a laugh.

"Jean-Jacques Sauvage is one of the most versatile, *superlative* musicians I've ever heard," John remarked finally and unexpectedly in a quiet voice, as he leaned companionably across the table, his eyes scanning the bar cautiously. "On the other hand, there's a But, and it's a big-up But. He's a *reckless* sort of fellow, always has been." John screwed up his face, adding, "Ah, he's young, and young men like t' feel their power."

"Let me loud up di ting, mon," Leroy interposed, "so you kan see it, and dis ain't no su-su. J-J's a perfectionist. Blows a righteous horn, big-up wicked, but he's his own worst enemy. Di ting 'bout J-J is, and I'm givin' it to you in Jamaican *Patois*, which will sum it up best– *nuh romp wid 'im, mon*. Don't mess with him! Don't vex 'im. Whatcha heard 'bout his temper is odds-on true. It. Kan. Be. Lethal, mon. *Lethal*."

Several minutes later, when Beau and Thaddeus were walking back to l'Hôtel Bakoua, the latter began deliberating over something that nipped into his head. Pausing suddenly on the sandy path, he pulled out his cell phone. "Hold up, there's one more thing we need to do."

Chapter Ten

"We still don't know if Antoine Li left Martinique for Rio," Thaddeus was saying to the Sisters and Beau as the coterie sipped sunset drinks at the *Coco*. "I tried to get the airline to divulge if Li was on that flight from Martinique to Rio, but they would not tell me. Because of security reasons, I didn't expect they would," he took a quick swallow of his *ti punch*. "Airlines have a variety of things to worry about today. However, at dinner, I'm going to ask Dorélia if she ever heard Li mention a Rio hotel. People who travel frequently, as we've been told Li does, usually have favorite hotels. I'll use the same ruse as I did with the airlines, that I have a time-sensitive business deal to convey to Li and need to reach him ASAP."

Since the sun had set, only a few people were in the *Coco*, but the Sisters and their escorts were being careful to hold their voices to undertones.

"Now that we've compared notes and discussed our findings, do you think we have enough to take to the police?" Beau asked no one in particular.

"Let's tie up a few loose ends," Raine advised, looking to Maggie, who nodded her red head in agreement. "I would say a trip into Fort-de-France would then be in order."

"No argument," Thaddeus put in with a nod, with Beau following suit.

Maggie traced the rim of her frosted glass with one beautifully manicured finger. "The passage we saw in that volume in the library is the provenance that proves, along with Jeweler Laperle's appraisal and the inscription on the inner band, that the bracelet in Historian Auteur's possession did, indeed, belong to the Empress Joséphine," she mused aloud.

Raine bobbed her head. "It's certainly another strong clue that it did. Though there was no mention of the word *bracelet*, the memoire did reveal that Joséphine lost something of value the night she and her little girl Hortense– who later became stepdaughter of Napoléon, Queen of Holland, and mother of Napoléon III– ran for their lives.

"Hortense's chronicle also related that Joséphine wrote her mother a telling communication after they returned to France, citing the lost item in the letter and apologizing for not bidding a proper farewell. In her memoirs, I think Hortense refrained from using the word *bracelet* to protect it from falling into greedy hands.

"Great Merlin's beard!" Raine exclaimed out of the blue. "If Joséphine's engagement ring sold at auction for over a million, what would that bracelet go for? With my own eyes, I saw Historian Auteur drop that handkerchief on the ground, then pick it up and stuff it into her pocket, after glancing slyly about to see if anyone was watching. Dorélia saw her do it too. Think about the sequence of events here. Odette Auteur learns what she did about the Joséphine bracelet from Laperle, then likely overhears him say he was thinking of reporting her to the authorities, thenceforth he plunges to his death from his balcony, a balcony on which the railing appears to have been tampered with."

Beau raised an ebony brow. "To echo our waitress friend, 'Coincidence? I think not.'"

The professor gave the Goth gal a sidelong glance with his bright blue eyes, but neither of them offered a comment.

"Things sure are lookin' bad for Odette Auteur," Beau remarked. He took a pull of his drink.

"Yet ..." Thaddeus stroked his beard, letting his thought drift away, though his reasoning was not lost– on the Sisters, anyway.

"Things are *looking* bad for Odette," chimed Raine and Maggie in harmony.

"But as Granny would caution, things are not always what they seem." Raine shook her dark head, remembering. "There's more than we know lurking behind the scenes."

"You don't think Odette killed Laperle?" Beau asked. "Is that what you're saying?"

"That's what I'm saying," Raine answered, trading looks with Maggie. "And that's why we have got to glean more information, real evidence, before we go to the police."

Nearly an hour later, the Sisters' party entered the candle glow of the hotel's la Sirène restaurant. No sooner were they settled in their chairs when Dorélia approached their table with the Bakoua's ribboned menus.

"Any news?" Raine whispered into the waitress' ear, when Dorélia bent to hand her a bill of fare.

The waitress shook her madras-wrapped head. "*Non, mon amie*, apparently the police still believe Pierre's death was an accident." She sent the Sisters a pleading regard. "*Et vous?* Have you found anything?"

The Sisters swapped the thought– *Careful*.

"We're checking into several things," Raine replied truthfully.

"Be patient," Maggie assured. "Our granny used to say that three things cannot be hidden– the sun, the moon, and the truth. The truth will prevail. It always does."

"Speaking of checking into things," Thaddeus began, "did Antoine Li ever mention a hotel in Rio, a preferred place he liked to stay?"

Dorélia thought for a long moment, before her face lit up with a recollection. "*Oui, je me souviens*. I remember one hotel he mentioned. The Copacabana Palace."

The professor stood, taking out his cell. "Be right back," he said. Swiftly then, he exited the area for the beach, where he placed a furtive call.

Within fifteen minutes, Dr. Weatherby returned to the table to relate in low tones to the coterie, "I asked to be connected to Antoine Li's room, and the desk clerk told me he checked out. When I queried if he left a forwarding address, I was told he had not. However, the person to whom I spoke mentioned that he might have flown to Bogotá. He was sure he heard him say 'Bogotá' while talking on the phone to someone. And he thought that someone may have been an airline's agent."

Later, over their langouste and avocado salads, the Sisters had another whispered exchange with their waitress. After describing the Creeper, they asked if she knew his name or anything about him.

"*Non*, but I know who you mean. I think he checked out. I haven't seen him in here for two or three evenings." She thought for a moment, and the Sisters could sense that the *Martiniquaise* was conjuring an image of the Creeper in her mind's eye. "I don't know his name or anything about that man, *mes amis*. All I know is, I wouldn't want to meet him in a backstreet on a dark night." After what appeared to be a worrying pause, the woman added in whispered French, "You must not waste time trying to prove someone else guilty. It was Odette Auteur who murdered my friend Pierre."

Meanwhile, at the hotel's reception area, the historian's name was on someone else's lips.

A well-dressed, silver-haired gentleman, with a goatee and thick, round, rimless spectacles approached the desk. Utilizing a fancy silver-tipped cane, he walked with a slight limp to address the concierge. "Good-evening," he said with pronounced British accent. "My name is Professor Prentis Hancock. I am wondering if you would afford me a great boon, my good man?"

The clerk gave a nod, responding in French-laced English. "It is my pleasure to serve, *monsieur*. What can we do for you?"

"Jolly good. I have heard that Historian Odette Auteur takes lunch here on nearly a daily basis. It is her habit between noon and 1:00, 1:30. Would you be so kind as to page her tomorrow, at ah … 12:20? Would that be feasible?"

"*Oui, monsieur.* However, may I suggest, she always sits," he pointed, "at that table semi-screened by those palms. You could introduce yourself, and–"

"*No*, I could not," the professor cut him short in a somewhat haughty manner. "That is simply not done whence I hail, what! I much prefer that you page her. I need only to speak with the author for a few moments, after which she'll be free to return to her lunch. I dare not request that the page be later for fear of missing her."

The concierge nodded again. "*Bien sûr.* Of course." He picked up a pen and wrote it down in French. Page for Odette Auteur to come to *la réception*, 12:20, with the next day's date. "It will be done, *monsieur*."

"Aye. Please do not forget, my man, eh? It is of the *utmost* importance. I have a book collaboration to propose to Historian

Auteur, but I am only on Martinique for the day tomorrow. I must put forward my proposal along with my contact information. I shan't take much of her time, five minutes tops."

"It will be done, *monsieur*," the concierge repeated with aplomb. "*Soyez assuré.* Be assured."

"Good man," the professor answered in his British intonation. "I might be browsing, perusing books in one of the hotel shops here in the lobby. But I'll be in the area, and I will hear the page and come straightaway to the desk."

"*Très bien, monsieur.*"

"Capital! Pip-pip, and cheery bye then."

With that, the imposing Englishman reinforced his limp with dignity, via his cane, to the main door where he exited the hotel.

***

"If only life could always feel like this," Raine sighed, snuggling against Beau's chest, "warm, balmy, and relaxed." She pointed her toes and stretched luxuriously under the cool sheet. Through the open windows, the tropical trade winds wafted to the room the aphrodisiacal scent of jasmine.

He kissed the top of her head. "You'd be bored out of your mind, Raine Storm."

One thing was certain. She always felt comfortable in Beau's arms. They were a perfect fit, and more and more, she was considering his proposal for a handfasting. He gazed at her face, the full, pouty lips turned up in a contended little-cat smile, the fair cheeks stained pink from lovemaking, the tousled, pixie-cut black hair, and the glittering green eyes that enchanted.

"I love you, Raine," he whispered. "More than you know."

Snuggling closer, she brushed the wispy bangs from her eye to peer up at him through the fringe of ebony lashes.

He stroked her flushed cheek. "What are you thinking?"

"I was thinking how comfortable this air mattress is. Hard and firm," she breathed in her throaty voice, sliding a bejeweled hand along his bare chest, the nails glossy black. "We've certainly christened this bed. Haven't we, big boy?"

"Every night," he whispered, tracing her full lower lip with a finger.

"Blessed be," she breathed. "That was very, very exhilarating, but this time, we'll go nice and slow."

"Whatever you like." As his hands glided over the curves of her body, he was remembering what she looked like when he unzipped her dress earlier, standing before him naked except for the black thong. "You have a kiss-me mouth." He pressed his lips against hers, kissing her deeply and basking in the sound of her desire. "If I may borrow from the Bard, you have witchcraft in your lips," he murmured. His mouth traveled upward. "And in these cat eyes."

She slid her hand over his shoulders and down his upper arms, reveling in his masculine appeal. A pleasurable shiver coursed through her, conjuring the familiar feeling of excitement and anticipation that brought back years of memories.

Beau's soul kisses never failed to make her squirm. Presently, he reached for her Serenity Now! Serenity Now!! oil on the nightstand before he flipped her onto her stomach.

With sensual caresses, he began with the back of her neck, rubbing the relaxing oil into the skin, into her shoulders and back, where he slowly worked his way down the spine. His fingers unhinged each vertebra gently from the others to produce a sensation of incredible relaxation. Over the rib cage. Over her thighs, legs, and feet, easing the muscles and tendons to dispel any defying tension.

Provocatively, he avoided the areas he knew would tantalize her into begging him for more. "That's good, little witch. Relax … re–lax. We've all the time in the world. I promise you'll feel good when I'm finished with you."

By this time, Raine was getting a bit drowsy with well-being. The aroma therapy of the oil combined with the sorcery worked by Beau's hands were rendering her deliciously cozy and calm.

He continued his massage, kneading the calves of her legs, working back up to the thighs, before his large, capable hands moved to the round globes of her derrière, palpating the cheeks to unclench any residual muscular tension in them.

She sighed.

"Yeah, baby, that's it. Free your mind, and let your body decide what it wants. It is my pleasure to serve," he teased, echoing the hotel staff in tantalizing velvety timbre.

"C'mon, sexy kitten, purrrrrr for me. Go–od. How does that feel?" he asked, his voice as soothing as a lullaby, his hands generating heat and– *magick*.

"Mmmmmm."

"Close your eyes," he crooned. "Re–lax. I'm going to take really good care of you."

"Witch it over me," the Goth gal crooned. "Mmmmmm, yes. Ye–es, you're a wizard." She sighed again. How pleasurable it was to have all the tension and tiredness released in such sensual style. "That feels sooooo good. Don't stop."

"I have no intention of stopping. Leave it all to me, my little witch. You need only relax and let your hot little body feel the love." He carried on, kneading his fingers into the yielding flesh. "There's magick in these hands. But you know that, don't you?" He poured oil into his palms. "I want to concentrate the Serenity into the back of your neck and the soles of your feet for the most relaxing results."

All she could do was continue to purr her response in the hypnotic trance he was casting upon her.

"Oooooooh," she whispered coyly, when minutes later, he "accidently" brushed a hand between her legs. "I can't help it. You're turning me on, Dr. Goodwin." She drew breath deeply and waited, with a rapidly beating heart, for what was to follow.

Beau gave a low wicked laugh. "*Très bon.* That's the express purpose of this session, *mademoiselle*– to relax you enough to let your body have its way. It's quite health-giving, you know. My goal is to set your wildest fantasies free, so we can enjoy a wonderland of erotic adventure … *together*."

"Mmmmmmm," she exhaled, "you know better than anyone, I'm a *very* adventurous girl."

"Indeed," he agreed. "You are."

"Turn over now, Raine. Do you mind?" he enticed some time later.

"Not at all, Doctor, I want the full treatment," she replied in her husky voice.

"And you shall have it," he said in an almost gruff manner, reaching a hand under her to roll her over, unto her back, and trap her beneath him.

Despite all their years of intimacy, she felt utterly wanton as she lay gazing up at him with a half-smile, while he tipped more of the fabulous oil into his palms. Then she closed her eyes, letting Beau slide his hands along her sides and down her firm thighs and shapely legs.

The Serenity oil, along with her lover's mystic massage, was increasingly sending a warm, relaxing sensation through her body. She moaned again when he spread the oil over her breasts, working it in slow, circular motion. Delightful flutters erupted in her stomach, as her relaxed breathing became faster and more pronounced. Presently, his fingers sank into her belly, stirring her internal organs excitedly.

"Let's take it up a notch," he rasped. He knew just what to do, and his oiled finger tips continued to do it like a virtuoso.

"Oooooooh, Beau," she breathed, her fair cheeks infused with heat. "You're so good. Mmmmmm, I needed this."

"I always know what you need. Relax, Raine, take it slow. Take all the pleasure your body and I can give. What I'm going to do to you, you're going to love. I promise."

"Then do it," she whispered. "Oooooooooooooh, yes ... ye—es ... yes ... YES!"

Through half-closed eyes, she gave him a sultry smile. "Dr. Goodwin," she purred, "I'm afraid what you're giving me is addictive."

Straddling her, he answered, "You're absolutely right, baby." His deep voice was like a caress. "It *is* addictive, so you'll have to keep coming back for more."

She clung to him without answering. The moment was beyond mere words. It was two bodies, one shared soul. And it was– *magick*.

The witchcraft that swirled in the shadowy room was of a very ancient kind, and it wrapped the lovers in the most powerful of spells.

Maggie and Thaddeus, meanwhile, were reaping the benefits from a lazy, moonlight walk on the hotel's private beach. It was, as is so often in the tropics, *glorious*, the trade winds cooling after the intense heat of the day. Fireflies floating like miniature lamps in the sultry night, the purling surf, the tropic-night sonata of the tree frogs and crickets, their symphony accompanying the day's descent into darkness– it was all so soothing. In the cloudless night sky, the waxing moon rode high in the dark indigo of the heavens, and the delicious scent of the small, white blossom of the Antilles, half tuberose, half gardenia, permeated the balmy air.

"The aroma of flowers is everywhere on Martinique," Maggie inhaled, as the professor took her hand to press it to his lips. Her tissue-thin caftan fluttered in the breath of warm wind, and her dark red hair blew softly back from her face.

"Sweet, the heady scent of flowers and rum," Dr. Weatherby pronounced wistfully. "It tends to wrap itself around a person like a gauzy cloak, a cloak woven of spun sugar."

They ambled along, close to the water, for several minutes without speaking, savoring the silence and serenity of the Martinique night.

After some time, Thaddeus said, "So the plan is to go to the buffet breakfast in the morning, then walk over to the Village Créole to pay a surprise visit to Historian Odette Auteur."

"Right," Maggie replied. "Did you have any difficulty finding her address?"

"No. When you told me the curator at la Pagerie mentioned that the author lives in the Village, it was a piece of cake to light on her address."

Maggie took a moment to reason. "A pop-in visit is the best idea. If we rang her ahead to ask if we might pay her a visit, that would give her an out, and our time here on Martinique is fast slipping away. Raine and I need to meet Odette in person to put our empath skills to work. *It won't take us long to glean what we need.*"

She danced her fingers over the jewelry at her throat– the ancient talismans, hers and Aisling's, bequeathed by Granny, along with the two sacred items she'd gained during her recent trip to Montana, their secrets shared only with her sisters of the moon. *Won't take long at all to glean what we need from Odette, especially since I've got the Nirumbee crystal with me,* she thought. *There's no better flim-flam detector. Cuts through deceit like nothing else.*

Aloud Maggie said, "It's lucky Raine speaks French as well as she does."

"And that she's always had a penchant for Empress Joséphine," Thaddeus agreed. *"Voilà* the perfect *raison d'être* for our visit." He began tickling her palm and the underside of her wrist.

"Raine is planning on opening discussion with the mixed feelings the *Martiniquais* have exhibited about Joséphine. What I'm getting at," the redheaded Sister went on, "is the slavery issue and the beheaded statue. Raine has always believed that History has not treated Joséphine fairly. Well, not completely, at any rate."

"That should win us points with the historian," Thaddeus stated. "Yes, let's get her talking about the two-year period when Joséphine made her visit home to Martinique, the perfect preamble to bring up Queen Hortense's memoirs. That, in turn, will open the door for mention of the loss of a valuable item the night mother and daughter had to run for their lives during the uprising."

"Voilà the plan," Maggie answered. "Raine can handle that part of it. All she need do is ramble on, as she's prone to do. We'll sit back and glean what we can from Odette's feelings and reactions." *And that's when I'll put my special crystal to work,* she told herself.

"If," Maggie talked on, "we discover Odette is not home when we call, we can kill time doing tourist things at the Village, then try again a bit later. Whatever it takes, we *must* talk with Odette Auteur tomorrow. As I said, it won't take Raine and I any time at all to size her up. I might even get a vision whilst we're there."

A sudden thought struck Thaddeus, and he said, "I was thinking how *passionately determined* Dorélia is that Odette is Pierre Laperle's murderer. I wonder if our waitress is–"

"What?" Maggie interposed, "a woman scorned? You're wondering if *she* could have killed Pierre? Was Dorélia lying when she said she and Laperle were no longer lovers? Hmmm, while forbidden fruit is said to taste sweeter, it usually spoils faster. You know what I'm saying. Hot fires burn out the fastest. Was Dorélia jealous over–"

"But assuredly you and Raine would've picked up clues with your empath radar," he amended.

Maggie made a little sound in her throat. "Normally, yes, but you recall there *was* one case when the killer was so adept at veiling emotion that we nearly missed feeling out the real person hidden beneath a beautiful veneer. However, Raine and I both picked up that our waitress friend was overly possessive of her jeweler paramour. Thus far though, neither of us believe she's a murderer."

Surely the Nirumbee crystal would've alerted me if Dorélia were not on the up-and-up, the Sister told herself. *On the other hand, I do suspect she is keeping something from us.* "It's my educated guess the woman is harboring a secret," Maggie said aloud. "Needless to say, I *hope* Dorélia is not the guilty party."

"I hope we glean something substantial, so we can take it to the police. There's that word again. But *hope*," Thaddeus mumbled, "is a prayer, not a strategy. Right now, all we have is circumstantial evidence. What?" he questioned. "Raine and Dorélia saw Odette drop a handkerchief on the ground, then put it back in her pocket. Dorélia's Voodoo sister-in-law saw Odette at Jeweler Laperle's chalet in her crystal ball. And we broke into the murdered man's home to spy. No, we can hardly present the Martinique police with *that*."

"Not to worry, darlin'," Maggie responded rather swiftly. "After Raine and I observe and interact with Odette in person, we'll have done enough legwork to consult our own crystal ball. And by then, our ancient oracle will show us precisely what we need to know at that point of time in our investigation."

"Yes, then we can talk to the police," the professor stated. "At any rate, I think we've done a good night's work."

She put her arm out to stop him in his tracks. Stepping close to run her fingers through his hair, she kissed him deeply. "Not yet we haven't."

"Your body is made for love, Maggie," Thaddeus whispered later that night. A dim light burned, casting their room in silvery shadows, whilst the sound of the surf soothed.

A low laugh rolled from her throat. "I think your assessment is *witchily* correct, professor. I can never get enough."

"We'll have to remedy that then, won't we?" he murmured, adjusting himself next to her on the rumpled bed. "I must amend something you said earlier. Hot fires can burn out quickly, unless," he reached for her, "they are stoked. Stirred often and stoked."

"You really know how to handle me," she breathed between kisses, and she was like hot, flowing amber in his arms.

He played with her a long time, as a musician plays a fine instrument. Certainly, the symphony he was creating was one of great talent and passion, with crescendo after crescendo, whilst he reveled in each moan, each breathy whisper and gasp of bliss.

"Oooh, that was heavenly," she exclaimed in near exhaustion, and she couldn't help but think of that line delivered by their skipper. "Happiness comes in waves."

"I have never known a woman who enjoys sensualities as much as you do, my Maggie." He kissed her ear. "You truly are a sorceress."

"And you are a maestro," she sighed, stretching in the feline manner that was her habit. "A wizard maestro. Witches believe that passion is natural and good. With us, it's not a guilt-laden subject."

"Nor should it be," he replied, kissing her full lips. "It's the most natural thing in the world. Let me pour you a glass of champagne to revive you." Standing, he did so, handing her a flute of the French wine, after which he poured some for himself.

Watching him, Maggie smiled her Mona Lisa smile as she sipped the bubbly and a new excitement tingled within her. "You used the word *revive*. Would you care to explain? It sounds as if you are planning to recommence our, shall I say, *gratification*."

The professor cleared his throat. "Well, my dear, it is such a rewarding pursuit that I thought we might. But, of course, I defer to your wishes."

"Uh-humm," she gave her low laugh. "Dr. Weatherby, I can answer your suggestion without deliberation." Again the mysterious countenance that was hers alone. "I *want and welcome* that pursuit over and o'er until I collapse– utterly satisfied." Setting her empty glass on the bedside stand and stretching in her graceful feline way, she fixed him with her McDonough eyes whilst he drank what was left of his champagne. "I love you partly because you can do that to me." Her words were like a purling stream of warm honey.

He arched a brow, and his bright blue eyes flashed. "Why else do you love me?"

She considered his query. "I love how you witch over me." She made a soft little sound. "You do, you know."

He eyed her meditatively, saying nothing. She was such a glorious creature, with the voluptuous body of a goddess, with her hair of dark fire, tip-tilted eyes of glittering emerald, the luscious mouth, and her skin of flawless cream.

"What?" she questioned his stare, then smiled in an almost deprecating fashion. "Do I torment you, darlin'?"

"You do, in a way." His gaze rekindled, and his voice deepened. "But I will settle the score for it."

Her eyes widened slightly. "Oh, and how will you do that, pray tell?"

"I will play with you in such a way that you will beg me to finish you off, and then, *then*, I plan to continue your torment until you scream for mercy."

"How medieval," she said with sexy intonation. "I believe that was a sort of challenge, my darling, and one I shall be most happy to accept."

Hence, things progressed. As usual, she reacted quickly to his stimulus. Within moments, her long, crimson nails were clawing the bedcovers, as wave after wave of pleasure washed over her.

"Oh, darlin', darlin', you just keep getting better and better. Better all the time," she whispered.

He answered her with familiar words. "This is only the beginning. Before the night is over, you will beg me to stop."

Maggie's insatiable desires posed no problem for Dr. Weatherby, PhD, a man who engaged in a lifetime of research and preparation. Intense study was so much a part of his life, that lovemaking was no exception to the rule, beginning with the Kama Sutra and ending with the sacred sex magick of the Craft.

"On second thought," he said, tracing a wet finger over her lower lip, "you won't know whether to beg me for more, or beg me to stop."

Within a minute or so, she was writhing, breathless and adrift in her witch's world of ecstasy. "Ooooooooh, professor. Oooooooh, you know just what to do. How *extraordinary* you are," she declared in sincere honesty.

"You know, don't you," she stopped to draw an uneven breath, "that the French call the big O *le petit mort*, the 'little death.' 'Tis the idea that *the* moment doesn't just trigger a physical release," she gulped a mouthful of air, "but a deeply spiritual one. Ah, but now you'll think me fanciful."

"*Bewitching*," he said simply, after which he began kissing her face, lips, cheeks, eyes, until she stretched her arms to pull him into a soul-reaching kiss that aroused her o'er again. "And, yes, fanciful."

The woman was a force of nature.

"Shall I renew my ministrations, my dear?"

"*Please*," she urged, her breath coming in short expectant gasps. "I *beseech* you to continue, professor. I need your ... very special nurturing more than you know."

"Oh," he gave a half-smile, thinking that her touch felt red-hot, "I do know, because I know you, inside and out. And how can I resist so enchanting a plea?"

He set about the task before him, and it wasn't long before Maggie was trembling in his arms, as he stroked her hair, and she surrendered to the intimate demands of her body. Things proceeded thus for another hour, when a panting Maggie gasped for breath and cried out, "Oooooooooh, professor, you'll kill me off!"

"There, there, ever so slowly," his mellow voice hummed, soothing and sensual.

"Darlin', I think now, to continue the magick, I am going to need your wand."

She trembled again in anticipation, as he drew her on top of him. "Too much of a good thing can be wonderful." Her lips curved in a seductive grin. "But I am really looking forward to *this*."

"Good, let me feed that fire." A pleased expression spread over his face. "Now then ... how are you feeling, my darling?"

"Mmmmmm," she purred. "Mmmmmmmmmmm, hmmmmmmm. Darlin', you are a wizard. Mmmmmmmmmmm. Oooooooooooh, yes ... yes ... YES!

"A wizard who wields a wand of magnificent beauty and *power*."

"Just like the moon,
your greatest magick will come in times of darkness,
when you have no choice but to trust your own power."
~ Grantie Merry McDonough

Chapter Eleven

The following day turned out to be eventful for the Sisters and their loves. After attending the hotel's buffet breakfast, the foursome walked to the neighboring Village Créole, where Historian Odette Auteur resided. However, when they arrived at her door, they discovered that the author was not home.

"We'll come back later," Raine huffed, disappointment edging her voice. "She's bound to be home sometime today. In the interim, we'll amuse ourselves in the Village shops and such."

Odette Auteur left her cottage townhouse an hour earlier. She had errands to run, after which her plan, per her habit, was to take lunch at l'Hôtel Bakoua's terrace café.

Around noon, the historian ordered a crab salad with a glass of white wine. When lunch arrived at her table, she picked up her fork and had just dipped it into the food when a heavy-set *Martiniquaise*, passing by, did a double take.

"*Mon Dieu!* Aren't you the author, Odette Auteur?" she exclaimed in French.

The middle-aged woman wore a golden-yellow, loose-fitting cotton dress that made her look round and jolly as a harvest moon. A madras head-wrap, tied in distinct Martinique fashion with two knots, covered her hair, save for a few dark curls that framed the moon-shaped face. Large gold hoops adorned the ears, and a huge straw purse was slung over one shoulder.

"I can't believe it," she continued, *à la* Kathleen Turner, her distinctive gritty voice prompting Odette to deem the woman a heavy smoker. "I've lived on Martinique all my life. I heard you lived here too, but this is the first time I am seeing you. *Sacre bleu,* please forgive *mon audace,* but when I caught sight of you, I couldn't help but speak. You are my favorite author." Her *café-au-lait* complexion appeared to take on a slight blush, as she brought her hands together in a sort of pleading gesture.

Odette gaped, saying nothing, for the excited woman, without pause, prattled on, whilst she began rummaging in the straw carryall. "I have one of your books in my bag. Would you mind signing it for me? It would mean so much. *Je vous prie.*"

"*Certainement,*" the author replied, continuing to carry on the conversation in French, "I would be happy to do that for you." Though she was taken aback, Odette couldn't help but be flattered by the woman's overt exhilaration over the chance encounter.

"I know the book is in here," the *Martiniquaise* said in an apologetic tone, frantically searching through the jumble in her bag. "Oh," she suddenly remembered her manners, laying a hand over her generous bosom, "forgive me," she uttered, directing the conversation into a social channel. "My name's Marie Duval. I live close by. Every so often, I treat myself to lunch here at the Bakoua. Sometimes, I even come here to enjoy *un spectacle.* I especially like the hotel's *Danses de Martinique* program, which, *au fait,* is tonight. I plan to attend. Where *is* that book?" she grumbled. "I know it's in here."

It was then a hotel bellboy, strolling through the terrace café, began paging, "*Madame Odette Auteur, à la réception, s'il vous plaît. Madame Odette Auteur est recherchée à la réception!*" The uniformed young man announced the page thrice, before heading back to the lobby.

The historian sat up straighter in her chair. "Now, *who* could be paging me at the reception desk?"

"Don't mind me," *Madame* Duval replied. "It might be important. I'll make sure the waitress doesn't run off with your salad. You can sign the book when you come back, then I'll leave you to finish your lunch."

"Thank you," Odette answered, rising from her chair. She scooped up her notes, stuffed them into her bag, and started off, in the direction of the adjacent reception area.

Madame Duval could not resist peeking through the potted foliage to see what was happening at the desk. Then she resumed her task, her searching fingers finding the item she was seeking in the muddled depths of the outsized straw satchel.

"Has your friend finished her salad?" the waitress asked, coming up behind and startling her.

"No, she has not," the *Martiniquaise* responded with a faint gesture of annoyance. "Could you bring me a glass of sauvignon blanc, please?"

"*Bien sûr, madame.*"

When Odette walked back to the table, she found Marie Duval sipping a glass of wine and leafing through one of the historical romance novels from *The Empress Series*.

Looking up from the book, Madame Duval took note of the expression on the author's face. "I trust it wasn't bad tidings."

"*No* tidings," Odette replied. "The person who had me paged didn't show up at the desk to meet me." She sat at her place, set her purse down and leaned back in the chair with an audible sigh. "I didn't recognize the name. *Le plus perplexe, ça.*"

Madame Duval shrugged. "Perhaps whoever it was got delayed or detained. If it's important, the person will surely try and connect with you again. I found the book," she smiled, holding it up. Rather than handing it to Odette to sign, however, she re-opened it to continue her perusal, in obvious attempt to draw out her time with the author.

"Such compelling stories, *The Empress Series!*" Marie enthused. "Do you think you'll be adding more books to the succession of Joséphine tales? I'm looking forward to more. I read … *savored* each and every one. At risk of sounding melodramatic, I'm totally *wretched* when each book ends." She took a sip of her wine, scrutinizing the historian over the glass. "I hope you don't mind," she said, raising the goblet a tad, "but I didn't know how long you'd be, and I wanted to make sure the waitress didn't make off with your salad."

Seeing through the fan's ruse for extending their *tête-à-tête*, the flattered author returned the smile. "Thank you." She picked up her fork, feeling unexpectedly magnanimous. "While I finish my lunch, why don't you tell me why you like *The Empress Series* as much as you do? I very much value reader feedback."

Marie's expression mirrored her delight. "I like so many things about your writings." She raised a finger, asking for a moment. "Allow me to organize my thoughts." The devotee took another sip of wine, saying in a trice, "When I start reading one of your novels, I can't *stop* turning the pages till I've completed the read. It's quite easy to get caught up in the immediacy of the events. I can envision everything clearly in my imagination." She tilted her turbaned head in deliberation. "I always feel as though I am *there*, in each scene, witnessing, and not just reading about what's happening. And I must say, you have a captivating way of presenting your characters as real flesh-and-blood people, and not just names on the pages of the books. Your historic figures come across *vividly*, and as a result, I feel like I know them, know them better than I do living, breathing people around me today. After all," she gave a slight giggle, "I'm not privileged to read other people's mail or diaries as I can the private papers of historic figures in your books. And another thing– I appreciate the research you do for the historic milieus of the tales. It's quite evident you do *beaucoup de recherches*."

The reader's words were gratifying, and as she ate, Odette nodded and smiled and interjected an occasional remark, thinking Marie Duval would make a great character for her next book. After several minutes, with fork hovering over her near-empty salad plate, the author said, "*Merci, madame.* It's readers like *you* who make all the research, the writing, *re*-writing, the fine-tuning and polishing, and all the endless hours of proofing worthwhile. I'm grateful for your patronage, as well as your feedback."

Madame Duval looked exceedingly pleased, and the corners of her mouth turned up in a broad beam. "When I noticed you, I saw you were working, so I apologize for interrupting both your lunch and your work. But I just *had* to speak to you. I hope you'll forgive me."

"It's quite all right. I needed a break." She thrust her folk into her salad to finish eating.

"There's something else too, *Madame* Auteur. I've absorbed a lot of history, reading your novels," Marie divulged. "Truly. The historic backdrops in your books have allowed me to understand our past, which, in turn, has afforded me a better understanding of the present. Your writing lets me– How can I express it?– climb right into history and be *moved* by what happened. What's more, so many of your settings have given me insight into less familiar cultures, hereby increasing cross-cultural awareness and … yes, yes, even open-mindedness." Marie Duval sat back to take a long sip of her wine.

"*Bon. Très bon!*" the historian grinned, thinking that the woman was much more intelligent than her provincial looks bespoke. "You mentioned historic research." She reached for the pepper to sprinkle on the remaining shreds of salad. "I think people tend to believe what they see in print, so I feel a duty to give my readers accurate milieus. Of course, I have taken a bit of dramatic license, here and there, for the sake of art in my fiction works, but not much, and not too often. And then only with circumstances or incidents that could well have happened."

When the historian had extended a hand for the pepper, the sleeve of her gauzy tunic rose to reveal the Joséphine bracelet. Odette had taken to wearing it when she went out, figuring that her wrist was the safest place for it. Nights, she hid the treasure at the bottom of a tea box, caching it on and under the pillowed mound of teabags.

"Tell me, Marie, which book of *The Empress Series* was your favorite?" Odette took the final bite of her lunch, dabbed delicately at the corners of her mouth with her napkin, and sat back to finish her wine.

"Oooooh, I loved them all. Each and every one," Madame Duval answered without wavering. "I don't think I could choose a favorite." Marie thought for a moment before asking, "Have *you* a favorite, *madame,* as the author?"

Odette laughed. "*Mais non*, indeed I do not. I pour my heart and soul into every book I write, and each is special to me. My books are my children."

"I can tell." Marie slid the book she was holding toward the author. "*Please.* I will be most grateful."

"*Avec plaisir.*" Odette signed the book and handed it back to the ardent fan. "Your kind words regarding my work have deeply touched me, *madame*. In fact," she gave a lighthearted little laugh, "they have made my day. I needed a lift. Thank you."

When the waitress stopped by the table to take the dessert order, the *Martiniquaise* stood, reaching out to pat the author's hand, which was resting on the table. "*Madame* Auteur, our little *tête-à-tête* has indeed been an honor and a privilege, one I shall remember fondly for the rest of my life. I wish I could express myself better, but I haven't your gift for words," she said very much *la grande dame*. "You've been very kind to allow me to intrude upon your lunch, but I shan't interrupt your dessert too. Rather, I'll bid you *adieu* and take my leave. Please go on writing, and you can be certain, I shall continue reading."

"I will do that," Odette said with a slight nod of her dark head. "*Adieu, madame.*"

No sooner did Marie Duval vacate the seat across from Odette, when the stalker, who was spying on the historian the previous day, skulked across the terrace café to watch her again. He gingerly peered through the foliage, then slunk back to sit in the dimly lit bar, where he could observe without being noticed.

A short time later, Odette returned home to her cottage townhouse at Village Créole. Once inside, she sank shakily down into a chair with a grimace of intense pain. "Damn this colitis." *This is the worst attack I've ever had.* "AH!" she gasped. *I must've brought it on with my worries over the bracelet.*

The agony was becoming insufferable, and she forced herself to rise and go to the bathroom cupboard for her medication, praying that would assuage her misery. With shaking hands, she poured herself a glass of water and swallowed two pills, groaning loudly when another severe pain ripped through her gut, nearly sending her to the floor. She clutched her stomach in torment. It felt as though someone was tearing through her lower abdomen with a razor-sharp knife.

The doorbell sounded.

Who the hell could that be? she wondered, remembering the mysterious futile page at the hotel reception. *I hope it's not a visitor. I can't deal with that now.*

Dragging herself to the door, she pulled it open, her face white with pain. "*Je suis désolée.* I'm sorry, I'm not feeling well. What do you want?" she asked more bluntly than she normally would have spoken to a caller.

The uninvited guest pushed his way inside and locked the door behind him, to stand menacing before the pain-ridden Odette with a strange, baleful light in his eyes. "*This,*" he slammed the historian down on the couch and quickly removed the bracelet from her wrist, slipping it into his pocket, "is what I want."

"*Non, non, pas ça,*" Odette choked in a sob. "Please don't. *C'est à moi!* It's mine. It's *mine.* It's always been mine. You can't," she whimpered. "*Please.* You don't understand. You can't take that from me! *Non, non, pas ça!*" She stood and tried to move forward but collapsed onto the tile floor, as her tormentor loomed over her with an evil sneer.

Without a word, the fiend went quickly into the bathroom. Using his handkerchief, he lifted the colitis medication from the shelf, returning to the living room, where he set it out in plain view near Odette's lifeless body. Grasping the author's wrist, the villain felt for a pulse, smiling in satisfaction. With sangfroid coldness then, via his handkerchief, he opened and relocked the door to let himself out.

About twenty minutes later, Odette's doorbell sounded again.

"I have a feeling she's home now," Raine said.

When no one answered, the four Americans waited patiently for several seconds.

"Perhaps she's in the bathroom," Maggie remarked, adjusting the turquoise tunic she was sporting over a white skirt. "Wait a bit and ring again."

When the author still did not respond, Raine moved to the window to shield her eyes and peer inside through an opening in the drapes. What she saw gave her a start. "Oh no!"

"What is it?" Beau asked.

He and Thaddeus squinted through the glass to catch sight of the historian sprawled on the living-room floor, whilst Maggie braced herself for what she knew would be a body.

'*No use cryin' over spilt potion,*' as Granny used to say. From the deep pocket of her beachy dress, Raine whipped out her phone to dial 15 for an ambulance, then she rang 17 for the police.

Now there was little doubt that an invisible hand had scribed over the whole mysterious mess– *Murder*.

It didn't take the paramedics long to pronounce Odette Auteur dead. *Capitaine* Michel Renard pontifically announced who he was, after which he immediately rang the coroner and proceeded to perform his duties as the principal *Inspecteur de la Police Nationale*, Fort-de-France.

Raine sighed and looked up to find the inspector's dark, intelligent eyes watching them.

"*Mademoiselle*," he said, addressing that Sister, "tell me again why you were here to call on Historian Auteur." His eyes scanned the Americans. "Just routine you understand."

The Sisters' party had introduced themselves to *l'Inspecteur de la Police* upon his arrival at the scene, and they were relieved that he spoke perfect English.

"Tell me, *mademoiselle*," the inspector repeated a soupçon stronger.

To tell or not to tell? That is the question, Raine thought. "We," she tossed a glance to her companions, "were hoping, in a manner of speaking, to discuss history with Odette Auteur and," she caught Maggie's eye, "discern what kind of person she was."

The man behind the badge furrowed his brow. "What kind of person? Please explain, *mademoiselle*. Your remark has," his voice morphed ominous, "*piqued* my curiosity." He was looking at the Americans with suspicion. But, then again, suspicion was the inspector's natural state of mind.

Capitaine Michel Renard was a middle-aged man of medium height and weight, but there was nothing middling about his personality. He had a smart, soldierly appearance, strong jawline, a neat mustache, swarthy complexion, and crisp, near-black hair over a low forehead. His face was chiseled, harder than stone, every edge sharp. The Sisters could sense straightaway that he was an intense, aggressive man with a keen intellect– perceptive, quick and alert– who possessed the hallmarks of a fine police chief. He made them think of something their granny used to say–

"The sleeping fox catches no chickens."

"Inspector," Raine began with determination under Renard's still watchful eyes, "we were planning to pay you a visit at your office in Fort-de-France, but we didn't want to come to you, hat in hand, wasting your time with gossip, our suspicions, and only circumstantial evidence to back it up. Now, after Historian Auteur's death, we have no choice but to share what we have with you, circumstantial or no."

The adroit Renard raised his dark brows, indicating that they sit. "I'm listening," he said, giving a huff of what could have been annoyance, though the tone of his voice screamed attentiveness. "Start from the beginning."

Raine did just that, relating what she had seen Odette Auteur do in regard to the handkerchief at la Pagerie. She told him Dorélia had witnessed the same thing, recounting all that their waitress friend had confided in them, including what the *Quimbois* sister-in-law had seen in her crystal ball. She even told him how sure Dorélia was that Odette Auteur had murdered Jeweler Pierre Laperle, ending that segment of the story with the waitress' entreaty that she and Maggie help solve the mystery to allow her ex-lover and good friend to rest in peace.

All the while, the inspector listened keenly, and the Sisters suspected he was making brief notes in his orderly mind.

Picking up Renard's thought, Raine said, "Of course *we* convinced Dorélia to talk with you. However, contrary to what she believes, *we* do not think Odette Auteur murdered Pierre Laperle," the Goth gal concluded. Noting the dour expression on the inspector's face, she softened her tone to take a different tack.

"Look, we never meant to get entangled in Martinique affairs, *Monsieur l'Inspecteur*," Raine pronounced with sincerity, "but mysteries have a way of dropping into our laps." To vanquish the cloud she sensed hung over their credibility, she dashed off the names of those he should contact to prove they were genuine psychics, not charlatans.

"We've worked with law enforcement at home in Pennsylvania, in our hometown and beyond." Raine met the inspector's withering look with resolve. "We've worked with the FBI and even Interpol."

"This is most unusual," Renard mumbled, lowering his head and shaking it.

"I beg pardon, *Monsieur l'Inspecteur,* but it is *indeed*," Raine quipped.

"Please check us out," urged the Sisters fervidly, with Maggie wondering if their faces matched the sincerity of their purposes.

"To get back on point," Raine hurried on, "what are the odds that the very next day, after we witnessed Odette Auteur doing that handkerchief trick out at la Pagerie, she turns up on la Rue Victor Hugo in Fort-de-France, at Pierre Laperle's posh antique shop, with a very old, very valuable bracelet that turns out to be connected to the Empress Joséphine?" The Goth gal recounted everything Dorélia told them had transpired in the store.

"Then three days later," Raine persisted, "Odette comes back to the shop to pick up the bracelet. Dorélia is again in the backroom, behind the curtain, along with a Chinese antique dealer who stops there about once a year to buy and sell, and they both overhear Laperle tell Odette that the bracelet is authentic, good quality rubies, with high gold content and an inscription that links it to a previous owner from the mists of history– none other than *the Empress Joséphine*," she pronounced with dramatic flair.

"Dorélia believes she heard someone enter the shop when Laperle was making the statement that he might be wise to report the whole thing to the proper authorities," Raine plowed on without qualm or quibble. "And now the plot thickens.

"That same afternoon, Beau and Thaddeus," she indicated her companions, "are nearly run down by Odette's auto when she peels out from the curb near Laperle's shop, and it looked to them," again she gestured toward the men, "that the historian was tailing someone. That *same* evening, the jeweler plunges to his death from the balcony of his cliffside chalet."

The inspector listened in silence, sitting very still, his expression stoic, though the Sisters could sense that his interest was growing. At one point, however, he did reach his hands to his head, as if the whole thing were becoming too much for him. At another point, he frowned impatiently.

Raine kept talking, filling the uniformed officer in on everything except *their* visit to Laperle's chalet.

"Then," she threw a glance at her sister of the moon, "Maggie and I go to Schoelcher Library, and what do *we* find?" She proceeded to tell Renard about the reference book, *The Memoirs of Queen Hortense*, that Odette had perused. "Opened to the period when Joséphine made her one and only return visit home to Martinique, a time-period that matches the era of the bracelet. *And* on that page of the memoirs is a passage stating that Joséphine lost something of value the night of the slave uprising when she and her daughter hurriedly fled Martinique."

"Look, Inspector Renard, let us be frank," Maggie stepped in to succinctly make the point to which Raine was leading. "We feel *strongly* that Jeweler Laperle's death and Historian Odette Auteur's are *connected*."

"And each is shadowed in foul play," Thaddeus adjoined in sinister timbre.

"But, to repeat, we don't believe, as Dorélia Sauvage and her sister-in-law do, that Odette murdered Laperle. We have other suspects, and we'll share these suspicions with you now, circumstantial or no," Raine declared. She breezed on to report all their apprehensions and hunches, everything surrounding Jean-Jacques; Antoine Li, the Chinese antique dealer; and even the Creeper. *For now anyway, I'll continue to have faith in Maggie's Nirumbee crystal and refrain from counting Dorélia among our suspects,* she told herself.

"Speaking of Odette and the Joséphine bracelet," Beau ventured with sudden urgency when Raine finished talking. "The historian had it in *her* possession, so it should be *here* at her residence."

"She could have cached it away in a safety deposit box at her bank," Thaddeus interposed.

"Could have, yes, but our psychic instincts," Raine looked to Maggie, "are telling us she did not. However, Inspector, you could easily find that out."

"We *urge* you to rummage this cottage for the bracelet," Raine and Maggie pleaded.

The Goth gal was flushed and a little breathless from her long earnest speech, but she leaned forward to fix the inspector with her witchy stare. "I'll describe it to you," she prompted.

After nearly two hours of careful search, no bracelet was found, nor any clues to make the inspector think the historian's death was caused by foul play.

"Except," Raine and Maggie pressed, "that the valuable historic bracelet has gone missing. Whoever killed Odette Auteur did so *to get that bracelet.*"

"Inspector Renard," Thaddeus began, "I'm going to go out on a limb and prevail on you to check out the bolt holes on Pierre Laperle's balcony. I'll wager you'll find evidence that someone unscrewed the bolts or whatever that held the railing to that balcony. We also entreat you to order an autopsy on Odette Auteur's body, and lastly, to see if she placed that bracelet in a safety deposit box at her bank. But first of all, please check us out, so you know we are honest individuals on a respectable course."

"My head," *Capitaine* Renard expressed with a look of intense frustration. He lifted his hands to his ears, "she is spinning."

For an instant, Raine was afraid they had overdone it, until the inspector spoke again.

"Let us go over everything *encore une fois. Slower* this time, and don't leave anything out. Start at the very beginning, and try and put everything in chronological order; I beg of you."

Over an hour later, Raine sat back to blow out her breath. "There, we've wearied you long enough, *Monsieur l'Inspecteur,* but I hope now we have earned the privilege of your time."

En route back to the hotel, Thaddeus remarked, "Do you know what I find most disturbing about this case?" Before anyone could respond, he said, "None ... er, almost none of the pieces fit together very well."

The Sisters did not respond. Rather, they were thinking that to solve this Caribbean mystery, they would need to call on their arts and wits more than ever before.

"Beware of people who brag about who they are.
A lion will never have to tell you he's a lion."
~ Granny McDonough

Chapter Twelve

"It's time we looked into our own crystal ball. The moment seems highly promising," Maggie stated, when the foursome entered her cabana after having dinner in the hotel's candlelit dining room. She lifted Angel Baby from her bag. "Raine, let's prepare her for scrying."

The Sisters set about, giving their mini-crystal ball, gifted them by their beloved Grantie Merry, a nice cleansing, bathing her in the bathroom sink with a soft cloth in tepid water and the mild, good-smelling liquid soap gratis the hotel. They were careful to begin by lining the sink with face cloths, so that the Baby would not get chipped.

"Keeping a crystal ball physically clean, cleanses the ball's energies as well," Maggie affirmed.

Reviewing aloud strengthened the programming of their oracle. It was the Sisters' way.

"As we do at home with our large crystal ball, Athena, we must always address this oracle by her name," Raine reminded. "And, as in the past, you lead us, Mags. You're the most gifted with scrying."

The redheaded Sister placed her hands lovingly on each side of the clear orb, whilst she spoke quietly. "Before we program Angel Baby today, we'll also have to smudge her with white sage. Remember, we'll need to smudge her before *and* after *each* session, so no negative energies will ever do her *or us* any harm."

As a rule, the McDonough witches made certain to travel with any magickal tools they might need. 'Twas no problem, for instance, to tuck a packet of loose white sage, incense cones, and a few small, all-purpose white candles into a pocket of their suitcases.

Maggie again took the initiative. "Before we actually begin, let's make physical contact with Baby," she directed. "Stroking the ball before using it energizes the crystal and reinforces our psychic bond with our oracle. We need to do this now."

Thaddeus and Beau were joining the Sisters for the session so the coterie could subsequently brainstorm the outcome; but since the ball belonged to the McDonough witches, not to confuse the energies, only *their* hands would ever come in contact with it.

For several moments, in succession, Maggie and Raine caressed the clear ball, gently passing their hands over the cool, smooth surface, as the former chanted softly, "Angel Baby, eye of the Fates, part the veil and the Otherworld gates. Bless our vision to awaken threefold– past, present, or future for us to behold."

Maggie used her extended pointer finger, in lieu of a wand, to draw a circle of protection around the room, calling upon the God-Goddess; the spirits of the four elements, the guardians of the watchtowers; as well as their angel and spirit guides, to secure a sacred space.

Raine was busying herself with the lighting of four small, white candles, after which she touched the lighter to a frankincense-and-myrrh incense cone she pulled from the same pocket of her valise, setting it into a cleansed hotel ashtray. The Sisters found the ancient purifier, "frank and myrrh," to be a powerful magickal tool for releasing stress and opening the Third Eye, in addition to cleansing.

Thaddeus and Beau helped by fanning the smoke with their hands, allowing the aromatic fragrances to permeate the entire area before placing the activated cone on a nearby stand.

In turn, Maggie lit a mini-bundle of white sage in a big, fan-shaped seashell she found on the beach that morning. Carrying the smoking sage in a clockwise motion– the natural and positive flow of energy– and chanting a smudging mantra, the Sister began cleansing the room of negativity.

"Negativity that invades this designated place, we banish you with the light of our grace. You have no hold or power here. We stand and face you with no fear. Be you gone forever, for now we say– this space we consecrate, and you will obey!"

"Together we cleanse," Raine charged, activating another chant, to which Maggie, Thaddeus and Beau joined in. "We cleanse this area completely free of any and all negativity!"

Maggie continued walking deosil/ clockwise. In addition to the fact that it was the natural and positive flow of energy, it was the direction associated with the movement of the sun across the heavens, and it was the course linked with blessings and good fortune. She chanted and cleansed in perfect accord, as the cabana room took on the combined scents of burning white sage and candle wax, along with the woodsy, earthy aromas of the good frank and myrrh.

Presently, Raine opened the Sisters' travel *Book of Shadows* to thumb through it to a ribboned section, after which she perused the handwritten page before switching off all the lights save one, a small table lamp she set on the stand behind the crystal ball.

Maggie reached for the Lemuria oil she'd placed on the table earlier, dabbing a touch on the Third-Eye area of her forehead, then passing the ampoule round to Raine, Beau, and Thaddeus, seated with her at the table.

The fiery-haired Sister smoothed the skirt of the tropical-print dress she was wearing, as she adjusted herself more comfortably in the chair. Comfort, ease and relaxation all were important when casting magick, almost as important as belief and intent. Thenceforth, she initiated a breathing pattern, allowing all the stress and negative energies to flow completely out of her body with released breath.

Raine followed suit, breathing deeply, "Healing energies in … negative energies out …"

"Healing energies in … negative energies out," the coterie echoed in concert.

There was a hushed silence as the magickal McDonoughs applied themselves to the task. It was always at this juncture of the ritual when Raine, especially, felt eager. Quickly, she did her utmost to tame her ardor. It would *not* do to be eager or excited– not for crystal-ball scrying.

After several minutes, Maggie opened her eyes to fix them on a section of the ball that expressly drew her. "Focus," she articulated in her silky voice, "focus on an area of Angel Baby's crystal depths that pulls at each of you."

Several quiet, peaceful moments lapsed, after which Maggie intoned softly, "Baby, as we go into a trance/ Bestow on us the magick glance/ Take us back in time today/ Reveal what happened come what may/ À la Pagerie, a bracelet found/ A fall from a balcony to rocky ground/ Take us back so we might find / A killer's two deadly crimes/ For dark secrets to be unlocked/ Within the hours of the clock/ That you have chosen for us to learn/ ***The facts!/*** For ***that***, we now return."

As the crystal ball's powerful energy commenced to flow, the seated witches imaged their vibratory levels rising to harmonize with the charged sphere, henceforth to craft their needed psychic link.

*The magick was working. Both Maggie and Raine could **feel** the oracle's power coursing around them and through them like an electric current.*

Within seconds, the witchy pair experienced a tingling sensation. The Sisters were adjusting to the ball's vibration– each in her own way. As in previous crystal-ball sessions, a swift surge of heat flared through Maggie, whilst a cool wave broke over Raine, prompting her to reach behind her for Granny's shawl, which, maintaining her gaze, she pulled over the bare shoulders of her strapless island dress.

"Expectation and anticipation are *not* helpful," Maggie reminded softly, keeping within the trance. "We know from experience, we must clear away any and all expectancies. We will see, at this point in our investigation, what Angel Baby wants us to see, nothing more, nothing less."

Thrice Maggie chanted their petition. When, for the third time, she repeated the line "… dark secrets to be unlocked," Raine could not help but think– *strange, sinister secrets.*

"Let us allow our minds to become as clear as the crystal. *Relax*," Maggie murmured, "and look into the ball's mysterious crystal cavern to remain entranced. Grantie Merry counseled that sometimes making connection with a crystal ball takes what seems like eons, other times not. We *know* we can do this. We've *done* it several times. *Re–lax*, we shall see what we shall see," the redheaded Sister crooned. "And we *know* that we shall *see*."

Keeping their gazes on the ball, not blinking an eye or moving an inch, the Sisters smiled inwardly as, within a few heartbeats and the crystal ball's mystical depths, a ghostly mist was rising.

"Our connection has been made," Maggie drawled softly. "The door is opening. Keep your focus. Let us allow the ball's mists to lure us in. That's it," she droned. "*Good. Ver-ry good.*"

Inside the orb, the ethereal mist swirled, slowly at first, then faster, then slowly again, before the crystal commenced clearing.

"Now we drift," Maggie hummed with composure. "Light as feathers, let us float inside Angel Baby's crystal cave, for like Merlin's, it will divulge Truth and only Truth.

"Soon now, the light and sound images, indestructible and eternal to the universe, will reveal to us what we seek. At what the Baby lets us peek.

"*Whatever* will be," Maggie whispered, "whatever we see, remain calm," she completed her thought, "*calm*, not to break the trance, or lose aplomb."

As the mists cleared, Maggie was careful not to elevate her voice. "We might see and hear what we do not anticipate. Quite often this is so, but Baby knows best what, at this point, we need to know," she rhymed smoothly.

"A spell in rhyme works every time," Raine put in softly.

Maggie's full lips parted as she gave a gentle sigh, "Mmmm. Do not attempt to make sense of anything till everything has faded away, for attempting to sort out will our spell doth flout.

"Simply *allow* the scenes, one into the next, to flow. *Ca–lm and centered as we go.* That's it, fellow scryers, keep emotion at bay. When the magickal movie ends, everything will fade and slip, slip, s-s-slip away." Maggie drew a fresh breath, freeing it as she kept her gaze.

The Sisters were gratefully discovering that each scrying session was easier than the last.

Meanwhile, out of the waning haze inside the crystal ball, a scene was emerging. In a trice, the gazers were seeing Historian Odette Auteur, on her knees, digging in a flowerbed at la Pagerie. They watched, in suspenseful silence, as her trowel hit something in the loose dirt, and since they hardly dared draw breath, they heard the distinct clink of metal on metal. Then, leaving not a shred of further doubt, *they actually saw Odette unearth the Joséphine bracelet.*

Dipping both hands into the hole in the flower bed, the historian ardently began freeing the treasure of as much dirt as she could, after which she pulled a handkerchief from a pocket of her Bermuda shorts, glanced furtively round, then stuffed the hankie-wrapped bracelet down into the pocket.

In an instant, the scene was effaced by the renewed smoky mists.

Hoping the magickal movie had not ended, the coterie reined in their emotions to remain calm and centered.

In a twinkling, another tableau began taking shape inside the crystal. This time, the image that seized unified attention was their top suspect at the door of Jeweler Pierre Laperle's chalet. The foursome watched as the killer, wearing surgical gloves and carrying a pouch of some sort, expertly used a set of lock picks to let himself inside, where he hastened to the balcony. There, taking a pillow from a rattan chair, he knelt at one end. Placing the pouch he was holding beside him on the balcony floor, he unrolled it to lay flat.

The watchers noted that it was a portable tool kit, from which the killer extracted a wrench. Next, he loosened the nuts from the bolts that held the railing onto the balcony and flung them to the rocks below. By using a screwdriver from the pouch, he succeeded in removing one of the two large bolts on that side of the rail, pitching it too off the balcony, down onto the rocky beach. Working fast, he unscrewed the second bolt almost entirely, leaving only about an eighth of an inch remaining in the wood. Then, hastening the pillow to the other side of the balcony, he knelt and repeated what he'd done opposite, tossing the nuts onto the rocks, along with one of the bolts, subsequently finishing the dirty deed by unscrewing the remaining bolt nearly the whole way, so that the slightest pressure would cause the railing to fall away from the wooden balcony.

Without delay, the killer replaced the tools to the pouch, re-rolled it, and tucked it under the arm of his pristine white suit.

Rising, he brushed off the knees of his pants and returned the pillow to the seat of the rattan chair. Then he went back into the chalet, closed the sliding-glass door after him, and locking the front door from the inside, took hasty leave.

Again, Angel Baby's swirling grey mists obliterated the scene within her crystal depths, whilst Maggie's soft tone helped keep the Sisters and the men centered. "*Relax*. Angel Baby will show us anything more she wants us to know. *Re–lax*."

Another scene was beginning to take form within the crystal ball. The Sisters watched as what looked to be l'Hôtel Bakoua's terrace café shimmered in and out of the ball's gathering "smoke." The scene wavered, revealing Historian Odette Auteur sitting at a table screened by tall, potted plants. Then it was gone, lost to the mists.

Unexpectedly, a beloved face appeared in the fog, and the scryers heard Grantie Merry's unmistakable voice speaking to them, though the image and words were faint and indistinct.

A beat of silence followed, broken only by the sound of the pounding rain, as an out-of-the-blue tropical storm broke boisterous in all its fury. An ear-shattering bolt of lightning, and into the crystal ball **burst** the snarling, growling face of a tiger, the mouth open to flash the deadly teeth, the eyes glowing red as a demon's!

Before the Sisters could let out their held-in breaths, the vision abruptly vanished, obliterated by Baby's effacing grey mists– to leave the orb crystal clear.

Several seconds passed with no further scenes emerging. The watchers knew now, for certain, that Angel Baby's magickal movie had ended.

Driven to respect proper procedure, the McDonough witches thanked God and Goddess, the guardians of the watchtowers, and their angel and spirit guides, completing the scrying ritual by smudging the crystal ball and returning it to its protective case.

"Not really a surprise," Maggie commented to her cohorts with a sigh. "The killer I mean."

Thaddeus poured them each a glass of red wine. "To ground us," he pronounced. "Drink."

Raine's green eyes found Beau. "I don't fancy pointing the finger of blame, baby, but I could sense your anticipation. That's why the last scene blurred and vanished." She kissed his cheek. "You're not used to scrying. Live and learn." She took a sip of wine. "We'll simply have to–"

"What was Grantie Merry trying to tell us when the scene faded?" Maggie interposed.

Raine ran a bejeweled hand through her wispy ebony hair. "Sounded like she said, 'Tiger's whispers.' But what sense does that make?"

Thaddeus' bright blue eyes twinkled, and he stood so suddenly his chair nearly overturned before Maggie's hand shot out to steady it. "It makes perfect sense. **Of course!**" the professor gabbled, setting his goblet of wine on a table with such a start that a bit sloshed out onto the wood. Then, with the air of a conjurer, he exclaimed, "Not tiger's whispers. Tiger's *whiskers!*"

With that, he spun on a heel and dashed for the door to the cabana's sitting area, tossing over his shoulder to his cohorts, "Need my laptop. Be right back!"

Several minutes later, Dr. Weatherby sat back from the computer screen to say, "I believe we have our killer."

The Sisters and Beau exchanged looks.

"Now the pieces of this puzzle are starting to fit together," the professor mused. "And very nicely too."

"Let's consult Angel Baby again," Raine charged. "This time," she pitched a reproving look to Beau, "we'll all be careful to stay calm and let our ancient oracle show us what she was about to reveal when that last scene vanished. I believe," her pouty red lips turned up in her little-cat smile, "since we've just uncovered what we did, Baby will be most obliging."

"Right," Maggie concurred. "Then we'll ring Inspector Renard."

Chapter Thirteen

Whilst the Sisters and their men were thus engaged, Jean-Jacques Sauvage was again working late in his office at the Fort-de-France bank that employed him. His band wasn't scheduled to play at the hotel this night, due to the Bakoua's *Danses de Martinique* program, hence he wanted to tidy up phone calls and paperwork at his desk. Both were routines connected to his job that invariably put him in a bad mood.

He was nearly finished with the dreaded tasks when his desk phone rang. "*Allô*," he spoke sharply into the receiver.

The disembodied male voice answered in French, "Have you opened your mail today?"

Thinking, at first, that it was the bank manager, Jean-Jacques said in questioning response, "*Monsieur* Argent, *c'est vous?*"

"Have you checked your mail?" the caller repeated, the timbre taking on a downright sinister tone.

"Who is this?" Jean-Jacques demanded, sure now the person on the other end was *not* his boss.

"Let's just say I'm a friend. Open your mail, *Monsieur* Sauvage. I think you'll find one *communiqué* in particular of great interest to you."

Jean-Jacques hadn't time to even go through his correspondence that day, so busy was he with client appointments, phone calls, and the endless paperwork he so despised that kept him from his music. He picked up the pile of things that had come in the afternoon post. Sorting through the various envelopes, his attention was immediately captured by one, *sans* return address, with large scrawling print in pencil that looked as though it had been written by a child.

His curiosity incited, he ripped the envelope open to extract a photograph of his wife kissing Pierre Laperle, one slender hand resting against the lapel of the man's elegant suit. There was no question in Jean-Jacques' mind that the blissful woman in the photo was Dorélia, and the date at the bottom of the image told him the kiss was captured only a few days prior. Though the kiss did not look to be that of a lover, and the jeweler was by now dead, a consuming anger seized the already-vexed man.

His voice rose in wrath. "***Who is this?!***" he boomed into the phone.

But the only response he received was a dial tone.

Uttering a tirade of oaths, he slammed the receiver into the cradle. Then, in his haste to complete his work and vacate his office, Sauvage tipped a paper cup, spilling the remains of his coffee onto his white suit. "*Merde!*" he roared, before hurling the cup into the dust bin to stalk with a thunder of profanities to the door.

Meanwhile, in Maggie and Thaddeus' cabana, the Sisters had just completed their second session with the crystal ball. What they observed reinforced Thaddeus' Internet discovery.

"There," Raine declared. "Angel Baby is again cleansed and properly put to bed."

"Let's ring the inspector right now," Maggie reminded. "Before another minute goes by."

The Goth gal quickly rang Renard at the cell number he'd given them, filling him in on their latest findings. Then she urged him to contact the morgue, explaining why in as much detail as she could. On her end, she could literally *feel* the inspector thinking, turning the case over in his mind, hashing out details.

For a long moment, there was silence on the line before he replied, his utterance indulgent, almost fatherly, "*Le matin* … in the morning, *mademoiselle*. The thing is as good as done. *Merci bien.*"

"Renard was either stunned by what we said, or he simply needed a few moments to process it first before thinking it through. I know not which," Raine informed her coterie. "Nonetheless, he assured me he'll contact the morgue straightaway in the morning, and I feel he's a man of his word. Unfortunately, no arrest can be made until the inspector does what we asked of him."

"There's nothing more we can do tonight, except," Thaddeus remarked, "and I strongly suggest we–"

"Warn Dorélia!" the Sisters and Beau cut in together.

When they arrived in the hotel's main dining room, *le Chateaubriand*, where the *Danses de Martinique* performance was underway, they found the area crowded with attendees– hotel guests, as well as those, by reservation, from the surrounding area, including *Madame* Marie Duval, who blended in perfectly with the large audience of happy spectators.

On the dance floor, the troupe of what looked to be about thirty traditionally costumed dancers, singers, and musicians were putting on a spectacular display of the music and dances of Martinique, to the hip-swaying rhythms of beguine and mazurka.

Sitting at the hotel's Gommier Bar, adjacent to the dance floor, was a simmering Jean-Jacques. He was waiting to catch a glimpse of his wife, and while he waited, he was drinking, which only served to fuel his already-stoked temper.

The Sisters spied him as soon as they arrived on the scene. Keeping him in sight, they glanced round for Dorélia. It was only a few seconds later when she breezed by the bar en route to the lobby, where she was planning to exit for home, her dinner shift over.

Faster than lightning, Jean-Jacques's hand snaked out to snare his wife, jerking her toward him to flash before her startled face his murderous glare, along with the photo he received in the post.

"If it's one thing I cannot abide, *chérie*, it's a liar. Have you anything to say?" His words, in their native French, sounding slightly alcoholic, came out loud and with force, causing those nearby to turn their heads and stare, including Madame Duval, who put a hand to her ample chest in shock.

Dorélia could see the raging storm in her husband's dark eyes. As if to block out his scowl, as well as the appalled looks they were receiving, she closed her eyes. "Please, Jean-Jacques, please don't do this. Please don't be angry," she pleaded in a rasping whisper.

He scoffed, his voice lifting with every syllable, "Angry? I'm way past being angry!"

"I could not put an end to my friendship with Pierre," she ventured in a soft tone, "but I swear to you, that's what it was at the last–*friendship*. Please let go, Jean-Jacques," she tried unsuccessfully to wrench away, "you're hurting me."

Raine's right fist clenched, and in a heartbeat, the Sisters and their escorts moved forward to intervene. Dorélia's husband, however, released her, the abrupt action nearly causing the frightened woman to lose her balance and fall sideways.

"Do you think you have not hurt *me*?" The pain was visible in his eyes. "I suspected you were still seeing him. I wish," he said in a low tone, "I could understand the ways of women. Sorceresses, all of you. You twist men's souls about your clever little fingers just to see what shapes you can craft." His voice abruptly rose. "I do know *this*. *You* are a selfish witch! A liar and a cheat. I'm going to a friend's. I want to find you gone when I return tomorrow!"

Sauvage shouted at his wife in a virtual red mist of fury, causing several more curious faces to turn their way. "Do you understand?!" he finished in a hunt-cat's snarl.

Staring dumbly at her husband, Dorélia stood for what felt like an eternity before she mouthed quietly in French, "What loathsome things to say."

Jean-Jacques laughed bitterly, a sardonic, derisive expression. "The truth, in many cases, *is* loathsome."

"Pierre's dead," she whispered. "It's finished."

"*Oui,* **fini**," Jean-Jacques repeated with a malevolent light in his eyes.

The way he spoke the word made her suck in her breath with a gasp.

"When I get home from the bank tomorrow evening, I want to find you gone! **Gone from my house!** *Forever!*"

She shrank from the evil peering from his eyes and the mad blast of his words. Words that held all the hurt in the world, along with a terrible disbelief.

The music stopped, and the rustle of interest in the crowd turned to a buzzing shockwave. Glancing round to see that everyone in the place was now staring at her and her crazed husband, the mortified waitress burst into tears. Without a word, she turned to bolt through the lobby and out into the tropical night.

The Sisters ran after her to find her sobbing in the shadows on the far side of the parking area. They greeted their friend with a rush.

"Dorélia, you must *not* go home," Maggie said forthwith. "You're in danger!"

"He's impossible, I know. The situation is impossible. I must pack my things," she answered in her Martinique way of thought. "I have to work tomorrow. Unless I start tonight, I won't have the time to do it all," she finished, sniffing back tears in a washed-out voice.

"No, you don't understand! You can't do that," Raine said, echoing her sister of the moon's urgency. "You can't go back to the house! You must *not* be alone–"

"I have no choice." Her voice sounded dead as a graveyard. "He meant what he said." Wrenching away, Dorélia melted into the jungle darkness beyond.

"And therein lies the problem." Raine knew Martinique well and was familiar with the island's gender roles. She was aware that marriage put wives in a vulnerable position in the household, where they often submitted to male chauvinistic attitudes and behavior, lest their husbands abandon them and/or take mistresses. "Despite modern feminist challenges, it's been a longstanding practice that Martinique husbands take mistresses, but woe to any wife who takes a lover," she recounted, looking disgusted. "Compounds the wretchedness of this whole mess."

An anxious Maggie's skin prickled. "It's all a ruse! The killer," she burst firmly into speech, "is lying in wait for Dorélia as we speak!"

The Goth gal's psychic gifts shot to full tilt. In the same single-minded way she did everything, she "felt for" their best option, rapidly formulating a plan. "I'm going to ring Inspector Renard again," she charged, already putting through the call.

"Tell him where to meet us, and tell him to hurry!" Beau urged.

"Thank the Goddess, Dorélia told us the other day where she lives," Maggie interjected.

"It's close," Thaddeus roused. "Let's go!"

In less than a minute, the foursome piled into the rented Renault and, with Thaddeus at the wheel, tore out of the hotel grounds.

"There's her house!" Raine shouted, pointing to a sea-blue bungalow with creamy-white shutters. "I know because she told me there was a little fountain with cupids in the side yard."

The Sisters, Beau and Thaddeus bounded from the vehicle and started running toward the palm-shaded cottage, just as Maggie's Nirumbee crystal flashed from yellow to red then black, the warning of danger confirming an exceptionally evil presence.

As they reached the front door, a loud scream issued from the house with matters instantly speeding to fast-forward. Bursting inside, they saw the killer backhanding their friend across the face before seizing her by the throat to choke the life from her— and there was no denying the look in those murderous eyes, dark and stony as shards of obsidian. The Sisters felt Fear's echo as—

The terrified Dorélia let out a strangled cry, and Thaddeus, stepping forward to subdue the large woman, thundered "Stop!"

Marie Duval's voice was low and harsh, and it bore the unmistakable discord of madness as she flashed a superior smirk, one hand holding tight to her victim, the other whipping out a gun. "It's only fair to warn you, I brought backup."

A slight noise caused Raine, whose ears were sharp as a fox's, to snap back with, "So did we."

At that express moment, the police surged into the room from the home's rear entrance, surprising Duval from behind, the supercilious expression dropping from her face. Feeling the killer's taut violence, the Sisters literally held their breaths.

As the tactical unit seized the culprit, the gun went off, the shot, in the confines of the small cottage, sounding like a blast from a cannon! Minus a second's hesitation, Beau and Thaddeus shielded the Sisters, though, by the Goddess' grace, the bullet smashed through the floor boards, mere inches from the magickal pair.

But the real shock of the night was the ominous Creeper, a dark lethal shadow in jeans and linen shirt, the sleeves rolled to the elbow. In he strolled with Inspector Renard, big as you please, as though he belonged there or anywhere, flooding the Sisters with a sensation of surprise all the way to their toes.

Without a word, the formidable man advanced upon Marie Duval with a professional zest and a cold look in his probing blue-grey eyes. Yanking the madras head-wrap from "her" head, he exclaimed, "Aha, the Tiger! Interpol has finally snagged you!"

The subsequent evening found the Sisters with their loves comfortably seated at the *Coco* for what Raine called "their merited sunset drinks."

"Who would've thought the Creeper would turn out to be Interpol?" she commented. "Goes to show, to echo Granny, things, and people too, are not always what they seem. When Grantie Merry said 'Tiger's whiskers,' and that ferocious tiger face burst into our crystal ball, I admit, I was baffled."

"Tiger's whiskers were an ancient Chinese torture," Dr. Weatherby related. "Seventeenth-century. The purrr-fect poison, excuse the poor pun. Finely chopped in food, they're tasteless, odorless, and there's *no* recovery. Rather fast-acting, even faster on someone like Historian Odette Auteur who suffered from acute colitis. The barb-sharp tiger's whiskers puncture the intestines, causing hemorrhaging. Dreadful business, that. It's an excruciating death. *Agonizing*."

"*Beastly* wicked murder!" Maggie exclaimed with a bit of a shiver. "Absolutely macabre, but it certainly gives us insight into the amusements of our mysterious antique dealer."

"Amusements such as murder," Beau quipped.

"Fair enough," Raine nodded her raven head. "Amusement to constantly prove he was smart enough to get away with what he deemed 'perfect crimes' were very likely a part of his motive for killing, for his crimes in general, though I'd say money ... *greed* was the real motivation. Let's review. Antoine Li, known by the code-name 'the Tiger,' is a notorious international killer, smuggler and thief. *Beastly*, to use your word, Mags.

"The man's a meticulous murderer who always did his homework. He researched Odette Auteur and learned she had colitis. Then he stalked her and found out she took lunch most days at l'Hôtel Bakoua's terrace café. He knew she wrote both fiction and history, knew her penchant for Empress Joséphine, and he discovered in his research that she loved hearing from her readers. I'd wager he found out, too, that Odette was impressionable. For those reasons, he disguised himself as a fan, a *Martiniquaise*, the disguise he used when he returned to Martinique from Rio. He gathered everything he needed to stage her death as a tragic end due to her colitis issues," Raine declared, pausing briefly to sip her *ti punch*.

"Inspector Renard said Li, whose real name is Antoine Hû, killed at least three people– three of whom Interpol is aware– using tiger's whiskers as the lethal poison. The surname Hû, by the bye, translates Tiger. Most likely how the fiend *got* the idea to use the ancient Chinese torture. The man is *ruthless*. And all of this together is how and why the International Police came to give him his ferocious handle," Thaddeus remarked. "Seven long years Interpol's been trying to snag the elusive Tiger. The master of disguise had suitcases with false bottoms holding a spectrum of fake passports and IDs, and he speaks several languages."

The professor grew a bit pensive. "*Elusive*," he repeated. "For one thing, no one, including Interpol, ever had an accurate description. When he was here on Martinique, as in several other places, he blended right into the mixed-race culture. Interpol Agent Sournois, our Creeper, wasn't certain he had found his man. He couldn't make an arrest based on mere suspicion, and he didn't want to blow his cover, so all he could do was shadow the Tiger and wait for him to make a move."

"Or make a mistake," Raine laughed. "Like messing with the Sleuth Sisters."

"If *you* hadn't thought of tiger's whiskers," Maggie told Thaddeus with admiration in her voice, "the French authorities, in all probability, would have attributed Odette's death to her colitis. Unless they knew specifically what to look for in an autopsy, they would *not* have discovered the real cause of her death. Her murder would have gone undetected." She leaned closer to kiss his cheek. "You're amazing."

The professor shrugged. "Hardly that, my Maggie. Your Grantie Merry's words and that tiger face triggered a memory is all. Years ago," his expression waxed wistful, "longer than I care to say, when I was a young man at university, I made a backpacking trek through China the summer of my junior year."

Maggie kissed him again. "You're still a young man, darlin'."

Thaddeus chortled. "I'm toting a lot of miles, but most of the time, I feel I've quite a few left in me."

Yes, Virginia, there is a Santa Claus ... and maybe even a wizard. Raine giggled. "I find you amazing too, Thad. You and Beau both, and don't think your qualities go unnoticed by Maggie and me." She took a long pull of her drink, sending Beau a look sated with promise.

"Goes both ways," Beau acknowledged in return, reaching over to squeeze the small, bejeweled hand resting on the table next to his.

"It's appalling that the Tiger got away with his crimes as long as he did," Raine commented.

"Inspector Renard pointed out that he was the cagiest criminal Interpol has ever had to deal with," Maggie replied. "He evaded capture for so long because he was incredibly clever ... with an exceedingly black spirit." She paused for a pensive moment, adding, "Born without a conscience that one, the way someone might be born without an arm or a leg."

"The inspector will be taking the Joséphine bracelet to *Madame* the Curator at la Pagerie. He found it hidden among the Tiger's things in the killer's efficiency apartment at Village Créole, central for spying on his victims, Odette and Dorélia," Raine informed.

"The Tiger made a full confession," the Goth gal reminded her coterie. "Admitted to Renard that he tampered with Jeweler Laperle's railing before he caught that flight to Rio, after which there were two more people, in his crafty criminal mind, he had to get rid of, two others who knew about the historic bracelet– Odette and Dorélia. As we said, his plan was that Odette's death would look like she died from a severe attack of her colitis. The Tiger plotted and schemed so that the hot-headed Jean-Jacques would get blamed for both Laperle's death, *if* it turned out the police realized the railing had been tampered with, and Dorélia's. So many people knew about J-J's rages. Knew about his flaming jealousy too.

"Let's not forget that it was the Tiger who posted the picture of Dorélia kissing Laperle to Jean-Jacques at his bank office. The Tiger captured the photo in the work area of Pierre Laperle's shop. Remember our waitress friend told us, right before she left the shop that day that the Chinese antique dealer she knew as Antoine Li was doing something on his phone. She thought he was texting, but he was taking that picture. The Tiger knew the image would *enrage* Jean-Jacques, and that he'd make a beeline to the hotel and– cat among the pixies– attack his wife in front of dozens of witnesses during the on-going *Danses de Martinique* program. Remember too, Dorélia told us she often confided in Laperle. We also heard her say the antique dealer visited the jeweler's store when he was on Martinique, soooo he must've heard dribs and drabs of Dorélia's woes with her hot-tempered hubby." Raine paused to take another swallow of her *ti punch*.

"Yep," Beau reasoned, filling the pause quickly, "both Laperle's death and Dorélia's could have been attributed to jealousy and revenge on Jean-Jacques' part. I guess the cunning Tiger thought of everything."

"Well now," Raine retorted with a feline grin, *"everything*'s a really big word. He didn't know Dorélia confided in *us*." The Goth gal thought for a moment, remembering something else. "I reckoned early on that Jeweler Laperle's murder was plotted and schemed by a man. That death did not fit the MO of a scorned woman. After I mulled it over, it did not seem to me to be a crime of passion."

"Angel Baby showed us that it was the Tiger, posing as the British Professor Hancock, who had Odette Auteur paged at the reception desk. Henceforward, disguised as Marie Duval, he could sneak the tiger's whiskers into her salad when she answered that page. The inspector said the evil man acknowledged that he always carried the finely chopped whiskers with him in a fancy antique pill case," Maggie put in. "Thanks to Baby, we saw him in the guise of Marie Duval liberally sprinkle the barbs into Odette's salad, then mix them in with her fork." Maggie's smile was sad. "It was at *that* point, we became fairly certain two … er *three* people when you consider Antoine Li … *four* when you consider Interpol's slippery Tiger, were all the same person– and the unerring finger pointed to *one killer*.

"The Tiger seduced Odette into thinking he, posing as Marie Duval, was an ardent fan. For the most part, women are more vulnerable than men. More emotional and impressionable too. Creative women especially." The Sister reflected, reaching back in time to add, "Obviously, the woman in my flash-vision, a woman who felt threatened by Dorélia, was Marie Duval, aka the Tiger."

Raine grimaced with the memory. "We didn't notice him as Marie Duval in the audience of the *Danses de Martinique* program because, in our singlemindedness, we were focused on warning Dorélia."

"Right. Completely absorbed in it." Maggie shook her head. "Great Goddess, I never thought we'd get the poor woman calmed down after the police collared the killer. She was absolutely hysterical. But understandably so.

"Our Baby showed us the Tiger's dirty work, but it's still hard to digest," the redheaded Sister quipped. "I don't like to speak ill of the dead, but what Odette Auteur did was wrong, taking that bracelet from la Pagerie property. Nonetheless, to die like that ... *ugh*," she quaked. "Honestly, I don't think the poor woman realized it was a valuable historic antique when she took it home with her. Afterward, I figure, she was too ashamed to return it, and," Maggie gently nodded her head in contemplation, "by then, she was so attached to the bracelet—"

"Yes, it became *une idée fixe* to keep it as her own," Raine cut in, completing Maggie's thought. "And she began rationalizing how the bracelet was *meant* for her, convincing herself that she did nothing wrong and should, by all rights, keep it."

"I'm astonished the Tiger confessed anything to Inspector Renard and the Creeper ... er," Beau corrected himself, "Interpol Agent Drago Sournois."

"Hoping for better treatment is my deduction," Thaddeus replied, after which he chortled, "What else *could* he do but cooperate with the authorities? Obviously, he knew the game was up. The inspector had him dead to rights, so it made no sense for him to tango with the police. To echo Raine, let's not forget that Renard told us the Tiger, overweening chap that he is, *bragged* about his actions, reiterating how clever he was and how stupid the police were."

"Great balls of fire!" Maggie exclaimed. "How did he think *that* would win him points?"

"We know from experience that bragging is something murderers can't help doing a lot of the time," the professor returned. "The sonsabitches are like that, carried away by their own egoism, by admiration of their own cleverness."

Raine looked to Maggie. "Granny always warned us to beware of folks who brag about who they are. 'A lion will never have to tell you he's a lion,' and I could substitute the word *tiger* there. As for murderers, we never met a murderer who wasn't vain, and that is ofttimes their undoing."

"Yes," the professor reflected, "I think some murderers seek out public notoriety and actively engage in the creation of public image. In any case, all of it was incredibly easy for the Tiger, as easy as falling off a log."

"Or sprinkling chopped whiskers into a salad," Beau cracked wise.

Stroking his beard, Dr. Weatherby was deep in private thought. "Interesting case. Very interesting case, this."

"I wonder if the Tiger wasn't a little mad ... *bonkers*," Maggie asked.

Thaddeus' hand dropped from his van dyke. "Pathological cases are the devil, even for Interpol, but my Maggie," he ventured after a moment, "we're all a trifle mad. It's human nature. Each and every one of us have gone or will go round the bend to some degree."

"I don't know about that, but I do know that both Chief Inspector Renard and Interpol Agent Sournois were grateful to us," Raine declared with pride. "Warms my heart how appreciative they were."

"Yes," Maggie agreed. "Fancy that. The staid Renard actually had tears in his eyes when he thanked us." She smiled. "And our ex-Creeper was very like a teddy bear." *Had I been able to get close enough to him to allow my Nirumbee crystal to do its job, I'd have known that,* she told herself.

"Seemed to me," Thaddeus commented, "Renard and Sournois are each routinely of a serious turn of mind, so you two made quite an impression."

"Well, I imagine there's quite a satisfaction in getting your man," Beau interjected. He took a swallow of *ti punch* and thought for a second. "I'd wager Renard and Sournois are both first-rate poker players. Do the French play poker?"

"*Bien sûr*, they do. What do you suppose will happen between Dorélia and J-J?" Raine abruptly wondered aloud.

"I predict we'll find out. She's scheduled to work the dinner shift," Maggie remarked.

Raine's phone began to vibrate. Answering it, she whispered to her cohorts, "Jeanne Gardien." The Goth gal listened for a minute or so, then rang off, "*Au revoir, madame, à demain et merci.*" To her coterie, she translated, "I told her we'll see her tomorrow. *Madame* the Curator has invited us out to la Pagerie to thank us in person."

"That's thoughtful of her," Maggie said. She took a sip of her drink, then rested an affectionate hand on Thaddeus's arm.

"What time?" Beau asked. "Thad and I were thinking we could all go up to the breakfast buffet in the morning." His look was positively puppy-ish.

"We can do both," Raine giggled, patting his cheek. "Jeanne asks that we meet with her late morning, eleven-ish." She signaled for the waiter to bring them another round of *ti punch*.

"You're a devious, scheming woman, and I love you," Beau returned.

Raine grinned. "Just keep loving me. I'll keep loving you, and the rest will fall into place."

"I never grow tired of the sunsets here," Thaddeus spoke soulfully, taking Maggie's hand. "Positively restorative."

"Nor do I," the redheaded Sister sighed in utter nirvana.

"Softly comes the evening from the western horizon, like a magician extending a red-golden wand over the landscape," Raine mused.

Sky, sea, and the greeny-black smudge of lush jungle in the not-too-distant mornes seemed suddenly on fire at the touch of that wand, melting and mingling together in the passionate burst of another Martinique sunset.

"I'll miss this island." Beau sent Raine a wink. "It's bewitched me."

"We've a few sunsets yet," she replied. "Let's make a pact to enjoy, *to the hilt*, every moment we have left."

"I'll drink to that," Thaddeus rejoined, raising his glass.

"Hear, hear!" the others toasted.

At dinner that night, the Sisters' party was not surprised to learn that Dorélia had reported off work.

"She's probably sorting out her life," Maggie said wistfully, remembering the sense of loss she felt when, years before, her own marriage was on the rocks. "You know what? My keen witch's intuition is telling me that she and Jean-Jacques will work things out.

Perhaps what happened will serve as a wakeup call for both of them."

"If they love one another, I hope you're right," Raine rejoined. "And I sense they do, for I believe theirs *is* a love match." She flicked a crumb from the bodice of her black, gauzy dress. "And you know what they say about love. It always finds a way."

The following morning, after bringing healthy appetites to the breakfast buffet, the Sisters, Beau and Thaddeus motored out to la Pagerie, where the curator was waiting for them with a lovely surprise.

Handing the magickal pair a beautifully wrapped package, she said without preamble, "For you. Open it, *mes amies.*"

The raven-haired Sister, especially, loved presents, and her excitement was clearly mirrored on her face– cheeks pink, eyes bright– as she tore away the blue, white, and red wrappings– representative of the French *Tricolour.*

"The gift is for you both," *Madame* the Curator told the Sisters. "I recall you mentioned that you live together. The set is for four, so it's actually for all of you to enjoy," the genial Jeanne Gardien declared. "The board and I went together on this to illustrate our deep appreciation for what you did for our beloved Pagerie. If it weren't for you, la Pagerie would not be in possession of the fabulous Joséphine bracelet."

Raine lifted the lid to exclaim over what the opened box revealed. "Wizzz-zzzard, it's gorgeous!"

The passionate Maggie was momentarily unable to speak, as her emerald eyes became moist with emotion.

Deeply touched, the Sisters thanked the curator profusely, each tossing aside protocol to give her a warm hug of sincere gratitude.

A subtle Jeanne confessed, "I overheard you say how much you admired the antique set we have on display here in the museum. Yours, circa 1965, is an exact copy. We were lucky to find it. These sets are becoming more and more rare, but Destiny intervened, and *voilà!*" she enthused, extending a graceful hand to the prize.

La Pagerie's gift to the Sleuth Sisters was a French *demitasse* set of green and gold Limoges porcelain. The small, delicate cups, bearing the Empress Joséphine's image, held exquisite, swirly gold handles, and inside the bowl of each cup was a hand-painted gold honeybee.

"What significance do the bees have?" Beau asked the curator. "I figure they must have some meaning."

Jeanne smiled. "Indeed, they do. Although Napoléon was never a beekeeper, he chose the honeybee as one of the most important symbols of the power and prestige of his empire."

"There are two schools of thought about why he desired that particular symbol," Raine put in.

"That's right," Jeanne concurred. "The first is that the honeybee is representative of the Merovingian kings, the founders of France, the dynasty started by the Franks, the barbaric tribe that settled what is now *la Belle France*. This was the dynasty with whom Napoléon thought to align himself– with Charlemagne, the great Frankish king and founding father of France."

"Tell the other school of thought," Raine urged. "It's the bee's knees, as our granny would say."

Jeanne laughed. "I believe I've heard that American phrase. *Eh bien*, as legend has it, when Napoléon established himself into the Royal Palace of Tuileries, he refused to spend money on new décor. However, he could not allow the drapery– with its embroidered *fleur-de-lys*, the French royal emblem of the overthrown monarch– to continue to hang in the windows of the palace. His solution was to order the rich, elegant drapes turned upside down. The inverted symbol resembled a bee. From then on, the tenacious bee became the emblem of Napoléon Bonaparte. As I'm certain you history professors know full well, his red coronation robes were also embroidered with gold bees."

"Both schools of thought are true shades of Napoléon," Dr. Weatherby asserted with quip. "I've always believed both have credence."

The Sisters readily agreed, after which *Madame* the Curator said, "*Oui, c'est exact.*"

"When will you be putting the Joséphine bracelet on display here in the museum?" Raine asked.

"Not until we get a custom security case for it, airtight, fireproof, with UV protective film, and as climate-controlled and burglar-proof as humanly possible. Then there's the matter of insurance, added-to alarms and lockdown. But it won't take us long; I can assure you. This is the most exciting thing to ever happen to us." Jeanne showed them a photograph of the bracelet that she took from her desk. "We are ecstatic, as you can imagine."

"Oooh, we can well imagine," Maggie dreamed. "I'm in love with that bracelet. It's absolutely gorgeous."

Thaddeus stroked his van dyke. "It certainly tallies with *your* taste in jewelry."

The curator seemed to be ruminating over something before she again spoke. "I just wish we had *documented* provenance connecting that bracelet to Joséphine. The museum will command our own appraisal and assessments, of course. I was thinking we could have *The Memoirs of Queen Hortense* open to the page where Joséphine's daughter mentions that her mother lost something of value the night the two of them hastily fled Martinique. I just wish we had the cited letter– what could be the key missive that Joséphine wrote *her* mother about the lost item. Perhaps there's mention of the word *bracelet* and perhaps even a description therein."

Jeanne Gardien tilted her dark head in a pensive pose. "That letter has never surfaced any place that I'm aware. You know, I've always believed that Joséphine's mother, Rose-Claire, had a hideaway here at la Pagerie, a secret nook for concealment of valuables. It only stands to reason that she would have a place to hide the jewelry bestowed on her by her mother, an important document *peut-être*, a few francs stashed away for a rainy day, or an important letter. People did that in those long-past days.

"Remember, Rose-Claire's husband Joseph, Joséphine's father, was a gambler and womanizer, thus Joséphine's mother would've wanted ... *needed* a hiding place to keep certain things out of his hungry hands. *She* was the glue who held this plantation together, not him. We've done a lot of renovations to this property over the years, however, and never have we come across a hidey-hole with treasures. But I have always believed there was ... *is* one, a secret niche yet undisclosed."

Raine shot Maggie a cunning sideways glance, and Thaddeus and Beau could almost hear the sleuthing switches snap to fast-forward.

***

A couple of hours later, in Maggie and Thaddeus' room at the hotel, the latter checked his laptop for the date of the upcoming full moon. *"Tomorrow night,"* he said, as if pronouncing a decree.

"The night of the slave uprising is the date with which we need to program our Time-Key," Raine directed. "If Joséphine's mother indeed had a secret nook for important and valuable items, she surely would've put a few things in there the night they were warned about a slave uprising."

Maggie and Thaddeus traded looks. "We agree."

"History tells us the date, 31 August 1790," Raine reiterated. "We wouldn't be guessing."

"Time-traveling to the night of the slave revolt, we will see how Joséphine came to lose the bracelet," Maggie realized, "and we'll spy on her mother, mistress of la Pagerie, to see if she caches anything away in a hiding place. By dint of Destiny, if that hidey-hole still exists, who knows what treasures it might hold?"

"Wiz-zard! It's decided then. We time-travel tomorrow at midnight, the hour of the clock we customarily embark on a time-trek," Raine stated with punch. "Now," she looked to her cohorts, "where will our portal be this trip?"

"That's a no-brainer," the professor answered. "It has to be la Pagerie."

"That settles that then," Raine grinned in what looked like feline contentment.

Beau, who was silent up to now, merely groaned, running his hand through his dark hair. "Surely you guys aren't planning to break into the museum grounds after hours."

"Oh, Beau," Raine huffed, "don't be such a rabbit! Be the lion that you are."

When Beau started to reply, the professor cut in.

"We won't have to break in," Thaddeus said reassuringly. "We'll Time-Key, under the veil of night and jungle, as close to la Pagerie as we can get. At the 1790 plantation, there won't be cameras or alarm systems, except perhaps for a dog."

"If there's a dog or dogs," Raine interposed, "I'll use my animal-communication skill to take care of that, no prob."

"When we land, so to speak, at our target time-and-place," the professor went on, "we'll tramp to the *sucrerie*, where the family was then residing– remember, after a hurricane destroyed the mansion, they lived on the second floor of the sugar refinery– and spy for all we're worth till we get what we went for."

"We can't all three slither into the *sucrerie*," Raine declared with vigor. "I'm the smallest and most agile, so I should be the one to do it."

"We'll decide together when we get there and assess the situation," Thaddeus said, absently rubbing the back of his hand over his beard. "I'm sorry, I've been assuming I'll be accompanying you ladies again on this time-trek." His look was almost pleading.

"You absolutely will," the Sisters replied at once.

"Beau can go with us to our portal, aid in our prep and send off, and wait for us there as a sort of lookout," Raine commented, grasping her lover's muscular arm and snuggling close. "Don't worry, baby, we've used our Time-Key with success several times now. No worries."

He raised an expressive ebony brow. "There're always worries."

"*No*," the Goth gal countered. "*No!* Worrying is like praying for what you don't want. It goes against the Secret. We are always careful to program what we *want* to happen, *never* what we do not want. The universe, the Law of Attraction, doesn't compute negatives, such as Don't, Not, or No. For instance, when you say or think, 'I don't want something or other,' that *something or other* is what the universe is receiving, and that's what you'll get. Example: If you think 'I don't want anything to go wrong,' that's exactly what you'll get– something or everything will go wrong. You *should* be thinking, 'I want everything to go right.' Or, better yet, 'Everything will go right.' The Law of Attraction gives you what you're thinking about, *period*."

Acquiescing to her witchy rationale, Beau took her face between his large hands, kissed her forehead, and replied, "*Touché!*"

Chapter Fourteen

The following day found the Sisters, Beau and Thaddeus lounging on the beach, reading the paperback pamphlets and books on Joséphine and the history of Martinique they purchased in the hotel gift shop. Though the books– which they intended to leave at *la réception* for future tourists– contained nothing new for the three history professors, they did want to review everything they could before they time-traveled. Too, they wanted to reap a bit of ease and amusement before their trek, which they knew from experience would be challenging.

At noon, they lunched in the shade of the bakoua-roofed Coco Bar on the turquoise water of the bay– fish fritters called *accras* seasoned with green onions and hot pepper and enjoyed with chilled white wine. Then they spent the remainder of the afternoon relaxing and reading before they revisited the Coco for their sunset rendezvous, sipping *ti punch* till shadows lengthened and the sultry air began to cool.

At dinner, they discovered that Dorélia had still not returned to work, but the waitress filling in for her told them that their friend would be back the next night. "She's staying with her sister-in-law," the substitute disclosed. "I think she and her husband are trying to resolve things. Jean-Jacques was so relieved that Dorélia was not hurt in the chaos the other night, he decided they should try again."

The stand-in, whose name was Salomé, went on to say that she was a cousin of Jean-Jacques. "He means well, but he takes after my uncle with that temper of his. He's never hurt Dorélia, but he does make her crazy at times ...*de toute façon*, she acts crazy." The woman immediately pulled back, as if she said too much, the gesture not quite believable. "*Je regrette*, I should not have said those things."

Maggie tossed a fleeting look to Raine. *Every slip of the tongue has meaning.*

Salomé lowered her voice to a whisper. "Might as well be honest. Dorélia can be ... er, um ... *une fille effrontée.*"

Raine sensed that Dorélia's replacement felt no *real* reluctance unburdening herself. She felt, too, that Salomé had substituted a polite phrase for *bitch* and conveyed the thought to Maggie.

"I remember once," the waitress went on in a mélange of French and English, "after *une dispute*, I posed her *la question*, '*Vous me détestez.* You detest me, don't you?' Do you know what she answered?"

The Sisters shook their heads, waiting.

"Dorélia shrugged and said, 'If I ever gave you any thought, I'd probably agree with that.'" Salomé scrunched up her face. "*Imaginez? Quelle audace! Elle fait souvent la maligne!*"

Says Dorélia can be a smart-mouth, Raine translated telepathically to Maggie.

"*Mais*, I hope the faerie princess and J-J can patch up their differences," Salomé concluded. "I'm fond of him, and er, I … I want to see him happy at long last." She paused, and her face clouded.

"What is it?" Raine could not help asking in French.

"I just remembered a curious thing Dorélia told me not long ago," Salomé replied in her native tongue with a strange, almost mourning emotion on her voice, though her words took suddenly a derogatory tone with a hint of acid. "It seems to me, Dorélia has always been blessed. She's always gotten everything she ever wanted. Take this job, for instance. She doesn't need this job, not like me. She and J-J don't even have children, and he makes a good living for the two of them."

The Sisters studied the older woman for a private moment. They could tell she had once been a beauty, though now her looks were faded, they intuited, from hard work and worry.

I'll bet she could spill a mouthful if she chose, Maggie thought-connected to Raine.

"What is it that she said?" the Goth gal pressed Salomé. "What did Dorélia tell you?"

"She said, 'I think the truest thing I have ever heard spoken about human beings on this earth is that it's quite easy to be happy— once you know you never will be.'"

How dreadfully morbid, Maggie shot to Raine. *God-Goddess wants us all to be happy. Genuinely happy.*

When the waitress moved off, Raine whispered her judgment. "Her demeanor spoke something more than her words."

"Something that smacks of jealousy," the redheaded Sister replied devoid of hesitation.

"With undertones of wickedness," Raine saw fit to interject. "Those Voodoo-woman eyes! At one point, I sensed her sharpening her claws. Mags, could Salomé be the woman you saw in your vision, the woman whom you said felt threatened by Dorélia? We thought your vision-woman was Marie Duval, but as it turned out, she wasn't a woman. Perhaps ..."

At that express moment, the redheaded Sister envisioned, on the movie-screen of her mind, a naked woman dancing under the full moon, her firm, café-au-lait body shining from the heat of the night and the flames of a fire that sputtered and crackled before her. She danced with thrust and power, her large hoop earrings catching the firelight as she whirled, her long, dark hair swinging round to hide her face.

When the four Americans finished eating, they progressed to the terrace for the hotel's *Soirée de Salsa*, the sensual Latin music to the Sisters' taste. Raine had been trained in Spanish dance, during what she called her "salad days," especially in flamenco and tango, hence she was looking forward to this night's scheduled entertainment.

Relaxing to the music, the Sisters could not ease from their minds the stand-in waitress' heavy words. Was Dorélia safe? Were their friend's words regarding happiness prophetic?

I suppose it all depends on how you define happiness, Maggie conveyed to a brooding Raine.

Using the pretty fans brought from Granny's trunk, the Sisters sat, gently fanning themselves after a dance. Across the way, two *Martiniquais* observed them with sultry stares. In a moment, they crossed the floor to petition the McDonoughs for a dance.

"Would you mind?" the magickal pair asked their loves.

"Enjoy," came the combined response.

The Sisters found the lithe native men to be terrific dancers, as well as gentlemen, and a good time was had by all.

When the band began an Argentine tango, Maggie returned to her seat, but Raine, who especially loved that particular tango for its beauty and drama, dazzled her partner and everyone on the terrace with the excitement and electricity of her movements.

She was lucky to have landed such a skilled, strong partner, who guided her round the rapidly-cleared floor with the power and grace of a panther, signaling the embraces, walks, leg hooks, and dips for which the style is celebrated. 'Twas fortunate too for the Goth gal that the black, form-fitting, off-the-shoulder dress she was sporting had a deep-slit for the intricate leg moves and extensions the sultry dance demands.

As the energy flowed, the created tango, enhanced with apt facial expressions, told a story of passion and seduction, of both the pain and the pleasure of love, the flames round the candle-lit terrace seeming to enliven the dancers even more– making them sizzle.

At one point, the *Martiniquais* who had been dancing with Maggie returned to the floor, signaling Raine's partner, who spun her into his friend's arms. In one fell swoop, both men were partnering with the raven-haired Sister, who, locking eyes with them, splayed her hands on each of their chests, pushing them backward in a smooth tango walk. The dance slinked into a sexy three-way that brought the audience to their feet at its finish in a burst of applause, along with vibrant shouts of Latin approval.

"*Olé! Olé!*"

One of Raine's partners whirled her, flushed and glowing, to the other, and the three dancers linked hands to execute an elegant bend to the spectators, after which each man kissed the Sister's hand he was holding.

Upon escorting Raine back to her table, the two *Martiniquais* accorded her a courtly bow, then with a nod of thanks to Beau and Thaddeus, they moved off with the unbroken grace and agility of the panther.

Beau, who had been sitting in a wash of pride, watching Raine with a deep intensity, leaned over to whisper something in her ear that prompted a kiss in response.

Long about ten o'clock, the coterie left the terrace for their rooms. It was time to prepare for their time-travel.

"We'll have to change out of our current clothes," Raine suggested, "and these heels."

"For sure," Maggie answered. "Let's hurry."

Some minutes later, the Sisters were wearing tissue-thin tunic tops, with three-quarter-length sleeves, over skirts of the same gauzy material. They had no access to period clothing, but the skirts were ankle-length, and the fabric and colors would suffice, Maggie's pale-peach, Raine's jungle-green. Having traded their strappy high heels for flats and gathered together a few magickal tools, in addition to their travel *Book of Shadows*, the girls were ready. At dinner, they'd handed their waitress a handful of teabags, asking that she prepare them a big pot of their special Tea-Time-Will-Tell brew to go.

Eager, as always, for yet another adventure, Thaddeus slid behind the wheel of their rental; and the coterie, armed with a mass of mettle and magick, drove off in the direction of la Pagerie.

"The last time we left the plantation, I noted a couple of places where I can pull this car off the road into the cover of jungle," the professor commented when they neared their destination. "We'll get as close to the *sucrerie* as we can, out of range of the cameras and alarms."

Raine laughed. "I knew you and Beau read our minds about the time-travel."

Beau guffawed heartily. "Didn't take a Gandhi to do that."

Raine mussed his ebony hair. "Very good, big boy. Gandhi is considered one of the greatest empaths who ever lived."

The coterie didn't talk much on the way, but when they were almost to the entrance of la Pagerie, Thaddeus delivered a heads-up.

"It's a dark night with this cloud cover, so it's going to be difficult to see, but watch for a side lane into the bush. I'll pull off to get us out of sight."

He slowed the Renault to a crawl, as they all strained to see a way into tropical forest.

"There should be a place … right about here," the professor mumbled.

"***There****!*" Beau hollered. "To the left."

Thaddeus backed up, then drove onto the narrow, unpaved path that led into utter jungle and layered darkness.

"Near as I can figure," the professor began, "we'll have about the length of a football field to walk to the *sucrerie*."

Once he was certain the car was completely invisible from the road, he stopped, and they got out.

The air seemed to sing softly with the nightly serenade of the tree frogs, otherwise it was a quiet, balmy night, humid, the air heavy with the threat of rain. In the night sky, the full moon slid behind the clouds, making their jungle cover even murkier. For several moments, the foursome stood, waiting for their eyes to adjust to the total darkness, which, coupled with the heavy atmosphere, felt like a smothering wet blanket.

"Night," Maggie breathed, "has the luminosity of the supernatural here." There came the sudden snapping of a twig, and something darted past. "Shhhhh …" She leaned her red head a little to the side, "*Listen.*" Whilst the witching hour drew nigh, the dark soul of night engulfed her, and the Sister felt a strange, primeval terror of she knew not what, causing her to shiver as though of an ague.

The soughing breeze moaned through the swaying palms to tremble the surrounding trees like castanets. In the trade wind, sugarcane rustled and whispered like the sheer lawn skirts of la Pagerie's mistresses from the distant past. Released by the darkness, fruit bats whistled a lonely tune, their presence enhancing an already eerie atmosphere– as the tropical night gave up its ghosts the island round.

"Raised on the folktales of her black nurse, Joséphine once said that Martinique nights unleash a procession of phantoms," Raine murmured. "I know now what she meant. It's as though the spirits are dancing, with all abandonment, the forbidden calinda."

All the scary, shadowy fancies she had ever heard about Martinique, a hideous throng to be sure, bolted from the cobwebs of her mind to recollection.

Glancing about, the Sisters took note. Vegetation that seemed innocuous in sun morphed frightening and grotesque under the moon to certain malevolent Voodoo mysteries. A tree that in daytime was merely a woody perennial changed, in the witching hours, to one of the zombies the *Martiniquais* called *tims-tims,* the living dead that walked the cane fields with staring, unfocused eyes that never close. Or, Goddess forbid, they'd encounter *la Diablesse,* the Devil-Woman who steps forth from behind a tree on a dark, lonely path, her cloven feet hidden under a flowing gown, to lure unsuspecting passersby to madness– or their deaths.

Then there was *Loup-Garou*, a shape-changer, who, having made a sinister deal with the Evil One, was given power over Nature, power to change form to that of a brutish werewolf. And if that were not enough, there was the *Soucouyant*, an evil crone who flies through the night sky as a ball of flame– to suck the lifeblood from her victims.

Intuiting his cohorts' uneasiness, Thaddeus whispered, "Ladies, ladies, don't let that extra-sensory splendor of yours run away with you. You'll scare one another to death with those tales. We've work to do."

Sure, the witching influence of the place had rendered them even more imaginative– to dream dreams and see apparitions– a contagion in the very air that blew from that haunted region to infect all who dared venture out once Martinique descended into darkness.

Maggie shivered again– both from zombies and the fact that the professor had seized their private thoughts. *Oh, I suppose it was easy enough to guess what Raine and I were thinking,* she told herself.

Coming abruptly out of reverie, Raine pressed her hands together. "Spot-on, Thad," she answered. "Let's find the right site to weave our magick."

They hiked farther down the dark path into what seemed like a yawning, black void. Moving through the night like specters, their hands in front of them, they felt their way till they came to a clearing, a small, circular glade that would perfectly serve the purpose of their ritual. Truth to say, it was *such* a perfect spot for magick, the Sisters wondered, simultaneously, if others had used it for that end.

Magick exudes from this site, from the earth, the trees and foliage, from the very atmosphere, Maggie sent telepathically to Raine, whose tip-tilted eyes glittered completely green, pupils dilated, as though they belonged to a cat negotiating its way in total dark.

The Goth gal stood still, using her empath ability to sense all she could about the place where they halted. *Nothing nasty*, she cast in conclusion to her sister of the moon.

Maggie echoed her thought. *No, no evil vibes here.*

Raine gazed through the tall palms to check the moon, but it was still behind the driving clouds that repeatedly hid it from sight, whilst the stars seemed to sink deeper into the sky. Skilled witches and practiced time-travelers that they'd become, the Sisters had ample time for preparation before the midnight hour, the most auspicious time for utilizing their Time-Key.

They sucked in a deep breath of air to center themselves, releasing it slowly.

Thaddeus, meanwhile, was straining his sharp ears for any noises he might pick up. "The tree frogs dominate, but if you listen really hard," he whispered, "you can hear birdsong. One is a monotonous, almost constant tweeting, but others chime in, now and again, with a variety of sounds. They blend so well with the 'koo-keeeee' chorus of tree frogs it's easy to miss them."

Beau was busy checking the security of their surroundings, being careful not to make any noise or attract attention from anyone near or passing by.

Raine tilted her face to the sky to again check the moon. It was something she did before every time-trek. The large pink orb was gliding free from a patch of clouds. *One of the names for June's Moon is Rose Moon*, she remembered. How fitting! Rose is the name to which Joséphine answered during the era we'll be time-trekking.

To the Sister's solace, there were no rings nor blood on the moon. Her relief was palpable as rain in tropical heat. Solemnly, she raised her arms, releasing her usual full-moon petition, *Oh hail, fair moon, leader of night! Protect me and mine until it is light.*

Opening her bag, Raine began rummaging inside until her fingers found the small lamp-like lantern she borrowed from her hotel room. Reaching into her pocket for the lighter she used when smudging, she lit the candle inside and set it down on a flat rock, taking a seat next to it. "Checking for essentials," she said. "Pepper spray. I make a point of carrying it everywhere, as well as an ampoule of Granny's healing potion. Just in case."

"With the great Goddess' help and protection, let's get started on our quest," Maggie advised.

Raine opened the big straw carryall, purchased at the *marché,* wide enough to extract the thermos the hotel kitchen lent them, handing it to Maggie. Then the Goth gal groped briefly through the bag's contents to locate and draw out the small stack of plastic cups they brought from their rooms.

"You recall, after our last time-trek, that I was right about the amount of Granny's flying potion we should use. Hence, this time again, *two* drops of Easy Breezy Flying Potion; and we indulge, as last trip, in two cups of our calming tea, one drop of Easy Breezy per cup."

After pouring their Tea-Time-Will-Tell special brew, Raine extracted a glowing vial of Granny's silvery flying potion to shake a drop into three of the cups.

"I haven't forgotten about you, Beau," the raven-haired Sister said a few moments later. She dove into the straw bag for the airline-miniature of rum, gifted to them on their flight, she had included in their repertoire of things, pouring it into the fourth cup. "To wish us safe passage."

After handing Maggie and Thaddeus a filled vessel of tea laced with flying potion, Raine smiled. "As always, this calls for a special cheering cup. Thaddeus, you do the honors."

Their cohort pondered a moment before raising his cup in a most succinct toast. "To the safety and success of our mission! So mote it be!"

"So mote it be," the Sisters and Beau stirred in response.

"Blessed Be!" the group chorused in unified voice.

Presently, the time-travelers drained their second cup, as thoughts turned to their task at hand.

"Before takeoff, let's review some important data," Maggie said. "We don't plan on dallying. We'll get what we need and get back as quickly as we can. Beau, as you've seen with our previous missions, you will see with this one. From takeoff to the moment of our return, not one second will have passed."

Raine hurriedly checked her belt pouch for an item that popped into thought. It was the trusty, lion-faced compact that had belonged to the lionhearted Granny McDonough. The charged item had become a good-luck charm to the Sisters, providing an extra measure of the magickal mix of protection, assurance and conviction they carried with them on each of their journeys into the past. Both she and Maggie were sporting "travelers' belts" with zip pouches over their tunic blouses.

"As we have for former time-treks," Raine reminded, "we'll cast the magickal spell to deal with the era's speech."

After momentarily conferring with Maggie on the ritual they would be performing, Raine continued, "Within our secret chant, we'll weave a spell that will *witch* speech– *hear and tell.* In other words, our speech will be heard by everyone we might encounter as dialect familiar to them. For this trek, in French, of course. The enchantment will work in the reverse as well, so that *everything* spoken to us and around us will sound … that is, will *translate* to our ears like our own modern English dialogue, including slang and patterns of speech.

"We are aware, the enchantment is not perfect," Raine recapped. "Some words and phrases may flee the charm, but the spell *will* work." She gave a sigh. "We don't plan to be exchanging dialogue with anyone this trip. At least, I hope we won't. It's just a precautionary measure. However, we do want to be able to *understand* everything we hear. I think that just about covers it. I believe we're ready to begin."

It was at this juncture of their preparations when their poppet, Cara, would bless them with a kiss blown from her magickal mouth but supplied by their granny, a rush of crystalline faerie dust, all silver and gold and shimmering, that wafted comfortingly to the time-trekkers to settle over them, brightening and polishing their auras to a Divine brilliance– an ultra-strong Light of Protection. The farewell kiss had become a pre-takeoff tradition that the Sisters set great store by. Nonetheless, though their poppet was not with them, they could still *feel* Granny McDonough's presence infusing them with power. Their thoughts and the love vibration had drawn her.

It was time.

"Are we ready?" Raine asked.

"We are," Maggie and Thaddeus responded at once.

"Let us spiritually and mentally prepare ourselves for our passage," Maggie stated evenly.

Looking at Beau, Raine could tell, via her empath capability, he was feeling apprehensive. "By all rights, this trip should go off without a hitch. I'll say again, we'll be back in a literal flash, with no actual lapse in time, for we are scientifically mindful, as well as spiritually aware, that the past, present, and future are simultaneous."

She glanced up, through the tall, swaying palms, at the moon. Having slid from cloud cover, it was directly overhead.

"Raine," Maggie bade, "douse that lantern now, and let us proceed." She delved into the straw bag for the magickal tools they would need when a sudden anticipation, like a bolt of electricity, sent shivers up her spine. She experienced similar feelings before each time-trek, though each pre-flight sensation was different from the others. The excitement that currently seized her wakened the imagination in a strange new way.

Both Sisters, concurrently, felt a telltale tingling of the skin. Something exhilarating was going to happen, something beyond the actual time-travel!

Rooted to the spot where she stood, the redheaded Sister listened intently. The trade wind had kicked up a bit since their arrival, and for a moment, it felt cold as ice. She thought she heard a voice on those gusts. "I'm here … I've been waiting for you. Waiting … waiting for you …"

The entity was speaking in French, but Maggie understood perfectly.

She inclined her head, hardly daring to breathe– expecting to hear the voice again. But now only the wind whispered, and on its breath floated a name.

This wood has a ghost. She turned to regard Raine, who sent her a questioning look.

You heard the voice too, didn't you, Mags? Raine tele-communicated with quickened breath.

*I did. Joséphine **wants** us to do this. She's calling to us from the other side of the veil. I just know something wonderful is going to happen!*

In contrast, the spectral presence seemed not to have the slightest effect on Thaddeus, who, in an effort to bring Raine and Maggie out of trance, was waving a hand before their faces. "Hello! Sisters!"

They looked up, quite startled to be thus roused, and smiling inwardly– focused.

"Our chant will incorporate all the particulars. The date we've chosen to visit is Tuesday, 31 August 1790," Raine stated. She turned to Maggie, standing close on her right. "'Tis good that our target date is a Tuesday, for this is the day of the week ruled by Mars, the planet of energy and action. As an Aries and a Scorpio, we are each overseen by Mars." A thought struck her. "As a Scorpio, Thad, too, is governed by Mars, though Scorpios are also ruled by Pluto. Anyway, Mars-ruled people, Mars-ruled day– this trek will be successful in every possible way," she programmed.

"It's almost midnight," Thaddeus prompted. "Let's make haste."

"Right," Maggie replied. "We're encoding to reach this same spot at eight in the evening of our targeted date. We want to make certain it is dark enough for our sleuthing." She cleared her throat. "Beau will be right here, waiting for us upon our return."

At a signal from Raine, Beau handed that Sister the container of sea salt, a lighter, and a small bundle of white sage. With the salt, she drew a circle around herself and her companions. Flicking the fire-starter, she lit the sage. In an instant, the air around them filled with the pungent tang of the good smoking essence.

Walking a circle with the smudge deosil– clockwise– the brunette Sister cleansed the area of negativity as the coterie chanted a strong incantation of protection, ending with the petition, "God-Goddess between us and all harm."

As one, the Sisters and their men charged, "Wind spirit! Fire in all its brightness! The sea in all its deepness! Earth, rocks, in all their firmness! All these elements we now place, by God-Goddess' almighty strength and grace, between ourselves and the powers of darkness. So mote it be! Blessed Be!"

In keeping with her practice, the raven-haired Sister began bracing herself for the Time Tunnel's bluster. For the third instance, she checked her belt for the few little things she might need, then she re-zipped the deep pouch, feeling beneath her blouse for her talisman. *She was ready to fly.*

Taking her cue from Raine, Maggie did likewise, preparing herself for takeoff.

"Talismans at the ready!" Maggie, the slightly older Sister commanded. She pulled her amulet and that of Aisling's free from their resting place beneath her gauzy tunic to lift the silver chains over her fiery hair. The talismans' center-stones, hers ruby, Aisling's sapphire, along with the scatter of tiny jewels on each amulet, glittered and flared energy in a beam of moonlight that streamed through the greeny-black cathedral of stately palms.

Raine removed her amulet from around her neck. In addition to their talismans, each Sister wore a medieval ring of great significance and deep-seated arcane forces. Hundreds of years old, worn and dulled by Time, the rings' brass shafts bore faded secret symbols etched into the sides of the mounts that individually held a large blue moonstone.

Already, the ancient rings were beginning to emit a shared bluish luster, a glow that looked particularly eerie in the murky shadows of their ritual circle. Known as the "Travelers' Stone" and specifically gifted for pathfinders, moonstone illuminated dark pathways and especially protected those who travel by night.

Under their unified protection, the Sleuth Sisters held out and fit together the trilogy of necklaces bequeathed to them years before by Granny McDonough, whose influential presence her granddaughters sensed more keenly with every passing moment. In those Sisterly hands, the powerful talismans actually warmed the skin as they verily hummed with energy.

"Fellow believers and practitioners of the Craft," Maggie enunciated in her mellifluous voice, "for the archaic definition of *talisman*, we hark back to ancient times. Before it was known as a magickal symbol, *talisman* carried a far older meaning. From the Greek word *telesma*, meaning 'complete,' a talisman in olden times was any object that completed another– *and made it whole.* I say this to remind and assure us, here present this night, under this arboreal cathedral of the great Goddess– of the majestic Power of Three."

Maggie looked to Thaddeus. "In addition to Aisling's talisman, which I will be wearing with my own to complete the Triquetra, *you* have been charged with the honor of standing in for our absent Sister, Aisling."

It would not be the first time Dr. Weatherby time-traveled with the Sisters in Aisling's place. He was a worthy substitute, though only the Sisters could wear the ancient McDonough talismans.

The full moon, sliding from beneath a cloud, whence it had briefly cached itself– as if waiting for just the right moment to make its debut– flashed a timely and quite dazzling blaze of light off the fitted talismanic pieces as the Sleuth Sisters united their voices to invoke in perfect harmony, "With the Power of Three, we shall craft and be granted our plea. With the Power of Three, so mote it be. With the Power of Three, so Blessed Be."

Raine and Maggie embraced Thaddeus for a long, loving moment, as memories of all they'd shared and accomplished together came flooding back to each of them. The Sisters, seasoned to the Craft, knew the love vibration to be the most powerful of all, that magick works best when vibrations are high and stress low. Love was the "juice" that enabled and energized their magick!

In the moon-drenched radiance of tropical jungle, it was a moment of supreme empowerment.

The Sisters slipped the amulets back over their heads, safely securing the sacred pendants under their clothing, Maggie with her own and Aisling's.

With careful expression, then, in the directed glow from Beau's keychain flashlight, the Sisters and Thaddeus intoned aloud the ancient Gaelic words, the arcane phrases Raine and Maggie had, over the years, so diligently ferreted out, the secret text neatly handwritten across their small *Book of Shadow*'s final pages– the ordaining language that programmed and powered their sacred travel through time.

The Time-Key.

Since the ancient chant was in Old Irish, in order to get it letter-perfect, it was best for the Sisters to *read* the words from their *Book of Shadows,* though the mantra had virtually imbedded itself, by this juncture, into their collective memories. In fact, Thaddeus' eidetic memory had snagged and saved the incantation the very first time he recited it with the Sisters, and as Time proved, it was a good thing he had.

Their unified voices rising with each line in crescendo, the Sisters closed the current segment of their ritual. "To honor the Olde Ones in deed and name, let Love and Light be our guides again. These eight words the Witches' Rede fulfill– 'And harm ye none; do what ye will.' By moon and stars, this spell is cast, bestow anew the Secret we ask. **Energize the Time-Key!** So mote it be! Blessed Be!"

In perfect stillness did they wait.

Not a sound broached the silence save the pounding of hearts. The night, at some point, had become hushed, their surroundings quieting even of night creatures and wind, exclusive of a gentle island breeze. The moon cast shadows through the tree tops to the ground, as the towering palms, swaying in the prevailing trade winds, seemed to *breathe* a message that was just beyond hearing.

The Sisters knew from past experiences not to fluster, hence they used the interval to further center themselves, drawing in their breaths and breathing out slowly, sustaining the placid mood conferred on them by the relaxing tea and their granny's sanctification.

And as it had been with their previous time-treks, it was as though something momentous were about to unfurl within the established circle. Here waited wise old Chronos, and in his fingers, the glittering coiled thread of past, present and future, a magickal yo-yo made to rise and fall to the hand of Time.

"Let us restate the passage. The power is in the word," the Sisters prudently advised.

"We have made our choice, and now we must focus," Maggie ordained. "We've woven our intent within the charm. We *will* arrive at our programmed destination. Let us put aside– each of us– any and all doubts, fears, and *impatience*. Witches know magick cannot be rushed. When the time is right, wishes, desires, and blessings come to pass."

The redheaded Sister paused a moment. "We need to free ourselves from all negativity– and simply allow the Great Secret to happen. For happen it will. Let us give ourselves up to it."

Once more, the Sisters chanted the ancient evocation, arms upstretched in calling forth. Prompted by Raine, they added at the last, **"Now is the time! This is the hour! Ours is the magick! Ours is the power!"**

Having repeated the afterword *thrice*, the Sisters' talismans, resting against their skins, radiated with heat– and the super Power of Three– as the conjured energies sparked, swished and swirled around them like something enlivened by the touch of a wand, a wand infused with the magick of powerful ancestors and elders.

They could feel those energies mounting in a great cone of power– *a huge witch's hat, omnipotent and unstoppable*– beginning slowly but steadily to rise above their heads. It was the way of strong magick, and thus it did not frighten these winning witches or their cohorts the least bit.

For a fleeting moment, both Sisters thought they detected something filmy white and vapory above the soaring palms. They raised their eyes to the moonlit sky.

The vapor, clouds, or spectral image was shaped like a beautiful woman, a woman in a diaphanous white gown of centuries past.

Could it be la Belle Créole, Joséphine? they asked themselves, the brainwave bouncing from one Sister to the other. There came next a whispering, a soft, low voice; and this time, all four people in that tropical glade listened intently. What was it they were hearing?

Though they strained their ears, they could not make out what the enchanting drawl was attempting to convey. There was nothing more– only the reawakened wind soughing through the trees and, beyond, the textured darkness with no sign of the apparition.

All they could do was wait in sharp anticipation.

Out of the blackness and expanse of that memorable night, they heard the captivating voice once again, speaking to them in velvety French.

"I'm waiting … wait—ing …"

"Wiz–zard," Raine exclaimed, a glimmer of a smile flitting over her features to kindle her emerald eyes in the moonlight.

At this point, like the tingle of a rising tropical storm on the horizon, they all sensed the escalating magick.

In the bat of an eye it came, softly at first, then louder, an electrical crackling sound, as gleaming flashes and orbs of white light zigged and zagged above and around the witches' circle, turning the tree-shrouded scene increasingly eerie.

Magick snapped and sizzled in the very air they breathed, as gaining strength, their established cone of power rose higher.

Closing her eyes, Raine could actually see, on her mind's eye, the silvery gold cone of energy rising in that huge witch's hat above their heads.

No sooner had Beau, at Raine and Maggie's signal, taken a step back, outside the circle of time-travelers, when a terrific gust of wind rushed across the area, lashing the tall trees and dense jungle wildly with creaking, sharp sounds as branches crackled and rubbed together, and clouds grazed the ghostly face of the moon.

Otherworldly in its timbre, the gale bore on its breath the bewitching flutes of the mysterious race of people gifted with supernatural powers who invaded and ruled Ireland over four thousand years ago, the mystical *Tuatha De Danann*, from whom the Sisters had gained the coveted Time-Key.

Like the wail of the banshee, the mesmerizing music grew louder whilst the squall whistled and moaned a siren's song of its own. Moonlight shimmered in the Sisters' hair, the stiff breeze whipping it about their faces.

So strong grew this tempest, howling and whirling with accelerated ferocity– *Like a lost soul hunting for a grave,* thought Maggie– that she grasped Raine to the right and Thaddeus to her left, gripping their arms hard. "Steady on now!" the redheaded Sister called above the din, though the gale tore at her long skirt, and the balmy air bore suddenly a glacial chill. "We know what's coming!"

The words barely left Maggie's lips when, in a jet stream of light, a bevy of ethereal faces, skeletal figures, and vaporish human forms appeared in the rising mists, their gaunt arms widening imploringly, their mouths opening in what looked to be silent screams. As the strange beings zeroed in, the time-travelers caught snatches of the Time-Key's magick formula of words.

A millisecond more and another surge of light! The figures' claw-like hands snaked tightly round the time-trekker's ankles, heaving them with supernatural strength toward the vortex of a pitch-black tunnel– a twister of helical wind that threatened to pull them into its infinite void with the force of a gigantic vacuum.

Undaunted but not wanting to be separated, Raine, Maggie, and Thaddeus held fast to one another, strengthening their power and protection with the concentrated love they shared, the action setting off a riot of magickal sparks.

"Your sorcery has done its work. The power is strong tonight!" The professor's mandate rang out– "***Let it happen!***"

Simultaneously, just outside the circle and their established Doorway of Time, Beau disentangled himself from clutching foliage to thrust his arms skyward, ebony hair blowing violently about his upturned face, his eyes bright as gas flames burning blue, whilst the wind spun the ancient charm round the Sisters and Thaddeus– faster and faster and faster!

For a magickal moment, the steely time-travelers were limned in silver– each a nimbus of light that overlapped, one to the other, with stunning brilliance.

Through the crashes of sound, they could still hear the chant. Knowing that "three's a charm" and propelled by the love vibration, the chrononauts raised their joined arms, keeping cadence with the wraithlike figures– to repeat the last line of the arcane passage for the third time.

A thick, vaporous cloud was rising from the depths of the ground– that started rolling and rumbling beneath their feet– even as the air around them continued to swish and swirl like the mightiest of whirlpools. A jagged streak of lightning split the sky behind them to smote the ground just outside the circle. A great tree shivered and splintered from the impact, and a tremendous roll of thunder walloped their ears with a commanding **RO——————AR!**

Maggie squeezed her cohorts' hands. "It's happening!" she called out, determined to stay calm.

"Make ready," Raine shouted, "we'll soon be on our way!"

An ear-shattering clap of lightning momentarily transformed the shadowy glade to brightest noon. A crash of thunder that shook the earth, and–

Suddenly, in the vortex' hellish battle with Time, the churning atmosphere opened with a violent suction, causing the Sisters and Thaddeus to feel as if they were being swept down a giant drain, as Beau disappeared from their view in a brilliant burst of blue-white light. Rapidly then did the Tunnel wholly swallow the trio of time-travelers, their voices rebounding after them–

"Bles————————sed Beeeeeeeeeeeeeeeeeeeeeeeeee!"

Quicker than any one of them could answer "Blessed Be," the threesome was plunged into blackest darkness, forcibly hauled deeper and deeper– into the interminable Tunnel of Time.

Above the din, Maggie's voice echoed through the dark corridor, **"Hold tight to one another! Can't chance being sep— arrrr—aaaa—teddddd!"**

Raine's words followed, rumbling down the mysterious passageway. **"To—geth—errrrr weeeeeeeeeee goooooooooooooooooooooooooooooooooo!"**

"Remember always:
Your heart is made of moonbeams,
and your soul is sated with stars."
~ Grantie Merry McDonough

Chapter Fifteen

With a loud swish and a flash of light, the time-travelers found themselves in a moon-splashed glade of tall palm trees.

"Ooooooooooh, **yes**!" Maggie exclaimed, grasping Thaddeus for support. "I'm so glad we finally hit on the right formula for our pre-Key ritual. I don't feel shaky and dizzy as I did on earlier trips through the Time Tunnel."

"And look at us," Raine exhaled with satisfaction riding on her words. "We've landed on our feet. We did the last couple of times, yes, but we were a tad queasy. Not any more we aren't!" She looked to Thaddeus, who appeared to be already checking out the setting. "You OK, Thad?"

"I'm good." His gaze skimmed across the space where they touched down. "Looks like we hit our mark, but at this point, it's damn near impossible to say."

From beyond the trees and foliage came the sound of black voices singing, accompanied by the insistent drum beats that throbbed of dancing the voodoo calinda.

"Shhhhh. Did you hear that? It's coming from the slave cabins on the other side of this jungle. One thing we know for certain is that la Pagerie's slaves and slave cabins have gone the way of history." Scanning their surroundings, Maggie noted, "Beau is nowhere to be seen. Another sure sign we've time-traveled."

"Let's just hope it's Tuesday, 31 August 1790," Raine said, her eyes probing the encompassing dark jungle.

Glancing about, Thaddeus whispered to the Sisters, "Stay put and keep your voices down. We don't want to entertain company in our modern mufti," he jested. "In all seriousness, our biggest concern is the slave uprising. Things could turn nasty real fast. *I'll* scout the area quickly. Be back in a flash."

"Be careful," Maggie and Raine cautioned.

"Always," the professor answered.

In Thaddeus' absence, the spooky sensations of the surroundings were heightened by the sounds from the slave quarters. Through the foliage, only flickers of their fires were visible, but their drumming and singing drifted fervently on the evening air.

"Night is the slaves' time, their only real period of leisure," Raine whispered. "All their living is done in hours of darkness, the time when their masters felt least secure ... a time of revolts and mysterious disappearances."

"Though there are historical indications la Pagerie's slaves were not mistreated, and there're clues Joséphine was kind to them, there's no *real* evidence to suggest that la Pagerie was any better or worse in their treatment of slaves," Maggie answered *sotto voce*.

"I know," Raine had to agree. "I guess we could say la Pagerie was a place of disturbing contrasts, the pretty gardens and shade trees of the family compound against the thirty-eight squalid little huts that made up the slave quarters– dark, airless hovels with dirt floors and straw beds."

She thought for a moment. "The household was trumpeted awake each morning by the slave master blowing his conch shell at sunrise. Slaves labored in the cane fields, bent under the lash in the searing sun, from sunrise to sunset, six days a week, all year long, since cane could be planted any time. And on their one day off, the poor souls were expected to work on their own plot of land."

"A hard, hard life," Maggie lamented, shaking her head, trying to fathom the evil that was slavery. "Perhaps not here on la Pagerie, but for so many slaves, I imagine death was a welcome release."

"Sex made the already intense atmosphere even more heated," Raine added. "It was a widely accepted practice for male plantation owners to take liberties with their female slaves. Plantation wives were expected to live with their husband's concubines and offspring."

Maggie responded with a brisk nod. "It was no mystery why Créole women developed a rep for vindictiveness toward female slaves. Talk about a complicated situation! To plantation wives, female slaves were at once property, constant companions, and rivals." She considered for a moment, saying, "Though terrible, slavery was a norm of those times. But as we progress as humanity, terrible norms are righted."

Raine heaved a sigh. "Well, Mags, you and I never soft-pedal history, nor does Thaddeus. Burying history leads to the repetition of age-old events. People need to be aware of the past, to acknowledge it, no matter how horrible it was. To forget or bury the past is to cheapen the lives of those who lived it, who struggled through it, both for those who were persecuted and those who did good. Thank the great Goddess, times change, norms change, and yes, Right eventually wins out. Blessed be."

"Blessed be," Maggie concurred.

Thaddeus returned at that moment from his reconnaissance to report, "I didn't see any trouble brewing over at the slave quarters ... *yet* anyway. I did see the balcony that Joséphine's father built on the *sucrerie*, and we're in luck. There's a trellis right next to it. I crept close to check it for strength. It seems strong, but it might not support my weight or," he looked to his beloved, "even Maggie's for that matter. Raine, I think you just might be the best choice to go into the residence. The fact that you're wearing dark clothing is good too."

The daring Sister was afire with eagerness. "Suits me." Her pouty lips curved in her little-cat smile. Clearly, she was pleased with the situation.

"Scale the trellis to the balcony. The louvered doors are open," the professor directed. "I'm assuming the balcony is off what we would call the 'master bedroom,' and that's, I believe, *precisely* where you want to spy. Hopefully, Lady Luck will continue smiling on us, and the mistress of la Pagerie will see fit, in a manner of speaking, to reveal her secret stash-away this night of the slave rebellion."

Thaddeus looked skyward. "The moon keeps sliding in and out of cloud cover, so we'll have light and shadow, which we'll put to good use accordingly."

"Let's not waste any time," Raine insisted. "We don't know when trouble will arise."

"Quickly and quietly," Dr. Weatherby alerted. "As I estimated, we're about a football field away from the *sucrerie*." He grasped an arm of each Sister, and they started off as fast as they dared.

A few minutes later, the trio was peering through the thick foliage– a tangle of bamboo, rubber trees, and towering hardwoods with vines and hanging vegetation– at the sugar refinery, the second floor of which was the family residence. The air was even heavier than before.

"Going to pour cats and dogs any minute now," Maggie said in a whisper.

Glancing round, Raine was just about to start for the trellis, when Thaddeus reached out to stop her. "Wait till that capricious moon slips behind the clouds. You don't want to be seen from a window, running across the lawn. When you get up to the balcony, be sure to peek inside those louvres to see if anyone's in that bedroom. Better safe than sorry. Oh, I nearly forgot to mention. I heard someone talking when I was checking the trellis. Seems Joséphine's father is not at home. He's in Fort-de-France, where he's expected to spend the night. Another break for us." He took Raine by the shoulders. "As soon as you get what we came for, *get out*. Be vigilant, and don't take any chances." It was but a short wait before he prompted, "*Go!*"

As Raine raced across the open expanse of lawn toward the *sucrerie*, she picked up her consorts' unified thought– *Be careful!*

A witch knows how to deflect attention, the Sister sent back through the ethers. *A witch knows how to hide in plain sight.*

Arriving at her destination, she straightaway began climbing the trellis. It was then a large, black dog appeared out of nowhere to station himself at the foot of the lattice and begin barking loudly.

Holding fast to the trellis whilst flattened against the *sucrerie* wall, Raine prayed the rung would sustain her stationary weight as she fixed him with her witchy stare to immediately send a telepathic message to quiet himself, that he had nothing to fear– she was a friend. *Tais-toi! Sois calme! Pas de danger. Je suis une amie.*

The dog instantly stopped barking, tilting his huge head in wonder to emit a friendly sound of compliance. However, at that express moment, the door opened, and a rough male voice, Raine supposed of a servant, called, "*Dauphin, viens ici!*"

With that, the dog trotted inside, and the man closed and bolted the door.

He's not just a guard dog, Raine told herself. *I'd wager he's used to track runaway slaves too.*

Breathing a sigh of relief, she scampered up the lattice's remaining cross-boards, hoisting herself over the wooden railing as gingerly and quietly as she could. *Thank the Goddess the soles of my shoes are rubber,* she thought.

From the balcony, she peered warily through the partially open louvered doors to a dark bedroom. Fickle moonlight showed the room to be empty. Ducking inside, she was just about to look around, when she heard the distinct sound of approaching footfalls.

There was only one thing to do. She scooted under the bed, an old-world bed with a high tester, to lie flat on her belly.

Thankfully, the lace coverlet came down far enough to hide her, though she could see through it.

A moment later, the door opened and Raine recognized, from her portrait in history books, Joséphine's mother, carrying a lit taper and, in the other hand, something else, that the Sister was unable to detect. She wore a chatelaine at her waist, from which hung keys and what looked to be a small change purse. The thing made a slight jingle-jangling sound when she moved.

Striding to the stone wall, the stately Rose-Claire set the taper down on a stand and, with both her hands, pulled a large stone from the wall, put it aside, and extracted, from the crevice, what looked to be, in an obliging beam of moonlight, a small, silver chest with a domed lid. Opening it, the mistress of the manor deposited something inside. By the sound it made, Raine immediately thought *Coins.* Then, *madame* snapped the lid shut, replaced the box to the wall, slid the stone back into place, and picking up the taper, exited the room, pulling the door closed with a clang after her.

What luck! the Sister thought, beaming with the discovery as she crept out of her hiding place beneath the bed. Standing, she advanced to the spot, committed to memory, where she'd seen Rose-Claire pull the stone free from the wall. Using the keychain flashlight from her belt pouch, she scanned the wall to see a crudely etched *fleur-de-lys* in the upper corner of a large stone. The mark was hardly noticeable. With her fingers, she felt to ascertain if that was the loose stone. Satisfied that it was, she was just about to exit the room for the balcony, when she heard frantic pounding at the door below, followed by a man's excited petition.

"I have an urgent message for *Madame de Beauharnais.* I need to speak with her at once."

"*D'accord, monsieur.* I will call her," a female responded with swift compliance.

Groping her way, Raine cat-footed it to the flower-flanked balcony, where she ducked down behind a rattan chair to eavesdrop, crouched there, unmoving and grateful she understood the French she was hearing. In a moment, a swishing of skirts, and the Sister was privileged to hear Joséphine's legendary voice.

"What is it, *mon ami?* You seem anxious." Then after a slight pause in which the gentleman caller started to speak, the listening Raine heard again the seductive, beguiling drawl, mellifluous as warmed honey. "Oooooh, but this is such a pleasant surprise. Shall we walk in the garden? The balmy scent of tropical flowers has never been so sweet."

A soldier's instinct made him glance quickly about before seizing her around the waist to taste the burning ardor of her lips. For the next moment or two, Raine could just barely hear their exchange of words.

"Mmmmm, kiss me again, *mon capitaine*," came the honeyed drawl. "I am hungry for kissing tonight."

He yanked her closer. "You need kissing badly, Rose, and I am just the man to do it, but now is not the time."

"Ooooh, *mon capitaine*," came the breathy teasing response, "how can you be so cruel as to ignite a fire you intend to smother?" There was a beat of silence. "And so hot a fire. So hot …"

Fasten your seatbelts, the Goth gal thought à la Bette Davis' Hollywood, *it's going to be a bumpy night.*

From her years of research on the future empress, Raine knew that the young officer at the door was a man who had a way with women, a charismatic and commanding aristocrat whom Joséphine had often fluttered her eyelashes and danced with abandonment at Government House across the bay, where her uncle was port commander. The dashing captain quite likely rendezvoused with the sensual Créole, nights, at a secret spot on la Pagerie. Certainly, they were acting as though more existed between them than a nodding acquaintance.

Without preamble, *Capitaine* Tercier released his embrace to deliver his news. "Danger is afoot, *chérie*. The slaves are out of hand, burning and pillaging; and led by a group of revolutionaries from Paris, they have overrun Fort-Royal and captured the shore batteries. Your uncle has been taken hostage. If you wish to–"

This was a thunderclap! Joséphine's hand rushed from the lapel of the military uniform to her open mouth, "*Oh!*" Staring in stunned disbelief, her heart hammering against her chest, the easily roused woman struggled to fight the tides of emotion sweeping through her. "*Mon Dieu!*" she exclaimed, fear heavy on her voice. "*Que faire?*"

"There is only one thing *to do*," he answered flatly. "You must board a ship and leave Martinique tonight. I have secured passage to France on the *Sensible*."

"But how? How will–"

"I know the captain. I met with him secretly before I came here. He kindly agreed to take you aboard. The *Sensible* sails for France at midnight. If you do not leave tonight, you might find yourself stranded here in the midst of chaos. Likely there'll be little or no shipping between Martinique and France after the *Sensible* sets sail. I know of what I speak, *chérie*." In an attempt to keep her calm, there was little emotion in his tone. It was a simple statement of fact– which, to his listener, sounded all the more ominous.

Joséphine was beginning to feel desperate. "Come in. I will pack my bags," she answered with an effort to sound composed.

"There's no time for that," Tercier stressed, his voice taking on urgency. "If you're coming, we must leave now, *at once*. Do as I say, Rose! The situation here on Martinique has already turned foul."

"I cannot leave without my daughter and my … Euphémie!" Taking note of the exigence on his face, she switched gears. "*Wait!* I will be but a few moments."

"*Dépêche-toi!* **Hurry!**"

As is common in the Sugar Islands, it started suddenly to rain, a cloudburst, with the wind kicking up. The raven-haired Sister, cached on the roofed balcony above the entrance, had only a short wait until, again, she heard the voices below her.

"*Allons!*" *Capitaine* Tercier shouted above the din of tropical storm. He took his lover's arm in a firm grip. "Let's make haste!"

From her position, Raine watched Joséphine– holding a frightened little Hortense's hand and accompanied by their faithful servant and companion, Euphémie, each of them enveloped in a shawl– dash toward the lawn with the uniformed officer. The Goth gal noted, too, that Joséphine had a small bundle tied and tucked under one arm.

She must have tossed a few things into another scarf, she told herself, remembering the future empress' insatiable penchant for shawls.

Joséphine ran but a few steps, abruptly stopping in her tracks.

"What's wrong?" Tercier yelled above the wind. "We **cannot** dally!"

"My bracelet is caught in my wrap," she yelled.

A surge of impatience made him shout even louder, "Hurry, there's no time to lose!"

Raine watched as the frantic woman jerked her arm free.

"My bracelet!" she screamed. "It fell off. Help me find it!"

Euphémie stooped to the ground, where she began feeling with her hands, at which time, the four people about to flee heard suddenly the roar of cannon from the captured battery.

"We've no time for this nonsense. Look!" the captain flung out an arm in the direction of Fort-Royal, to the scarlet haze in the night sky, the blood-hued smoke reflected in the waters of the bay and lighting Joséphine's dark hair with a fiery red glow. "And there!" he pointed to what appeared to be a mass of lit lanterns moving toward them from a distance. Fervid voices carried on the wind. "Slave gangs coming here to recruit la Pagerie slaves for the rebellion."

Joséphine's hazel eyes widened in panic. *"Mon Dieu!* I should feel like a traitor. A traitor! I cannot leave my mother, my–" she broke off with a sob, wrestling mentally with her fears.

"No one will harm them," Euphémie assured, taking her half-sister firmly by the shoulders. She knew her temperamental sibling well, knew that even under normal circumstances, she was inclined to cry at the slightest provocation. "The slaves here are not treated cruelly," she persevered. "The family is well-loved."

"But the danger, the gangs!" Joséphine burst into a flood of tears, hating herself for her cowardice. *"Maman and our sister ... Manette is not well, and Papa is away–"*

"When the captain arrived," Euphémie interposed truthfully, "I told *madame* to bolt the doors and stay inside."

Joséphine stared at her half-sister with an air almost of madness, then started piteously to protest, when again Euphémie stopped her short. **"Listen to me, Rose!"** she shrieked, gripping the sobbing young woman's shoulders tighter as though to shake sense into her. "You and I both know your mother will *never* leave this plantation!"

Before the hesitant Joséphine had a chance to respond, Tercier, having run out of patience, grasped her arm painfully to yank her forward. "Enough! *Allons!*"

She seemed surprised and inclined to protest, but yielded to her lover's insistence.

The rain, too, was falling with persistent heaviness as the four resumed their race across the expanse of lawn– to escape.

Crouched yet on the balcony, Raine told herself, *That's how the bracelet came to be lost. And their hurrying feet tramped it into the mud.* She thought for a beat. *This happened at the start of the tropical storm and hurricane season, so the heavy rains ... and more and more traipsing feet pounded it farther and farther down into the earth until another hurricane, that last one, well over two centuries later, brought it to the surface.*

The empathic Sister felt Joséphine's tumultuous fear and stress, the feelings warring within her heart. What she did not know is that less than two hours later, when the frigate *Sensible* set sail for France, fired upon unsuccessfully by the insurgent cannoneers, the pent-up emotions of the future empress would release themselves in a deluge of the bitterest tears she would ever shed.

The Rose of Martinique knew she would be penniless in Paris, but her tears of grief were the result of a keen sense of loss, the kind of loss she was not destined to suffer again till the end of her life, when, in delirium, she would cry out for the only man she would ever truly love.

Raine quickly descended the lattice, leaping to the ground and nearly slipping on the wet grass. As suddenly as it had started, the rain stopped. Dashing for the cover of jungle to rejoin a drenched Maggie and Thaddeus, she caught the flashes of light from the lanterns, as well as the excited shouts from the marauding gang homing in on la Pagerie's slave cabins.

"Any luck?" Maggie breathed, when her sister of the moon rejoined her cohorts in the foliage.

"Wizard luck, Mags. I'll tell you everything as soon as we Time-Key home." Secretly pleased with herself, the plucky Sister peered through the hanging vines of a mahogany tree to see that the mob had reached its destination.

"We're not going *anywhere* till that gang moves off," Thaddeus whispered. "Keep low and don't make a sound. Don't stir an inch, no matter what you see or hear. Cover your mouth if you have to."

"They're speaking *Patois*," Raine whispered. "Ordinarily, I'd only be able to make out a few words, but we're picking up most of it due to the speech-charm we cast."

The chatter in harsh native Créole gave the impression that the two slave factions were quarreling.

"I don't think that bunch is going to convince the slaves here to throw in with them," Thaddeus reasoned in a low voice. They'll be moving off in a bit."

"Sister, we just got something else we came for," Maggie said softly. "Looks like la Pagerie's slaves will remain ... *did* remain loyal. It's what you always believed, Raine. In the face of the sins of slavery, this tells us something about how the slaves on this plantation were treated by Joséphine's family."

Within twenty minutes, though it seemed like an eternity to the time-travelers, the angry voices subsided and faded, as the gang retreated from the domain of la Pagerie.

"Let's just wait a few moments more," Thaddeus cautioned.

"History tells us the slaves were defeated not long after Joséphine returned to France," Raine put in quietly, leaning her back against a tree to gently fan herself with a banana leaf. "It was a horror here. An absolute horror. The ringleaders were beaten to death and their heads propped on posts around the island."

"Nevertheless," Thaddeus said, "the seeds of change had been sown."

"Martinique," Raine pronounced, "would never be the same."

Some minutes later, the history-pilgrims hastened back to the jungle glade where they had begun their adventure. Here, they took a few moments to center themselves in preparation for their flight through the blustery Tunnel of Time.

"Thaddeus, wait," Raine breathed, as a thought plagued her. She hurriedly related to him and Maggie what she'd seen the mistress of the plantation do, being as descriptive as she could be. "I'm trying to picture the ruins of the sugar refinery as they are today. The *sucrerie* wall with the hidey-hole. Is that particular wall still there ... in our time? I'm asking you because your mind records and stores everything."

Thaddeus stroked his van dyke a moment before answering. "That would be the south wall," he stated, his blue eyes crinkling in happy thought. "It's still standing."

With a sigh of relief, Maggie drew from the pouch of her belt their small, travel *Book of Shadows*. Opening the grimoire to the ribboned final pages, she, Raine and Thaddeus clasped hands tightly to begin the ancient Gaelic invocation, *the magickal Key that would unlock the door of Time–*

And take them forward once again.

***

When the time-trekkers piled into the Renault to head back to the hotel, Raine whipped out her phone. "I think we should ring *Madame* the Curator at once to tell her we *must* meet with her first thing in the morning."

"It's after midnight," Beau reminded. "You don't want to call her now."

"I most certainly do. Anyway, I doubt she'll answer," Raine said. "She probably turns her phone off before she goes to bed, but we could leave a message that she'll hear as soon as she wakes up." She leaned forward from the back seat to poke her head between Thaddeus and Maggie. "We've only what? Three full days left on Martinique? Suppose she has a commitment that takes her away, and we don't get to meet with her?"

"You're right," Maggie replied. "Go ahead and ring her."

Raine quickly put through the call. "Jeanne, Dr. Raine McDonough here. We must meet with you early tomorrow morn–"

"*Allô!*" Jeanne Gardien's voice sounded, as she picked up. "Dr. McDonough?"

"*Oui, c'est moi,*" Raine said, continuing to speak in French. "I hope I didn't wake you. Never expected you to answer. I was leaving a message."

"You didn't wake me," the curator replied. "I was working on the museum's webpage. I just wrapped up and was about to go to bed, but you didn't wake me. What's wrong? You sound rather strange."

"We must meet with you first thing in the morning, *madame*, at la Pagerie," Raine blurted. "It's a matter of the *utmost* importance." She listened for a few moments. "No, I cannot discuss the matter over the phone, but you know you can trust us. I entreat you, if you have anything scheduled for the a.m., please reschedule it. We must rendezvous with you first thing on the morrow. Oh, and please make certain to have a maintenance man there with an extension ladder and a few basic tools." She stopped briefly to listen again. "*Oui, à 9 heures du matin. Merci, madame. Bonne nuit.*"

Raine rang off with her cat-who-ate-the-canary grin and a euphoric knowledge blazing within her Crafty essence. "Now, that wasn't difficult to arrange. Not at all, at all. At nine in the morning, we make *Madame* the Curator's longtime wish come true!"

"If you need something to believe in–
start with yourself!"
~ Granny McDonough

Chapter Sixteen

When the Sisters' party pulled up to the museum at la Pagerie the following morning, Jeanne Gardien was waiting for them with an expectant look on her pleasant face.

"I must say," she stepped forth to greet them as they exited the Renault, "I am more than curious as to what this is all about."

Raine's eyes swept the area. "You remembered what I requested, a maintenance fellow with extension ladder and tools?"

"*Oui*," the curator replied, completing the exchange in English. "He's here on the property. All I need do is page him with my phone."

"It's best we talk first inside, in your office," Raine said with a satisfied nod.

"This way," Jeanne gestured, ushering her guests before her.

It was pleasantly cooler in the museum's office, for it had rained that morning, and the air was heavy, the atmosphere sticky and uncomfortable.

"I'll begin," Raine said truthfully, "with the cue that Maggie and I, along with our other cousin, Aisling, are psychics, as well you know by now. Each of us has different gifts. In addition to her scrying … crystal-ball skills, Maggie is often gifted with visions. But lest I get ahead of myself. You said a couple of things, when last we met, of great significance. You said that you wished you had documented provenance for the Joséphine bracelet, and then you told us you always believed Joséphine's mother, Rose-Claire, had a secret hiding place here at la Pagerie in which she kept keepsakes, coins," the Goth gal raised an arched ebony brow, "an important letter perhaps."

"We knew, from Joséphine's daughter's memoirs, that there *was* a letter about a lost item of value that Joséphine penned her mother upon her return to France," Maggie put in. "And we figured that Rose-Claire just might have *saved* that letter to prove ownership in the event the lost item was ever found. You said yourself you never knew the letter to turn up anywhere over the years.

"Anyroad," Maggie concluded with the white lie she and Raine had agreed to tell, "to make a long story even longer, the thoughts about this letter brought on a vision, an image so vivid that Raine and I consulted our crystal ball. *Madame*, we believe we know where Rose-Claire's hidey-hole was … er *is*. Since Raine is the more fluent Sister," Maggie smiled, "in both English and French, *she* will point you in the right direction."

The Sisters did not often tell a lie, but when they found it necessary, they made certain it was something, in keeping with the Witches' Rede, that would not harm anyone. They simply could *not* divulge the secret of their Time-Key, *that* they were committed to protect at all costs, hence the concocted revelation.

Madame the Curator's face took on a look of anticipation as excitement broke on her voice. "Shall we look?"

Raine and Maggie answered in sync, "Call your maintenance man, and let's get to it!"

La Pagerie handyman Chance Latour positioned the tall ladder against the *sucrerie* stone wall Raine and Thaddeus pointed out to him. The maintenance man was sporting khaki Bermuda shorts and a cotton tee over which he wore a tool belt. Suspended from his ladder was a basket with hooks. And sticking out of his pocket were gloves used by the museum for handling artifacts.

"Move the ladder a little to the left," Raine directed. "Yeah, that looks good, right there."

Chance climbed to the top of the ladder, to what would have been the second floor of the structure, his dark eyes perusing the wall. "*Eh bien*, what am I looking for?" he called to the curator in French.

"A very small, crudely etched *fleur-de-lys*," Jeanne answered, "in the upper, right-hand corner of one of the stones, which should be loose."

"We're in luck," Chance said, keeping to his native tongue. "It rained a little while ago, and the walls are wet. The moisture's doing a good job revealing any marks on these stones."

For several minutes, the maintenance fellow searched as far as he could see from the position his ladder afforded him. Shaking his head, the *Martiniquais* yelled down to the Sisters' party and Jeanne below. "I don't see any *fleur-de-lys* anywhere."

"Try moving the ladder," Raine proposed. "I think I may have told you wrong. Move it down that way," she pointed.

Chance descended the ladder, then repositioned it to the direction the Sister indicated. Once he ascended again to the top, he began anew to search the stones for the royal French mark.

"Ah!" he exclaimed after several moments. "I think I might've found something." Taking a handkerchief from the pocket of his khakis, he rubbed an area on one of the stones. *"Je l'ai trouvé … I found it!"* He polished the stone for several more seconds. "I almost didn't see it. Weather and dirt over the years have nearly obliterated it."

"Try lifting that stone out," Jeanne said, trying her best to remain calm. She was recording everything on her smart phone, for she completely trusted the Sisters and just *knew* that today would be an occasion to record for posterity's sake.

Chance attempted to loosen the stone, but it stubbornly remained in place. "Not moving," he shouted down to his watchers. *"Attendez! Une minute."* From his tool belt, he extracted a flat-tipped screwdriver. With precision then, he began tracing the perimeter of the marked stone.

"Ça y est! I think this stone *might* be loose. All that appears to be holding it in is dirt." He continued scraping with his screwdriver. "And lots of it."

Finally, the worker was able to pull the stone free from the wall, after which he deposited it, for the time being, into the basket secured to his ladder. Next, he took a flashlight from his belt, directing the dazzle into the crevice. "There's something in here," he said loud enough for the others to hear.

"Put the gloves on and take it out as carefully as you can, Chance, then bring it down to me," Jeanne ordered, struggling to contain her exhilaration. She commenced pulling a pair of the artifact-handling gloves onto her own hands.

Reaching inside the hollow, the maintenance man extracted a small silver box with a closed, domed lid. "Looks like an old jewelry box," he said, starting down the ladder. At the bottom, he handed the engraved, antique casket to Jeanne. *"Voilà le prix!"* he smiled, flashing even, white teeth.

"Merci, Chance," she said, emotion flooding her essence. "Now, go back up and before you replace the stone to the wall, make sure there's nothing else in the crevice. If there is, bring it down."

The man reclimbed the ladder, aimed the beam from his flashlight again into the fusty cranny, then plunged a gloved hand into the space to feel for anything else that might be cached there, just to make sure. "Nothing more in here," he reported. "I'll put the stone back in place."

***

When the curator ushered the four Americans into her office several minutes later, she could no longer contain her eagerness. Setting the silver box on her desk, she took a deep breath and attempted to lift the domed lid. It fused to budge.

"Stuck." She blew out her breath. "*Mais pas de problem.* I have some plastic tools here in my office that I can use to open this box without damaging it." Unlocking a drawer of her desk, she chose one of the small instruments mentioned. With a bit of finagling, Jeanne was able to open the small chest without harming the closure or the silver.

The Sisters, Beau and Thaddeus stepped in closer. Inside the box were a garnet and pearl brooch; a fancy gold ring set with a large cabochon ruby; several old coins; and at the bottom, a folded parchment.

"It's my educated guess that Rose-Claire inherited this jewelry from her mother," the curator ventured. "Joséphine's mother was born into an ancient and noble aristocratic family. There you see her maiden name, the proud, elite des Vergers de Sannois emblem," she indicated the family's initials worked with *fleur-de-lys,* "on the domed lid of the box. It's my speculation, too, that over the years, she was forced to sell her jewelry to keep this plantation going. This was likely all she had left when she died here in 1807, at the age of seventy." Jeanne looked closely at each item. "I believe both the brooch and the ring are gold and the stones real. The box itself appears to be sterling silver." She examined the coins. "These are called 'livres,' from the Latin word *libra,* a unit of weight."

"I thought *livre* was the French word for *book*," Beau queried.

"Correct," the curator answered. "The difference is the gender. The monetary unit is feminine, while book is masculine. *Une livre* I could liken, for your understanding, to the British pound that uses an ornate L for its symbol, representative of the Latin *libra.* These antique coins are much more valuable today than they were back then. This box is, indeed, a treasure chest."

"And," Jeanne smiled, her voice taking on a bit of drama, "we have yet the document. 'Tis my wish we saved the best for last." With gloved hands, she gently removed it from the bottom of the silver box, while the Sisters waited with pleasant anticipation.

When *Madame* the Curator carefully unfolded the single page, they saw a parchment, pale yellowish-brown and stained with moisture, though the ink was still legible. "Vellum," she pronounced. "A fine quality parchment, generally smooth and durable. *It's a letter*," she breathed, her words catching in her throat. "Written in Joséphine's own hand and signed by her." Jeanne's dark eyes scanned the page. "She wrote it to her mother. The brief *communiqué* is dated Sunday, 31 October 1790. I'll read it to you in English, so you'll all understand what I'm saying.

"'*Maman*, I write to you in sadness, for I did not want to leave you that night of the slave rebellion when I fled Martinique on the *Sensible*. To leave the way I did, with such a hurried *adieu,* has pressed heavy on my heart since that fateful night. As for the crossing, it was the most difficult journey possible. The storms! Our ship rode the waves and wind like a bucking horse! The sea washing over the ship rendered the decks too-often forbidden and walking in the passageways dangerous, but I shan't dwell on that *cauchemar* for fear its monstrous character will reproduce the feelings of anxiety and terror in my dreams again this night.

"'I pray this missive finds you well, *maman*, and as always, I send you all my love.

"'I will write a longer letter later, for now I am in the process of finding a place to live, and I think I'll be residing with another Créole. She, however, is truly a woman of revolutionary sympathies. *Eh bien*, a sign of the times. She too has a daughter, who gets on well with my own Hortense, so I shall be happy, *maman*.

"'Everything here in Paris is different from the past. I hardly recognize the city that I left over two years ago. The changes are exciting and worrisome at the same time. But I shan't frighten you. Never fear, I have influential friends and protectors.

"'I have acquired a funny little dog, a pug that I've named Fortuné. He is somewhat temperamental but loyal, and I hope, as his name denotes, he will bring me good fortune.

"'I don't want to neglect to tell you that I lost a valuable gold and ruby bracelet the night I fled la Pagerie. It fell from my wrist as I was crossing the front lawn. Fashioned much like a rose, it bears my name on the inner band. If you find it, keep it to sell, for it is my fondest wish that you make use of it to help the plantation we both so keenly love. I know, *de l'expérience de la vie*, that everything in life happens for a reason, and I feel strongly that my lost bracelet is destined to help la Pagerie.

"'I will write soon again. Please know that your daughter, your namesake, loves you with her whole being. Take care of your health, *maman*. I pray you, *papa*, and Manette are well. God bless and keep you safe.

"'Your Rose.'"

Raine sighed with pleasure. *The Wheel of Fate ... turns as it turns, eh? We were summoned to Martinique by the empress' spirit,* the Goth gal imparted telepathically to Maggie, *a spirit with unfinished business.* Aloud, she said, "I feel strongly that our Joséphine is very, very pleased that, finally, her bracelet *will* be helping her beloved la Pagerie."

"Looks like our work here is done," the Sisters recited as one voice.

Jeanne Gardien came immediately forth to warmly embrace the magickal pair with the traditional French *faire la bise.* That is, she leaned in to touch her cheek to the cheeks of each Sister, kissing the air, whilst her lips produced a kissing sound. "Your work, as you called it, will put la Pagerie in a whole new status among the museums of the world. I thank you, *mes bonnes amies.* My board thanks you. *Eh bien*, Empress Joséphine and– *la Belle France* thank you."

Chapter Seventeen

Upon leaving la Pagerie, the Sisters' party decided to drive to the Fort-de-France area to visit le Jardin de Balata.

Finding the appropriate section in their guidebook, Raine was reading aloud to her companions from the backseat of the Renault, "… about a twenty-minute drive from Fort-de-France, one of Martinique's most famous sites. Beautiful, tropical botanical gardens in the mountains above the capital."

Her green eyes skimmed down the page. "Begun in 1982, the gardens are the masterpiece of famed horticulturist and poet Jean-Philippe Thoze, who designed the land surrounding his grandparents' home to reflect his childhood memories and celebrate Martinique's natural beauty. Three thousand different tropical plants from around the world, including– Galloping gargoyles, get this– 300 varieties of palm trees. Bamboo, mahogany, begonias, wild orchids, *et cetera*. Stunning views of the mountains and harbor. Winding paths … bla bla. Tropical birds and lizards. Hordes of energetic hummingbirds.

"Wiz–zard, listen to this bit. There's a hanging rope bridge above a portion of the gardens that gives a whole different perspective." The Goth gal turned the page to speed-read further. "Great, this guide lists a couple of restaurants nearby where we can get a decent entrée and a good glass of wine. Since we didn't have time for anything but a continental breakfast this morning, I'm starved. How about you guys?" Without waiting for an answer, she pressed, "Let's eat lunch first, then we can hike the botanical gardens to work off the calories. What say you?"

The coterie chose an informal eatery, next to a verdant park overlooking the sea, that specialized in Créole food. With great satisfaction, they enjoyed fresh, grilled fish served with local vegetables, curried rice, and an excellent salad, washed down with a crisp white wine.

"That was one of the best meals we've had on the island," Thaddeus noted. "Exceptional. Shall we indulge in dessert?"

"Why not?" Maggie replied, surrendering to her sweet tooth.

"Hecate, yes!" Raine put in. "We'll walk it off at the gardens," she reasoned, eyeing a scrumptious-looking slice of coconut cake that a passing waiter was taking to an adjacent table.

When their server inquired if they had ever sampled a traditional Martinique dessert called *Blanc Manger Coco*, and they admitted they hadn't, he insisted they could *not* leave Martinique without trying this creamy delight prepared with, among other things, coconut milk, cinnamon, vanilla, and lime.

"Mmmmm … MMM!" Beau enthused. "That was good. Let's see if we can get Ian to whip it up for us at home. This would probably be a snap for him."

When the foursome arrived at le Jardin de Balata, they began their long, pleasant walk through the garden's rain forest segment.

Some time later, Maggie remarked to Raine, "I'm glad we had sense enough to wear these straw hats and comfortable walking shoes today." She adjusted her outsized sunglasses. "That sun is scorching, and many of these paths follow hilly terrain."

"Good workout for us; that's for sure," the raven-haired Sister returned. "This place reinforces why Martinique is known as the 'Isle of Flowers.' I think I'm partial to the wild orchards and hibiscus. Though," she hesitated in flora quandary, "the begonias and bougainvillea are lovely too." She turned slowly round. "The profusion, size, and scent of these flowers … 'tis a glimpse of the Summerland!"

But the most joy that day was the enchanting experience of the bird's-eye-view had from a stream of hanging bridges suspended between the park's giant mahogany trees.

"We'll never forget this treetop trail," Maggie proclaimed, "with its rustling tropical leaves and dramatic views. The lush Carbet Mountains and the vistas to the sea are absolutely breathtaking."

There were Zen moments of peace and tranquility at the waterlily-covered ponds, where the Sisters and their menfolk rested in the shade to soak up the gardens' blissful enchantment. Splashes of vivid color were everywhere, and a timely trade wind cooled them after nearly two hours of non-stop hiking. It was there the Sisters spotted Dorélia, sitting alone in quiet meditation.

"Don't bother her," Maggie whispered to Raine, who was just about to call out to their friend. "She comes here to reflect and mull over matters. I'm sensing strongly that the water burbling over those rocks helps her to sort things out."

"Quite so, Mags. We'll see her tonight at dinner," Raine agreed. "C'mon, let's move off before she sees us."

"Raine," Maggie paused her Sister, fixing her with the McDonough stare over the rims of her designer sunglasses, "she's going to give him one more chance. It's his last. Of that, she has made up her mind."

"Then he had better make the most of it, hadn't he?" Raine thought for a moment. "Isn't his band playing at the hotel tonight?"

"Yes," Maggie answered. "I wonder ..."

"I know," Raine snatched the thought, "a leopard can't change its spots, but broken people *can* fix themselves."

"Do you think J-J is broken?"

"No, but he does."

"I agree with Raine," Thaddeus put in. "*He's* the only one who can fix his problem."

Maggie's voice was soft. "He needs to find his center and his quiet." The Sister was remembering the sage advice of a Cheyenne elder they had met one long-past summer when she and Raine had accompanied their archeologist parents on a dig in the Powder River Basin of Montana.

"Yes," Raine concurred, snatching her sister of the moon's thoughts. "J-J needs to listen with his heart. He needs to allow his music to mend the wounds in his heart and heal his soul, to live each day as it comes, and to learn life's lessons from experience."

"A lesson learned means a change in behavior, or the lesson was not learned," Maggie said, thinking yet of the Cheyenne elder. "A good smudging ceremony of purification and healing would benefit him greatly." Closing her eyes momentarily, she could hear the drums and the Native chanting that brought forth such a healing. She could hear the voice of the elder.

It is good.

Maggie was thinking, too, of the healing gifts of yet another very special Native American. His name was Joseph Nighthorse, and his magick had left an indelible mark on her soul, his love a permanent place in her heart. She felt for the Crow medicine necklace he had gifted her last spring in Montana. "We will send J-J healing energies, Sister," she stated firmly.

"Good thinking," Raine agreed. She sent Maggie an understanding look and the thought, *You were thinking of Joseph because he is thinking of you. That's how magick works. He will never stop loving you, Mags.*

Maggie responded with a subtle nod, closing her eyes as a powerful memory, complete with vision, flooded her essence, and her fingers lovingly caressed the medicine necklace. To change the subject, she repeated aloud her idea about sending the healing energies.

"Straightaway, upon our return to the hotel," Raine answered in perfect agreement. "We'll ground and center and make sure energy is flowing through all our chakras, then we'll send J-J healing Love and Light."

"So it shall be, Sister," the redhead responded with another nod. "We will send the energies to *both* J-J *and* Dorélia."

Last stop within le Jardin de Balata was Créole House, the actual home, within the widespread park, of founder Jean-Philippe Thoze's grandparents. With its period furniture and décor, the charming dwelling conveyed the colorful story of island life in bygone days.

All in all, the marvel of Martinique's botanical gardens created an enduring memory the McDonough witches would conjure for peaceful meditation the rest of their magickal lives.

Before they left the Fort-de-France area, the Sisters wanted to visit the capital's Rue Victor Hugo's high-end shops.

"Aren't you ladies tired of walking?" Beau asked with good-natured humor.

"Never too tired for shopping," Raine answered, looking to Maggie for support.

"And we never really had proper time to scout those shops," the redheaded Sister concurred, "not on the grand boulevard."

"That's right. Our shopping has been rather desultory," Raine stated, sending Maggie a subtle wink.

"Tell you what," Thaddeus proffered, "how about you both shop till it's time to head back to the hotel for our sunset aperitif, and Beau and I will explore again on our own."

"Fine with us," the Sisters responded happily.

When they motored into the capital, Thaddeus parked the Renault on the street in front of a sidewalk café. Looking at his watch, he said, "Enjoy your shopping spree, girls. Let's all meet back here at this corner in an hour and a half. We'll have to head back to the hotel directly then, or we'll miss the sunset."

"Fair enough," the Sisters chimed, as they started down the boulevard at a trot.

Some time later, whilst the ladies were browsing in a posh clothing boutique, Maggie stepped out of a changing room to ask Raine, "What do you think of this one? I really like the color."

Raine regarded the striking redhead, posed in an off-the-shoulder, turquoise beach dress with a witchy handkerchief hem. "That's the one, Mags. Take it."

The Goth gal moved to the counter where the shop girl could ring up her purchases. Glancing out the window, she exclaimed to Maggie, who set the items she was taking before the clerk. "What the–? Look across the street, Mags. Another mystery has manifested. Over there," she pointed, "Beau and Thaddeus. What do you suppose they're doing in that fancy jewelry store?" Her emerald eyes widened. "I'll bet they're buying us each a gift, and it must be something really special by the looks of that place."

Maggie peered out the window, then immediately stepped back so the men would not notice her. "If they are, it's to be a surprise, so don't mention that we saw them."

Raine's ebony brows rushed together, as her Aries temper rammed her rebellious streak full-awake. "I most certainly *will* mention it. *I want to know.*"

A half-hour later, when the couples rendezvoused at the Renault, Raine couldn't wait to pose the question that had tormented her for the past hour. "What were you two doing in that ritzy jewelry shop? Maggie and I saw you when we were in the ladies' boutique across the street."

"Having the battery changed in my watch," Thaddeus answered *sans* hesitation. "It wasn't keeping good time," he flashed her his wrist, "now it's running, dare I say it, like clockwork. Mine is one of those watches that requires a jeweler to replace the battery. No way can I do it myself. And no way can I do without my watch."

Raine's mien clearly mirrored her chagrin, which brought a tinge of humor to Maggie's eyes, that she struggled to veil so her sister of the moon would not seize it and be vexed.

"So how about you?" Beau inquired. "What did you buy? I see you've got packages. I just hope you two will be able to squeeze all your purchases into your luggage."

Meanwhile, the pouting Raine shot Maggie a thought: *Thad's story rings true. He did buy a watch battery. Ah well ... .* Aloud, she said in response to Beau's remark about luggage, "Don't worry about that, big boy. Maggie and I have been travel experts since we were witchlettes accompanying our parents, round the world, to archaeological sites. None of the McDonough clan were ever stay-at-home people."

"I have a hunch you ladies are planning to make use of *our* valises too," the professor remarked with a chuckle.

At eventide, whilst the foursome sipped their sunset drinks at the hotel's Coco Bar, they began discussing what they should do to make the most of their remaining time in Martinique.

"I think tomorrow we should drive down to Pointe des Salines, the spot where the Atlantic and the Caribbean meet. Les Salines is the longest sweep of beach in Martinique and said to be the most beautiful," Thaddeus suggested. "We've been down that way, but we never spent time on the beach there, and I think it would be a nice relaxing thing to do for a change."

"Sounds good to me," Beau replied. "You gotta admit, we've been keeping a hectic schedule. I'd welcome a day for unwinding."

The Sisters exchanged looks to speak at once. "Pointe des Salines it is."

Leafing through the guidebook, Raine found the section on Les Salines. "Wizard," she breathed, "the book says they have the best ice cream there. We'll have to try some." She returned the guide to her bag, satisfied with her find and looking no further.

"Darlin'," Maggie said, "I really don't know how you stay so slender. You eat twice as much as I do."

Raine grinned, breathing a singular, utterly succinct riposte– "*Witchcraft.*"

That night when the coterie entered the candle glow of the Sirène dining room, they were happy to see Dorélia approach their table. The waitress came straight over to greet the Sisters, stretching out her hands to them.

"*Mes amies, comment je suis heureuse de vous voir!* How happy I am to see you, my friends! Again, I must thank you for saving me. Bless you. Bless both of you," she ordained. "I owe you my life."

"Happy to help," the Sisters declared, pleased to see their friend in high spirits.

The woman, by this point, was squeezing a hand of each Sister, as gratitude shone in her luminous, almond-shaped, dark eyes.

"You don't have to thank us for doing what was right," Maggie replied.

"We simply followed our instincts and did what had to be done," said Raine. "It's what we do."

"It would never cross our minds not to help someone in jeopardy," Maggie finished. There was a slight gap before Maggie asked in her soft voice, "How *are* you?"

"*Très bien, merci,*" Dorélia answered. "Jean-Jacques and I have been talking, *really* talking, for the first time in our life together. First of all, we each gave up the need to be right. I think there is hope for us yet. *En tout cas*, we're both committed to try harder this time."

"That is really good news," the Sisters responded concurrently.

Once everyone was seated at table, Dorèlia handed them menus. "You're going to love the special tonight. *Lambi fricassée* served with rice pilaf and baked bananas." She smiled, looking like her old self. "*Magnifique!*"

"Just what is *lambi fricassée?*" Beau asked, looking up from the hotel's outsized menu.

"Conch stewed with local vegetables and spices in a good, rich sauce. I highly recommend this dish, *monsieur*. You will *not* be disappointed. I promise you."

The Sisters' party took their friend's advice and ordered the *lambi*, with the hotel's famous Créole salad to start, and the French house White to drink.

Later, when the music of Jean-Jacques' Trade Winds drew them to the terrace, they noted the obvious change in the band leader.

"He doesn't have that annoyed look about him anymore," Raine commented with satisfied expression.

"He's happier. I have a feeling he's thinking clearer," Maggie added after a moment of empathic scrutiny. "I sense," she broke off, allowing her empath radar the time to receive and process, "he's serious about implementing good changes in his life, *permanent* changes."

When J-J stepped to the microphone, he glanced across the way to his wife, saying, *"Bonsoir, mes amis, et bienvenu.* I wish to dedicate my first song of the night to my beautiful wife, Dorélia. *Une chanson sincère– Ne Me Quitte Pas."*

Raine leaned forward in her chair toward her cohorts seated at table to say, "The song title literally translates, 'Don't Leave Me,' but the more apropos translation is 'Never Leave Me.'"

It was apparent to all who heard him that night on the Bakoua's balmy, lantern-lit terrace that Jean-Jacques' song came from the deepest reaches of his heart. He made his horn *cry* for all the trials and tribulations of, what the Sisters sensed, was an unhappy childhood and youth. That horn cried for his tumultuous marriage too, and for his angry life.

As he sang Jacques Brel's fervent French classic, the empathic Sisters seized images and sentiments– like leaves fanned by the song of a melancholy autumn wind, *plaisirs du temps perdu–* souvenirs of the past that drifted from the impassioned musician via his voice and horn.

Reflections of flowers pressed in a keepsake book, old photographs hung on the wall of memory– a sleepy little fishing village, an old bell in the tower of a picturesque white church, gold rings on a heart-shaped wedding pillow. Along with moving pictures that breathed and challenged the fervid man still– of Dorélia's smiling face, her dark hair ruffled by a wayward wind, kisses blown from rosy lips, a sexy tango in the candle glow of an intimate café, the lovers' sandy footprints effaced by a sudden surge of sea– and all of it looking like the sound of J-J's soulful song.

"Like any true artist, he understands magick," Thaddeus commented unexpectedly. "It's apparent Jean-Jacques has experienced his share of life's vicissitudes … joy and pain."

"In his case," Maggie cut in, "there was a lot more pain."

"He was good before, really good, but now," the professor searched for the right words, "there's an intensity to his performance, a new depth to his entire repertoire. Now he's brilliant."

During the break, the band leader approached the Sisters' table, asking if he might join them for a few moments.

"Of course," they answered, "please."

Jean-Jacques pulled a chair from a nearby table between the McDonoughs to straddle it backwards and voice in charming

French-laced expression, *"D'abord,* let me say *Thank You* for saving my wife's life." He reached out to take a hand of each Sister. *"Merci bien.* You risked your own lives to save the woman I love, and I cannot express with words what is in my heart. I can only say it with my music. *Alors,* I will dedicate the songs in my next set," his lively brown eyes skimmed the coterie, "to … *mes amis américains.*

"I have made a career decision in addition to personal ones. In a week," he declared proudly, "I begin a new job. *Oui,*" he gave a nod, "at the Martinique School of Music in Fort-de-France. I will be teaching talent-blessed *Martiniquais, les jeunes et les adultes.* Youth and adults," he translated. *"Alors,* three nights a week, I will continue to play my music here at the hotel. And who knows?" He gave an expressive shrug, typical of his French spirit. "Who knows? We will see what happens, *eh?* Dorélia tells me I need to have more confidence in my own talent."

Crossing the terrace, the waitress paused for a moment to respond to her husband's words. "I tell him that *tout le temps,* all the time."

The Sisters swapped looks and feelings, culminating with Maggie's thought, I *can't help but think, still, that Dorélia is harboring a secret.*

"Your wife is right," Raine ventured to the band leader. "You need to believe in yourself. No one will ever believe in you if you don't first believe in yourself."

"That's right. Trust your instincts," Maggie interjected. The redheaded Sister placed a hand over her chest to thump her heart. "Everything you require is already within you."

"Be patient with yourself," Raine thought to add. "Just take one day at a time, and above all, be true to yourself."

Jean-Jacques managed a smile at that. "I wasn't myself in my old job. I was playing a role, and it was *exhausting.* But at my new post, I will be free to be me."

"You have a nice smile, *monsieur,*" Maggie returned. "Use it more often."

"I will do that," the band leader answered, his expression broadening to a grin. "I've decided to be happy because it is good for my health."

Raine recognized the quote. "Ah," she pronounced, "Voltaire."

The musician stood, smiling down at the Americans. "One of France's greatest writers. A very wise man to be sure."

"We wish you all the best, Jean-Jacques," the Sisters echoed. After which, Beau and Thaddeus put forth happy returns of their own.

Later, when the Sisters were dancing to *Chanson d'Amour* and *C'est Si Bon*, they felt the love vibrations radiating throughout the terrace setting. Contrary to his former vibes, these sensations emanated from a contented, serenely calm Jean-Jacques Sauvage.

"Life is good," Maggie sighed in Thaddeus' arms.

"So good," echoed a glowing Raine.

Unbeknownst to the Sisters, the situation back home at Tara was not quite so rosy.

***

Whilst Raine and Maggie were dancing the night away in Martinique, the Sisters' loyal housekeeper, Hannah Gilbert, and her husband, Jim, were sound asleep in Tara's guest room, Jim's snoring breaking the otherwise silence. The couple usually stayed at Tara in Raine and Maggie's absence, keeping watch over the property, in addition to looking after the animals and executing the chores in and about the house and stable.

Sometime after midnight, whilst Tara slept, the clanking sound of a heavy, metal object hitting the cement driveway abruptly rousted the Merlin cats, Black Jade and Black Jack O'Lantern, curled up together on a large padded chair in the corner. Leaping to the windowsill, Jack parted the drapes with a paw to see a shadow figure prowling around Jim's pickup truck.

Bounding on the bed, the muscular black cat began desperately to waken Hannah, kneading her shoulder and ranting his feline flak for all he was worth. It took only a moment, for the housekeeper was habitually a light sleeper. Consequently, the subsequent stream of actions unfolded rapidly and nearly simultaneously.

Jack sprang back to the windowsill, making the strangest noises Hannah had ever heard him emit. Throwing off the covers, she jumped out of bed and parted the drapes just enough to peer out, refraining from turning on a light. There, below, was a man wearing a ski mask and holding a tire iron, who appeared to be casing the doors and windows, looking for security cameras. Without wasting a beat, the quick-thinking woman called 911, at the same time, poking her husband to stir him awake. Unlike his wife, however, Jim was a deep sleeper. He merely rolled over and continued snoring even louder.

'Twas Jack who came to the rescue. Like a streak of lightening, he launched himself to the nightstand, strewn with Jim's wallet, coins, and truck keys, to *pounce* with carefully aimed paw on the key fob's red panic button. Just as the shadow man was about to strike the truck's passenger-side window with the tire iron, the loud, screaming alarm stopped him in his tracks.

Rushing downstairs to Hannah's shouts, Jim threw open the front door at the same time a police car screeched into the driveway. Flinging out his arm, the riled caretaker yelled to the uniformed officers, who were already out of the vehicle, "He ran into the woods! Get 'im!"

Wasting no time, the police charged after the culprit.

Meanwhile, Hannah, having snatched up her robe, came scurrying down the stairs after her husband to the front door where the couple met a second police vehicle. "You sure got here fast," she greeted the officer striding toward them.

"We were in the neighborhood, ma'am," he replied. "Yours was the third call we got tonight about a thief breaking into cars in the area. We were only two streets over when the dispatcher tipped us off. You're lucky the perp didn't smash the glass outta your truck," the policeman commented to Jim, who was circling his vehicle in an attempt to make certain it was unharmed.

"Yeah," Hannah answered, turning her head to gaze up at the guest-room window, where Black Jack and Black Jade were perched, staring down at the scene, their eyes gleaming pumpkin-orange in the police car's flashing light. "As my boss would say," she chuckled, "**CAT**egorically lucky."

Chapter Eighteen

When Raine woke in the morning, she sprang up like an alarm had gone off in her head. "I need to call home," she told Beau as she grabbed her phone to ring Hannah. "We've been so absorbed in the happenings here that I haven't given much thought to what might be going on back home. There's trouble of some sort. I feel it."

After chatting with the housekeeper for several minutes, she rang off. "Beau," she said to her love, who was coming out of the bathroom, "Jack is our hero again."

She quickly related what had transpired the night before, concluding with, "The man was just about to break into Jim's truck when Jack stopped him. If he hadn't, the culprit would very likely have broken into the garage, our stable, and who knows, perhaps even the house. He must have been desperate, because we have motion lights and cameras everywhere. Anyway, the police nabbed him in the woods, and when they searched his van, they found all sorts of stolen loot. He'd been breaking into vehicles in our neighborhood for a couple of hours. Other folks had already called 911, so that's how the police got to Tara so fast."

Raine grew wistful. "The Merlin cats, bless them, are always watching out for us, especially Jack. Do you know, he pointed out to me, just before we embarked on this trip, that the word **Home**ow**ner** is centered with *Meow*."

Beau's penetrating blue eyes crinkled at the corners. "I never thought of that, but he's absolutely right."

"Indeed," Raine returned. "A cat is at the center, the heart, of family life, and a house is not a home without a cat ... or two or three."

"There's no question Black Jack is Tara's rightful steward and guardian. He faithfully watches over it and all of us," Beau reiterated.

"*Witches* over us, you mean," Raine grinned. "How I love my Jackie boy!"

Meanwhile, back at Tara, Black Jack O'Lantern's pumpkin-hued eyes kindled, as his mouth closed from an epic yawn. *Witches, huh? Yes, I'm CATegorically familiar.*

***

Later that day, the Sisters were relishing relaxation on the beach at Pointe des Salines, at the site where the temperamental Atlantic Ocean meets the tranquil Caribbean.

Under her large straw hat, Maggie was penning a letter to her ex in Ireland, whilst Raine was reading one of the books about Joséphine they'd purchased at the hotel. Beau and Thaddeus were napping, having positioned their towels in the shade a few feet distant from the ladies.

As most days in Martinique, it was sunny with a welcome trade wind, the beach scored by ripples of sea and powdery white sand. Much less frequented by bathers, Pointe des Salines was a relatively untouched strand bordered by lush vegetation. At the beach's edge was a small intimate restaurant, and on the horizon, since it was a crystal-clear day, the Sisters could faintly discern the neighboring island of St. Lucia.

Maggie gazed out over the surging, foaming water, the steady swell breathing in the glint of sun like liquid gold on its surface. She stretched a hand to the curled, pink conch shell Thaddeus found for her earlier at surf's edge. Held to an ear, it whispered of the sea, of mermaids and ghost ships, of shipwrecks and sunken treasure, of swashbuckling pirates, of romance and spice. At present, the large shell was simply helping to hold her beach towel in place against the breeze. "Did Hannah happen to mention what all she and Jim accomplished these past few days?"

The Goth gal looked up from her book. "Bless them. She said she and Jim washed all the windows, inside and out, and she laundered curtains and the drapes she hadn't time for this past spring. Jim repaired the paddock gate and trimmed all the hedges and shrubbery round the place, whilst Hannah dusted and ran the sweeper through the entire house."

Maggie's ex-husband floated into Raine's thoughts. "Mags, my witch's intuition is telling me Rory's time to cross over is fast approaching, but you know that."

"I do," she commented, reaching up to brush away a tear. "I think I'm penning this final letter more for me than him. It's a strange feeling I've been having, as if Rory is looking over my shoulder as I write this."

"That well may be. I believe," Raine said as gently as she could, tilting her head in pensive gesture, "he's gone into a coma, and he's astral projecting. It's quite common really."

Maggie nodded, unable to say anything for several moments. "Yes," she breathed, her mind mobilizing at last, "I've been feeling it too. His time is drawing nigh."

Raine reached over to pat her sister of the moon's hand. "You're one of the finest people I've ever known, Mags."

Maggie gave her crystal laugh. "Well now, Raine Storm, that's a given for a McDonough, isn't it?" She pored over the past for a long moment. "I wish I could be with him at the last, but I've honored *his* wish that I stay away. Rory was always vain about his looks, and ..." she choked back a sob, "he doesn't want me to see him in Cancer's clutches. He wants me to remember him as he was."

Raine rose to tie the sarong she purchased the day before round her waist. The tissue-thin material was printed with ferns and vines in the deep-green color the Sister favored. She adjusted her big straw hat, then slipped her feet into her flip-flops. "I think I'll rouse Beau to take a walk with me to that little eatery down at the end of the beach for some of the ice cream they're so famous for in these parts. Any preference on flavor?"

Maggie thought for a moment, peering at Raine over the rims of her sunglasses. "Surprise me."

When Thaddeus heard Raine and Beau say they were going for ice cream, he stood. "Good, then I'll go for a swim now." He strode to the water's edge, walked into the rolling surf and plunging in, began swimming with easy strokes.

Maggie watched him for a moment, before picking up the forgotten guidebook Raine had used as an anchor on one end of the beach towel. The canting of the old days had left her a bit sad, and she needed to lift her spirits.

Leafing through the illustrative book, the Sister found the section on Pointe des Salines. She read for only a few seconds when her eyes lit on a passage that nearly stopped her heart.

You must be careful of the current at Pointe des Salines, for this is where the Caribbean and the Atlantic oceans meet, creating dangerous riptides.

With a start, she came to her feet, flinging her fiery hair back from her eye to gaze out to a sea that suddenly looked deep and cold and hungry. "Great Goddess!"

Thaddeus was becoming smaller and smaller on the horizon.

He's swimming so far out. A terrible feeling of dread surged through her, and though she knew better, she allowed Fear to obliterate everything else. "Oh, dear Goddess, don't let him drown. Please don't let him drown!"

Glancing fretfully round, she saw no one she could ask for help. When she returned her gaze to Thaddeus, now a mere speck on the horizon, she saw him drifting further still away from the beach.

"**No!**" she raised a cry that would have raised the dead had there been any about.

"**Thaddeus!!**"

Mustering her energy, she sent the man she loved all the strength she could. "Goddess, please help him. Please … please!"

Getting control of herself, Maggie put a hand on her talismans to chant with all her essence: "Bring forth the passion of love's fire! Goddess feel my true desire! With all my strength, I fight this fate! Make this danger obliterate! So. Mote. It. Be!"

After chanting the spell thrice, she released her breath and focused. Suddenly, the speck that was her beloved changed direction. *It looks like he's swimming off to the side*, she told herself with a flicker of hope. As she watched, the professor began swimming back to shore, hand over hand, like a man climbing out of a nightmare.

Running to the shoreline, Maggie waited with bated breath, while Thaddeus steadily made his way to her. When he started wading ashore, she splashed toward him, throwing her arms around his neck, laughing, crying, and so sated with emotion, she could hardly speak.

"Why did you go out so far? What happened out there?!" She began kissing his face, his lips, sobbing out her fears in huge gulps.

"It was a riptide, Maggie. When a rip starts taking you out to sea, you go along for the ride till it weakens. Then you swim off to the side and start back to shore. No big deal." He lifted her chin with a finger. Smiling warmly, he said, "I felt the energy you witched me. Felt it good and strong."

"No big deal? You could've drowned! I was so frightened, Thaddeus. My heart was in my throat." She couldn't stop kissing him.

He took her by the shoulders to stop her shaking. "Listen to me. People only drown in rips when they fight them. You never, ever want to do that. Fighting results in exhaustion and drowning. Just go with the flow. Rips usually weaken fairly fast, then, as I said, you swim to the side and back to shore."

Seeing that she was not to be quieted with explicative words, he enfolded her in a long, effective hug that soothed her soul. "Shhhh, it's OK. I'm fine. 'Twasn't anything. There, there, my poor little red bird. There, there."

By that point, Raine and Beau returned with the ice cream. Quickly then, Thaddeus related what had happened, during which Raine handed a still-snuffling Maggie her mango ice. "Eat this. It's melting all over me, and it'll make you feel better."

"Maggie," Beau said, handing her his handkerchief, "you should know that Thaddeus is *way* too smart," a twinkle leaped to his deep-blue eyes, "to let an ole rip get the best of him."

The foursome decided, unanimously, that it would be a grand idea to drive up the Atlantic side of Martinique, hugging the coast, to take in the pretty fishing villages on that side of the island.

"Fishermen usually return around noon," Raine said, glancing at her watch. "We'll get to see them, putting in, aboard their brightly painted *gommiers*. So picturesque these little fishing villages, with those colorful boats and nets."

"Let's be certain to capture some good pictures today," Maggie put forward. "I plan to translate a couple of photographs to oils for Tara. I know at least one choice for a painting will be la Pagerie, due to its special meaning for us."

"Tell you what let's do," Thaddeus said from his position behind the wheel of their Renault. "Let's drive up the Atlantic coast so far, then cut inland to jump on la Route de la Trace, the road that winds through Martinique's rain forest. Circle round to the Caribbean side and soak up the fishing villages on that coast en route back to the hotel. We'll be making a big scenic loop."

"To see as much as we can, let's skip a grand lunch today and just drive. We'll keep our eyes peeled for a little café where we can grab a spot of something to keep us going," Maggie suggested.

When everyone agreed, Beau said, "The rain forest should be an ultra-scenic drive."

"It is," Raine replied. "You won't be disappointed."

At the fishing village of Vauclin, the Sisters fell in love with its blue, palm fringed lagoon, where they saw several people kitesurfing.

From first sight it was the tropical village of one's dreams. Half-naked children squealed with delight at surf's edge before a rainbow of pastel-hued bungalows. Carefree young girls giggled and chattered with one another in the shade and beauty of graceful coconut palms. A group of old men were huddled together about a game of chance played with a board and numbers; and fishermen, singing rhythmic French shanties, serenely worked on their nets against a backdrop of foamy white breakers.

Behind the beach was a cute café where Beau and Thaddeus purchased a large to-go order of *accras*, the popular Martinique fish fritters, along with bottled water from France.

Eating on the run, they motored north to the village of Le François, enjoying the serenity and beauty of that seaside hamlet, before Raine convinced them they needed to stop and take in as much of the historic Habitation Clement as time allowed.

"Part rum distillery, part Créole plantation, part heritage site and museum, Habitation Clement, with its gorgeous gardens, is a *must-see*," Raine read with pleading voice from their guidebook.

"By the bye, as you probably figured out, the French word *habitation* means 'plantation.' I know we don't have time for the whole tour, which takes about an hour and a half, but at least, let's stop and have a quick look-round." She skimmed down the page, reading snatches of the text. "Historical site since 1996 ... where French President Mitterrand hosted American President George H.W. Bush to finalize the end of the first Persian Gulf War in 1991. Home of the method of rum production known today as *Rhum Agricole* ..."

After forty-odd minutes of driving along the Atlantic coast, Thaddeus cut inland to jump on the Route de la Trace and pass through the island's famous rain forest. At that point, he turned the wheel over to Beau with sagacious instruction to drive "dead slow."

La Trace was bumpy and full of twists and turns. "But like life, rough roads can lead to beautiful places," Beau said. Though it was very hot, the rain forest was lovely grandeur, the growth of trees and underbrush so thick they could hardly distinguish one tree from another in the luxuriant tangle of bamboo, fern and vine, of palms, mahogany and mango, of cedar, bay, and breadfruit.

"And all so *intensely* green. La Trace," Raine read from the guidebook, "was a trail first used by Jesuits in the seventeenth century ... traverses rich tropical forest with magnificent flora. Oh, would you look at those *giant* ferns!"

"This central region of Martinique is characterized by more rain and humidity, which supports the flora," Thaddeus remarked. "*Super*-flora by the looks of it."

"And listen to that rocky stream," Maggie pointed. "The voice of the Goddess. So soothing."

"Catch this," Raine interjected of a sudden, her finger saving the page in the guidebook. "Says here that motorists might not want to travel la Trace after dark ... lest they run into *la Dame Blanche*, the White Lady. For years, people from all over the world have claimed that they've seen the figure of a female ghost dressed all in white, standing in the middle of the road, nights. When they stop and exit their cars to see who or what it is– the lady vanishes."

"We have a similar ghost in our Laurel Highlands back home in Pennsylvania," Maggie said, jogging memories.

"Actually," Thaddeus interjected, "White Lady legends are found in many countries around the world. Common to these folklores are accidental deaths, suicides, or betrayals by husbands or lovers. The theme is almost always one of loss, and the sightings are more often than not near the place of death."

"Did you ever hear the famous Martinique tale of the *Quimbois* love spell?" Raine asked in witchy rhyme.

"No," came the unanimous reply.

"Well," Raine grinned, glad for the chance to tell it, "let me remedy that, and la Trace is the perfect setting for a good story of the occult." She took a moment to collect her thoughts, her mind speeding back through time for details.

"I heard this tale several years ago during my very first trip to Martinique. It's about a young *Quimbois* woman, very beautiful– and I could use the word *enchanting* without *any* exaggeration whatsoever– who became the mistress of a medical intern from Paris. Fauve was one of those amoral creatures of whom novelists and playwrights have always made fertile copy.

"In a couple of ways, she reminds me of Joséphine. By that I mean the graceful walk, like a feather dancing on a puff of breeze, and the smoky drawling voice, indolent, as if she'd never have the strength to carry a sentence to full stop." Raine paused. "Then, of course, there's the sexual prowess both women exerted over men. Lest I stray from the topic of discussion, allow me to present the other protagonist in my tale.

"The intern, it seemed, came from a prestigious French family of considerable wealth. The family had its prejudices, especially back in the old days. Let me think ... I seem to recall that this story unfolded sometime during the early 1900s. Anyway, when it came time for the young man to sail for France, he dreaded telling his *Martiniquaise* mistress that he would soon be departing for home, never to return to Martinique. He delayed the task as long as he could, finally bringing himself to relate the inevitable, that their relationship was soon to end and very likely, they would never see one another again. He expected that she would rant and rave, storm in utter madness and frenzy, since the young woman was prone to emotional outbursts, but to his surprise, she took the news calmly. Never turned a hair. Little did he realize, it was the calm *before* the storm.

"The next month passed without incident, bringing the sad day when he was to board his ship for the crossing to *la Belle France*. The morning of his departure, he became deathly ill. His skin burned with a raging fever, and sweat poured from him, though he shivered with cold chills. There was *no way* he could travel. He couldn't even rise from his couch to walk across the room, so tortured and weak was he from the virulent malady that racked his body.

"From his window, he watched, glinting in the bright Martinique sunlight, the gleaming white ship on which he had booked passage, as it sailed gracefully out of the harbor.

"His mistress, holding a cold compress to his head, began singing a strange song to him in the *Patois* language of her people, words he could not understand. Within minutes, his fever lifted, his head stopped aching, and his chills vanished. Miraculously, he was well again.

"This phenomenon occurred two more times. *Thrice* he missed passage back to France due to a severe attack of a mysterious ailment that ceased to exist as soon as his ship sailed– vanishing into the ethers with the strange *Patois* chanting of his mistress.

"Finally, the young doctor surrendered to the fact that he could not leave Martinique or his *Martiniquaise* lover. *It was impossible.* As a doctor, he could not explain it, and neither could the medical staff at the hospital where he worked.

"Legend has it– and I tend to believe legends, for they almost always emerge from a truth. Legend has it," she repeated, "that he spent the remainder of his life with the *Quimbois* woman, practicing medicine here in what was then a French colony.

"Now, my question is this: Was the *béké* Frenchman's illness psychosomatic? *Une maladie imaginaire* brought on himself because, in reality, *he* did not want to leave his mistress or his idyllic life on Martinique for a far more structured, demanding existence in

Paris?" The Goth gal's deep voice took on an eerie timbre, "Or was the malady caused by something significantly more sinister?"

Before anyone could respond, Raine rumbled in her throaty voice, "*A mystery insoluble.* This type of thing has happened all over the Caribbean, and heed my words, its history is not confined to the distant past. When you look around at this beautiful setting– the clear blue sky, the sparkling azure sea, the sun pouring its amber light over the tropical green of jungle, the lovely colors and scent of flowers, the happy, laughing people– it's difficult to believe." She raised a brow. "And yet ..."

"As professors of history and archeology," Maggie stated with conviction, "we know real magick does exist. Anyone who has ever fallen in love has been touched by magick. The world is full of magickal things patiently waiting for our wits to grow sharper."

"You know what was the most curious thing about that tale?" Raine asked rhetorically. "The doctor's mistress had a habit of sitting at his feet. After she cast her spell over him, it was *he* who sat at *her* feet. It is said people noticed the reversed position– or should I say *status?*– of their roles in the relationship.

"The mistress, as *I* said, was very beautiful, in the hour's fashion, *purringly* pretty like a well-stroked cat. Everything about her was catlike, movements and mannerisms, *everything.* Those who met her often commented on how mysterious she was. I remember when first I heard the story, I was told she was '... highly intuitive and as graceful and agile as any feline. She carried the mystery and intensity of the panther, a sleek black panther. People, even those who did not believe in the occult, could *feel* her power.'"

Maggie mused a long moment, saying finally, "Hmmm, I can't blame her for wanting to hold on to her lover; but interfering with free will, if indeed that's what it was– a big no-no."

"Whatever it was," Raine responded with a chortle, "Fauve– and by the way, the French name Fauve means Wild and Uninhibited– anyway, she was not the kind of gal to embrace an Oh-Well-Life-Is-Full-Of-Exits maxim. That's for sure."

Maggie's eyes shifted to the window. "Difficult to imagine that anything wicked goes on in a paradise like this."

"Wicked things go on everywhere," Raine returned. "Take our hamlet, for example. It's a lovely place to live. Quite pretty and quaint. There are some nice people living in it, but there are some extremely *unpleasant* ones as well. Why, just the other day ..."

***

An hour or so later, the foursome took the loop from the Trace round to the Caribbean coast, motoring south to return to their hotel in time for their evening drinks at the Coco Bar, where they were looking forward to another Martinique sunset.

When, en route, they came to the fishing community of Case-Pilote, Raine suggested they park the Renault to take a walk around the town. The place had dignity and charm with a surplus of color.

"One of the oldest villages on Martinique, known for its church that dates to the seventeenth century. Let's take a look at it. There it is," she pointed. "See, the roof is shaped like a ship's hull and the pediment like a scallop shell. Neat, huh? Inside is an amazing mosaic crafted from burnt crockery debris from the 1902 eruption of Mount Pelée. Oh, and the town square boasts a really pretty fountain."

As the Sisters walked along the battery, they began to feel the tingle that signified something significant was about to unfold. No sooner did Maggie mention the witchy intuition to her sister of the moon, when Raine's phone began to vibrate.

"Doctor McDonough," she rumbled huskily into the receiver.

"Raine, I need for you, Maggie, and your escorts, all four of you, to come out to la Pagerie in the morning. You must be here by ten. Please don't be late. It's *mandatory* that you be here," *Madame* the Curator said with what could only be termed French *vim*."

Raine's gaze lighted on Maggie, who was listening avidly, since the former held the phone for them both to hear. Speaking into the cell, she said, "May I ask what this is about, *madame?*"

"I cannot speak of it over the phone. All will be explained when you arrive. I remember that tomorrow is your last day on Martinique, but this is *too* important for you to miss. I *entreat* you, if you have anything planned, *please* rearrange your schedule. You **must** come out here tomorrow at ten, and please be on time."

"I don't understand," blurted Raine, bedeviled. "Has something bad happened?" The Sister did not sense anything negative in the offing, but she thrust forth the query anyway.

"*Non, non, rien comme ça. Tout va bien,*" Jeanne Gardien assured, dropping the words in her native French. "Please, this is all I am at liberty to say now, but again, *I beg of you*– please be sure to come out to la Pagerie *à dix heures du matin **précises*** ... tomorrow

morning at ten sharp. *Merci.* I must go now," she finished swiftly.
"*À demain.*"

And with those mysterious words, the curator rang off.

Chapter Nineteen

The next morning, since it was their last full day on Martinique, the Sisters and their loves rose earlier than usual. After treating themselves to the sumptuous breakfast buffet at the hotel terrace dining room, they piled into the Renault to motor out to la Pagerie.

"Have you an inkling as to why Jeanne has summoned us back to the museum?" Maggie put to Raine, as she buckled up. The redheaded Sister dipped a hand into her bag for her compact and lipstick.

"I haven't, no," the Goth gal answered. "Goodness, she's thanked us profoundly, and she and the board have gifted us with the lovely Limoges *demi-tasse*. I can't quite put my finger on what this is about ... unless the board wants to thank us in person. I'm feeling a sort of *gathering* out there today. That's probably it."

"I think you're right," Maggie agreed, freshening her glossy tangerine lipstick in the compact mirror.

"I guess you don't have any idea how much time we'll be at la Pagerie this morning," Beau asked, knowing full well the answer to his query.

"None whatsoever," the Sisters chorused.

When the two couples arrived at their destination, they no sooner parked their rental, when *Madame* the Curator strode briskly from the museum entrance to greet them.

"So glad you could make it on time, *mes amis*," she smiled broadly. "You must be bursting to know what this is about." Jeanne made a sweeping gesture toward the door. "*Alors*, let us go inside. I hope you'll be pleased."

Upon stepping into the museum's cool interior, the Sisters immediately exchanged looks, for as Raine's sentiment predicted, there before them, standing in what Americans would call "apple-pie order," was a gathering of official-looking people, only a couple of whom the magickal duo recognized– Principal *Inspecteur de la Police Nationale* Capitaine Michel Renard and Interpol Agent Drago Sournois. The Sisters also noted a television camera and members of what had to be the French press.

"We are met today to honor you for what you did for our beloved *Musée de la Pagerie, la Martinique, et la Belle France,*" Jeanne Gardien stated magnanimously. "Let me begin by introducing you to everyone." She ushered the invitees ahead of her. Then positioning herself alongside what was very like a receiving line, she commenced with the formal introductions, starting with *le Préfet de Martinique*, Monsieur Henri Beaulieu. Splendid in full dress uniform, black with a surplus of gold braid, the tall, solemn-faced préfet, representative of the national government, shook hands with the Americans, thanking each in perfect English for their service to France.

The next two officials to express gratitude to the Sisters' party were Chief Inspector Renard, also in full dress uniform, and Interpol Agent Sournois, who was attired in a light-grey suit. Both men wore countenances of deep approbation.

Surprising the Sisters even more, the austere Agent Sournois bent over Maggie's, then Raine's, hand in the courtly manner of an old-world gentleman to chivalrously kiss each.

And to think, Maggie tossed to Raine, *we used to call this charming man the Creeper!*

Following the French authorities, the five museum board members, presented by *Madame* the Curator, each thanked and shook hands with the four Americans.

All the while the *Télévision Martinique* camera was rolling, newspaper reporters from the *France Antilles-Martinique* and the English-language *Caribbean News Now* were capturing photographs and making copious notes.

Once the curator finished taking the Americans down the line of officials, she stood before the gathering to speak, the Sisters and their escorts next to her. For the Americans' sake, she spoke in English, laced now and again with French, as an interpreter translated in French.

When a museum assistant handed *Madame* Jeanne Gardien a large wooden plaque with brass trim, she slipped on her eyeglasses and began reading the commemorative text, which told the story of the Joséphine bracelet. The account related the Sleuth Sisters' role in the capture of the elusive criminal whom Interpol called the "Tiger," as well as their recovery of the bracelet and, by use of their psychic gifts, the discovery of the Joséphine letter that gave all-important provenance to the historic item. When Jeanne Gardien finished reading, she nodded to her assistant, who moved to stand to her right, holding two replicas of the museum's plaque. To *Madame* the Curator's left waited the Americans.

"This beautifully crafted plaque will be placed with the security case we, *le Musée de la Pagerie,* have commissioned for the Joséphine bracelet and letter, as well as the silver jewelry box, brooch, ring, and coins that belonged to Joséphine's mother. The case will also hold *The Memoirs of Queen Hortense*, open to the page where Joséphine's daughter made mention of a valuable item lost that stormy August night in 1790, when she and the future empress fled la Pagerie for France."

Gratitude filled Jeanne's voice. "Just as the inscription on the bracelet, the queen's memoirs, and the discovered letter document the bracelet's connection to Joséphine, this plaque will document our connection to these heroic Americans for all time– for posterity's sake."

She nodded to the assistant, who presented Maggie and Raine each with a replica plaque, the shiny brass trim seeming to flash a reflection of their bright and ardent spirits.

"Now, with your permission," the curator addressed the Sisters, "we would like to include a photograph in the security case with these treasures."

A thrill of good feeling surged through the McDonoughs who responded in the affirmative, "We would be honored."

The museum assistant stepped forward to capture several photographs, including a couple with Thaddeus and Beau.

"Once the security case arrives here at la Pagerie, and we have everything arranged therein, I will send you several images," *Madame* the Curator promised the Sisters.

Jeanne then completed the ceremony by stepping forward to execute the traditional *faire la bise.* "*Merci encore, merci toujours, mes chères amies américaines.*"

"*Nous sommes heureuses d'avoir pu aider,*" a blushing Raine returned in French, whilst a teary Maggie delivered the message in English. "We are happy we could help."

Afterward, reporters from *Télévision Martinique* and the newspaper *France Antilles-Martinique* ask politely if they might cut interviews with the Sisters, who graciously accepted, answering questions about their backgrounds and their psychic abilities, being ever careful to protect their Time-Key. At the end of the interview, the reporters garnered the magickal pair's impressions of Martinique.

When a reporter from the *Antilles* commented that he was impressed with the Sisters' strong sense of duty for doing the right thing, he finished by saying that they certainly did go "... above and beyond. Did you ever think," he asked, "when you first took on this mystery that you would, *could,* go as far as you did?"

The Sisters traded looks, with Raine answering cryptically, "To quote Napoléon, 'Until you spread your wings, you have no idea how *far* you can fly.'"

For the next hour, attendees enjoyed a champagne reception, with the French bubbly and *hors d'oeuvres,* in the shade of the stone pavilion on the museum's luxuriant grounds.

Once everyone was holding a glass of champagne, Monsieur le Préfet, Henri Beaulieu, raised his glass to propose a toast. *"Aux Soeurs Détectives!"* he enthused with a bright smile of camaraderie, to which the gathering responded in kind.

"Aux Soeurs Détectives! To the Sleuth Sisters!"
"Bravo! Formidable!"

When the Sisters, Thaddeus and Beau drove away from la Pagerie at half-past noon, by all rights, they should have been tired. On the contrary, the exciting event that morning invigorated the foursome, prompting them to follow the plan they had formed the previous evening at dinner.

Since it was their last day on Martinique, they unanimously voiced their desire to drive northeast to the *Presqu'île de la Caravelle* and explore that narrow finger of land, a wildlife and nature reserve, that jets six miles straight out into the tempestuous Atlantic Ocean.

"Traffic considered, it's about an hour's drive to the ruins of Château Dubuc," Raine read from their trusty guidebook. "We can walk around the castle ruins, then, since the hiking trail for la Caravelle starts there, trek at least one of the paths for the time we have left before our drive back to the hotel. We don't want to miss our last Martinique sunset this evening."

"What does the guide say about *le château*," Maggie queried from the front seat.

Skimming the text, Raine replied, "Overlooks scenic Baie du Trésor, Treasure Bay. Offers magnificent views."

Her eyes traveled down the page. "Was for many decades the property of the rich and powerful du Buc family. Ooooh, get this: Pierre du Buc fled France after a notorious duel and settled in Martinique in 1657. His victories over the Carib Indians earned him redemption at the French Royal Court, along with a land grant here in Martinique. His grandson built the castle between 1720-1725 ... a coffee and sugarcane plantation."

Her emerald gaze perused the subsequent passages. "Hmmm, in addition, it's believed the family engaged in smuggling. Certainly, the isolation of the castle was conducive to landing discreet boats." She read on. "Says the castle's nefarious past included slave smuggling.

"Anyway, the family resided there for seventy-plus years. Over time, several hurricanes damaged the house, which was gradually abandoned. Today, all that remains is a small museum, that traces the lives of the castle owners, and ruins scattered over a vast National Park."

Again, Raine skipped down the page. "Says the trail loop has some steep and slippery grades, loose rocks, even some large boulders to step around and over, but we'll manage OK."

When they arrived at Château Dubuc, Thaddeus brought the Renault to a stop on the parking lot, so the coterie could explore the ruins before striking the trail that hugged Treasure Bay.

A consummate illusionist, the professor began framing and capturing photos with the camera suspended with leather strap from his neck.

"Though we're not in Merrie Olde England, makes me think of the Castle of Torquilstone from *Ivanhoe*," Maggie said wistfully, "which I like to read every autumn round my birthday. It never fails to leave a drizzly November in my soul, but I can't help myself. It's such a *romantic* tale."

Gazing at the castle ruins, Raine responded to her sister of the moon, "Yes, I see what you mean. This place reminds me that another soubriquet for Martinique is Island of Ghosts."

The Goth gal tilted her dark head, trying to remember something she heard years before. After a few moments of reflection, she said, "I recall a story an artist shared with me the first summer I came to Martinique. He was an eccentric sort of chap,

English, but more like a Guy de Maupassant character, who was here, in his words, 'to find himself.' Anyroad, he told me he saw Paul Gauguin's ghost, not far from Château Dubuc, on one of the hairpin roads that descends from the clouds ... you know what I'm saying, from the mountains, before zigzagging down to the Atlantic seaboard. He swore it was true." Noting the look on Thaddeus' face, she exclaimed, "What?! What're you thinking?"

The professor chortled. "What I think won't raise the dead, but how did he know it was Paul Gauguin?"

"I suppose," Raine shrugged, "because Gauguin had a very distinctive look. Strong features, prominent nose, penetrating eyes, and a dark, sweeping cavalry mustache. The Englishman was an artist, after all, and he would've been 'acquainted,' so to speak, with Paul Gauguin."

"What was Gauguin's ghost doing?" Maggie queried.

Raine thought for a moment. "Walking along the coast road. The specter was carrying his folding easel and art supplies in a large satchel, worn cross-body like an oversized shoulder bag. My friend said he was wearing a paint-spattered artist's smock and a big, black beret. Oh, and he wasn't quite solid, but rather ethereal, parts of him almost transparent."

"We believe in ghosts because we've experienced them," Maggie commented. "And we're used to them, so we're usually not fearful. After all, when I look in a mirror, I see Granny in my own face and when she manifests. But you know what? I've never yet heard of a murderer who wasn't afraid of ghosts. Did you hear what Inspector Renard said this morning about the Tiger? He's been having nightmares of ghosts, of the people he's tortured and killed, I'd wager, come to haunt him."

"Doesn't make me feel sorry for the black-hearted scumbag," Raine retorted. "It should've dawned on him that Karma never forgets a name or address."

"'Tis the universal law of cause and effect," Maggie agreed. "People who create their own drama, create and deserve their own Karma. You reap what you sow."

"About Gauguin," Beau interposed, "isn't he the French Impressionist who painted Tahitian life?"

"Correct," Raine answered. "He sought out exotic environments, spending, toward the end of his life, over ten years painting in French Polynesia. On one hand, he was a sort of wolfish wild man, on the other, a sensitive martyr for the arts. He had been a stockbroker, if memory serves, then abandoned his wife and children, his job, *everything* in France for his art. His short stay on Martinique, in, I seem to recall, 1887, preceded his penchant for French Polynesia. He did about a dozen known paintings here on Martinique. Colorful, rural scenes of island life.

"In Tahiti, his penchant emerged for painting young girls. He took up with a thirteen-year-old Tahitian beauty who posed for many of his works there. He repeatedly entered into *liaisons* with young girls, 'marrying,'" she gestured imaginary quote marks with her fingers, "two of them and fathering a number of children, undoubtedly exploiting his position as a privileged European.

"Certainly, he made the most of the sexual freedoms available to him. As shocking as it may sound that the girl was only thirteen, in Tahiti, at that time, this was the age of consent. And it is said, Gauguin's little mistress had other lovers in addition to him.

"Anyway, Gauguin was forever having problems with the Catholic Church and government authorities, neither of which approved of polygamy. Too, he often sided with the natives against the Church and the authorities. In 1903, due to such problems, he was sentenced to three months in prison, but died of syphilis that same year before he could serve, his body weakened by alcohol and a dissipated life."

"Great Neptune's trident, the surf's wild here!" Maggie marveled with abrupt expression.

It was windy, and high waves constantly battered the Caravelle cliffs, which made for an awe-inspiring reminder of the unharnessed power of Earth Mother.

"Rocky outcrops and dark ocean water are characteristic of Martinique's Atlantic side," Thaddeus said. He picked up a stout tree branch to use as a walking stick.

"The cliffs here remind me of Ireland," Maggie remarked, as they continued their hike along the meandering trail.

"They remind me of Point Reyes, California," Thaddeus returned.

"Or Brittany, France," Raine put in. "**Stop!**" the Sister yelled with force. "Don't move! I want to show you something. See the red paint along the trunk of that tree?"

The others followed her pointing finger, responding in turn.

"That tree is a *mancenillier*," Raine asserted. "Don't ever touch one of them. Avoid the leaves, the trunk, every bit. And for Goddess' sake, *never* eat the little green apples. *Mancenilliers* are toxic to humans. The sap they produce is poison– *fiery* poison. Never stand under one of those trees when it rains. Even water running off their leaves will burn the skin like fire. *I know.* I stood under one in a sudden downpour my first time on Martinique, and I developed blisters all over me. The *mancenillier* is known here in the Caribbean as the Tree of Death; and trust me, there've been people who *have* died after eating the sweet fruit. Historically speaking, Christopher Columbus, learning the hard way, christened the tree with its name that means, literally, Little Apple of Death."

"Great Goddess," Maggie exclaimed, "why doesn't Martinique rid the island of these monsters?"

"Well, the trees actually protect wildlife," Raine remembered, though she couldn't recall how. "The red stripe makes it easy to avoid the buggers, and there are signs warning tourists. See," she pointed. "Be watchful. I wanted to give you a heads-up."

"I meant to ask," Maggie began, "does the guidebook give the reason this cove is called *Treasure* Bay?"

"It does," Raine answered. "This secluded paradise is thus named due to the jasper and other eye-catching gemstones that occasionally wash ashore. Found in an infinite number of colors and patterns, jasper is known as the 'Supreme Nurturer.' It sustains and supports in times of stress, and brings the owner or wearer tranquility and wholeness. It provides confidence, protection … absorbs negative energy, and balances yin and yang."

"I'm feeling lucky," Thaddeus declared. "Let's spread out for a bit and see if one of us spots a nugget."

After several minutes of combing the wave-battered beach, the professor shouted, "Found one!" He held out his hand to show the red, dark-veined stone that was about the size of a US twenty-five-cent coin. Polished by surf and sand, it was gorgeous.

"Red jasper is said to increase self-confidence and self-trust," the Goth gal stated. It also brings courage, calm, and relaxation. Not to mention," she winked at Beau, "sexual vibrancy."

"Then, good thing," Maggie rejoined, "that I thought to bring a small vial of Granny's love potion on this trip. It will enhance the natural energy to which you gave emphasis."

Thaddeus grinned as he stroked his van dyke in pensive gesture, locking eyes with Maggie. "Here," he handed her the jasper. "You and Raine know what to do to prepare this stone for tonight."

"I read in the guidebook," Beau shared, "that the lighthouse here gives hikers a stunning, 360-degree, panoramic view of the Caravelle and Martinique's Atlantic coast."

"Onward to the lighthouse, and then we must head to the car and drive back to the hotel for our rendezvous with Sunset," Thaddeus directed.

"The account I read in the guidebook last night was a harrowing description of the lighthouse keepers who braved category-five Hurricane David back in 1979," Beau declared. "Make sure you read it. Those fellas had one helluva spell ..."

***

"We meet one last time," Raine said sadly, "at the Coco, when sky and sea are set aflame."

"Each has been a *Merry* Meet," Maggie avowed, settling into her chair and adjusting Granny's lacy shawl over her bare shoulders.

As he held Raine's chair, Beau leaned forward to whisper in her ear, "I'd love to watch every sunset with you through the sunset of our lives."

"Beau, you're so incurably sentimental," Raine said, turning her head to send him an appreciative regard. Reaching up, she tweaked his thick, ebony mustache. "And that's one of the reasons I love you." Twisting further round, she placed her shawl over the back of her chair before smoothing the black, strapless dress over her knees. "I love the gauzy, tissue-thin material of the clothes they wear here," she said to Maggie. "Very cool."

Maggie's dress was a tangerine affair, similar in cut and style to Raine's. "That's the idea."

The foursome ordered what had become their customary *ti punch* then sat back in the bamboo chairs to relax, sipping and chatting as they waited for that supreme moment when the sun catches the ocean on fire and the world seems to hush in peaceful sanction.

"My fondest memories of Martinique," Maggie voiced softly, "will always include our sunsets. I know there will be times, back home, when I conjure these moments for quiet meditation."

"Let's all think of a good sunset feeling," Raine recommended. "It will help keep the memory alive."

"Serenity," Thaddeus began, "is watching a Martinique sunset and feeling *grateful*. The sunsets here have taken my spirit to a new place of quietude and peace."

"Caribbean sunsets are so breathtakingly beautiful, they're like looking through the gilded gates to the Summerland," Maggie proffered.

"Glowing, intoxicating words, those," Raine quipped. "No one can look at a sunset here and not dream," she added, catching Beau's eye.

"Sunsets are proof that endings can be beautiful," Beau determined with succinct aplomb.

"Often when we think we're at the end of something, we're basically at the beginning of something else," Thaddeus returned. "I've felt that. Many times." His bright blue eyes scanned the coterie, from face to beloved face, and a warm smile shone from his essence. "My desire for us is that 'the miles we go before we sleep' be filled with the feelings that come from deep caring– appreciation, joy, understanding ... wisdom. And beyond that, in all the endings in our lives," his gaze held Maggie's, "we'll be able to *see* the new beginnings."

Maggie leaned in to kiss the professor's cheek.

Softly the evening came then– with the Martinique magick of day's end, the most dazzling sunset of all. As the huge, red-orange sun sank sizzling into the azure sea, the McDonough witches felt their senses sharpening. At that supreme moment, both Sisters heard a distinctive Créole voice on the trade wind whisper, *"Bien joué, mes soeurs."* *Well played, Sisters.*

The pair looked to one another, whilst Raine sent Maggie the thought: *I believe, Mags, we've fulfilled our destiny here. I'm making a wish, on our last Martinique sunset, that Joséphine's ghost will come back to visit us. I'll definitely let her in.*

Tears shimmered Maggie's emerald eyes jewel-like. "I'm thinking that sunsets are not just scientific phenomenon. I believe they're strong evidence that somewhere out there, someone is smiling down on us, encouraging us and, taking my cue from Thaddeus, giving us hope ... telling us that everything is going to be fine."

"Yes, a sunset is the Goddess' goodnight kiss," Raine concurred with her moon sister.

As they watched, twilight fell. The fiery sky turned an inky-purple, sprinkled as it was with a myriad of glittering silver stars.

"A Martinique night," Maggie concluded, "never fails to surprise with its suddenness."

When the Sisters' party entered the candle glow of the hotel dining room, they were disappointed not to find Dorélia there. The stand-in, as previously, was Jean-Jacques' cousin, Salomé.

"I don't know why she quit, but she *has*," the woman told them tableside. "That's all I know, except that she won't be waitressing anymore."

The Sisters swapped anxious glances.

"I hope nothing bad has happened," Raine said, almost to herself. "You don't suppose she and your cousin are having marital problems again, do you?" she posed *sotto voce*.

The older woman gave a dismissive shrug. *"Je ne sais pas.* I know only that Dorélia has quit for good. The management told me if I want her job, I can have it." Triumph unquestionably carried on her voice.

"Hmmm," Raine murmured. *I'm still picking up jealousy, though I'm not sensing anything truly wicked as I suspected earlier on. More like simple female jealousy. But I wonder if ...* She decided to wait till Salomé moved off to discuss it with her coterie.

Before the waitress left their table, Raine drew from her purse an olivine gemstone, about the size of a US five-cent coin, that she had charged. "Here," she said, "I want you to have this."

"What is it?" the older woman asked with curious expression. She took the shimmering, pale green stone, turning it over in her dusky hand. "It's pretty."

"It's an olivine. The French word for it is *peridot*," the Goth gal replied. "Some call it the 'Evening emerald.' Olivine is peridot in its basic form, a precious stone, to be sure. It's found in comet dust, and was discovered on the moon and detected by instrument on Mars." Noting the incredulous expression on the waitress' face, she assured, "It's absolutely true. The ancients believed, quite literally, that peridot was ejected to Earth by a sun's explosion and carries its healing power. And because of its connection to the sun, it's one of the birthstones, the purr-fect stone, for Leos. Aren't you a Leo?"

Salomé's dark eyes widened, then fixing on the gem resting in her palm, she uttered the French for Wow. "*Waw!*" Realizing she hadn't answered the question put to her, she said, "*Oui.* I am a Leo. How did you know that?"

Raine smiled in her unique feline fashion. "Be certain to carry the stone with you at all times," she advised, reaching out to close the waitress' hand over the olivine. "It will assist you greatly in your life. *I promise.* Set it in the sun, or rinse it with clear, clean water once in a while to cleanse it. And put it on an east-facing windowsill in the energizing light of the full moon each month. Those things will keep the stone's powers strong. Oh, and don't let anyone else handle it. You don't want to confuse the energies. It's solely for you."

When Salomé moved to the next table of diners, Raine leaned close to Maggie to whisper, "Our wise little poppet instructed me to pack an olivine when we were preparing for this trip. That stone will aid Salomé in alleviating jealousy. It's an aid, but it won't interfere with free will. Working in harmony with the stone's metaphysical properties, I cast it for her last night." Continuing to hold her voice to a whisper, the Goth gal said, "Listen, I was wondering if ..."

"Well," Beau said a minute or so later, "let's order." He picked up his menu. "It's been a long day, and I'm hungry."

They took the waitress' suggestion and ordered the special that night, *l'Escalopes de Veau à la Normande,* accompanied by the house White. This after a fresh green salad.

"These Créoles really know how to prepare food," Thaddeus declared. "I keep eating like this, and I'll have to let my belt out a notch. However, I'm going to miss the delectable food here in Martinique."

"Can't beat it," Beau readily acceded. "This veal cutlet with cream sauce is out of this world." He took a swallow of wine. "I have to admit, I came to this island a skeptic about the food, since I'm a traditional meat and potatoes kind-a guy. I confess something else too. Though I was anticipating a restful vacation, I was wondering, before we got here, if there was anything to see in the Caribbean except sunlight. I gotta say," he sent Raine a look sated in meaning, "this trip has been wholly gratifying."

Raine sighed. "It pleases me no end to hear you say that. I am certain my colleagues, that is to say, my fellows from the history department," she looked to Maggie and Thaddeus, "would agree that, due to their long and layered history and the many fortunes of the Caribbean, the West Indian islands are all different, one from another. Therein is the boundless charm of the Antilles. Not only is each island singular, each has something new to offer. And speaking of traditional," Raine caught at Beau's word, "I suggest the traditional Martinique dessert tonight. It's our last chance to enjoy it."

Everyone agreed, and the popular Martinique *Blanc Manger Coco* was ordered by all.

As the coterie savored the white coconut flan, Jean-Jacques' Trade Winds band began setting up to play. When the Americans relocated to the lantern-lit terrace, he was singing the song that, excepting the Empress Joséphine, put Martinique on the map, "When They Begin The Beguine." It was not surprising that his rendition was exceptional. What was surprising was what happened next.

From *la réception* swayed Dorélia to join her husband at the microphone.

"Yowza!" Maggie sucked in her breath. "Is it–"

"It's Dorélia all right," Raine answered, "but I'll be a meddling muggle, it doesn't even look like the woman we know … knew."

The former waitress looked gorgeous in a floral, low-cut dress that revealed a curvaceous figure, her dark-brown hair, long and loose, her almond-shaped eyes made up seductive.

"Wow, she's a knock-out," Beau said.

"And listen to that voice, would you?" Raine observed. *So that's what the mysterious Dorélia looks like devoid of her flouncy waitress getup. No wonder her cousin-in-law is jealous.*

"I *knew* she had a secret," Maggie said with a shade of smugness. "That gal can sing!"

Husband and wife continued their duet, during which time the Sisters noted how in love they appeared to be. Their voices harmonized well, and the choice of songs in their repertoire complimented their new-found romance.

When the band took their first break of the evening, J-J and Dorélia made their way to the Sisters' table. After the initial greetings, Raine, who couldn't hold back any longer, blurted in French, "What a bombshell you presented us with tonight!"

Dorélia smiled prettily. "*Ouelle surprise* for me too! I remembered what you told Jean-Jacques, that no one will ever believe in you if you don't first believe in yourself." She gazed at her husband with love-filled eyes, patting his cheek to send him a popular Martinique endearment, "*Oui, doudou.*

"I feel different," she gushed. "I *am* different. *Vraiment,* I can't expect J-J to have more confidence, if I don't have it myself. My husband always told me I have a good voice. He tried his best to convince me to sing with his band, but never did I have *le courage,* the– *comment dit-on?*– the *poise* to do it. I could *not* sing before an audience. Now, I have proven to myself that I *can.*" She smiled again. "How did I do? *Dites-le-moi.*"

"Great!" came the unified reply.

"You made 'em sit up and take notice," Raine said truthfully.

Thaddeus sent her an avuncular beam. "You've got untapped potential," he pronounced with an airy confidence of his own. "I predict that soon, you'll have all of Martinique at your feet. A word, nonetheless, of advice, *mes amis.*" The professor fixed the couple with his brilliant blue gaze. "A duet cannot be in harmony with just one voice."

"*Pas de souci.* Not to worry. I'm finally breaking free of my anger," Jean-Jacques declared. "Making peace with life. I've got baggage, but I'm trying to shoulder life's burdens as a real man would."

"Unless a man's got somethin' to lift," Beau commented, "he can never find out just how strong he is."

Maggie shifted her gaze from Dorélia to Raine, sending the Sister a silent message, along with the conjured image of the naked woman dancing in firelight under the full moon. Maggie knew now that the woman had been Dorélia. Though she was not a full-fledged *Quimbois*, she had released a petition, of her own making, for help with her marriage.

Raine grinned at the happy couple. "Keep your eyes on the stars, your feet on the ground, and you'll do well."

Casting an eye over the Americans, Dorélia answered with soft expression, "And God keep you safe on your journey home. We will never forget you. *Jamais*. Never."

"I'm pleased we could justify the faith you showed us. Oh, that reminds me. We have something for you," Maggie remembered, reaching into her bag for the red jasper they found that day at la Caravelle. She proceeded to tell their friend how they came to find the stone, concluding that it was a "... special gift from the sea." Then she shared the metaphysical blessings of jasper, ending with instructions for keeping it cleansed and charged. "Let no one else handle it. Raine and I charged it expressly for you and J-J. It will bring you luck– the pair of you."

"It's already working," Dorélia beamed, stepping forward to warmly hug each Sister.

Raine and Maggie returned the glow. *Much more than you know!*

When the musical duo returned to front the band, Maggie and Raine looked to Thaddeus.

"It was almost as though you *knew* about this," Maggie intimated. "After all, you're the one who proposed blessing that stone for them."

"*Did* you know? About Dorélia joining her husband's band?" Raine pressed.

The professor's bright blue eyes crinkled at the corners, and he gave her a twinkling, shining sort of look. "Now, how in the world would I have known that?"

But the twinkle in those telling eyes hinted at something else.

It was very early the next morning when the Sisters' taxi started down the lane from the Bakoua. Gazing out the cab's rear window, Raine's eyes glistened with unshed tears blurring her vision, as the hotel receded in the distance, disappearing from view when they rounded a palm-lined curve in the road, the rays of sun shooting past her like golden machine-gun fire.

With a sigh, she swiped her eyes with a tissue to take one last look at the jungle-cloaked Pitons du Carbet, faint and misty across the water, their peaks shrouded by wispy clouds. "*Au revoir, ma chère Martinique,*" she whispered.

Taking her hand, Beau brought it to his lips, his mustache tickling her skin. "We'll come back," he said softly, and the promise on his voice heartened the simplicity of his words.

Chapter Twenty

A month had passed since Raine and Maggie returned home from their holiday on Martinique. Since it was Beau's birthday, the Sisters were in the Goth gal's vintage MG en route to the Hamlet's Gypsy Tearoom.

Ever since she was a child and polished off Nancy Drew mysteries faster than her granny could supply them, the impressionable Raine planned on having a vintage roadster of her own one day. When she was ready for the purchase, she searched everywhere for just the right car but to no avail.

Then the crafty young witch decided to *manifest* her target MG, the roadster on which she'd set her heart. She did research and got a clear visualization of precisely what she wanted, intensifying the energy every time she envisioned the 1953 model she desired. She was thoroughly and carefully specific, surgically precise with every detail, from the signature headlights to the wire-wheels, and she truly *believed in the power of her own spell.* Within a few short weeks, the MG TD of her dreams appeared in the classified ads of the *Hamlet Herald*– within the price range she had programmed into the enchantment.

The sports car's like-new red and black interior and grill were the Sisters' high school and college colors, and the pristine cream body was the perfect canvas for the wee magick wand Raine commissioned detailed on the driver's door, with her initials in fancy script on the wand's grip.

As she drove, Raine was looking forward to an intimate supper that evening with her lover at Tara. To give the couple privacy, Maggie was planning on spending the night at Thaddeus' house.

"Can't believe it's August already," Raine commented. She expertly shifted into low gear to descend Englishman's Hill. "Before you know it, we'll be resuming our teaching duties at the college."

"I was so busy neatening my bedroom closet today I forgot to ask. What're you preparing for Beau's birthday supper tonight?"

"I've gotten everything ready ahead of time. Going to throw a couple choice steaks on the back-porch grill. It's easy, and it's Beau's favorite meal, especially when I use that rub he likes. I've already chopped the salad. Have only to dress it. Washed and foil-wrapped a couple of potatoes to accompany the steaks. I plan on loading my potato just the way I like it, with sour cream and chives, a dollop of salad dressing, shredded cheese, chopped olives and hot peppers, topped by a sprinkle of peanuts, with the whole thing smothered in hot sauce. Dessert I'll buy at the tearoom."

"You've got a cast-iron stomach, darlin'. You know, you should have baked Beau a cake," said Maggie in a teasing fashion.

Raine snorted a scoff. "I should think it most unlikely that I'd bake anything to transcend our Gypsy friend's culinary delights." She could not contain a grin of expectation. "However, I will provide Beau with, shall we say, a transcendental treat of my own making after dinner."

Maggie's silvery laugh tinkled through the air like wind chimes on a summer breeze. "You know what they say. Intimacy is for magick or pleasure."

Raine tossed a wink at her sister of the Craft and chortled in throaty merriment. "Uh-hummm, it's for both."

Maggie spent the next several moments plucking choice intimacies from her abundant memory tree. "Passion's good, darlin'. Witches are meant to live a life of passion, purpose, magick and miracles."

Raine's bejeweled fingers flicked the air in witchy gesture. "The most incredible thing about both magick and miracles– is that they happen."

When the Sisters entered the cool, dimly lit café, they glanced round for the proprietress, Eva Novak.

Located in the lowest level of what had been the Hamlet's original armory, the Gypsy Tearoom was a romantic destination with its flickering wall sconces and the cozy seating that began life as horse stalls. The Gothic, 1907 fortress-like structure was purchased by Eva Novak when the new armory was erected several years prior. During renovation, the roomy box stalls were transformed into booths, ideal for the readings Eva's clientele frequently requested along with her special teas and delectable Tearoom fare. Like her ancestors, Eva read palms and tea leaves.

The Tearoom's ground floor served as the banquet hall, reserved for groups and events. Eva used the third floor for her private quarters. Her living room occupied one of the building's twin turrets, her bedroom the other, making her feel, as she often said, like a queen in a castle tower.

Renovation had been as the definition of the word affirms– cleaning, repairing, and reviving with as little actual remodeling as possible; for, like others who purchased old buildings in the historic Pennsylvania village of Haleigh's Hamlet, Eva was set on keeping the structure's integrity.

In the basement-level Tearoom, wood table-and-bench seating filled each horse-stall-turned-booth. The walls of the cubicles were covered with garnet-red, tufted leather, against which the occupants could comfortably rest their backs. Too, the booths' thick, padded walls provided additional privacy.

Gothic-style tables and chairs occupied the center of the room. Miniature stained-glass lamps topped the tables, and on the opposite wall from the stall-booths was an impressive, walk-in stone fireplace that conjured cozy reverie of olden times. The ceiling flaunted the original walnut beams; the walls, exposed brick, the same aged brick as the building's exterior. Massive, sliding barn doors, with medieval-style, black hardware, separated the dining area from an ample kitchen.

Hardly had Raine and Maggie entered the quaint establishment, when Eva, in bright Gypsy attire– lipstick-red, off-the-shoulder, low-cut blouse and flowing teal skirt belted with a fringed red shawl– emerged from the kitchen to sail toward them with open arms. "Merry Meet! Welcome, darlinks!"

The woman radiated a shining spirit. To look into Eva's face was to see her honest heart, and it enduringly filled the empathic Sisters with light and made them smile.

If you only knew how much we rely on your special Tea-Time-Will-Tell calming brew! Raine thought. "It's good to see you, sister," the Goth gal said aloud, returning their good friend's warm embrace.

"Your order is ready, Maggie," Eva stated in Hungarian accent. "Caviar, house salad with my special dressing, and pan-seared scallop dinner for two. Will you ladies be wanting dessert today?"

Raine's deep voice grew bubbly, "Do witches have familiars?" she jested.

"Or besoms?" Maggie twittered.

"I tell you the choices," the proprietress replied, adjusting the wide, red scarf tied round her short, fluffy blonde hair. Large, gold hoop earrings completed the look. Howbeit, she not only *looked* the part– Eva Novak was the real deal, and one-of-a-kind to boot.

The colorful sister had been married four times. For some unknown reason, the woman had a penchant for firemen, as well as the name *John*. Raine and Maggie didn't know whether the husbands' given names were each John, or if Eva just addressed each by her favorite appellation. The sum of what the McDonoughs knew is that all four of Eva's husbands had been called "John." All four had been firemen, and each, like Eva herself, was Hungarian.

Widowed twice and divorced twice, Eva always spoke kindly of her former mates. Indeed, when any one of her husbands was ever mentioned, she habitually yanked a paper towel from the bodice of the Gypsy blouse or dress she was sporting to wipe tearful eyes. The Sisters never knew her not to be prepared with that towel. Nor did they know the lusty woman to be without a gentleman friend for too long, though these days, Eva seemed partial to her independence.

True to form, the tearoom proprietress was a talented psychic, as conversation would prove anon.

Per the Sisters' prompt, she began listing the day's desserts. "To die for, each one! My famous Tearoom blintzes. Chocolate mousse cake. Traditional New York cheesecake with fresh berries, today blue. Anything else would not be a good choice for take-out. They would melt. It's hot out there today." Eva fanned herself with a menu she snatched from the sideboard. "Maybe just my hot flashes."

"For me, this is a no-brainer," Maggie remarked. "Please put two pieces of the cheesecake with my order."

"Three pieces of the chocolate mousse cake to go for me," Raine answered.

"Why three?" Maggie questioned.

"The extra is for Beau to take home," Raine explained.

Eva's heavily made-up eyes scanned the Sisters. The woman had the eyes of a leopard, and they could see deep into the very soul of those she looked upon. Bringing a bejeweled hand to her forehead, the action causing her curious assortment of bracelets to jingle-jangle, she said, "Ah, I see for you both a very special evening ahead. A golden time. Sit and dr-rink my tea, darlinks. *Sit, sit*," she indicated the nearest booth, "and I will see what messages the oracle reveals at the bottom of your cups."

Not in the least surprised, Maggie and Raine readily sat for a spell to chat with their good friend and experience her wondrous gift of tasseography, one of the most practiced fortune-telling processes for which Gypsies are known.

When the Sisters finished their tea, Eva gazed first into Maggie's cup, studying the remains for nearly a full minute. "Ahhh, a night of passion, my dear, is in store for you and a gift of gold, *which*," she raised a bejeweled finger, asking for the Sister's added attention, "could well be symbolic for that special *man* in your life." Her Sophia Loren eyes danced with fun. "*Enjoy*." And the radiance of her visage shone brighter than the noonday sun.

Turning to Raine, she bent her head to scry that Sister's cup. "Oooh, I'm getting a lot of signs. Looks more like *Samhain* than *Lammas*. I see a costume, a sexy witch's costume for a special event. You, my little witch, have visited a website," Eva revealed with naughty expression. "The Sexy Witch's Cauldron. Ah yes," she quipped, "brevity *is* the soul of lingerie. You are so happy. You found everything you needed, and as a result, *more* than one surprise is coming *your* way this night, both of which you will take great *pleasure* in. So to you, too, I say– *Enjoy!*"

Tugging a paper towel from her bosom, Eva dabbed at her eyes. "This reading conjures my John who liked to surprise me with little presents hidden all over the house." She rolled her hazel eyes and lowered her voice, leaning closer to the Sisters. "He liked to surprise me in the bedroom too. Oooooh," she said, snatching again the menu to fan herself as a memory quivered through her essence. "And how I loved it."

The proprietress stuffed the paper towel back into her bodice to take a hand of each Sister affectionately between her own. "Darlinks, I share with you something else." Eva peered at them shrewdly. "The tea leaves have told me that your gifts, the skill and power of your witchy ways will increase … a heap more."

It would not take long for the Sisters to discover that everything their Gypsy muse revealed to them was spot-on.

Nonetheless, as the MG purred out of the Tearoom's carpark, Maggie turned to Raine to say, "I can't help thinking that Eva saw more in those leaves than she told us."

"Hmmmm," Raine considered, her pouty lips tightening, "I believe you're right."

En route to Thaddeus' house, a hitherto-bemused Maggie confessed, "Raine, when I thought I'd lost Thaddeus that day on the beach, I started thinking seriously about a handfast, the old Pagan, Celtic custom of a year and a day. And after that?" She lifted her shoulders slightly. "We'll see. I wanted to tell you, for I want you to understand. A handfast has been on my mind of late, darlin', though I haven't *definitely* decided." Maggie's look was almost pleading, when–

Raine shot a swift sideways glance at her sister of the moon to say, "I know, Mags." The raven-haired Sister drove in silence for a few moments, saying presently, "Do what your heart tells you to do. Granny always advised us to listen to the heart."

When they arrived at Thaddeus' English Tudor home, Raine helped Maggie carry the food to the door. Then she drove back to Tara to prepare for Beau's birthday supper.

She showered and put on the new, black spiderweb thong-teddy, matching thigh-high stockings– Beau loved it when she wore black stockings– and her favorite spike heels with the witchy vamps. Then she stepped into a little black summer dress, wriggling to zip it up. Lastly, she rubbed her wrists with the love balm she and Maggie concocted from Granny's *Book of Shadows*, dabbing it behind her ears and along the sides of her neck.

Natural ingredients, such as apple, used in love philters and balms for centuries, were all edible. The thought made her tingle with anticipation.

Governed by that thought, she wanted to set the mood for powerful magick, thus Raine decided that music was just what the witch-doctor ordered. Flicking a switch, she sent Rowena of the Glen's *Book of Shadows* to the back-porch speakers. Rising from the mists, earthy and erotic, the album never failed to strike a chord in the Goth gal's witchy essence, stirring a tempest of emotions. Listening to the songstress' "Pagan Lover," she swayed to the enchantment. *Tonight especially, Rowena pulls me right into that sensual dance with her.*

Upon completing a few last-minute preparations for the dinner, she lit the flickering-flame lanterns on the screened-in back porch and opened a special bottle of Merlot, pouring herself a glass. Staring out at Haleigh's Wood, she sipped the wine, absorbed in thought.

It was the night of the full moon. The woods, close to dark, seemed to throb with excitement. A night bird called from afar. She was thinking about Maggie and Thad. She was thinking about Beau too, and like Maggie, she was thinking hard. The shuddering sound of Tara's antique doorbell interrupted her contemplation and sent her flying to answer it.

Their candle-lit supper came to a satisfying finale. As a romantic occasion, the meal was already a success. They drank the wine and enjoyed the steaks, after which Raine excused herself to freshen up and fetch the gifts she purchased for Beau's birthday. She had always wanted to get him a good gold pocket watch. His looks and personality were so suited to such a timepiece, with chain and fob, that it was something she had to satisfy. After careful searching, she found just the right one, then went a step further to have it engraved. So that he could sport the watch properly, she purchased a trilogy of Irish waistcoats in different color tweeds.

"The watch is worn suspended from the chain which fixes from the pocket of the vests," Raine instructed needlessly.

Beau's eyes crinkled at the corners. "Yes, I've heard tell." He pushed in the stem to open the ticking timepiece, and his eyes caught the inscription. *"Like Time, our love is endless."* When he raised his gaze to hers, she saw he was deeply moved by her gift.

She noticed, too, that he pressed the stem again before he closed the case, the proper way to prevent wearing out the closure.

"You like it." It was not a question.

"*I love it*," he stated, for the moment carefully returning the watch to its box. "Thank you, baby. I will treasure it always."

"Open this one next," she said, excited as a child and pleased by the emotion in his expression. With her little-cat grin, she handed him a square box. Like each of his birthday presents, it was done up in velvety black paper tied with silver ribbon.

Beau removed the wrappings and opened the box to reveal what she'd always called, with mysterious mien, a "Such-A-Night" hat, an Irish tweed newsboy cap that matched the deep blue of his eyes.

"To complete your sexy look," she declared. "Try it on." Raine bit her lower lip, hoping she'd chosen the correct size.

"Fits perfectly," he assured.

God, he looks good enough to ... Sometimes she forgot just how great-looking Beau was.

Raine stepped closer to adjust the cap. With a finger, she smoothed the errant strand of ebony hair that fell over his forehead. In the lantern-glow of the porch, his eyes fixed once again on hers. Pulling her against him, he breathed something in her ear followed by what could only be described as a feral growl. She drew in her breath. Her pulse raced at the naughtiness of the words, as she thought of what was to come.

"That's for later, baby. For now, let me say, I think your sleuthing skills are slipping," he teased. "You're usually alert, but you missed something very important here tonight."

"Oh, and *what's* that?" her voice rumbled deep in her throat as she toyed with his lower lip. His whisperings had released her desires, along with a thousand butterflies in her stomach.

"That's **what**," he pointed with play of words, endeavoring to control his need for her.

Raine turned her head to see a small, gift-wrapped box on the rattan stand alongside the lounge she'd occupied earlier. Moving briskly to pick up the tiny parcel, she asked with widened eyes, "It's *your* birthday, not mine. What might this be?"

His entire essence was awash with mystery. "Open it and find out."

Never one for patience, the Goth gal ripped off the green paper and ribbon to find a black velvet ring box, the jeweler's name and address from Martinique. She lifted the lid and, for the second time, sucked in her breath. Nestled inside was a glittering *Toi et Moi* ring, a replica of Joséphine's engagement ring from Napoléon.

"Except that I had the jeweler substitute the sapphire for an emerald. I couldn't see you blue," he bantered, skimming a finger over his mustache. "Emerald is *your* color and stone. However, if you would want the ring to hold a sapphire for a perfect match to Joséphine's ring, then I will take care of it for you."

"Hecate no, Beau. I wouldn't dream of changing a thing about this ring. It's lovely and perfect for me in every way." She was about to try the ring on, when she paused it in midair, tilting her head to ask, "Beau, what does this mean?"

He winced, and a flicker of hurt flashed in his denim-blue eyes but vanished almost as rapidly as it had appeared. "Raine," he began in a voice perhaps a dash too stern, "it means whatever you want it to mean." He got down on one knee and took her hand in his. "I will ask again, if that's what you want. Will you marry me in a handfast ceremony of your direction? Any way you wish to do it, I'm agreeable."

She bit her lip, saying nothing as Time waited, and once again, hurt flittered across Beau's handsome features.

"Or if you wish, we can call this ring, as my previous offerings, a promise for the future." He rose and leaned into her, his muscular body pinning her against the wall, his kisses slow and soft. She found herself crushed against his chest, her fingers splayed wildly on his shoulders as she kissed him back– deep kissing, a surging river of it.

"Don't answer tonight," he said against her lips, murmuring then something inaudible. With lusty breath, he ran his tongue along her neck, as a male lion might do to a lioness in the tall grass of the African savanna. "The ring's inner band is inscribed, in old-fashioned script, *Au Destin*, 'To Destiny,' as Napoléon's wedding gift to Joséphine. Think about this, about everything. Time, as you say, is endless, but life, each incarnation itself, is far too short." He waited a beat. "Life is going by all too fast, Raine."

Yes it is, she thought. *But I can't think about all this now. I'll go crazy if I do.* She slipped the ring on her right hand, and she could feel his power. "For now," she said aloud. "For now."

Her serious face morphed kitty-cat, and she kissed him with all the passion he had roused, one small dimpled hand skimming impishly up his chest. Reaching behind her, she unzipped the little black dress, letting it puddle at her feet. Stepping free, she stood before him in the spiderweb thong-teddy and thigh-high stockings, the stiletto heels rendering her just the right height for the job. "And right now," she demanded, and the green eyes flared for an instant, "you're going to keep that promise to me."

His eyes raked her, and he became wryly aware of a fierce sense of possessiveness. "You're a mite high-handed this evening," he said flatly.

The feline eyes danced with mischief. "Get used to it."

Beau raised his eyebrows inquisitively. "A sarcastic little witch at times, aren't thou? Come here," he snarled, a devilish glint appearing in his eyes. He ran a hand restlessly through his hair, his whole body seething with frustration as he grappled with wanting to throw her down on the settee. "Let's find out just how strong your spells are." He stared a moment longer before he suddenly grabbed her and, sitting on the nearest chair, deftly turned her over his knees. He heard the sharp intake of her breath before he thundered, "I've been wanting to do this for a long time!"

Raine gave a little yelp. Her entire life, no one had ever spanked her. Not really. It was a first, and for the first time too, she felt somewhat dominated and controlled— at least for the moment— by a man having his way with her, cheek to cheek. She could feel her bottom tingling, and she squirmed in spite of herself. It was a huge turn-on, playful, but attention-getting nonetheless.

"Birthday spankings are for the one whose birthday it is," she protested, though not with any believability.

"You've needed a spanking for years," he growled, continuing the stinging swats, first one side, then the other. Betwixt, he gently rubbed the glowing globes.

"That's not all I need," she babbled in wicked delight.

"Tonight, *I'll* decide what you need," he gritted almost fiercely. In truth, the thought brought him a savage satisfaction. To her surprise, he lifted her up and sat her on his lap facing him, giving her one last swat that made her tremble.

Tonight was a night of contradictions and confusion. Beau always had a certain plunging aggressiveness to him, but in the past he'd been in control of it, and that's what both confused and excited her. He was always ultra-masculine, though he did nothing overtly to control. Yet at the moment, he was dominating her completely, and he fairly throbbed with power.

Oh, the unabashed male arrogance of him!

On the other hand, it gave her an undeniable tingle to know that *she* was the cause of his wholly masculine gratification.

She trusted him with her life, and she was duly reminded that he had saved her life on more than one occasion. A new thrill of excitement shot through her, and she wrapped her arms around his neck to pull herself closer, watching him from under her lashes. He was gazing at her with an appreciative glint in his eyes as he gave her full concentration, and it seemed to her that he made love with a fierce energy that night, *As if,* she thought, *he's imprinting himself indelibly on my senses.*

At one point, she ducked her head into his shoulder and closed her eyes, almost embarrassed by the depth of feeling he had stirred, his witching woodsy scent rendering her dizzy.

"Do **not** look away from me, Raine," he ordered, catching her chin with his palm and studying her broodingly. She raised her head, somewhat stunned by the power in his voice. Sliding his hands along both sides of her face, he clasped her before him, and when he fixed her with his scorching blue gaze– *those eyes came right at her.*

Beau's eyes have always held unreadable mysteries, she deemed with startling insight, and she was at once grateful for his unrelenting honesty and for the happiness found in the tingling overtones of mystical sexual abandon.

"I want you to look straight at me, into my eyes, to my soul. Do you understand me?"

She nodded, unable to summon the words to respond. Prickling with secret pleasure, her face flushed hotly at the frankness and unrestraint of Beau's ardor, of the voluptuousness of his artful French kisses. Teasing, slow and sensual– they were releasing a frenzy of emotions. Sex was one thing, but their lovemaking went far beyond the physical. *It was spiritual. And yes,* she thought, *mystical.* It seemed more intimate somehow than even the first time they had made love years before, and did it fare delicious!

"Good girl." He spoke softly, the simple phrase like the power pulse of a wand.

From deep in her core, her inner-voice screamed, *Beau ... Beau, you're so powerful,* she thought in sweet confusion, *it's almost frightening ...*

She was at just the right angle, and in her lust-filled haze, she was swept into his passion like a leaf in a gale. *It's like he's witching it over me,* and the witch in her so needed what he was giving, the soft little gasps at the back of her throat sending ripples of fulfillment through him.

As the pleasure washed over them, their minds met, and two kindred souls became one, bringing a new feeling of connection—perhaps even a new understanding.

After dinner, Maggie and Thaddeus were enjoying a spell of leisure in the quiet of evening, snuggled together on his couch to enjoy the French music they purchased in Martinique. A magickal display of fireflies lent sparkle to the Laurel Highlands, limned in moonlight and visible through the wall of glass doors in Thaddeus' Great Room. Sipping wine, the couple chatted comfortably about a variety of things, from childhood reminiscences to vivid recent memories, to their future plans together.

When he rose to change the album, Thaddeus opened a drawer of the entertainment center to extract a square, gift-wrapped box about five inches deep and seven inches all round. With a glimmer in his bright blue eyes, he handed it to Maggie. "I think this will please you," he said.

"Oh, Thaddeus," she breathed, "what is it?"

The professor's mouth twitched, and he ran the back of his hand over his van dyke. "Only one way to find out," he prodded. "You know what I'm fond of saying, 'Each day comes bearing its gifts. Untie the ribbons!'"

Swiftly then, she tore away the gold paper to discover a red velvet box bearing the name of a Martinique jewelry store on Rue Victor Hugo. "Oh, Thaddeus," she repeated, as she lifted the hinged lid with a gasp. "Ooooooooooooh ..." A hand flew to her mouth, her excitement making it difficult to breath. "The Joséphine bracelet!" The hand dropped to her breast. "My heart rate must be a good two hundred."

"I'm afraid it's merely a replica," he stated, pensively stroking his beard. "Though, I must relate, it *is* an *exact* copy. I was adamant about that in my instructions to the jeweler. Exact except for the inscription on the inner band. Devoid of Joséphine's name, this one reads only *Pour ma belle rose*. Rose is not capped in your bracelet, since it is not your given name, but I had the jeweler replicate the old-fashioned script of the original." He took the bracelet from its rosy nest to slip it on Maggie's arm, then carefully secure the S-clasp. "Even the stones are old European rubies. Pigeon-blood stones in the deepest, most sought-after color. Just like the actual Joséphine bracelet."

"Great Goddess, darlin'," the overwhelmed Sister exclaimed. "You must have paid a fortune for this piece. Oh, my darling Thaddeus, what an enchanting surprise!"

"You treat me to love and romance in a spirit of true generosity, my dear. I can well afford to show my love for you with generosity of things that *you* value, whether it be material possessions, time, positive spirit of all sorts ... *love*. Not to say that love could ever carry a price tag, but if it did, I guarantee that the one I'd have for yours would be so dear, it would be totally unaffordable to anyone but me."

"*No one but you*," she breathed, pressing against him on the couch to kiss him, her tears wetting both their faces. "I love the bracelet," she said, accepting it for its true value, as a gift of adoration, "but more importantly, I love *you*. So very, very much." She gazed into his eyes before whispering in his ear.

"Can you be a bit more specific about that, my dear?" the professor queried with humor.

Maggie moaned and slid her hands along his chest to blow into his ear before conveying her request in explicit detail.

The professor cocked an eyebrow, studying her for a private moment.

She was wearing black, a floating, diaphanous black. It was the negligee he had gifted her for her last birthday.

"As I always say," he touted, "practice makes better ... and better and better. Do you agree with that hypothesis, my dear?"

Maggie kissed him, replying in a feathery whisper, "I wholeheartedly embrace it, professor, but I think you should continue to instruct me. Your lessons are so very exciting, and I greatly benefit from your tutorship. In truth, I would go so far as to say I can't live without it."

"Well then, I've given you what you fancied, hence I believe I should give you what you need." He proceeded toward that end when, breathless, Maggie said, "Darlin' ... darlin', let's give each other a night we'll remember for the rest of our lives."

***

The next morning dawned golden. The August sun shone bright, but the humidity was low, with a slight breeze that held the promise of autumn.

At breakfast, Raine and Maggie decided to go for a long horseback ride. The stable was situated far to the rear of the house, on Tara's triple-size lot, its cupola topped with a witch weathervane to match the one on the manse's highest gable. Before Beau attached either to the rooftops, the Sisters infused the witchy guardians with strong blessings of protection.

After saddling up, they headed into the woods, following the trails Beau and his father graciously kept clear for them.

Full of mettle and mischief and hot-blooded like his owner, Raine's jet-black Arabian, Tara's Pride, was a feisty gelding that always appeared to be in a hurry. Even his walk was hurried, if one could even call it a walk.

"The horses haven't been out for a couple of days thanks to those thunder storms," the Goth gal said, maintaining a tight rein till they could get to a clearing. "They're chompin' at the bit for a good run."

Maggie patted the sleek neck of her cherry chestnut mare. "You know," she directed to Raine, "I can't believe I was once thinking of changing her name owing to the craziness in this world. My Isis is named for the Egyptian goddess of magick and life. It suits her, and I'll never substitute it for something that would only be second best for her."

Raine leaned forward in the Spanish saddle to smooth Tara's ebony mane. "Who was that on the phone this morning? When I came in from getting the paper, you were just hanging up. I meant to ask you then, but remembered I needed to make a call myself, and afterward it slipped my mind."

"It was Thaddeus. He wants to take me out tonight for an intimate engagement dinner. Somewhere really special, he said. I have a keen witchy feeling we'll be driving up the mountain, deep into our Laurel Highlands, to dine at the Hidy-Holde. I've always loved the woodsy setting and medieval décor of the place, so Gothic and romantic, especially in their Round Room, the *perfect* ambience for him to slip *that* ring on my finger. I didn't want to begin wearing the ring until he does that tonight."

Maggie was referring to the emerald ring Thaddeus gave her at Yule a few years ago. She closed her eyes, reaching back in time to the moment Thaddeus presented her with the love token.

It was the most gorgeous ring she had ever seen– a large rectangular emerald surrounded by tiny, sparkling diamonds. Thaddeus commissioned the piece to match the necklace he'd given her a couple of months prior– an antiquity that, over a thousand years before, belonged to the Goddess-like Gormlaith, the stunning, red-haired queen and wife of medieval Ireland's Brian Boru.

She remembered what Thaddeus said when he gifted her with the ring. "Maggie, I know you do not wish to become engaged yet. Nonetheless, I want you to have a ring to match the Gormlaith necklace, which I've chosen, at this point in time, to call a 'promise ring.' Here is what it means: You have my promise that no matter what happens in our lives, whether or not we become engaged, whether we have a wedding or handfasting, no matter what– I will always love you. That is my promise to you, and that is what this ring symbolizes– my unyielding love for you. *Forever.*"

Maggie had placed her hands on either side of his noble face, kissed him full on the mouth, and thanked him from the deepest reaches of her heart. "And you have *my* promise of pure, unconditional love."

So much has happened since that Yule, she told herself. *We've all come so far. Sometimes it seems like just yesterday, other times ... other times ... it feels like far.*

The thought triggered something Granny once said. *Sometimes I can feel my bones straining under the weight of all the lives I've lived, of all the burdens I've toted.*

Coming out of reverie, Maggie glanced over at Raine. "Your ring is beautiful, Sister."

Raine grinned but said nothing. It was the sort of thing Maggie would do. In fact, the Goth gal was unusually quiet the past few days, prompting her sister of the moon to leave her to her thoughts, thoughts that encompassed a mélange of things this morning, including the night of intimacies with Beau after the birthday dinner.

Strong but never rough ... powerful but always tender. He certainly witched it over me, and truth be known, that's always been my secret desire ... at least in the bedroom. I loved it. And he knows I loved it. She looked up, amidst the leafy-green canopy of overhead branches through which the sun's sparkle flecked her upturned face and shoulders. *Beau's always known me better than I've known myself.*

They rode in silence for a while, save for the sounds of the horses, the creak of leather, or the occasional trilling song of a bird. A monarch butterfly fluttered nearby.

After several minutes, Maggie spoke wistfully, "Remember what you and I said to one another when we were leaving Ireland, after ferreting out the Time-Key? We talked about how nice it would be to one day have a double handfast there. Do you remember? Raine?"

"Hmmmm?" the brunette Sister replied, surfacing from her own daydream. She had been imaging Beau's hot blue gaze that had totally captivated and devoured her the evening before.

Maggie recapped what she just said.

"Yes, that would be wonderful, Mags. We should do that. Why not?" Raine sparked of a sudden. "Why not?!" She drew rein.

They had come to the clearing. Exiting the woods, the Goth gal whooped. When her mount took off, Maggie's shot forward like an arrow loosed from an archer's bow. As Tara's Pride broke into full gallop across the open field, Raine felt the thrill of elation she always did in the horse's smooth stretching and the wild rush of wind at her ears. Chucking her sister of the moon a glance, she shouted her usual meadow challenge, "Last one across is a mutton-headed muggle!"

Then she took a deep breath– and her own good advice, deciding to listen to her heart.

The small Potrera saddle provided close contact, whilst the thundering hoofbeats pounded out the cadence– *Life is good. Life is good. Life is good!* It was a oneness with horse and the universe, and it was the most *freeing* sensation in the world.

***

The Sisters were just about to enter the house, when they spied the mailman striding smartly up the driveway, whistling a happy tune. To Raine and Maggie, that whistling meant letters and/ or parcels.

"I'll go inside to put the kettle on," Raine tossed over her shoulder. "You get the mail."

"Morning, Danny," Maggie greeted. "I see you have something for us today."

"Glad I caught you," he answered, handing her several envelopes." He glanced down at the letter in his hand. "Registered Post from Ireland. You gotta sign for it."

Maggie's voice caught in her throat, and it was a moment or two before she could speak. Dashing off her signature, she said, her words rasping, "Thank you, Danny."

"Have a good day!" he called, as he happily hoofed his way back down the long drive.

When the redheaded Sister entered the house, Raine was putting the teacups on the kitchen table.

"What's wrong?" she asked, though she was certain she knew what the foreign letter in Maggie's hand signified.

The tearful redhead sank down in the nearest chair. "Rory's gone."

Raine came immediately to her Sister's side to enfold her in a warm embrace. "I'm sorry, Mags."

"There's more. Much more. This letter is from his solicitor." Maggie perused the single page for the second time. "Rory's left everything he owned to me. His bank accounts, the castle and everything in it. *Everything*," she repeated, as though she needed to for her own awareness.

Raine moved to pour the tea, then sat across from Maggie at table. "I remember you telling me he had no immediate family." She stopped there, unsure of what else to say.

"The solicitor writes that Rory hoped I'd take over, to run the business. Seacliff Castle hosts weddings and gatherings of all sorts; *ceilidhs* … Irish fun evenings with music and dancing once a week, Saturday evenings I think; psychic fairs; renaissance fairs; Celtic sports and such, all at different times during the year. I think there's a golf course. And I know there's a stable with horses and bridle paths. The castle itself is a five-star hotel. Oh, and the place is open to the public for tours at designated times. The solicitor asks that I fly over there as soon as possible. The staff is understandably apprehensive, worried about their jobs. And it's *that* which worries *me* the most."

Maggie got a sudden vision of rounding a curve in the road leading to the tall, wrought-iron Seacliff gates and seeing the medieval castle in its full glory.

"Didn't Rory live at Seacliff?" Raine queried, taking a sip of tea.

"Yes, the owner's living quarters occupy the wing that overlooks a roaring Atlantic. There's hardly any strand there. The sea crashes against the rocks below. It's quite lovely." Maggie closed her eyes, remembering the last time she had seen Rory. The visit took place nearly seven years prior, during the Sisters' Time-Key quest. "*Lovely*," she whispered, remembering, as new tears rose to her eyes and an unseen hand clenched her heart, squeezing till she wanted to keen for the dead in the ancient Irish way.

Pulling a tissue from the pocket of her riding shirt, she swiped at her eyes. "At least, I don't think he suffered. You, Aisling, and I took care of that. I was able to help him that way."

"Yes. He's at peace. He went with the greatest of ease to the Light." Raine's green eyes opened very wide, as a persistent fear peered out at the dear person across from her. "What will you do, Mags?"

"The letter states that I must go there straightaway to meet with the solicitor, sign papers, look over the property, go over the books, meet the staff, and ultimately decide what I am going to do. The sooner, the better." Maggie let out a groan. "I dread meeting with the solicitor. Absolutely dread it. You know what lawyers are. One can never get a straight answer out of any of them.

"Rory stated in his will that it would be entirely up to me," she rushed on, oblivious to Raine's expression, "but he hoped I would take over and keep things running. The place is in the black. Doing *well*, in fact. Rory was so proud of that." After a pensive pause, she said almost inaudibly, "I've always thought there's something enormously dramatic about a will. I realize now it was a *knowing*."

Contrary to her nature, Raine nearly burst into tears. On the other hand, she so wanted to support Maggie in whatever she decided to do. Torn, she could not voice what was in her heart. Not yet anyway, so, staggered into silence, she kept quiet, which was also contrary to her nature.

"I have dual citizenship," Maggie ruminated, aloud but to herself.

The statement drew a blank stare from Raine, who continued to regard her moon sister with a stunned silence. At that moment, the Goth gal looked very small and childlike. Her cheeks had lost their rosy flush, and her green eyes held a curiously absent look.

"Thaddeus wants to sell his house and retire," Maggie went on, "and he wants me to resign from teaching. I loved living in Ireland. The magick and all that. *Eire*, where the wind carries secrets to share with those who listen. Where the heather grows thick upon the hills, and the shamrocks not far from it." She took on a far-away look. "There's something indefinably mysterious about Ireland. Perhaps," she closed her eyes and leaned back in the chair, "it's the thick fog that rolls low across the leas even late in the day, or the ghostly sea mists, or the way the grass is incredibly green year-round. Or it could be that every pub, restaurant … *every cobblestone* holds a history most folks can't even begin to imagine."

She opened her eyes. "But the fact that I fell in love with the people, the history, the land is *no* mystery. *Heaven on earth.* Rory always joked that if he couldn't go to Heaven, he'd at least die in Ireland."

"Oh, Maggie," Raine sighed wearily.

"Oh!" Maggie beseeched in her soft manner of speaking, suddenly grasping Raine's forebodings. "Darlin', *please* don't fret. I'll likely end up doing what Thaddeus has been proposing for the last few years– and that's dividing our time between our bases. We could spend part of each year in Ireland, part at Tara and the mountain cottage here in the Laurel Highlands. Thaddeus wants to hold on to it. Eventually, you, Aisling, and I will inherit Grantie Merry's cottage at Salem."

Her beautiful face brightened. "That reminds me. We *must* visit Grantie again, and–" She broke off, saying abruptly, "Raine, I want Thaddeus to go on this trip to Ireland with me, of course, but I also want you and Aisling to come with me, to help me sort things out. This is a matter that requires reflection. A good deal of reflection.

"When we leave Ireland, we could fly to Boston, en route home, and visit Grantie together. I will want to share everything with her. I know I can convince Aisling to take a few days off, and you, Thaddeus and I have a month before classes resume at the college. What say you? *Please!*" Her look was positively pleading.

"Of course, Mags. You know I will."

"Oh, I must tell you," Maggie said in excitement, hoping to bring Raine out of her funk, "that Grantie Merry's taken to using a cane carved from black Irish bog wood, which you know has magickal properties. The bog oak, at least 6,000 years old, was carved by an awesome Irish druid and charged on the sacred Hill of Tara, home to the Old Ones, *the* faerie portal and the doorway to other worlds. A most mysterious wood, Irish bog," she envisioned. "The cane's handle is fashioned like a black cat. I don't know why we never saw Grantie with it before, but I can't wait till we see it. You especially, Raine.

"When you were at Beau's last night, I chatted with her in our Athena crystal ball, but I could hardly get a word in. She told me the cane was imbued with limitless magickal powers and can act like a vortex to the spiritual realm, helping to commune with spirits. She said the cane draws negativity out of its owner, and negative spirits and energies are magnetically sucked into the bog wood and destroyed. *Zapped*," she exclaimed with huge gesture, "utterly and completely destroyed!

"Then Grantie went on to say that the cane was a powerful good-luck charm, that it drew positive people, energies, and opportunities. It can manifest the owner's deepest wishes, providing those wishes harm none, of course. Great Goddess, Grantie said the cane can move from one place to another on its own, and it can assist in astral projection and travel, even past-life work. Did I mention that it stops evil spirits in their tracks?" Maggie could sense that her magickal cane dissertation was beginning to have an effect on her distraught sister of the moon. "And guess what? It protects against curses, hexes and misfortunes. What say you to that?"

Before the spellbound Raine had a chance to reply, their poppet, Cara, manifested on the kitchen table to say, "*Mo sheacht mbeannacht ort!* My seven blessings upon ya!" The doll pointed a rag-stuffed mitt at Raine. "You canna wor-rry 'bout changes comin', lass," their little friend propounded with her usual vim. "Ivery ting will wor-rk out th' way it's supposed-ta. Yer Granny *insisted* I tell you dat, f'r she kin feel yer woe."

"Thank you, Cara," the Sisters echoed in sync.

"I plan on conjuring both Granny and Grantie by evening tide," Maggie stated resolutely, tapping her full lips with a finger. "Raine, you didn't get to speak with Grantie last night, and we must talk things over with Granny too."

The trio of Merlin cats entered the kitchen then, walking side-by-side, across their domain with the aplomb of majestic black leopards.

Raine scooped up Black Jack to cover her hero's velvet face with kisses. "I love you, Jackie boy!" She held him close, bringing forth his Number-Three Purr, whilst Maggie picked up Black Jade. The more reserved Panthèra opted for Granny's cushioned rocker before the window, leaping into the golden light of afternoon for her nap, which she preferred any day to kisses.

"The kitties will miss you, Mags. Took Black Jade a week to forgive us when we returned from Martinique. But you can't take her away from Jack. You simply can*not* separate them."

A smidgen of hurt flickered in Maggie's McDonough eyes. "I wouldn't think of separating them, darlin'. *You know that.*"

With her face buried in Jack's soft fur, Raine bit back tears. Then she stood, squared her shoulders, and turning to hide her face, opened a cabinet door for a bottle of the Irish.

Noticing, Maggie chortled, "Darlin', it's not even noon."

"I figure it's cocktail hour somewhere in the world, Sister. It's not every day, you inherit a castle, now is it?" With a heart full of trepidation, the raven-haired Sister poured a healthy measure for each of them. Before she could raise her teacup, however, there came a decided cough from Cara.

"Ain't ya f'r-rgettin' sumpin', lass?"

Raine laughed, then poured a drop of what their poppet sometimes called the 'poteen' into the wee cup that was the doll's alone. Raising her teacup, she toasted with the traditional Irish salute to Health, "*Sláinte!*"

"*Sláinte!*" Maggie and Cara echoed.

Raine tossed the drink back with expert tilt of the wrist before her McDonough eyes found Maggie's, and a look passed between them. At that moment, everything they had ever shared flowed from one to the other, and for the first time, the Goth gal knew that nothing could ever break their bond. *Nothing. But what of the Sleuth Sisters?* She asked herself.

"To the Sleuth Sisters!" she cried with sudden proud fury, hoisting her cup high.

"To the Sleuth Sisters!" Maggie and Cara returned.

"Hey, can I get in on this?" a familiar voice sounded behind them.

Turning, Raine and Maggie blurted, "Aisling!"

"The door was unlocked," she answered, "so I let myself in."

"When we spoke on the phone last night," Raine began, "you said you had a busy schedule today."

"I do," the blonde with the wand answered, "but I had to stop in to wish you both Love and Light and everything Merry and

Bright." The senior Sister hugged first Maggie then Raine. "Ian, Merry Fay, and I are all so happy for you." She took a step back to study the two dear faces before her. "And you know how Granny always said that timing is everything in life."

Aisling looked to Raine, and the knowing McDonough eyes of the two Sisters held.

"This is a decision only *you* can make. You must look to your own soul for the answer. But for what it's worth, I sense *it's time*, and I think you do too," Aisling concluded softly. "My *wish* for you," her green gaze slid to Maggie, "is that you are both as happy as Ian and I."

The pink color was returning to Raine's cheeks, the emerald sparkle to her eyes.

"Thank you, Sister," chorused Raine and Maggie heartily.

"Sit for a spell," Maggie pulled a chair out from the table, "and join us for a drop of the Irish. We've something to discuss with you."

Raine poured another cup of tea, sweetening it with the smooth whiskey.

"Before you do, let me say, there's another reason I stopped by," the blonde Sister revealed. "I sensed your fears, and I knew you needed me." She looked each of her Sisters in the eye. "Don't you know that *nothing* will ever destroy our very special trinity, our Power of Three? We're bound together for all eternity, and we have a noble destiny to fulfill– *together*. A destiny ordained by the Triple Goddess. When Ian and I handfasted, my bond with you only grew stronger. You know that."

"We do, Sister," Raine and Maggie chimed.

"All right then!" Aisling beamed, and it was a golden sun coming from behind grey clouds.

"Aisling, *bless you*," Raine and Maggie cast as one.

"I've been tossing around an idea about the handfastings, another reason I *had* to rush over here," Aisling embarked. "I want you to consider what I have to say. Suppose ..."

***

In the subsequent minutes, the blonde with the wand shared her delightful inspiration, after which there was a brief interchange of thought between Raine and Maggie.

*Our Leo Sister is a **wizard** lioness. She always knows exactly what to do to make things right. A truly wise woman,* a grinning Raine swooshed to Maggie.

Yes, and we can always feel her power, Maggie swished back. Then she shared the news from Ireland, which, in turn, led to a most satisfying exchange of dialogue.

"This calls for another cheering cup." The senior Sister stood, raising her drink to declare, "The Sleuth Sisters! All for one, and one for all! It's not original, but that's our call!"

The magickal trio reiterated with all the love they could muster, "***To the Sleuth Sisters!***"

Everything is going to be all right. More than all right, Raine decided.

In a twinkling, it was like a weight had been lifted from Raine and Maggie. Glittering White Light swirled round the Sisters three in an energy field that danced with the force of the Uni-verse, a singular song of ecstasy that was so powerful, it created a warm glow, becoming as indestructible as the love vibration itself.

The rising, spiraling energies formed, above the threesome, the witch's hat Cone of Power– in which possibilities become infinite.

This was the Old Way– and, yes indeed, it was *formidable*.

Looking down, the Goddess smiled– and was truly pleased.

"Another purrrrrr-fect ending, Jack."
~ Dr. Raine McDonough, PhD

"You know, Raine–
Every ending is merely a new beginning."

~ Black Jack O'Lantern, PhD
(Puss of Hubristic Divination)

"Witchcraft offers the model of a religion of poetry, not theology.
It presents metaphors, not doctrines, and leaves open the possibility
of reconciliation of science and religion ..."
~ Starhawk

~ Epilogue ~

"OK," Aisling charged, "now that I've told you what *I've* done, I want to review with you both what *you've* accomplished. Then we'll go over the to-do list from the top," the senior Sister informed Raine and Maggie.

It was the first week of September. The Sisters three were sitting at Tara's kitchen table, where they were sipping tea and planning for the upcoming triple handfasting to be held at Seacliff Castle, County Clare, Ireland, at *Samhain*.

"It's such a wizard idea, Aisling," Raine began, "to renew your vows with Ian so that our handfasting will have the Power of Three."

"There be nothing more powerful," Aisling answered, "than the Love vibration augmented by the Power of Three in Celtic handfast on Ancestors' Night– *Samhain*– the Witches' New Year. Now, since last we met a few days ago, fill me in, Sisters. I can sense that a lot has happened." She settled into the kitchen chair and picked up her teacup.

"The paperwork is all done with the Irish solicitor," Maggie announced. "I daresay the castle staff was relieved that business will continue as usual. Again, I want to thank you, Sisters, for accompanying Thaddeus and me to Ireland. It meant a lot to us both."

She thought for a moment, adding, "As we speak, staff is preparing the owner's wing for Thaddeus and me according to my instructions. Before we left Ireland, I designated where all Rory's personal things would go throughout the castle. Some in the Great Hall, a few pieces in the dining room, others in the castle's pub, and so on. His clothing will be donated to a local charity. I'm keeping Rory's nice green Land Rover Discovery for our use in Ireland. He took really good care of it, so it should last a virtual lifetime."

Maggie pursed her full red lips. "Though I doubt very much *I'll* be driving there. Rory's Rover is a stick, and since the Irish drive on the left side of the road, I don't think I want to attempt it. Thaddeus wants to teach me, but," she giggled, "you know the only stick I drive is my besom." She looked to Raine. "Then again, as you say, 'When in doubt, rock the hell out,' so I may be tempted to give that stick a go.

"I'll have you know, Sisters, that Thaddeus is now officially retired, and I have resigned from my teaching duties. He listed his house only a fortnight ago, and yesterday, he told me he thinks he already has a buyer, a very pleasant young couple, both teachers at Haleigh High," Maggie finished.

"I've secured a semester off from my teaching duties at the college, without pay, but I'm certainly not complaining," Raine put in. "Haleigh College has been most understanding and co-operative through all this. Beau's secretary, Jean, has cleared his schedule for the two weeks we'll be in Ireland for the handfast and honeymoon. Emergencies will be directed, via phone message, to the animal hospital in Farmington.

"In a few months, Kitty and Raoul Duff will begin their internship with Beau at Goodwin Veterinary Clinic, after which there'll be a trial period to see how they work out. Beau is optimistic that, eventually, he'll take them on as partners, at which time they will reside at the Clinic; henceforth," she rambled on, "freeing him to finally have a life." The Goth gal thought for a moment. "Beau has moved a few personal items and all his clothing here to Tara. The clothes fit nicely in the hall closet across from my … our bedroom. You know men don't have as much in the way of garments as we ladies."

"Thaddeus has installed his wardrobe to Tara, some of which will go with us to Ireland," Maggie stated, "and some he took to our mountain retreat. He's selling all the furnishings with his house, save for a few items that he's already transported to the cabin.

"Eva Novak's niece, Beth Addams, who owns the travel agency we use here in Haleigh's Hamlet, has officially agreed to manage the castle for me," the redheaded Sister went on chattily. "The timing couldn't be more perfect. Six months ago, she and her widowed sister became partners. You remember Beth's sister. She used to supervise the tax office downtown. Now, she'll take over the management of their dual-owned travel agency here in the Hamlet, and Beth will oversee the castle for me.

"When Eva confided that Beth became a travel agent because she loves travel but was bored sitting at a desk, knee-deep in paperwork, I galvanized into action. Not that there won't be paperwork in her new position, but Beth is thrilled with the opportunity to live in another country, and in a medieval castle to boot. She's honest, intelligent, and more-than-capable, with the personality required for interacting with clients. She has just what it takes, and I can't tell you how relieved I am to have her on board. I don't feel nearly as overwhelmed."

"Has Beth left for Ireland?" Aisling queried.

"She has," Maggie replied. "There's a lot to learn, and she wants to get started as soon as possible so I can reopen the castle– the goal date two or three weeks subsequent to *Samhain*. Two of the older staff, a married couple who've worked at Seacliff forever, have volunteered to show Beth the ropes. Of course, Thaddeus and I will be there too. It warmed our hearts that the owner and manager of another castle hotel in County Clare has offered to let us shadow her to familiarize us with the intricacies of running such an operation."

"Well," Aisling smiled in satisfaction, "I'm impressed with how much you both have accomplished. Now," she adjusted herself in her chair, "let's go over, detail for detail, everything we can for our Power of Three *Samhain* handfast. We want it to be truly *magickal!*"

Aisling thought for a moment, adding, "*Samhain* is a time of endings and new beginnings. It's the perfect time for witchy handfasting. Most especially ours. *Samhain*'s also the time for honoring the ancestors, and oh, how Granny will love this! What could *be* more magickal than handfasting at *Samhain*? And in an Irish castle!"

"A *mysterious* Irish castle complete with its own ghost," Maggie saw fit to toss into the merry mix.

Maggie's words stirred in Raine a witchy presentiment. "I'm superbly grateful dear Grantie Merry has bequeathed her Irish bog cane to us for a joint handfast gift. After all, she only just acquired the magickal walking stick a few months ago," she reminded. "From a former lover, do you believe? A lover who was a *super*-witch, and great balls of fire, a lover so much younger than she!

Grantie must have made a powerful impression on him, for their *liaison* took place so many years ago." Raine grinned in spite of herself.

"What're you smiling at?" Aisling asked with a tilt of her blonde head, though she was already sensing the response.

"Grantie Merry was a cougar," the Goth gal replied.

"I don't think that's true," Aisling spouted defensively. "But as you said, she must've had an intense love affair and bond with Brother Gareth Knight. Goddess rest him. Apparently, their relationship spanned several years."

"Hot and heavy," Raine giggled. "That photograph she showed us ... what a hunk!"

Aisling was feeling so happy of late, she threw her head back and laughed out loud. "To borrow a quote from *Alice in Wonderland*, 'You're mad, bonkers, completely off your head. But I'll tell you a secret. All the best people are.'"

"I still can't believe Grantie gifted us something so special, so meaningful to her. *Now*, rather than ... you know what I'm saying, *after*," Maggie reacted with heartfelt appreciation. "The thing is so sated with magick, it virtually *vibrates*."

"She knows her time is nigh," Aisling said with sudden sadness on her voice. "I sensed that as soon as we entered her cottage. Thank the Goddess we spent time with her at Salem when we left Ireland. Grantie wants us to have the walking stick now because she knows, too, we'll have *need* of it at Seacliff Castle at *Samhain*, and she wants *nothing* to interfere with our handfast ceremony."

"I agree. I'm getting the same vibes. Grantie told us the bog stick will take on even more power in *our* hands," Raine reminded.

"What we give power– has power," Aisling concurred, her statement opening the door to several subsequent minutes of spellbinding symposium.

The blonde with the wand sat back in her chair to give an explosive sigh. "Let's get to it, Sisters. We've only a few weeks till the big day. I want us to have the Power of Three, yes, but," Aisling urged, "it's my solemn wish that you have everything *you* want, *each of you*, in this very special handfast ceremony."

"Hold your unicorns!" Raine stood to put the kettle on. "This calls for a second pot of our special witches' brew."

As she prepared their favorite green tea, she sang brightly to herself. "Still around the corner a new road doth wait. Just around the corner– another secret gate!"

"If you're going to do something,
do it well,
and be sure to leave behind a little witchy sparkle."
~ Dr. Raine McDonough, PhD

~About the Author~

Ceane O'Hanlon-Lincoln was born at the witching hour of midnight during an April thunderstorm, and she has led a somewhat stormy, rather *whirlwind* existence ever since.

A native of southwestern Pennsylvania, Ceane (SHAWN-ee or Shawn) taught high school French until 1985. Already engaged in commercial writing, she immediately began pursuing a career writing both fiction and history.

In the tradition of a great Irish *seanchaí* (storyteller), O'Hanlon-Lincoln has been called by many a "state-of-the-heart" writer.

In 1987, at Robert Redford's Sundance Institute, two of her screenplays made the "top twenty-five," chosen from thousands of nationwide entries. In 1994, she optioned one of those scripts to Kevin Costner; the other screenplay she reworked and adapted, in 2014, to the first of her spellbinding *Sleuth Sisters Mysteries,* ***The Witches' Time-Key,*** conceived years ago during a memorable sojourn in Ireland. As Ceane stood on the sacred Hill of Tara, the wind whispered ancient voices– ancient secrets. *O'Hanlon-Lincoln never forgot that ever so mystical experience.*

Fire Burn and Cauldron Bubble is the savvy Sleuth Sisters' second super adventure, ***The Witch's Silent Scream*** the sexy third. ***Which Witch is Which?*** is the witchin' fourth whodunit, ***Which-Way*** the spine-tingling fifth, ***The Witch Tree*** the haunting sixth, ***The***

Witch's Secret the scintillating seventh, ***Careful What You Witch For***, the gripping eighth, and ***Someone To Witch Over Me***, the sizzling ninth adventure in the bewitching *Sleuth Sisters Mystery Series*.

Watch for the anticipated ***Witch Upon A Star***– coming soon!

Ceane crafts each of her *Sleuth Sisters Mysteries* to stand alone, though it is always nice to read a series in order for the most surprises– and this author hopes you like surprises.

A prolific writer, Ceane has also had a poem published in *Great Poems of Our Time*. Winner of the Editor's Choice Award, "The Man Who Holds the Reins" appears in the fore of her romantic short-story collection ***Autumn Song***– the ultimate witchy-woman read.

William Colvin, a retired Pennsylvania theatre and English teacher, said of her ***Autumn Song***: "The tales rank with those of Rod Serling and the great O. Henry. O'Hanlon-Lincoln is a *master* storyteller."

Robert Matzen, writer/ producer of Paladin Films, said of ***Autumn Song***: "I like the flow of the words, almost like song lyrics. *Very evocative*."

World-renowned singer/ actress Shirley Jones has lauded Ceane with these words: "She is an old friend whose literary work has distinguished her greatly."

In February 2004, O'Hanlon-Lincoln won the prestigious *Athena*, an award presented to professional "women of spirit" on local, national and international levels. The marble, bronze and crystal *Athena* sculpture symbolizes "career excellence and the light that emanates from the recipient."

Soon after the debut of the premier volume of her Pennsylvania history series, ***County Chronicles,*** the talented author won a Citation/ Special Recognition Award from the Pennsylvania House of Representatives, followed by a Special Recognition Award from the Senate of Pennsylvania. She has since won *both* awards a *third* time for ***County Chronicles***– the series.

In 2014, Ceane O'Hanlon-Lincoln was ceremoniously inducted into her historic Pennsylvania hometown's Hall of Fame. Ceane shares Tara, her 1907 Victorian home, with her beloved husband Phillip and their champion Bombay cats, Panthèra, and Black Jade and Black Jack O'Lantern.

In addition to creating her own line of jewelry, which she calls Enchanted Elements, her hobbies include travel, nature walks, theatre, film, antiques, and reading "… everything I can on Pennsylvania, American, and Celtic history, legend and lore. Moreover– I *love* a good mystery! Historians, in essence, are fundamental detectives– we're always connecting the dots."

~~~

~ A message to her readers from
Mistress of Mystery and Magick–
Ceane O'Hanlon-Lincoln ~

"There's a little witch in every woman."

"I write because writing is, to me, like the Craft itself– *empowering*. Writing, as the Craft, is *creation*. When I take up a pen or sit at my computer, I am a goddess, a deity wielding that tool like a faerie godmother waves a wand.

"Via will, clever word-choice and placement, I can arrange symbols and characters to invoke a whole circuitous route of emotions, images, ideas, arm-chair travel– and, yes indeed, even time-travel. A writer can create– *magick*.

"I am often asked where I get my inspiration. The answer is 'From everything and everyone around me.' I love to travel, discover new places, and meet new people, and I have never been shy about talking to people I don't know. I love to talk, hence over the years, I've had to train myself to be a good listener. One cannot learn anything new, talking.

"People also ask me if there is any truth to my stories about the Sleuth Sisters. To me, they are very real, though each is my own creation, and since I have always drawn from life when I write, I would have to say that there is a measure of truth in each of their essences– and in each of their witchy adventures."

How much, though, like the author herself– *shall remain a mystery.*

~ ~ ~

A Magick Wand Production

"Thoughts are magick wands powerful enough to make
anything happen– anything we choose!"

Thank you for reading Ceane O'Hanlon-Lincoln's
Sleuth Sisters Mysteries.
If you enjoy Ceane's books, help spread the word about them!

The author invites you to visit her on Facebook,
on her personal page
and on her *Sleuth Sisters Mysteries* page.

May your life be replete with— *magick!*

"The most beautiful experience we can have is the *mysterious*.
It is the fundamental emotion that stands at the cradle of
true art and true science."
~ Albert Einstein

Believe!

"Somewhere, something incredible is waiting to be known."
~ Carl Sagan

Believe!

"To be yourself in a world
that is constantly trying to make you something else
is the greatest accomplishment."
~ Emerson … and Granny McDonough